The View from Here

The View from Here

CINDY MYERS

KENSINGTON BOOKS
www.kensingtonbooks.com

KENSINGTON BOOKS are published by

Kensington Publishing Corp.
119 West 40th Street
New York, NY 10018

All Kensington titles, imprints, and distributed lines are available at special quantity discounts for bulk purchases for sales promotion, premiums, fund-raising, and educational or institutional use.

Special book excerpts or customized printings can also be created to fit specific needs. For details, write or phone the office of the Kensington Special Sales Manager: Kensington Publishing Corp., 119 West 40th Street, New York, NY 10018. Attn. Special Sales Department. Phone: 1-800-221-2647.

ISBN-13: 978-0-7582-7740-4
ISBN-10: 0-7582-7740-7

First Kensington Trade Paperback Printing: December 2012
10 9 8 7 6 5 4 3 2 1

Printed in the United States of America

For Diane

Acknowledgments

So many people have supported me through the writing of this book. Thanks to my editor, Audrey LaFehr, for her faith in this book and encouragement. Thanks to Deborah Smith and Pamela Morsi for their support, and to my best friend, Diane, who has always cheered me on.

And as always, thanks to my husband, Jim. I couldn't do it without you.

The View from Here

Chapter 1

"Open it. What are you afraid of?"

A simple question, with lots of simple answers. Maggie Stevens was afraid of heights. Of snakes, deep water, dentistry, and needles. She was afraid of being stuck on a plane next to a guy who wouldn't shut up, of suddenly becoming allergic to chocolate, and of getting old and losing her butt.

And, apparently, of thick envelopes with the return addresses of law firms. She stood in the living room of the house in Houston where she'd lived for twenty years, her best friend, Barbara Stanowski, at her side. Sunlight poured through the curtainless windows, so that Maggie had to squint to read the embossed print on the heavy linen envelope: REGINALD PAXTON, ESQUIRE, 113 FOURTH STREET, EUREKA, COLORADO.

"What is Carter doing using a lawyer in Colorado?" she asked.

"You don't know it has anything to do with Carter." Barb perched on the edge of a packing box and lifted her heavy mane of dark hair off her neck. The two friends had spent all morning wrapping dishes and taping boxes, and still Barbara looked like the former beauty queen she was. Maggie should probably hate her for it, but then again, there were things about her that Barb could probably hate, too—that kind of history was the basis of a solid friendship.

"He's already taken everything worth anything," Barb said, looking around the almost-empty room, at the flat squares of carpet where furniture had once sat and darker sections of paint where pictures had hung—all the ghostly impressions of Maggie's former life. "What's left?"

"Maybe he wants the Steuben." Maggie glanced over her shoulder at the four boxes of Steuben glassware she and Barb had carefully wrapped in tissue and Bubble Wrap. Carter Stevens had given her the first piece on their wedding day and then a new piece on every special occasion thereafter. Four boxes of memories too valuable to break.

"Open the envelope," Barb said. "Maybe there's a house in Vail he forgot to tell you about and he's been guilted into giving it to you."

"Carter never feels guilty." Not about dumping her after twenty years for an older (richer) woman. Not about taking the retirement fund and leaving her with a house that was worth less than the mortgage owed on it. She slid her thumb under the flap of the envelope and ripped it open, then pulled out a sheaf of legal papers. On top was a handwritten letter on stationery that matched the envelope. It was dated May 18, only four days previous.

Dear Ms. Stevens,
I am very sorry to inform you of the death of your father, Jacob Charles Murphy.

The words echoed in her head like a snatch of song spliced into the middle of the stock market report, or one second of bad porn flashed on the screen during a Disney cartoon—out of place and unsettling.

"Maggie? Honey, are you all right?" Barb grasped Maggie's shoulders and led her to the only chair in the room—a fake

Eames armchair that was awaiting pickup by the Disabled Veterans. Maggie perched on the edge of the seat and stared at the letter until Barb took it from her.

"Oh, honey, I'm so sorry," Barb said. "I didn't know your dad was in Colorado."

"Neither did I. I didn't even know he was alive."

"I remember you said he and your mom split when you were little. You never talked about him."

How could she talk about someone who was more fantasy than reality? The laws of biology dictated that, of course, she had a father, but she'd never been sure she could believe science any more than she did religion.

"When was the last time you saw him?" Barb asked.

Maggie shook her head. "I never met him—at least not when I was old enough to remember." The only things she had of her father—besides his DNA—were three pictures from the album her mother had kept on the top shelf of her closet.

Maggie had taken the pictures after her mother died two years previously, and tucked them away beneath the bras and panties in her underwear drawer, where she could be pretty sure Carter wouldn't snoop. After twenty years together, he knew the story, but she'd been reluctant to share those photographs with him. Maybe even then she sensed she couldn't trust him with those treasured icons. If only she'd paid attention to those instincts.

"You want to talk about it?" Barb asked.

Maggie shook her head, then sighed. "He and my mom married and then he left for his second tour of duty in Vietnam. He came home long enough to see me born and to name me after his mother. As far as I know, we never saw him again. Mama always said the war messed him up." When Maggie was little, she thought that meant he'd been maimed or crippled. As she got older, she understood her mother meant the war had damaged her father's mind. She still couldn't pass a homeless man on a street corner without stopping to give him money, especially if he wore an old army jacket or fatigues, or had a sign that read: VIETNAM VET, PLS HELP. "I thought about trying to find him, but never did anything about it." That fear thing again—she'd been too afraid of what she might discover.

Barb turned back to the letter. "Who handwrites a letter these days?" she asked. She flipped to the legal-sized sheets following and let out a whoop.

"What?" Maggie stood, her legs still a little shaky. "What is it?"

"It says here Daddy left you a gold mine." She grinned. "Won't Carter eat his shorts when he hears that?"

Maggie grabbed the papers and scanned them, lines of crisp black type jumping out at her: *sole heir . . . all his worldly goods and possessions . . . French Mistress Mine.*

"It sounds more like a brothel than a mine," she said.

"It says farther down that it's in the Eureka Gold Mining District," Barb said. "And it belongs to you."

"Do they still mine gold in the U.S.?" Maggie asked.

"Why not? Do you know what the price of a troy ounce is up to these days?"

"No, do you?"

"Well, no," Barb admitted. "But I know it's a lot. Jimmy bought me these earrings for my birthday and whined about the cost for a week." She touched the large gold hoops at her ears.

Maggie read the letter through a second time, trying to absorb its contents.

> *I hope you will want to visit Eureka and see your new property. Please let me know if I can be of any assistance.*

"It says here there's a house and two vehicles in addition to the mine, and '*sundry personal belongings.*' "

"Sounds like your daddy did pretty well for himself. And he didn't forget his little girl."

Maggie swallowed past a painful tightening in her throat. She'd never even known the man and she felt like weeping over his death.

No, not over his death. The tears that threatened were for the missed opportunities he hadn't taken advantage of, to know her and to be there for her when she could have used a father in her life. He might have held on to her memory for forty years, but why hadn't he bothered to contact her? Why wait until he was gone and it was too late for him to be anything more to her than a collection of might-have-beens and what-ifs?

"What are you going to do?" Barb asked.

Maggie looked at the discarded furniture and piles of packing boxes—all that was left of twenty years of marriage to a man who had turned out to be a stranger to her. Her hand went to the chain around her neck, where she'd worn her mother's wedding ring for the past two years. The day the divorce was final, she'd slipped her own ring onto the chain. She told herself she should sell it or put it away in a jewelry box, but she wasn't ready to give up something that had been a part of her for twenty years. Twenty years in which she'd made Carter the focus of her life, living where he wanted to live, working where he wanted her to work. At the time, she'd thought of her actions as the requirements of love and devotion; now, she felt she'd been sadly duped.

He was gone and she was left with no family, no job, and no idea what to do with the rest of her life. Her only plans were to take a trip somewhere, anywhere. She'd fantasized about spending the summer exploring Europe, eating bread and pasta in intimate little cafés in Tuscany and walking cobbled streets in Rome, seeing new sights and discovering new things about herself, and eventually ceasing to mourn the end of her marriage. But so far all she'd managed was a one-way ticket to Las Vegas, where she had a vague notion of staying at the Venetian and pretending she was in Venice.

She could probably trade in that ticket for one to Colorado. "I think," she said, a shiver of excitement like incense smoke curling through her. "I think I'm going to Eureka." She'd see this gold mine, sort through the personal belongings, and try to take stock of the man she'd never known and the life she needed to lead.

On the flight to Denver, Maggie was seated next to a dentist who felt the need to impress her with his life story. She devoured an extra-large chocolate bar and wondered if the sudden urge to scratch was the first sign of hives. When the flight ended, she raced to the airport ladies' room and checked the mirror. No sign of her ass disappearing—if anything, it was bigger than the last time she'd checked.

The flight from Denver to Montrose, the closest town of any size to Eureka, was on a turboprop that held maybe thirty passengers. The flight attendant shepherded them up the ladder to the plane, then climbed down and directed the pilot out onto the runway. Maggie spent the flight trying not to think about falling out of the sky and wishing for more chocolate.

After the plane had leveled out, she opened her purse and took out the envelope with the three photographs of her father. All three pictures showed a tall, slender man with reddish hair and clear hazel eyes. He had a high forehead and thick brows, and a wide mouth stretched into a smile so genuine and warm it made anyone who saw the pictures smile in return. In one photo, he stood by himself in front of a white 1966 Mustang, one hand on the driver's side door as if caressing it.

In the second photo, the man stood with a blond teenage girl. The girl wore a white pique mini dress and white sandals, and carried a bouquet of orange blossoms and stephanotis. The man wore army khakis, a private's insignia on his shoulders.

In the last photo, taken with a Polaroid camera and faded almost pastel with the passing years, the man cradled a pink-swathed baby. The infant's face wasn't visible in the photo; the man's face was the focus of the shot. His smile was stretched even wider, the eyes filled with such tenderness and pride; Maggie had burst into tears the first time she saw the picture. Even now, though she had looked at the image a thousand times or more, she felt her eyes mist and hastily tucked the photo back into her purse.

Reginald Paxton, Esquire, had offered to meet her plane, so while she waited for her suitcase, she scanned the crowd for anyone who looked like a lawyer. She'd about decided he was the fat man in the dark suit when someone tapped her on the shoulder. "Mrs. Stevens? I'm Reggie Paxton."

Reggie was a forty-something biker with a silver ponytail; small, square, granny glasses; and a black leather vest. Maggie managed to pick her jaw up off the floor and offer her hand.

"Hello, Reggie," she said. "I'm Maggie Stevens."

"I'd have known you anywhere," he said. "You look just like old Murph."

"I do?" The idea made her heart beat a little too fast.

"Well, you're certainly prettier than Murph, but you've got his eyes and the red hair."

She put a hand to the auburn curls she'd pinned up for travel. These days the color came straight out of a bottle; no sense telling Reggie her original shade was something her mother had always disparaged as "mouse."

"We've got about a forty-minute drive, but I can use the time to fill you in on all the details of your father's estate and answer any questions you might have," Reggie said, when she'd pointed out her suitcase and he'd snatched it from the belt.

To her relief, he didn't drive a Harley, or at least he hadn't brought it with him to the airport. Instead, he loaded her suitcase into a dusty blue Subaru with vanity plates that read: LGL EGL.

"I'm very sorry about your father's death," Reggie continued when they were buckled in and headed toward the airport exit. "Murph was a great guy, and a good friend of mine."

"I—I didn't really know him well," she said. "Not at all, actually. He and my mother split up shortly after I was born."

"Yeah, he told me the story. His side of it anyway. His biggest regret was never getting to know you."

"He could have picked up the phone or got on a plane anytime," she said, unable to keep the iciness from her voice.

"Yeah, and he should have." Reggie adjusted the visor to block the worst of the sun's glare as they turned west onto the highway. "He knew it, but he couldn't make himself do it." He glanced at her. "Murph was a great guy, but he wasn't perfect."

How great could a guy be who abandoned his wife and child, and never even tried to get in touch with them? she thought. But she kept the idea to herself. "The papers you sent said he left a gold mine?"

"The French Mistress." Reggie chuckled. "Heck of a name for a mine, ain't it? No one knows if there ever really was a mistress, or if it was just wishful thinking on the part of some lonely miner."

"So my father didn't name it?"

"Oh no. All these old mining claims were named over a hundred years ago. There's some pretty colorful ones: The Etta May, Colorado Princess, Last Chance—there's even one over in Lake County called the Codfish Balls Mine."

A hundred years ago. "So there's not actually any gold?"

"Some people say there still is, but it's hard to get to, and not worth the money it would take to get at it. Some of the mines never had any to begin with. Though there were always rumors about the French Mistress."

"What kind of rumors?"

"You'll understand better when you see the place. Your dad was quite a character."

Characters were people in plays and books. They weren't real—just as her father had never been real to her.

"What is it you do in Houston?" Reggie asked.

"I was the office manager for a shipping company." Carter's company, actually. "I was laid off a few months ago." Divorced, but the result was the same.

"Ah," Reggie nodded. "The economy's hitting a lot of people hard."

Carter's business was still booming, just without her. She'd thought about scrambling all the computer files before she left, but she hadn't had the heart to wish disaster on the woman who'd taken her place in the office.

Francine Dupree, aka the future Mrs. Carter Stevens, had no need to risk her manicure working in an office. The Dupree millions left to her by her first husband afforded her a life of shopping, spa treatments, and sleeping with other women's husbands.

How long before a forty-something shipping magnate with thinning hair and the beginnings of a paunch began to bore her? Carter had his moments, but the man had definitely been absent when charisma had been handed out. Maggie had always thought of him as "comfortable," a quality she thought desirable in a marriage partner. Unlike her adventurous soldier father, Carter had seemed guaranteed to stick around for years to come. A man who insisted on staying in the only house they'd ever owned, who drove the same model of car year after year, and who wore clothes until they were threadbare seemed a good bet for stability.

So much for thinking she knew anything about odds. Maybe it was a good thing she wasn't headed to Vegas.

"Do you have any children?" Reggie asked.

"No." The single syllable caused a tightness around her heart, the pang of deep regret. Carter hadn't wanted children, so they'd never had any. Of all the things he'd stolen from her, Maggie regretted this sacrifice the most.

"I've got two daughters," Reggie volunteered. "And two granddaughters. Girls run in our family."

"That's nice," Maggie said. What else could she say?

"Do you have reservations at one of the hotels in town?" he asked. "I can stop by there if you want to check in before we run up to Murph's place."

"Your letter said there was a house. I thought I'd stay there."

Reggie flushed. "I'm not sure you'd like Murphy's place. I mean, it's not really fit for a woman like yourself." He glanced at her gabardine slacks and matching jacket.

"I know my father was a bachelor and probably not much of a housekeeper, but I can clean the place up. It is mine now, right?"

"Yes, it's yours. And it's pretty clean. My wife and I emptied out the refrigerator and took out the trash so you wouldn't have to deal with that."

"Then what's the probl—Oh, he didn't have a girlfriend living there, did he? Or a wife?" The weight of the idea pressed her down in the seat. No one had mentioned anything about this, but her dad had only been sixty. Why shouldn't he have remarried? Oh God, did she have brothers or sisters running around somewhere?

"No, no, there was no girlfriend. And Murph never remarried after your mother, at least as far as I know." He nodded. "Yes, I'm sure I asked when we wrote up the will, and he was positive your mother was his only wife and you were his only child."

Maggie felt weak with relief, but disappointed, too. A half brother or sister might not be such a bad thing. When she was seven, she'd invented an imaginary sister, who slept in bed with her and shared half her chair at the table. The sister listened to all her whispered secrets and finished off the peas Maggie didn't like. A hollow space in her chest ached at the memory. It would be nice to think she had some remnant of family left in this world, now that both her parents were gone, but apparently her father had been as reluctant to take a second stab at marriage and parenting as her mother.

Which led to the question that had been nagging at her since she'd stepped on the plane to come here. "Reggie, what was my father like?"

"Murph was a great guy."

Right, as if that told her anything. Did that mean he paid his bills on time and liked the same sports teams as Reggie? "My mother always gave me the impression he came back from Vietnam, well, *different.* I never knew if that meant he suffered from post-traumatic stress or a drug problem or what." She went through a phase in high school where she read everything she could about the war and its veterans. She'd learned a lot, but nothing that gave her a clearer picture of her father.

"He didn't talk about his war experience much," Reggie said. "He drank too much sometimes, but he didn't make a real habit of it. He liked his privacy and all, but he wasn't really a hermit. He had plenty of friends in town. You'll meet some of them, I'm sure. They'll want to stop by and pay their respects." He glanced at her again, a twinkle in his eye. "And they'll want to get a look at Murph's girl."

"Then he wasn't . . . crazy? Mentally ill, I mean."

Reggie's expression sobered. "Jacob Murphy was as sane as you or I," he said. "Every once in a while he'd get to feeling down—he'd go off into the mountains for a while until he got to feeling better. I guess some people would label that depression, but Murph got through it his own way and didn't seem the worse for it."

She felt a surge of relief, accompanied by threatening tears. She blinked rapidly and dug her nails into her palms. "That's good," she said. "My mother said there were problems when he first got back from the war. I guess she meant the drinking."

"So you don't have any memories of him at all?" Reggie's voice was gentle.

"No, I was only a few days old when he left." She cleared her throat. "I was shocked when I got your letter—surprised he remembered me, or knew where to find me."

"Apparently he'd been in touch with your mother. We found a few letters . . . they're in a box up at his cabin."

"I—I didn't know." Her voice sounded watery, and she clamped her lips shut, willing herself not to break down. Her mother had talked about Jake a lot in the last weeks of her life, but she'd never mentioned any letters, or even suggested Maggie try to get in touch. Was that because he'd asked her not to?

They were silent for the next few miles, rocketing past pale green fields dotted with wildflowers and clusters of grazing cattle. Then they topped a rise and Reggie pointed toward the horizon. "That's Mount Winston there. The one that looks kind of like a mastodon tooth, with snow on top."

Mount Winston jutted from a range of slightly smaller peaks, stark silver and white against a sky so smooth and blue it reminded her of a porcelain plate. "It doesn't even look real," she said. "It's like a movie set or something."

Reggie chuckled. "It's real, all right. If there weren't all the trees in the way, you could see your dad's place, on the slopes of Mount Garnet."

"Are there garnets there?"

"I don't think so. The story is it's named after a miner's wife. Though another version says Garnet was a prostitute." He shrugged. "The truth gets muddied up sometimes."

Especially when men are involved, she thought, but kept her mouth shut. "Tell me about my dad's place," she said. "What did I inherit?"

"There's thirty-two acres," Reggie said. "Most of one side of Garnet Mountain. A house and a couple of outbuildings. A Jeep—it's old, but it still runs good. Oh, and a 2006 Polaris Switchback."

She blinked. "A what?"

"Snowmobile. Really nice one, too."

Understanding dawned. "That's the second of the two vehicles you mentioned in your letter?"

He nodded. "Murph used the Switchback as much as the Jeep in the winter."

Maggie's dreams of newfound wealth were melting as fast as ice cream on a hot sidewalk. "Tell me about the house."

"It's an old miner's cabin. Not much to look at on the outside, but Murph fixed it up pretty nice over the years—new roof and windows, insulation and everything. It's got a good wood stove, so it's warm in the winter, and up on the side of the mountain like it is, you can't beat the view. 'Course, it's not the easiest place to get to, especially in the winter. And there aren't any neighbors to speak of. You'd probably be more comfortable in town."

"It's not winter now," Maggie said, curiosity building. "Why couldn't I stay there? Is there electricity? Plumbing?"

"The electricity comes from solar panels on the roof and a generator for backup. There's a propane stove and refrigerator. Bathroom with a shower and composting toilet Murph put in a few years ago. Said he got tired of digging his way to the outhouse every time it snowed."

"A composting toi—" She felt a little queasy. If only Barb were here. She'd find something witty or crass to say to lighten the moment. She'd make Maggie feel better about the mansion in the mountains and two sleek vehicles, which had all burned to the ground, replaced by an aging Jeep, a snowmobile, and an off-the-grid miner's shack with a composting toilet.

"I want to see the place," she said. "Then I'll decide."

"No problem," Reggie said. "Like I said, the view alone is worth the trek up there, and there's probably a few things in the house you'll want to take with you."

Maybe she'd find some rusty miner's relic to remember her dad by. She'd come here hoping for treasure, but really, that would be more fitting—some worthless antique to commemorate their non-relationship.

A cluster of buildings came into view. "Welcome to Eureka," Reggie said. He flipped on his blinker and turned the car off the highway, onto a wide dirt road flanked by wood-front buildings that looked straight out of an old John Wayne western. One weathered wooden front bore the legend: DIRTY SALLY SALOON.

Maggie clamped her mouth shut, not wanting to be caught gaping like some yokel. "How big is Eureka?" she asked. "I mean, what's the population?"

"Four hundred or so permanent residents, though it can be ten times that many during tourist season." He pointed a long finger at a weathered two-story building with a false front. "My office is upstairs there. Downstairs is the Last Dollar Cafe. The Laundromat and grocery are one street over, and the library is behind there. If the librarian, Cassie Wynock, approves of you, she'll let you use the library computers to e-mail. If she doesn't, come by my office and you can use mine."

"If she *approves* of me?" Maggie did let her mouth drop open now.

Reggie shrugged. "Cassie's kind of particular. And she and your dad got in a tussle once over a book he checked out and never turned in."

"Oh, come on, now. She held a grudge over a late library book?"

"Well, apparently it was kind of a rare book on Eureka's history, and he kept it checked out for something like five years. He said he just forgot about it, but I suspect he did it because he knew it drove Cassie nuts."

Maggie sympathized with Cassie. She didn't have a lot of patience with people who broke rules simply for the sake of breaking them. Then again, she'd spent her life walking carefully inside the lines.

They passed a driveway flanked on either side with stone

columns and a large, colorful sign: LIVING WATERS. A tall wooden fence obscured the property from view.

"What's that?" Maggie asked.

"Hot springs," Reggie said. He grinned. "Clothing optional, hence the fence. It's open to the public, if you want to try it out."

"Um, no thanks."

"You can wear a suit if you're shy," he said. "The water's real relaxing."

He spoke with the voice of experience. A sudden image of the stocky lawyer in the altogether flashed through her mind; she quickly banished it. "How much farther to my dad's place?" she asked.

"Fifteen minutes or so," he said. "From here on out we'll be driving pretty much straight up."

She settled back in her seat as they left the last of the town behind. She didn't know what she'd expected, but clearly there wasn't much here for her in Eureka. She'd visit her dad's shack, collect a few mementos, and catch the next plane back to Houston, another chapter in her life closed. She and Barb would have a good laugh about it later. With any luck, Reggie would be able to sell the whole lot for enough money to at least pay for a good vacation.

One far away from the men who insisted on screwing up her life, both past and present.

Chapter 2

"Cassie, do we have any books on reincarnation?"

Cassie Wynock, librarian at the Eureka County Library, looked up in surprise at the shriveled knot of a man who stood before her desk. "Bob, why do you want a book on reincarnation?"

"Danielle told me in another life she used to be an Egyptian slave girl, and it got me thinking, wondering if I had any past lives."

In another life, Cassie would have been a wealthy woman of consequence—a queen or, at the very least, a prime minister. Certainly not a librarian who spent her days catering to people like Bob Prescott.

Then again, Cassie didn't believe in nonsense like reincarnation. The only past that shaped a person was the life she'd lived, and the lives of the ancestors before her. Cassie's forebears had been among the first to arrive in Eureka County and had made their mark all over this land. The very plot where the library now sat had once been Wynock property, as had the school and the bank and just about everything else in town. Most people had forgotten that, but not Cassie.

"The New Age books are over here," she said, leading Bob to the small section of shelves.

"Thanks, Cassie. Say, did you hear Jake Murphy's daughter's coming to town? Supposed to be arriving today."

Cassie stiffened. "I didn't know Jake had a daughter."

"Surprised the heck out of me, too." Bob studied the shelf. He needed a shave, and the bristles of his beard stood out like salt scattered across his chin. "Now, which one of these books is gonna help me figure out my past lives? Danielle said knowing what we were in the past can help us figure out what we're supposed to do in this life."

Bob was seventy if he was a day. If he hadn't figured out what to do with his life by now, why worry? But Cassie kept her mouth shut and returned to her desk. If he wanted to take life advice from a waitress at the café where he ate breakfast, Cassie wasn't one to tell him different.

She tried to focus on putting together the next issue of the library newsletter, but her mind kept wandering back to the other bit of news Bob had shared: Jake Murphy had a daughter.

The idea caused a pain behind her eyes. Thinking about Jake always hurt. She'd made such a fool of herself over the man.

Cassie was not a foolish woman. She'd graduated at the top of her class at Eureka High School and had been poised to head to the University of Colorado to major in international studies when her mother was diagnosed with cancer.

Cassie had done the right thing and stayed to nurse her mom while the rest of her classmates, including the boy she'd been dating, went off to college. When her mother died two years later, her father had been a complete wreck, so Cassie had stayed and enrolled in college at Montrose, commuting back and forth between the red brick campus and the Queen Anne home on Fourth Street where she'd grown up.

Montrose didn't offer international studies, so Cassie had let a counselor talk her into pursuing a degree in library science. She'd planned to transfer to CU in a couple of years and change her major, but that never happened.

Her father died, leaving her the house and not much else. The county had decided to build this library and had offered her the job, so she'd taken it. It wasn't what she'd planned for her life, but she'd made the best of it, and done a good job. She had no illusions about herself. She knew she was fast becoming a stereotype of the old maid librarian who lived alone with two cats. She'd dated some in her younger years, but the men who asked her out were of a type she secretly disdained—soft and studious, weak in a way that was too much like her father and his father before him. Wynock women had a history of being attracted to men without backbones—the main reason all the land they'd once owned was no longer theirs. Cassie wasn't going to follow in her mother's and grandmother's footsteps.

Then Jacob Murphy had turned her head completely, and played her for such a fool.

She'd seen him first at Hard Rock Days, an annual celebration of Eureka's mining heritage. Local men competed in feats of strength like racing, pushing loaded ore carts, and driving spikes in solid rock.

Jake had stepped up to take his turn swinging the hammer, a tall, lean man with coppery hair and beard. He'd stripped off his shirt to reveal rippling muscles—Cassie knew she wasn't the only woman in the crowd who drew in her breath at the sight. She hadn't been able to take her eyes off him as he swung the hammer. One, two, three blows and the spike was in. He accepted the trophy with a crooked grin.

The moment was burned into Cassie's memory. The sight of him had haunted her dreams for the next few nights. It didn't matter that he was older than her—fifty-five to her forty-five. He was exactly the kind of man she wanted. The kind who never gave her a second glance.

And then the man himself had stepped into the library and walked right up to her desk with that same crooked smile and asked if she could help him find some books on local history. He'd cast a spell on her, one from which it had taken her months to awaken.

"Cassie, are you gonna help me out here or not?"

Bob's voice broke into her reverie. She jumped up from the desk and hurried to the front counter. "Did you find the book you wanted?" she asked.

"Nah, found some stuff about other people's past lives, but I don't give a damn about any of them. Maybe I'll ask Danielle what she recommends. In the meantime, I got this instead." He held up the latest Dan Brown novel.

"Hello, Bob, Cassie." A tall woman dressed like a gypsy in a patchwork skirt and peasant blouse emerged from the stacks and approached the counter.

"Afternoon, Madam Mayor." Bob grinned, probably because he knew how much Lucille Theriot hated her title. One more example of how she didn't take the job seriously, Cassie thought. Look at the way she dressed. She looked more like a bag lady than the mayor of a small town.

"Lucille, what do you reckon you were in your past life?" Bob asked.

Lucille didn't even blink at this non sequitur. "I have no idea, Bob. I have enough trouble keeping up in this life without worrying about the last one."

"But you do believe in it? Reincarnation, I mean."

"I'm at the age where nothing surprises me."

Cassie pulled forward the stack of books and began scanning them—*Parenting the Adult Child, When Your Adult Children Move Home, Healing Broken Families*. She looked up and met Lucille's gaze with a questioning look.

The mayor flushed. "My daughter is moving in with me for a while."

What was this, secret offspring week? "I didn't know you had a daughter," Cassie said.

"She's been living in Connecticut with her father since she was a teenager. Now she's lost her job and wanted a change of scenery, I guess." Lucille opened and closed the top book on the stack, fidgeting. "She needs my help. It will be a good opportunity for us to get to know each other again. And she has a son, a little boy."

"I was just telling Cassie I heard Jake Murphy's daughter is coming to town, too," Bob said. "You reckon she's here to stay?"

"I believe she's coming to look at the property she inherited," Lucille said. "Reggie's picking her up at the airport right now."

Reggie Paxton was the town's only lawyer, so Cassie guessed he'd handled Jake's will. "Did you know Jake had a daughter?" she asked Lucille.

The older woman shook her head. "Apparently he and the girl's mother split years ago and he hadn't seen his daughter since. But he left her everything in his will, so she's coming out to take a look."

"If she needs someone to show her the French Mistress, I can help her out," Bob offered. "I spent almost as much time up there as Jake."

"She might not appreciate the fact that you were trespassing," Lucille said mildly.

"A man shouldn't let a few obstacles get in the way of a dream," Bob said, rubbing the side of his face. Cassie remembered Jake had given the old man a black eye once, when he'd caught him in the mine uninvited.

"One look at the mine and Jake's old place will send her running back to wherever she's from," Cassie said.

Lucille shrugged. "You never know. This country can take hold of a person. That's what happened to me."

"Plenty of people think they like it, until they spend their first winter here," Cassie said. It took a certain toughness to thrive in these mountains, a toughness that had been bred into Cassie.

"We'll all get a chance to meet her," Lucille said. "Danielle and Janelle are talking about holding a kind of memorial service for Jake over at the café while she's here."

"I thought they already had a service," Cassie said.

"Not really. Some of Jake's friends got together and scattered his ashes, but we never had a real ceremony. I think it would be nice for his daughter."

"Why should she care, if she hasn't seen him in years?" Cassie asked.

"If it were me, I'd want to know what my old man was like," Bob said.

Cassie sniffed. "She should talk to me. I could tell her what he was like."

"Not everyone feels the way you do," Lucille said. She gathered up her books. "See you around."

Lucille and Bob left together. Cassie gave up on the newsletter and stared out the window. She had a view from here of Mount Winston. This time of year the crown of the mountain was heavy with snow, shining silver in the afternoon sun. Her family had once owned a good part of the mountain, and neighboring Mount Garnet, too. They'd probably even owned the land where the French Mistress stood, though she'd never been able to prove it. Her great-grandfather had thought all that rock useless and had been happy to sell it to the miners who came looking for gold. Fool's gold, he'd called it, though he'd been the fool when so many of them found the precious metal and became rich.

The money in the family came from her great-grandmother, who'd had the foresight to open a restaurant and laundry to cater to the miners. Later, she'd added a general store and a hotel. She was the one who built the house Cassie lived in now.

Cassie came from a line of strong women who made a habit of falling for weak men. Jake hadn't been weak, but he'd definitely been wrong. Cassie should thank her lucky stars she'd discovered his true nature before it was too late.

* * *

The house struggled up the steep slope like an old woman in long skirts, in danger of falling over with one good shove. The exterior was unpainted wood, weathered the soft gray of pencil lead. The roof was rusted to the color of dried blood. A silver stovepipe jutted from the peak of the roof, a tattered scrap of cloth fluttering from it.

"Is that . . . a windsock?" Maggie asked, squinting at the once-red tube of fabric.

"Yep." Reggie pulled a set of keys from his pocket. "I'd better give you these before I forget. The keys to the Jeep and the snowmobile are on there. House key, too, though I doubt Murph ever used it."

Maggie accepted the keys and climbed out of the car, which was parked on perhaps the only flat section of ground on her father's property. Every other square inch slanted precariously. As she braced herself with one hand against the car door, a chill wind tugged at her clothes. "Whatever possessed him to want to live up here?" she asked Reggie as he joined her beside the car.

"It was probably just a matter of convenience at first. He needed a place to live and the house was here when he bought the place, though he's done a considerable amount of work on it."

She stared at the shack. One end of the front porch was supported by a pillar of dry-stack rocks, while the other jutted into thin air. On closer inspection, the siding was of varying widths of wood held together with rusting nails, and no two windows were the same size. "He did?"

"It's a lot more sound than it looks," Reggie said. "Why don't we go inside?"

She followed him up a stone path to the porch, which, despite its appearance, felt solid enough underfoot. Reggie pushed open the door, then stepped aside to let her enter.

She hesitated, suddenly nervous. She'd wanted to come to

Eureka to discover what her father was like, but what if she didn't like what she found? A person's home was so personal. Her mother had had a little embroidered picture on her bedroom wall: *Home Is Where the Heart Is.* Was she really ready to see her father's heart, which she had at various times in her life pictured as black, or merely empty?

The house was not empty. Furniture and possessions crowded the front room, which, as it turned out, was the only room except for the little bathroom tacked on the back and the loft bedroom overhead. Maggie stood on a square rag rug just inside the door and tried to take it all in.

Directly in front of her was an overstuffed love seat and matching chair, each covered in old quilts, arranged in front of a polished black wood stove. Behind the love seat was a square wooden table with two chairs. A tall bookcase stood against the wall opposite the woodstove, while the back wall of the cabin was filled with kitchen cabinets, an old-fashioned refrigerator with rounded corners, and a narrow gas stove and deep enamel sink.

"Bedroom's upstairs." Reggie pointed to the steps next to the bookcase. "There's a king-size bed up there and more bookcases. Murph was a great reader. The bathroom's through that door in the corner."

She nodded and moved a little farther into the house, like a swimmer acclimating to cold water.

"He put all these windows in about four years ago," Reggie said. "You've got a terrific view now from every room—even the bathroom." He nudged her a little farther into the room. Now she was standing directly behind the love seat, staring out at the world falling away—sky and clouds and distant mountains, like the view from an airplane.

But she wasn't in an airplane. She was in a house, standing on a solid floor, though that, too, suddenly seemed to be falling away, as she tumbled over in a dead faint.

* * *

When Maggie came to, she was flat on her back on the hard wood floor, staring up at her own distorted reflection in Reggie's glasses. "Wh-what happened?" she gasped.

"You fainted. Easy now." Reggie supported her as she sat up.

"That's ridiculous. I never faint." She looked around, as if she might spot the culprit who was responsible for this embarrassment.

"It's the altitude," Reggie said. "You're at ten thousand feet above sea level here. It takes some getting used to. I can take you back to the hotel in town. That's only eighty-five hundred feet, so you should feel better there."

"I feel fine," she said, ignoring the buzzing behind her eyes. She struggled to her feet and stared out at the view again. "Are we really hanging out in space like this?" she asked.

"In a manner of speaking." Reggie kept one hand on her arm, as if he expected her to tumble over again at any moment. "But remember, this house has been here at least a hundred years. And Murph installed all-new anchor bolts not long after he moved in. Two-inch-thick steel drilled into solid rock. You're in no danger of sliding off into space, even if it feels that way."

She continued to stare at the expanse of sky and rock spread out before her. She was reminded of the IMAX movies she'd seen as a kid, when the helicopter carrying the camera suddenly swooped over a canyon. She had that same stomach-dropping sense of the world falling away. Of flying. "It's incredible," she said.

"The view from the bedroom's the same, while the kitchen and bathroom look up the mountain."

"I want to see."

She admired the view from the kitchen and dining windows of silver rock and gold aspen. A crabapple tree grew at the corner of the house, sheltered between a lee of rock and the old outhouse. "The outhouse still works," Reggie said.

"Murph kept it because it was convenient when he was outside working."

She couldn't decide if this proved her father was lazy, practical, or just eccentric, though she was leaning toward the latter. She climbed into the loft, sat on the edge of the quilt-covered bed, and stared at the dizzying view once more. Reggie sat beside her, silent for a long while. There was something to be said for a man who knew when to keep his mouth shut.

A dark speck appeared in the sky and moved closer. A bird of some kind soared in lazy circles—some kind of hawk, or maybe an eagle. In all these books filling the bookcases, was there a volume that would tell her?

"Do you think, living with a view like that every day, you ever come to take it for granted?" she asked after a while.

"I don't think Murph ever did. He always said he didn't need a church as long as he had that view. For him, this place was heaven. That's why he stayed here, even through the rough winters."

She tried to imagine her father, a vague figure with features that weren't clear to her, alone in this cabin surrounded by mountains and sky. What had he found here that had kept him here despite the hardships?

She'd felt empty since Carter left, but maybe before that, even. People made jokes about midlife crises, but was it really so surprising that someone should reach middle age and wonder if they'd really fulfilled their purpose in life? Other women her age were raising children, some even had grandchildren. Maggie had produced no family, built no career. Even before Carter left, she'd wondered sometimes if working in an office and cooking balanced meals each evening was the best use of her talents. She'd signed up for a yoga class, but whenever the teacher told her to lie still and focus on her breathing, she'd always ended up making a mental grocery list or replaying inane commercial jingles—as if her breath just wasn't interesting enough. As if *she* wasn't interesting enough.

That was her big fear, right there in a nutshell. Carter had left her because she was boring. And if she didn't do something to change, she would bore herself right to death. She'd thought travel abroad would help broaden her perspective and inspire her to try new things—to be a different sort of person.

She gazed out the window at the world spread out below her. She doubted a person could find a broader perspective than this, or a place more unlike what she was used to.

"You don't need to drive me back to the hotel," she said. "I'd like to stay here."

"Are you sure?" Reggie studied her face. "It gets cold up here at night, even in summer. You'll have to start a fire in the stove. I don't imagine you've done that much in Houston."

"I'll figure it out."

"All right, then." He stood. "Do you have a cell phone?"

She nodded.

"You might have to walk up the road a ways to get a good signal." He fished a card out of his wallet. "My number's on there. You call me if you need anything at all."

"Thank you. I'll be all right. Really."

She climbed down the ladder after him and walked with him to the door. She waited while he retrieved her suitcase, then watched out the front window, until the plume of dust from his car disappeared into the distance. Then she sat on the love seat and stared out at the view, alone in a silence deeper than she'd ever known, but for the first time in a long time, not really lonely. The view was a kind of companion, as if the world itself was embracing her. She wondered if this was what her father had felt when he said he was in heaven here. She didn't know if she believed in heaven, but maybe spending some time here would help her find out.

Chapter 3

Maggie woke to the hazy gray light of dusk, cold seeping over her, and her stomach growling with hunger. She sat up, aware of another growling, too. A deep rumble, echoing through the house. It sounded like . . . a motorcycle?

She hurried down the stairs and looked out the front window at a black and silver motorcycle squatting where Reggie's car had been parked earlier. A man in black leather—leather jacket, leather chaps, black leather boots—straddled the motorcycle. As she watched, he took off his helmet, revealing a shaggy mass of hair a shade darker than the chestnut goatee that framed his frowning lips. He stared up at the house, his frown deepening.

An icy fist of fear clamped around her heart as she realized she was literally in the middle of nowhere, alone, without even a telephone to call for help. What if this was some crazed serial killer who'd decided to take advantage of her vulnerability?

She looked around the room for some kind of weapon. Oh, why hadn't she taken that self-defense course that had been offered at the Y last month? She picked up a stick of kindling from the bucket by the wood stove. Was it thick enough to knock a man out? Even if it was, how would she get close enough to hit him before he overpowered her? Oh God, what if he had a gun?

She crept to the window for another look. The motorcycle was silent now. And empty. The man in black had disappeared.

She fumbled in her pocket for her cell phone. Maybe . . . She flipped it open. NO SERVICE. Dammit! Who in their right mind lived in a place with no telephone? Then again, obviously her father had not been in his right mind. Men in their right minds didn't desert their wife and infant daughter for no reason and without a glance back.

The scrape of gravel outside the other side of the house made her catch her breath. With the stealth of a cat burglar—or maybe just the caution of a terrified female—she crept to the window on that side.

The man was there all right, on the path that led toward the old outhouse. He had a stick in one hand and was poking at something on the ground. Watching him, anger began to edge out Maggie's fear. She stalked to the front door and yanked it open, then ran to the end of the porch. "Who are you and what the hell do you think you're doing?" she shouted.

The man dropped the stick and whirled around, the frown replaced by a look of astonishment. "I could ask you the same question, lady," he barked.

"I own this place, and you're trespassing. You need to leave before I call the police."

"Call them on what? There's no phone up here."

Why did bluffing work in books and movies, but never in real life? "What are you doing here?" she asked.

"I came to check on the place, make sure everything was all right." He took a few steps toward her.

She held out the stick of kindling. "Don't come any closer."

He glanced at the wood, which, come to think of it, was pretty thin, and seemed to be fighting back a smile. But he stopped moving toward her. "You said you own this place?" he asked. "Who sold it to you?"

"No one sold it to me. I inherited it from my father."

All humor vanished from the man's face. "I knew the owner of this place and he never said a word about any daughter," he said. "So try telling the truth this time."

Maggie didn't know whether to be more upset that this stranger was accusing her of lying, or that maybe he was telling the truth about her father never mentioning her. "Jacob Murphy was my father," she said. "He and my mother split up when I was still a baby, but he left me everything he had in his will. If you don't believe me, go talk to Reggie Paxton."

Blinking back tears, she turned and headed toward the front door.

The stranger was on her with lightning speed. He grabbed her arm, pulling her away from the door. Maggie screamed and lashed out, and he stepped back so quickly she stumbled.

"Hey, it's okay," he said, holding both hands up as if to ward off a blow. "I didn't mean to scare you. And I'm sorry I accused you of lying. You just startled me is all. I didn't expect to find anyone up here."

"Thought you'd be free to snoop around, didn't you?" she said. "Maybe help yourself to whatever you wanted."

"Hey, I said I was sorry for calling you a liar. No need for you to accuse me of being a thief."

"Then what are you doing up here, especially this time of night?"

"I was on my way back from Telluride and thought I'd swing by and make sure everything was all right. And I was thinking about Murph, missing him. I thought it would be good to come up here and remember a bit."

He was a very good actor or was telling the truth. Maggie relaxed a little. Up close, the man was a little older than she'd first taken him for—early thirties, maybe. "What's your name?"

"Jameso Clark."

"I'm Maggie Stevens."

"Pleased to meet you, Maggie." He offered his hand, still clad in fingerless leather riding gloves.

His hand was big and warm, the leather soft against her palm. She tried to remember the last time she'd been this close to a man, and couldn't. She reluctantly slid from his grasp. "Hello, Jameso."

He peered into her face. "I can see the resemblance to Murph now. You've got his eyes."

"I do?" Her mother had never mentioned she looked like her father, but then, her mother never talked much about Jacob Murphy, at least not until the end. And then those ramblings had been focused on the past—on a time before Maggie existed.

"I'm sorry for your loss," Jameso said.

"Thank you. But I really didn't know him. You two were friends?"

"Yes and no."

The cryptic answer puzzled her. Was he her father's friend or wasn't he? But before she could probe further, he put his hand on her shoulder. "It's getting cold out here. Why don't we go inside."

"It's not much warmer in the cabin," she said. "I need to start a fire." She still couldn't get over the idea that it felt like February at the end of May. In Houston, she'd already been running the air conditioner for two months.

"I can do that for you."

He followed her into the cabin, filling the tiny room with his presence. He squatted in front of the stove and began feeding wood into the box. "You want to surrender your weapon now?" he asked.

She glanced at the wood in her hand. "Oh, sure. Do you want some coffee? And maybe something to eat? I'm starved. I don't know what's in the kitchen. Well, I do know there's a bunch of Lorna Doones. My dad must have really liked them." She was babbling but couldn't seem to stop herself. Silence felt too charged between them.

Jameso smiled. "Coffee would be good."

She escaped to the kitchen side of the room, determined to pull herself together. A single electric bulb lit the small space. She found the coffeepot, an old-style percolator, and lit a burner on the gas stove with a lighter she found hanging on a nail by the sink. The coffee was in a canister in the freezer. Soon the comforting aroma of brewing French roast filled the air.

In the refrigerator she found a loaf of bread, mustard, and a package of deli ham. Bless Reggie's wife.

"The house will be warmer soon."

Jameso spoke from behind her. She turned and found him filling the space between the love seat and table. He no longer looked menacing, but still, he made her nervous. She took two mugs from hooks under the cabinet and set them on the counter. "Do you want a ham sandwich?" she asked.

"No thanks. I've already eaten. But you go ahead." He moved past her to open a cabinet. "Where are you from?" he asked.

"Houston."

He reached into the cabinet and took out a tall bottle. He smiled at the label, then unscrewed the cap and poured a generous slug into one of the mugs. "Irish whiskey," he said. "Do you want some?"

She nodded. "All right."

Jameso poured the whiskey and left the bottle on the counter, then turned to contemplate the expanse of starlit sky in the picture window. "I was in Houston a few years ago," he said. "A lot different from this."

"Yes." Houston was another world compared with this mountaintop.

"You plan to stay here?" he asked. "Or are you just checking the place out to sell?"

"I'm not sure." She didn't have much to go back to in Houston; then again, she didn't feel like she really belonged here.

"You should give it a try. Murph must have thought you'd like it, since he left you the place."

"Or maybe the place is mine now because it's customary to leave your belongings to your only relative."

"Murph never did anything because it was customary." He switched off the flame beneath the coffeepot and filled their cups. It felt odd to be in a home that was supposedly hers, yet this stranger was so much more at ease here than she felt she ever would be.

He moved into the living room. She took her sandwich and followed, sitting on one end of the love seat, knees together, plate on her lap, while he sprawled beside her, long legs stretched in front of him. "What were you looking at out there, before I startled you?" she asked.

"What do you mean?"

"You were poking at something with a stick. What was it?"

He made a face. "I was just looking at a pile of scat, trying to figure out whether it was fresh or not."

"Scat?"

He laughed. "A pile of animal feces. Shit. Bighorn sheep shit, to be exact. I wanted to know if the animal that left it had been around recently."

"Are you some kind of tracker? Hunter?"

"No, I just live in the mountains, and I'm interested in everything else that lives up here."

"What do you do?"

"Whatever I can." He shrugged. "In the summer, I drive tourists around on all the Jeep trails. In the winter, I give ski lessons to other tourists over at Telluride. Sometimes I tend bar down in town."

"At the Dirty Sally." She remembered the saloon.

"That's right. It's named after a mine."

"Speaking of mines, what do you know about the French Mistress?"

"You mean this place?"

"Is there more than one?"

He shrugged. "I really don't know anything about it."

"It was a gold mine, right? Was there any gold in it? Reggie said there were rumors. . . ."

"There were rumors, all right. I think Murph made up half of them himself, to keep people guessing."

"Why would he do that?"

"He didn't like people knowing his business. That included me." He leaned forward and set his mug on the coffee table in front of the sofa. "I don't know about the gold. Murph had money from somewhere." He gestured toward the picture window in front of them. "It may not look like much to you, but it cost a lot to fix up this place. Whether he paid for it with gold or some other way, I don't know. He was good at keeping secrets."

"What kind of secrets?"

"You, for one." He stood. "I'd better go."

She didn't want him to leave. In the dark, she was so much more aware of her loneliness.

Unlike Reggie, Jameso didn't seem too concerned about leaving her alone in the remote cabin. He was probably used to rugged mountain women who looked after themselves. Maggie had always thought of herself as independent; she always held a job and had her own money, her own friends. But here, in this alien landscape, she felt weak, unsteady on her feet.

Or maybe that was just the shot of whiskey in the coffee. "I'll be fine," she said, though she hadn't meant to speak the words out loud.

Jameso gave her a curious look. "Why wouldn't you be?" He headed toward the door. "I'll stop by again sometime, see if you need anything," he said.

"Thanks." She stood in the doorway, one hand clutching at the rings on the chain beneath her shirt. She watched him climb onto the motorcycle and roar off into the night, the taillight a single red ember disappearing down the mountain.

"I'll be all right," she said again as she closed the door and turned back to the fire. But just all right wasn't going to be enough. She wanted to be happy again, to remember what that contentment felt like. She contemplated the star-spangled view and felt a swell of something inside her; it was not yet strong enough to be called hope. She'd label it possibility.

Lucille smoothed the plaid quilt over the twin bed and frowned. Was the plaid appropriate for a thirteen-year-old boy? Would he rather have rocket ships or baseballs or something else entirely? Should she have waited for him to get here and let him pick out the furnishings for his room?

She sat on the end of the bed and looked at the mismatched dresser and chair, and the student desk shoved under the eaves. Everything was gleaned from the antique/junk shop she owned. The things were donations or items she'd picked up at auctions or even out of alleys on trash day. She wouldn't bother telling Olivia that, or Lucas. If the boy took after his mother at all, he was sure to be embarrassed by his grandmother, as Olivia had always been embarrassed by her mother.

She had no idea what the boy was like. The last time she'd seen him he was seven months old. The last time she'd seen him in person, she amended. Olivia sent photographs from time to time. The last was of an owlish-looking boy with pale blue eyes behind round, wire-rimmed glasses, his close-cropped blond hair almost invisible against his pink scalp.

Lucille had no idea what Olivia herself looked like these

days. The young woman changed her appearance like a chameleon, blending in with whatever crowd she associated with at the time. She'd gone through a Goth phase, dying her hair ink black and wearing Kabuki white makeup. Another time, she'd bleached her hair platinum and donned pencil skirts and round-toed pumps and rolled curls à la Veronica Lake. Still later, she'd added pink streaks to the blond and taken to wearing baggy jeans and skintight baby T's and listening to loud, angry rap music.

Maybe having a child of her own had settled her down some. Lucille hoped so, though she couldn't call this latest move settled.

The call had come out of the blue, while Lucille was working at the store. "Hey," Olivia said, an abrupt, sharp syllable that was more a command for attention than a greeting. "The kid and I are thinking about coming out to see you for a while."

Lucille's heart pounded at the words, but she told herself not to get too excited. Olivia had promised visits before and they hadn't materialized. "You know I'd always love to see you and Lucas," she said.

"Yeah, well, I lost my job and D. J. moved out, so I thought it was a good time to come stay with you a while."

Lucille took it D. J. was the latest boyfriend, though she'd never heard him mentioned before. The last she'd heard, Olivia was living with someone named Allen. Lucas's father had disappeared from the picture so long ago, Lucille could scarcely remember his name. Bryan, maybe?

Then the news about the job sank in. Olivia had been working as a receptionist at an electronics manufacturing business for the last five years. "You were laid off?" Lucille asked.

"Fired, actually. I was sick of the place anyway. You've got room for us, right?"

Physically, Lucille had two empty bedrooms, if you counted

the little room up under the eaves where she stored luggage and extra inventory from the store. Emotionally, she was less sure she had room for her daughter's always disruptive presence. But she had the boy to think of. Maybe this would be a chance for her to get to know her only grandchild.

"How long do you think you'll stay?" she asked.

"Don't know. 'Til you and I can't stand each other, I guess."

Lucille winced. When Olivia had last lived in her mother's home, she'd been a strong-willed fifteen-year-old who balked at Lucille's curfew, requirements she do her homework before watching TV or visiting friends, and her refusal to buy Olivia cigarettes or a car. She'd run away on a bus to her father, and he and Lucille had decided their daughter would be better off staying with him.

Lucille had been secretly relieved Mitch was willing to take over the burden of dealing with the obstreperous teen, but that relief was coupled with guilt that she'd somehow failed her daughter. "All right," she said. "I'll look forward to seeing you."

They were driving in tonight, and Lucille supposed she was as ready as she'd ever be. She went to the window and stared out at the darkened street, as if that would make Olivia drive up any sooner. A single headlight appeared in the distance, approaching fast. A motorcycle with a dark figure crouched on its back. Lucille recognized Jameso Clark. Handsome, wild Jameso, the kind of man-boy she had chased after time and time again when she was a girl. Unless things had changed, Olivia would waste no time picking Jameso from the herd here in Eureka. Lucille felt no qualms about this. Jameso was a good man, if a little restless. He might be a positive influence on Olivia, and at least he would give her one more reason to stay in town.

She looked down the street again. Two houses down, every light blazed. Cassie Wynock kept her house lit up as if she were hosting a party every night, though she lived alone with two cats and enough old books and pictures to fill a museum. Lucille had been inside exactly once, when she delivered a desk Cassie had purchased from the shop. Cassie had claimed the desk had been her father's and she didn't know how it ended up in Lucille's shop, but she wanted it back in its rightful place.

Lucille knew exactly how that desk had ended up in her shop. A woman who had bought it from Cassie's father had sold it to her, but she didn't argue with Cassie. If the woman wanted to pay double what the thing was worth to have it back, Lucille wouldn't argue. As it was, the two of them had a hard time wedging the piece in among all the other relics stuffed into the downstairs parlor.

Lucille imagined Cassie in her crowded house, wandering through the rooms and turning on all the lights. Was the illumination so she could see all her treasures better? Or because she was afraid of the ghosts that surely lurked among all the flotsam and jetsam from the past?

Two more headlights appeared in the distance, wobbling as the driver navigated the railroad tracks at the end of the street. A dark, blocky SUV glided into view, hesitated, then slid to a stop in front of Lucille's house.

She had no recollection of flinging open the front door and running out into the darkness. Only Olivia's look of disdain told her how foolish she looked. "Couldn't you wait a second for us to get out of the car before you start hovering?" she asked.

"Obviously not," Lucille said drily, once again biting off words of reproach about the lateness of the arrival. She turned instead to the boy who had climbed out of the backseat and come around to stand beside her. Her grandson was an unimpressive specimen, peculiarly buglike with his long, bony arms and legs and oversized eyes behind the round glasses. "Hello, Lucas," Lucille said. "How are you?"

"Tired and I have to pee," the boy said, his voice a clear tenor that was neither plaintive nor strident. He was merely stating facts.

"You'd better come inside, then." Lucille led the way into the house. She pointed out the downstairs bathroom to Lucas, then turned to her daughter. In the bright glow of the foyer light, Olivia looked older than Lucille had expected. A double furrow arced across her forehead, and twin grooves etched either side of her mouth. Her blond hair had a dry, over-processed look, and the multiple piercings in each ear looked out of place, like a Halloween costume. Then again, Lucille reminded herself, no one looked their best after a cross-country drive. "You must be exhausted," she said.

"Yes," Olivia said. She glanced over her shoulder, toward the SUV. "Is it okay to leave the car parked there overnight? I don't feel like unpacking right now."

"It should be fine," Lucille said. Not that Eureka was immune to crime, but what thieves there were rarely ventured onto this quiet street. "If you lock it, it should be fine."

"I'll move it in the morning," Olivia said. She pressed a button on the keychain, and the car chirped and blinked its lights at her. "I really don't want it out where everyone can see it."

Something in Olivia's voice made Lucille wary. "Why not?" she asked.

"Don't look so alarmed. It's all right, really. I'm sure D. J. won't mind that I borrowed it."

"D. J. I thought you said D. J. was gone."

"He is. He's in Iraq, on some big-money contractor's job. He asked me to look after the car while he's gone. So that's what I'm doing."

"So he knows you drove it to Colorado."

"No, but hey, when he needs it, he can come get it." She dropped the keys back in her purse. "I'm too wiped to talk anymore. Where am I sleeping?"

Lucas emerged from the bathroom, wiping his hands on his jeans. "You want me to bring in the suitcase, Mom?" he asked.

"In the morning. Lucille is going to show us to our rooms."

Lucille winced at the sound of her name. Whatever happened to Grandma? "Lucas, you're all the way up at the top of the house. There's another stairway at the end of the upstairs hall that leads to your room. There's no bathroom up there, so you'll have to share with your mother." As she talked, Lucille made her way up the stairs. She showed Olivia the pink and white guest bedroom and bath, and pointed out the stairs to Lucas. "Do you want me to go up with you?" she asked.

"No, I'm okay," he said. And without another word he climbed the narrow flight of steps and disappeared.

Lucille heard the door open, then shut with a click. "He seems to be a very independent boy," she said.

"Does he?" Olivia scraped her too-long bangs out of her eyes. "I guess that's a good thing. I never could have stood a clingy child." She moved into the bedroom, one hand on the doorknob. "I'll see you in the morning."

"Wait." Lucille hated for the evening to end on such an abrupt note. "Do you want something to eat? Or I could make tea."

"I'm dead. I just want to go to bed."

She did look exhausted. Lucille wanted to fold her in her arms, to comfort Olivia as she had when she was a very little girl. But Olivia hadn't allowed that kind of closeness in many years.

"I'm glad you're here," Lucille said, the verbal equivalent of the hug she wanted to give.

Olivia's eyes met hers for the briefest instant, before flickering away again. In that moment, Lucille saw another emotion between the weariness, something almost like . . . gratitude. "I'm glad, too," she said. "It'll be good to stop for a while. To think."

Then she shut the door, leaving Lucille to stand in the hall and wonder. Olivia hadn't said she was glad to see her mother, or glad to have another chance for the two of them to bond. But she was glad to be here, in this house, whatever her motives. It was a start.

Chapter 4

Maggie had Lorna Doones and coffee for breakfast, and found a pad of paper and made a list. She needed food besides ham and cookies. Cash, if she could get it. Did Eureka even have a bank? She should get a map of the area. Maybe Reggie could tell her where to pick one up. She'd have to ask him where the mine was. Even if it was empty, she wanted to see it.

As the list grew, she began to feel a little more confident. Making a list—having a plan—gave her the illusion of control. In the days following Carter's announcement that he was leaving her, she'd filled notebooks with lists: things she needed to do at work, items she needed to pack, questions to ask her lawyer—and one very long list of every bad name she could think of to call Carter. She'd started with A, "addlepated asshole," and worked her way all the way to P, "pinheaded prick," before she'd abandoned the task.

Her new list tucked into her purse, she stepped onto the front porch. Now that the sun was up, the chill wasn't so pronounced, though the air still held a freshness unlike anything offered by the humidity of Houston. Reggie had said the cabin was at 10,000 feet. She supposed that far above sea level it never really got warm.

She dug out the key ring Reggie had given her and locked the cabin behind her, then walked around the side of the house to the Jeep. It was an older model, with fading red paint and worn leather upholstery. The dash was littered with old gas receipts, a half pack of spearmint gum, and what might have been a speeding ticket, but the ink was so faded Maggie couldn't read it. She shoved everything into a plastic bag she found on the floorboard and stuffed it behind the seat. She also found an oversized bath towel, a pair of rubber boots—size 11—and three yellowish rocks. Curious, she tucked one of these into her purse and left the other two on the floorboard.

The Jeep organized, she turned the key. To her relief, the engine started right up, purring smoothly. She fastened her seat belt, adjusted her mirrors, then realized she was going to have to back the unfamiliar vehicle down a considerable slope before she had room to turn around.

Heart in her throat, she inched the Jeep back, one foot on the gas, the other on the brake, fighting images of hurtling backward down the mountain into space.

Going forward wasn't much better once the Jeep was turned around. On the way up here with Reggie, she'd been too focused on the scenery and the mystery of her inheritance to notice the lack of guardrails on the winding two-lane road—no guardrails and a heart-stopping drop-off a scant two feet from the driver's side tires.

She thought of Jameso traveling this road on a motorcycle at night. Was that as reckless as it seemed to her—or did people here measure danger on a different scale than someone who'd spent her whole life in a place as flat as a flip-flop?

Maggie felt a long way from the humid, level world where she'd spent so much of her life; more than the ground beneath her feet was tilted here. She'd hoped coming to Eureka and seeing her father's house would answer some of the questions she had about the man, but so far he was more mysterious than ever.

With a shaky sigh of relief, she reached the main highway, with its broad lanes and sturdy guardrails, and was able to relax a little. She passed the Living Waters compound, a fog of steam floating above the fences like low-lying clouds.

It was just after seven when she cruised down Eureka's main street—too early to visit Reggie at his office or to attempt to find a map. The Lorna Doones already seemed a distant memory to her stomach, so she found a parking space near the Last Dollar Cafe and went inside.

A sign just inside the door instructed her to seat herself, so Maggie slipped into an empty booth against the far wall. The interior of the Last Dollar felt so familiar: red linoleum floor and gold leatherette booths mixed with oak ladder-back chairs. The tabletops were white Formica sprinkled with gold stars. Framed black-and-white photographs lined the walls: miners in hard hats with picks, solemn-faced families arrayed outside hand-built cabins, and a group of women in long dresses on impossibly long wooden skis. A pair of those skis was mounted beside the photograph. Elsewhere, on the walls and ceiling and on the pillars between the booths, hung pickaxes and miners' lanterns and hard hats and tin lunch pails. On the wall behind the cash register were six of those singing fish that had been popular gag gifts a decade before.

Maggie took this all in and realized why the place felt so familiar: this was the kind of decor that theme restaurants in Houston were always striving to emulate. But this was no work of a Hollywood prop shop. The Last Dollar was the real deal. She could imagine customers cleaning out the basement and finding Grandpa's old hard hat—or a singing fish someone had given them for Christmas—and donating it to the walls of the café.

"Good morning, hon. What can I get you?"

The woman spoke with the easy warmth of the older women of Maggie's youth, who addressed everyone as "hon" and "dear." But this woman was young—not yet thirty—with a thick fall of dark brown hair to the middle of her back. She wore low-slung jeans and a black T-shirt that said, WELL-BEHAVED WOMEN RARELY MAKE HISTORY. The shirt stretched over her not inconsiderable breasts, and she wore multiple rings in each ear and another in her nose.

"I don't have a menu." Maggie looked around the table, wondering if she'd missed seeing one amidst the clutter of condiment jars against the wall.

"Oh, we don't have menus." The waitress pointed to a chalkboard near the pass-through to the kitchen.

Maggie read through the list of omelets and pancakes and muffins, her stomach growling. "What do you recommend?" she asked.

The waitress studied her, her look far more intense than Maggie had expected for such a simple question. "How about two eggs, over easy, with wheat toast, some of our homemade elk sausage, and grits. Unless you prefer hash browns."

"No, grits are fine." Her mouth was already watering at the prospect.

The waitress smiled. "I'm Danielle, by the way," she said.

"Maggie." She'd never felt compelled to introduce herself to a waitress before, but this didn't feel like an impersonal encounter.

"Welcome to Eureka, Maggie. I'll bring you some coffee right away."

Thirty seconds later, Maggie sipped coffee from a squat blue mug that looked handmade, and watched Danielle circulate among the other patrons. She seemed to know at least half by name, and treated everyone to warm smiles and a motherly concern.

After a few minutes, she was joined by a second waitress, a slender blonde with rosy cheeks and ice blue eyes. She wore a pink paisley bandana over her short hair, and a red apron over jeans and a T-shirt. She was even younger than Danielle, maybe early twenties, and when she refilled Maggie's coffee she spoke with a slight accent that hinted at Germany or maybe a Scandinavian country. "I am Janelle," she said. "You're Murphy's daughter, right?"

"Right." Maggie didn't even bother asking how she knew. Apparently she resembled her sire, Reggie liked to talk, and if that wasn't enough, she was driving her father's Jeep.

"Dani and I were hoping you'd stop by," Janelle said. "If there's anything at all you need, you let us know."

Danielle arrived with Maggie's breakfast: two picture-perfect eggs arranged beside a neat stack of toast points, two fat sausage patties, and a pool of creamy grits dressed with butter and flecked with black pepper. She set the plate in front of Maggie and beamed. "One of our chickens, Arabella, laid those eggs," she said. "I've been saving them for someone special."

"You know which chicken laid which eggs?" Maggie tried to determine if they were putting her on.

"Arabella is an Araucana chicken," Janelle said. "She lays blue eggs, so we always know hers. Usually we keep them for ourselves, but sometimes we share them with special people."

"Oh. Well, thank you."

"Murphy built our chicken house," Danielle said. "We always gave him Arabella's eggs. He said they were the best."

They left together, and Maggie stared at the unlikely connection to her father on her plate. But hunger won out over the bizarre nature of the honor of being presented with prized blue eggs by strangers, and she picked up her fork and dug in.

Arabella definitely laid wonderful eggs—or maybe it was only that Maggie had never had eggs so fresh before. The toast was made from homemade bread, the sausage better than any she'd ever had, and the grits smooth and buttery. She wiped up the last of the egg with the last of the toast and decided if she had no other reason to stay in Eureka, she would linger to enjoy more breakfasts like this.

She looked around to tell Danielle or Janelle so and spotted them by the register, their arms around each other as they chatted with a patron.

Maggie thought of a fairy tale she'd loved as a child, about Snow White and Rose Red—in this story of a Snow White without dwarves, she'd been blond and ethereal, counterpart to the dark-haired Earth Mother Rose. Janelle looked down at her companion, such obvious affection in her eyes that Maggie felt a sharp stab of envy. Would a woman know how to love her better than the man she'd mistakenly given her heart to? Too bad her inclinations didn't run in that direction.

She was about to signal for her check when a bent, grizzled man slid into the booth opposite her. He wore a green plaid flannel shirt and bright red suspenders, with wisps of white hair combed across a perfectly round head. "Bob Prescott," he said, offering a knotted hand. "Your old man came close to killing me one day, then two weeks later he saved my life."

Maggie sagged back in the booth. "He did what?"

Bob grinned, revealing teeth too white and perfect to be real. "Thought that might get your attention."

Danielle arrived to take away Maggie's plate and refill their cups. "I'll tell Arabella you liked the eggs," she said, eyeing the polished plate.

"Them girls believe in talking to animals and all that nonsense," Bob said. "But they're the best cooks in three counties, so I don't care if they ride broomsticks in their spare time or sit around chanting mantras or whatever it's called." He sipped his coffee, eyeing Maggie over the rim of the cup. She waited for the inevitable comparison to her father.

"You don't look much like him, and you can be thankful for that," Bob said. "He was an ugly son of a bitch, with a temper to match."

"Yet he saved your life?"

"After trying to kill me first."

Was the old guy legit? Or some local crazy who got a kick

out of making accusations to strangers? His somewhat beady eyes were fixed on her, the washed-out blue of age, though the light behind them wasn't the least bit dim. He was clearly waiting for her response. "Why did my father try to kill you?" she asked.

"I told him to his face I thought he was a lying son of a bitch." Bob grinned. "He didn't like that much."

"I don't think anyone would like that much. What was he lying about?"

"I'm not sure he told the truth any day since he got here," Bob said. "He was a man with a lot of secrets. You're proof of that."

"There's a difference between secrets and lies." Didn't they all have things in their lives they'd prefer to keep to themselves? Maybe her father hadn't told people about her because he was ashamed of the way he'd abandoned her and her mother.

"Murph said there was no gold in the French Mistress," Bob said. "I say he was lying."

Maggie hated the wild flutter in her chest that proved how shallow and materialistic she was. Yes, she'd come to Eureka wanting to know about her father, but a big lure had been the promise of wealth—gold. She was still trying to process that disappointment, and here was this old man teasing her with hope. "What makes you think he was lying?" she asked, trying to brace herself for the answer.

"Murph always had plenty of cash, and he never did a lick of useful work that I could see. He spent weeks holed up there alone on that mountain, then he'd disappear altogether for a while, and when he showed up again, he'd have plenty to spend." Bob leaned toward her, his expression feverish. "I say he was taking gold out of the mine, hauling it to Denver or Salt Lake or some other big city to sell, and putting the proceeds in the bank." He sat back. "You do some checking and see if I ain't right."

"I certainly will check on that," she said, disappointed in spite of her determination not to be. If her father had a fortune sequestered away somewhere, Reggie would have told her. After all, the lawyer was apparently the only one who'd known about her.

"The fact that he got so upset when I called him a liar proves I was on to something, too," Bob continued.

"Maybe he just didn't like being accused that way," she said. "You said he had a hot temper."

"He hit me so hard he broke my jaw." Bob rubbed the side of his face, as if he still felt the blow. "I fought back, but Murph was bigger and younger. If some others hadn't pulled us apart, he would have killed me for sure."

"Where did this fight take place?" Maggie asked, trying to picture it.

"The Dirty Sally." Bob grinned, an unexpected response considering the grave nature of his charges. "We'd both had a few at the time, but I stand by what I said then—Murph lied about the gold."

Right. And the moon was made of green cheese and her ex-husband would spend the rest of his life regretting leaving her. Nice fantasies all, but without a snowball's chance in hell of being true.

"What about him saving your life?" she asked, not sure if she really wanted to hear the story, but sure Bob wouldn't leave until he'd told it.

"That was me being stupid," Bob said. "I wasn't paying attention to the weather and got caught out in a blizzard. I was already half froze to death when Murph found me and hauled me in. I reckon there were other men who would have left me there to die, considering the circumstances."

"What circumstances?" He wanted her to ask, though she figured he'd tell her anyway.

"He found me at the mouth of the French Mistress mine. I'd snuck up there to do a little prospecting of my own."

Maggie blinked. "You were going to steal from him?"

Bob shrugged. "I figured he owed me for breaking my jaw."

"So after he saved your life, you two became best friends," Maggie said. She could practically hear violins playing.

"Hell, no. He threatened to whoop my ass if he ever caught me on his property again." Bob shook his head. "Then he put a big iron gate over the mine entrance so nobody else could get in."

"And you know this how?"

Bob chuckled. "I had to check, don't you know."

She'd have to find that entrance and have a look for herself, Maggie decided. Though what would she be looking for, exactly? She remembered the rocks she'd found in the Jeep and reached for her purse. "I have something I'd like you to take a look at." She pulled out the rock and pushed it across the table.

Bob picked up the misshapen yellowish lump, then pulled a pair of wire-rimmed glasses from his shirt pocket and examined it closer. "Nice ammonite," he said, and handed it back to her.

"What's an ammonite?"

"Fossil." His gnarled finger traced a faint outline in the stone—an oblong creature that looked like a cross between a giant pill bug and a centipede.

"Then it's not gold," she said.

Bob laughed. "You might get a few dollars for it at a tourist shop, but people find them all the time up here. It'd make a nice paperweight."

"Thanks." She dropped it into her purse and looked around, ready to make her escape.

Janelle glided over. "Would you like some more coffee?" she asked.

"No, thank you. I'd better get going. I need to find a bank and a grocery store." Was Eureka even big enough to have these things? "And is there somewhere I can buy some drapes, or the fabric to make them?"

"The bank is at the end of this street," Janelle said. "The grocery is on Pickax, one street over. There's a hardware store, too. They sell curtain rods and things like that, but I don't know where you'd find drapes or fabric." She wrinkled her brow, then brightened. "You should try Lacy's, next door to the grocery. There's a little bit of everything in there."

"Thanks. I will."

"Can I get you anything else?"

"Just the check," Maggie said.

"It's already been taken care of," Janelle said.

"Oh, I can't let you do that," Maggie said. The special eggs had been one thing, but the two women obviously made their living here. She didn't feel right accepting freebies from them.

"I didn't do anything," Janelle protested. "Jameso paid your check."

"Jameso?" Her cheeks felt hot, and she looked around trying to spot the motorcycle rider.

"He already left," Janelle said. "He said he owed you for scaring you last night." Her smile was knowing. "You don't have to be afraid of Jameso. He is like a big, friendly dog—more bark than bite."

"I'm not afraid of him," Maggie said stiffly. She was annoyed. Now she'd have to find him and thank him for buying her breakfast. And why hadn't he bothered to say hello when he was in the café?

Chapter 5

Lucille was eating breakfast at the little table in her kitchen when she heard the stairs creak. A few moments later, the door opened and Lucas entered. He wore socks but no shoes, and the same clothes he'd had on last night, the T-shirt untucked from the baggy jeans.

"Good morning," Lucille said. "Would you like some breakfast?"

He nodded and pulled out the chair across from her at the table. "Do you have cereal?" he asked.

"I have Cheerios."

"That'd be okay."

She poured the cereal and milk, and set the bowl in front of him. He was probably old enough to do it himself, but he looked barely conscious still. "How long did it take you to get from Connecticut to here?" she asked as she set the bowl in front of him.

"Three days."

"That's a really fast trip." It had taken Lucille five days from California, ten years ago.

"Mom drove until she couldn't see anymore, then we'd

stop the car and sleep for a while." He spoke around mouthfuls of cereal. Not a pretty sight, but Lucille wasn't in the mood for etiquette lessons this early in the morning.

"You stayed in a hotel," she said.

"No, she just pulled into a rest area or a parking lot and I'd crawl in my sleeping bag and she'd lay the seat down."

What had driven Olivia to travel that way? Was she too broke to afford lodging? Or was she running from something—or someone? "If the car you're in belongs to D. J., where is hers?" she asked.

"She sold it." More slurping of cereal. "D. J. won't mind if we use his car. He's a nice guy."

"And he's your mom's boyfriend?" Olivia had never said, exactly.

"Yeah." Lucas looked glum. "They had a big fight before he left. She didn't want him to go to Iraq, but he said he could make a bunch of money there. Then Mom lost her job, so that's when she decided to come see you."

Any port in a storm, Lucille guessed.

"What are you going to do this morning?" Lucas asked her.

"I have to go to work. Is your mom going to take you to school to get enrolled?" If that was the case, maybe she'd better wake Olivia.

"She said I can wait until Monday. I don't see why I have to go at all. There's only a few more days left in the school year anyway."

"More like two and a half weeks." But it wouldn't hurt for the boy to wait a couple of days. Lucille could sympathize with Olivia's desire to rest today. "What will you do if you're not in school?" she asked. "Do you want to come to work with me?" Prowling through the miscellaneous junk in her store might keep him occupied one day at least. "We can leave a note for your mom." No telling when Olivia would awaken; she'd looked completely beat last night.

"No, I don't think so. I'll look around on my own."

"You should stay here with your mom."

"She won't care if I go look around," he said. "She doesn't worry about me."

Lucille couldn't believe that. Every mother worried about her children, even long after they were grown and gone. "All right. Stop by my shop at lunch time and we'll get something to eat."

"How will I know which store is yours?"

"The name of the place is Lacy's. It's on Pickax Street."

"That's a funny name for a street."

"A lot of places around here have names related to mines and mining. The people who first came here—well, the first white men—were all miners.

"Were there Native Americans here before that?"

Not "Indians" but "Native Americans." So politically correct and strangely adult sounding. "The Uncompahgre lived in the area before it was settled."

He nodded again, focused on the cereal.

"Are you sure you'll be all right by yourself?" she asked.

He nodded. "I'm used to finding my way around in new places. And Mom says Eureka is pretty small, right?"

"Yes, it's pretty small."

"Then I shouldn't have any problems."

Where did he get that outsized sense of self-assurance? Not from her. Not from his mother either. Olivia had been shy to the point of being tongue-tied until eighth grade. Even then, she'd never been a social butterfly. Left to her own devices for a day, she'd have retreated to her room to read science fiction, write in her journal, and listen to dark, incomprehensible music.

"There's a bicycle in the shed out back if you want to use it," Lucille said.

"Okay."

They were definitely going to have to work on his manners. "When someone offers you the use of something they own, you should say thank you," she said.

"Okay." Pause. "Thank you."

"You're welcome." What the hell had she gotten herself into? "I'd better go now. See you at lunch." She left him at the table and went to get her purse and her keys. She took one last peek at him before she went out the door. He'd gotten up and was pouring a second bowl of cereal. As if waking up in a house with a grandmother who was a virtual stranger, in a town on the edge of nowhere, was really no big deal at all.

Maggie found the bank and withdrew some cash from the ATM. She didn't have a lot of money, but it ought to be enough to see her through a few more weeks. Of course, there was always the Steuben, which was insured for $20,000, but it wasn't exactly a liquid asset. And it was the one good thing she'd taken from her marriage.

Eureka Grocery was a surprisingly well-stocked market with a deli in the back and three check stands by the door. She filled a basket with frozen dinners, canned soup, bread, cereal, and skim milk—the single woman's shopping list. Add a few tins of cat food and she'd be a full-fledged stereotype.

When she was married, she'd prided herself on her cooking skills; she'd made her own soups and bread, even homemade pasta. Such effort seemed pointless when you had to eat the results alone.

Next door to the market sat a long, low building. Bright red letters in the front window identified it as Lacy's. A stout blonde in a long, red flowered skirt and black ballet slippers was sweeping the front porch when Maggie approached. "Good morning," the woman said cheerfully, not pausing in her work but turning to sweep her way toward Maggie. "Come on in and look around. I've got a little bit of everything."

This was no understatement. From her spot just outside the open doorway, Maggie spied a circa 1950s sofa and chair, a gilded mirror, a box of canning jars, three teddy bears, and a mounted elk with only one eye. "I'm looking for some curtains," she said. "Something to cover a big window."

The woman—Lacy?—leaned her broom against the porch railing. "I don't know," she said. "But let's go see."

She led the way into the shop, down narrow aisles lined with everything from old Barbie dolls to sets of Haviland china. Garage sale castoffs sat side by side with what Maggie suspected were valuable antiques.

But she didn't see so much as an old tablecloth or faded bedspread, much less a set of drapes large enough to cover a wall-wide window.

They reached the back of the shop and a row of six dusty, wine-colored velvet theater seats. Beside them sat an old-fashioned movie projector. "How big a window are you looking to cover?" the woman asked.

"A big one."

"Then I may have just the thing." She reached behind the row of seats and dragged out a large cardboard box—the kind that might have once held a washing machine. She opened the top and began pulling out yards and yards of wine-colored velvet. "Theater curtains from the old Ironton Theater," she said. "Do you think they'd work?"

Maggie grabbed two fistfuls of the velvet and stretched it out before her. It was dusty and a little faded, but still sturdy. And there was certainly plenty of it. "How much?" she asked.

The woman eyed Maggie, then the box of velvet. "Thirty-five dollars."

"I'll take it."

Together, they stuffed the fabric back in the box. "I'm Lucille Theriot, by the way," the woman said. "I own this place."

"Maggie Stevens." Maggie took the offered hand. "Who's Lacy?"

Lucille laughed. "I have no idea. It was supposed to be

Lucy's, but the sign painter goofed. Come on. Let's drag this up front."

All that velvet proved heavier than Maggie had anticipated. By the time they reached the front of the store, both women were red-faced and out of breath. "What . . . brings you . . . to Eureka?" Lucille asked.

Maggie waited a few seconds more before she answered. "My father was Jacob Murphy," she said. "He left me his place, and I came up from Houston to settle his affairs."

"Ah. I heard you were coming to visit. Welcome to town."

"Thank you."

"Are you trying to cover those windows in his cabin?"

"Just the ones in the bedroom. You've seen them?"

"Not exactly. And certainly not the ones in his bedroom."

"Oh, I didn't mean . . ."

Lucille laughed. "I'm not saying I wouldn't have taken him up on the offer if he'd asked. Murph was a good-looking man, and he was only about eight years older than me, but we were just friends. I'm the one who sold him the windows."

"You did?" Maggie glanced around her, wondering if there was a hardware department she'd missed.

"I bought out an estate over near Rico and the guy was a glazier who had all these odd sizes of windows someone had ordered for a custom home and never built. Murph had mentioned he wanted some new windows for his place, so I hooked him up. Murph always said he owed me for those windows. It was our running joke that someday I'd collect." Her expression sobered. "It was a big shock when he died. He seemed like the kind who'd go on forever."

"How did he die? No one told me." She'd been so consumed with mapping out the details of her father's life that she hadn't thought to ask about his death.

"I heard it was a heart attack," Lucille said. "He was working up at his place, stacking rocks or something, and just keeled over. You could ask Jameso. He's the one who found him."

Jameso again. Did the guy make a habit of lurking around the cabin? Why? She fought annoyance—at Jameso, and at her father, for dying before she had a chance to get to know him, and for not letting her be a part of his life while he was alive. After all these years, that rejection still hurt.

True to her claim of having "a little bit of everything," Lucille unearthed a packet of needles and three spools of black thread to go with the theater curtains. Maggie added a pair of scissors and surveyed the pile. "What the heck am I going to hang these with?" she asked.

"Hardware store up the street sells steel pipe and plumbing fittings," Lucille said. "That's the only thing sturdy enough to support these heavy things, plus they'll cut them to size for you."

Maggie nodded. After she measured the windows, she'd make another trip. She paid for the purchases with her credit card; then the two women wrestled the box out to the Jeep and Maggie headed back up toward Garnet Mountain, determined to spend the rest of the day looking for the French Mistress Mine and studying whatever papers her father had left behind.

She'd just passed the hot springs when her cell phone erupted with the opening notes of Vivaldi's "Spring." *Barb*. She knew before she glanced at the phone, and guilt washed over her that she hadn't yet called her best friend. She pulled over onto the side of the road and answered the phone.

"You had better have been held hostage by Yetis or be in bed with some gorgeous, rich stud."

Barb's husky drawl filled Maggie with an unexpected wave of homesickness. "I'm sorry I haven't called," she said.

"So, no Yetis? And no stud? I'm disappointed in you, woman."

"Give me a chance. I've only been here one day."

"You must have been busy doing something, if you couldn't even be bothered to call me."

"There's no cell service at my dad's place. And no land-line." No electricity or cable or Internet . . . Barb would be calling for men in white coats to take Maggie away when Maggie told her she planned to stay.

"Back up. You're staying at your dad's place?"

"Yes, it's a cabin on a remote mountain—a *real* cabin, not some real-estate developer's idea of a weekend getaway for the Ralph Lauren set. This is an old mining shack my dad remodeled."

"Uh-huh. And what about the gold mine? And the two vehicles?"

"There's no gold in the mine." Bob had been very definite about that. "And the vehicles are an old Jeep and a snowmobile."

"A snowmobile!" Barb's laughter rang loud in Maggie's ear. "Oh, darling, it sounds like you are having a real adventure. What's the town like—Eureka or whatever the name is?"

"Eureka is beautiful. Not very big, but what's here is lovely. Gorgeous scenery. Very different from Houston. Very . . . rugged." The mountains, but the people, too, had an informality and individuality she hadn't encountered before. As if living isolated from crowds and city conventions had allowed each person to assert whatever aspects of her personality she wanted, whether as a motorcycle-riding lawyer or as chicken-raising lesbian café owners. She smiled at the thought.

"You sound as if you like it." Barb sounded amused.

"I don't know what I think, really. It's all so different."

"Maybe different is what you need."

"Or maybe if I stay here I'll end up as crazy as my father was."

"Was he crazy?"

"I don't know," Maggie admitted. "I've been here less than twenty-four hours and I've learned he may have had a drinking problem. He probably never remarried after he and my mom split, and he apparently never had any other children. He was eccentric enough to live up on a mountain all by himself, yet he seems to have had plenty of friends. I met a man who said Murph almost killed him, then a few weeks later saved his life, and the librarian apparently doesn't like him because he kept a library book out for five years just to annoy her."

"He sounds like a really interesting guy," Barb said. "And I must say, you've learned a lot in one day."

"Everything I learn only leads to more questions. The only person he seems to have told about me is his lawyer. He went to all the trouble to leave me everything he owned, but why?"

"It's sort of traditional for people to leave their belongings to their only living relative. You qualify."

"Nothing else about my father or the way he lived was traditional."

"Maybe he felt guilty about abandoning you and your mother, and this is an attempt to make up for it. Guilt can be a powerful motivator, you know."

Such as her own guilt that she hadn't done more to try to make contact with her father after she was grown. She'd vowed plenty of times to look for him but had never done so. "The more I find out, the worse I feel," she said.

"So keep looking until you know everything," Barb said.

"I think it's probably impossible at this point to know everything, since my dad isn't here to tell me."

"Then keep searching until you find enough to make you feel better. Him leaving you and your mom was a shitty thing to do, but from what little you've told me so far, it doesn't sound like he was a complete asshole. That has to be worth something."

"I guess you're right. I'm going to stay here a little while longer anyway."

"Let me know if you need me to send you anything from Houston," Barb said. "Better yet, let me know when I can come visit."

"Give me another week or so to get settled; then I'd love to see you." The thought of having Barb here to bolster her spirits—and maybe her nerve, if need be—cheered her.

"Is there anything interesting to do in Eureka, Colorado?" Barb asked. "Besides look at the gorgeous scenery?"

"There's a hot springs. Clothing optional."

"Ooh, now that does sound interesting. We must try it out when I visit. Any good-looking men?"

Maggie thought of Jameso. "I've been too busy to look for men," she said. "Why would I want one, anyway? The only ones I've known have been more trouble than they're worth."

"True. But they have their uses."

"I don't have any use for one right now."

"Have fun solving the mystery of your father," Barb said. "It will be good for you to be on your own in a new place—one without so many unfortunate memories."

What about the good memories she had of Houston—and even of her marriage? There had been some, B.F.D.—before Francine Dupree. But maybe Barb was right. After her divorce she'd wanted to travel to exotic places in order to gain a new perspective on and new ideas for her life. Eureka wasn't Tuscany or Nepal, but it felt worlds away from Houston and her problems there.

Cassie had not slept well, and this translated into a fouler than usual mood that made most patrons avoid speaking to her. They approached the counter warily and handed over their library cards and books to be checked out or turned in without comment. Word spread through book readers that Cassie was "having one of her days," and those who could, decided to wait until another time to visit the library.

A city council member had dared to complain once about Cassie's surly attitude toward the patrons and taxpayers who were, after all, paying her salary, and had felt the full brunt of the Wynock wrath. He had endured a stern lecture on the role of the Wynocks in the community, the fact that the land upon which the library sat had once been Wynock land, and the sacrifices Cassie herself had made to make the library the thriving community resource it was today. If patrons wanted the equivalent of a cocktail hostess behind the desk, they could certainly have one, but she believed they were better off with a woman who knew the collections like the back of her hand and the history of the county better than anyone else. This library was more than the building and the books within its walls. This library was Cassie Wynock's life, and he would do well not to forget it.

The man had left, cowed and quiet, and the townspeople had accepted Cassie and her moods as much a part of the library as the uncomfortable chairs at the computer stations and the dusty collection of birds' and hornets' nest in the front display case. Cassie enjoyed the respect she felt was her due and things ran smoothly.

So she wasn't pleased when, shortly after lunch a skinny boy with a head as round as a light bulb and wire-framed glasses sliding down the end of his nose ambled up to the counter and stood there, staring at her. Cassie ignored him, and he shifted from one foot to the other, watery blue gaze fixed on her. He cleared his throat. Cassie continued to stare fixedly at her computer screen, though she was so distracted by the boy's strange presence she couldn't focus on the words printed there.

"Ma'am, could you help me?" he asked.

With her most forbidding scowl fixed in place, Cassie turned to look at him. She definitely didn't recognize him. His was such a striking collection of physical attributes, she couldn't have forgotten him. "Yes?" she asked frostily.

"Do you have any books on the Native Americans who lived in this area?"

She'd expected some inquiry about video games or graphic novels or use of the computers—the usual interests of boys his age. "Shouldn't you be in school?" she asked.

"No. Do you have any books on Native Americans?"

"To which Native Americans are you referring?" she asked.

"All of them that used to live here," he said. He seemed completely uncowed by her forbidding tone and manner, a novelty in itself.

She stood. "You may find some books in the Juvenile Nonfiction area."

"I don't want kids' books," he said. "I want real books. History books." He glanced around him. "Do you have a local history section?"

Intrigued, Cassie led him to the history collection and the half-dozen books about the Uncompahgre tribe and their impact on the area. "These books may interest you, but you'll need a library card to check them out," she said.

He pulled a biography of Chief Ouray off the shelf and opened it, holding it close to his face. "You can give me one," he said. "I'm going to be living here now."

She tried to hide her surprise. She'd assumed he was a visitor, perhaps from one of the families who spent the summers in one of the guest cabins along the river. "Where will you be living?"

"With my mother and grandmother—Olivia and Lucille Theriot."

So this was Lucille's grandson. Cassie had almost forgotten. She'd seen the expensive-looking SUV parked in front of Lucille's house that morning, but in a fog of sleeplessness had failed to make the connection. "How long are you going to be staying?" she asked.

"A while, I guess. Mom says I have to start school Monday."

"What grade are you in?"

"Seventh." He closed the book and met her with that disconcerting, unblinking gaze. "Can I have a library card or not?"

Not, she was tempted to say, solely on the basis of his impertinent tone. But it wouldn't do to discourage a kid who actually wanted to read. "Your grandmother will have to sign for you and I can issue a card on her account," she said.

"Does that mean I can't take the book with me now?"

"That is exactly what it means."

His lips pushed out in a pout, and she could almost see him weighing the merits of putting up an argument. He decided against it; he was definitely a bright young man. He replaced the book on the shelf and scanned the other titles nearby. "Is there anything here about mines in the area?" he asked.

The phrasing of his question caught her off guard. The last person to ask her that was Jacob Murphy. "What do you want to know about mines for?" she asked, as she had asked Jacob.

"I just think it would be interesting to know more about them."

"Mines are dangerous places. Don't go getting any ideas about exploring them. You'd be trespassing, and besides, you could fall in and get yourself killed."

He scowled at her. "I may be a kid, but I'm not stupid."

"Don't talk to me in that tone of voice, young man."

His gaze slid away. "Yes, ma'am." But there was no hint of humility in his words. Oh, this one would be a handful indeed.

Without another word, he turned and shuffled out of the library. Cassie felt an uncharacteristic pinch of guilt as she watched him leave. Could she possibly sound any more like an old maid librarian? Really, what business was it of hers if the boy wanted to go looking around in dirty old mines? That was for his mother and grandmother to worry about, though the two of them didn't have any qualms about letting him wander all over town by himself. Not that Eureka was dangerous or anything, but people should have standards.

That was the difference between Cassie and most other people, she thought as she returned to her desk. She had standards. Protocol and decorum needed to be observed. Failing to do so was the first step down a slippery slope to the bottom.

Chapter 6

Back at the cabin, Maggie put the groceries away and thought about starting her search through her dad's things. But the silence pressed in around her, too heavy and weighted with grief and regret to allow her to sit still. She fled instead out of doors, pausing to pull on a denim jacket she found on a hook by the door. The jacket smelled of wood smoke and leather, and a scent decidedly male but not unpleasant. As she slid her arms into the sleeves, she thought this was as close as she'd ever come to a hug from her father.

She rushed out the door, as if to leave such sentimentality behind, and followed the path that led up behind the house. In less than a minute she was breathing hard, but she pushed on up the hill, anxious to see where such a well-worn trail would lead. She cleared the house, then circled a clump of knotted evergreens and emerged on the side of the mountain, looking out over a valley not visible from any of the windows in the house. She recognized the snow-covered profile of Mount Winston in the distance, a silver ribbon near its base that might have been a road.

She continued hiking, less winded, though her heart pounded

in her chest like an engine laboring up a grade. The trail leveled and she followed it along a ridge between two uplifts, the gravel a pinkish gray beneath her feet. The sun streamed down in a brilliant, clear light unlike any she'd ever seen before. It was more silver than gold, illuminating every detail of each flower petal and blade of grass. She imagined this was a light artists and photographers would rave about—the kind of light a recluse or depressive would have hidden from.

If this path was any evidence, her father had spent a lot of time on this mountainside, in this light. It was almost funny, the idea that someone who lived in a place like Eureka, that others would see as a retreat, would need to get even farther away. Maggie knew plenty of people in Houston who vacationed in Colorado every summer to escape from the heat and humidity of the Gulf Coast. For years she'd lobbied Carter for a trip to the mountains. The closest she'd come was getting to tag along on a business trip to Denver about ten years ago.

She'd suggested they take a few extra days and drive to the mountains, but Carter had refused to leave the office that long. He'd placated her with talk of a return one day on a real vacation, but like so many of his promises, that one was never fulfilled.

At the time, she hadn't even felt particularly bad about that. That was simply how Carter was. She'd accepted it, the way she accepted that fiber cereal tasted bad but was good for you, or that mammograms were something she was supposed to get every year.

Love, or an emotion she mistook for it, had blinded her to all the other possibilities out there. So here she was in Colorado at last, looking for possibilities.

One very large possibility loomed ahead of her right now. She stopped and studied the yawning black hole in the side of the mountain. Could this be the entrance to the mine? As she drew nearer, she could make out the iron grate set across it and the large padlock affixed to that. She stopped in front of the lock and read the sign posted on the rock to the left of the entrance: NO TRESPASSING. VIOLATORS WILL BE SHOT. SURVIVORS WILL BE SHOT AGAIN. Handwritten underneath in black marker: THIS MEANS YOU, BOB.

She laughed. Despite Bob's assertion that her dad had tried to kill him, Jake apparently had a sense of humor about their feud. How had Bob gotten to the mine, anyway? she wondered. The only path she could see led right past the cabin, and all those windows.

Windows reminded her of the curtains she still had to work on. If she wanted to sleep past dawn tomorrow, she ought to try to tackle them.

She pulled on the gate, but it was fixed fast. She'd have to look through her dad's things for the key and come back later. She started back down the trail and had almost reached the cabin when she saw a large, fawn-colored animal on the path ahead. She stopped, transfixed, and stared at the bighorn ram, horns curled like nautilus shells on its head. It stood not more than ten feet away from her, regarding her with calm, golden brown eyes.

She had never before been so close to a wild animal, unless one counted the copperheads she'd killed with a hoe when they invaded her flower beds in Houston, and she did not. She stared, transfixed by the soft thickness of the animal's pelt. It had almond-shaped eyes and a nose that looked like black leather.

But after several minutes passed and the ram showed no inclination to move, Maggie began to feel impatient. The wonders of nature were all well and good, but she was ready to get back to the cabin. She had curtains to sew, and she was thirsty. Hungry, too. And she was probably getting burned, standing out here in the sun so long. "Shoo," she said, motioning with her hands.

The ram blinked and shifted its feet. Then, instead of moving away from her, it took a step toward her.

Maggie began to feel nervous. Though the ram wasn't terribly tall—only about three and a half feet at the shoulder—it was stocky and clearly muscular. And those horns looked really hard. Was it upset because she was trespassing on its territory? Did it plan to fight her, the way she'd seen on nature shows? Would it try to knock her off the mountain?

She looked around for some sort of weapon with which to defend herself. There were plenty of rocks along the path, and this close, she could probably land a good blow on the animal's side. But that might only make it mad. And she didn't want to hurt it; she only wanted it to move.

"Go on, now," she said, raising her voice. "Shoo!"

The ram kept walking toward her, very slow and deliberate, its feet picking delicately among the rocks in the path. Maggie backed up but didn't compensate for a bend in the path, and before she knew it, she was pressed up against a large boulder, the ram between her and any kind of freedom. Oh God, what was it going to do to her? She squeezed her eyes shut, thinking this would probably be a good time to remember some of the prayers she'd learned in childhood Sunday school.

Something wet and slightly rubbery swiped across her neck, like being swabbed with a large wad of already-chewed gum. She opened her eyes wide and stared at the ram, who moved his attentions to her cheeks, licking like an overgrown dog happy to greet its master.

Maggie couldn't help it; she began to giggle. How absurd that the first kiss she'd had in months and months was from a sheep!

All fear banished; she shoved the ram hard in the side. It moved away, reluctantly, the way on oversized dog who'd been begging at the table would move. Obviously, it wasn't wild. Had her father made a pet out of this beast? Leave it to her old man not to be satisfied with anything as mundane as a dog or cat.

She made it to the cabin, the sheep following her right up

onto the porch. She had to shut the door in its face. Then it stood with its nose pressed to the front window, bleating pitifully.

Ignoring the animal, she hauled one of the theater curtains out of the box she'd deposited in the middle of the living room and dragged it up the stairs to the loft bedroom. In lieu of a measuring tape, she found a ball of twine in the kitchen and cut lengths equal to the height and width of the bedroom window. She marked the velvet and cut it, then began to hem.

The rhythm of the task soothed her, and after a while she let her eyes wander from the work to the room around her. A low bookshelf under the window held half a dozen battered Louis L'Amour paperbacks, a field guide to birds, and a brown hardback book that had a look of age.

She set aside the sewing and fetched the book from the shelf. *History of the Mining Regions of Eureka, Colorado, and the Surrounding Territory,* by the Reverend A. J. Kirkland. The cover was faded brown cloth, water spotted, and frayed at the edges. The inside pages revealed a copyright date of 1923—and the kind of paper checkout card Maggie associated with the libraries of her childhood. *Eureka County Public Library* was stenciled across the bottom of the page.

She closed the book and replaced it on the shelf. So this was the book that had gotten her father on the bad side of the local librarian. She wondered if she should return it. Maybe she'd meet the woman first and then decide.

On the bottom shelf was a steel lockbox, the kind used to store canceled checks, tax receipts, or other important documents. Maggie looked away and picked up the sewing again, but the box seemed to stare at her accusingly. "Don't be such a ninny," she said out loud, and hauled the box onto the bed beside her.

The box was locked, but thirty seconds of jimmying with the sewing needle and scissors popped the lock. She lifted the lid and sorted through the top layer of papers—titles to the

Jeep and snowmobile, old bank statements, and property tax receipts. Next came what appeared to be every automobile license permit her father had ever paid; receipts for iron, lumber, and other building materials; a doctor's bill from 1996 that showed he'd been treated for a broken hand; and a traffic citation for reckless driving from two years before. Why had he deemed these items important enough to save?

She set all this aside and peered into the box again. At the very bottom lay a brown five by seven envelope. Across the front, in what she could now recognize as her father's handwriting, was the single word, *Angie*.

Angie was Maggie's mother. Her hands shook as she folded up the brass brad and lifted the envelope's flap. Inside were two white envelopes, addressed in her mother's slanted hand. She opened the first letter and read:

> *Dear Jake,*
>
> *It was good to hear from you again. I'm glad you're doing well. Your place sounds really pretty—I'm glad you've found a spot where you can feel at home. I know you said Houston reminded you too much of the jungle, so it seems right you should end up in the mountains.*
>
> *I am doing as well as can be expected. Maggie came by this morning and I wish you could see her. You would be so proud of our little girl. She has your eyes, and sometimes when she's really serious and she tucks her chin in a little when she's speaking, it reminds me so much of you I almost expect to hear your voice coming out of her mouth.*
>
> *She is married to a good man, Carter Stevens. They never had children, which makes me sad, but it is their choice, so I tried not to say anything. He has his own business, a shipping company, and Maggie is his office manager.*

I will send you a picture when I find a good one. I want you to see how pretty she is, all grown up. Can you believe it's been almost forty years? Sometimes when I close my eyes it seems like yesterday.

I'm going to close for now, but hope to hear from you again soon.

Love,

Angie

The letter was dated the year before her mother's death. Her mother's cancer had been diagnosed by then. Had the illness prompted her to hunt down Jacob Murphy? And how had she managed to find him, hidden away here in the wilds of Colorado?

Or had Jake contacted her?

She opened the second letter. It was much like the first, full of praise of Maggie and her "wonderful" husband. What would Angie have said if she'd known the decision not to have children had been Carter's, not Maggie's? Letting him bully her—yes, that was what he had done; she could see it so clearly now, though she hadn't before—was something she would regret the rest of her life. Maggie wished she'd had the courage to confide in her mother about that; Angie might have offered some words of advice or comfort. Then again, Maggie was glad her mother hadn't lived to know Carter's betrayal. She had died believing Maggie had found happiness in her marriage, something that had eluded Angie.

No mention was made of Jacob's long absence from their lives. Maggie read both letters again, hoping for some explanation of her father's actions, why he had left them the way he had. But none was forthcoming. The second letter mentioned that a picture of Maggie was enclosed, but it was missing from the envelope.

She stared into the now-empty metal box, wishing for more. She had carefully sifted through all her mother's papers after Angie's death and had found no correspondence from her father. Why not? Had Angie burned the letters?

These communications contained no mention of her mother's illness. Had she kept that a secret from her ex-husband? *Maybe I'll make it to Colorado one day,* she wrote. *You know you're welcome to visit me in Houston any time.*

Why hadn't her dad made the trip? Maggie felt her heart squeeze as she stared at the writing. She wished more than anything that her mother was with her at this moment, to explain to her why she'd written the letters and what they meant.

A loud rapping shattered the silence. Maggie gasped and the empty box almost slid from her lap. She rescued it and stood, then hurried downstairs to answer the knocking.

She opened the door to find Jameso fending off kisses from the ram. It was a comical sight, the grown man struggling to shield himself from the amorous attentions of the bighorn. "He won't go away until you feed him his Lorna Doones," Jameso said, shoving the animal away.

"Until I what?" She held the door open wide enough for Jameso to slip inside.

"All those Lorna Doones in the cabinet aren't because Murph was so fond of them," Jameso said. "He fed them to Winston."

"Winston?"

"That's what he called the beast. After Mount Winston."

"My father made a *pet* out of a bighorn sheep?"

"Well, he's still a wild animal. But he's crazy about Lorna Doones. Give him a few and he'll leave you alone—at least until tomorrow when he starts jonesing for them again."

Incredulous, she went to the cabinet and fetched the package of cookies she'd opened for her breakfast. She started toward the door, but Jameso pulled her back. "Don't take the whole package out there," he said. "He's liable to trample you to get at them. Just take three or four."

She grabbed four cookies and slipped out onto the porch, Jameso following. As soon as the ram spotted her, Winston clattered up onto the porch and nudged at her arm. She held out the cookies, palm flat, the way she'd been taught to give treats to horses at a friend's ranch when she was a little girl.

The ram swept up all four cookies with his tongue, then trotted a few feet away, where he stood chewing contentedly. Maggie shook her head and went back inside. "I'm sure there's a story to go with what just happened," she said, looking at Jameso expectantly.

"It may have involved a dare," Jameso said. "Or maybe Murph just got lonely and decided to make friends with one of the only other creatures living up here." He shrugged. "Stories associated with your dad have a way of, um, *evolving* over time."

"So I'm beginning to realize." She crossed her arms over her chest. "What are *you* doing up here?"

"Danielle and Janelle want to have a little get-together in honor of your dad. Sort of a memorial."

"Oh. Well, sure. I mean, they don't need my permission for that. They knew him better than I did."

"They want you to come."

"All right. Where will it be? Is there a church, or—"

"They're going to have it at the Last Dollar. Tomorrow about seven. It'll be more of a wake than a service, really. They just thought it would be good if everybody got together to talk about your dad and have a few drinks in his honor."

"Of course." This might be her best chance yet to find out more about her dad. "Tell them thank you for me. And thank you for breakfast this morning. You didn't have to do that."

He shoved his hands in his pockets. "I felt I owed you one for scaring you last night."

"I wasn't scared," she lied.

"I didn't think about what it might be like for you, coming upon a strange man up here all alone." He looked around the cabin. "How do you like it up here? Are you settling in all right?"

"I'm getting used to it." The silence still bothered her, but it was getting better. "I'm making a curtain for the bedroom window so the light won't wake me in the morning."

"Yeah, Lucille mentioned she'd sold you the old theater curtains. Murph would have got a kick out of that."

"He would? Why?"

"He used to say he didn't need movies or television when he had the view out his windows. He would have thought theater curtains were appropriate."

"You said the other night he wasn't really your friend, but you seem to know him as well as anyone. So what was your relationship?"

His gaze shifted. "Do you really want to go into this?" he asked.

"Yes, I never met my father, so the only way I can learn what he was like is through other people's impressions of him."

"Fair enough. As long as you don't expect to hear only the good things."

"I don't. Why should I?"

"All right, then. There were a lot of things I really liked about Murph. He had a good sense of humor. He was smart. He could be really generous when he wanted to be. But he had a selfish streak, too. I didn't always like the way he treated people." His eyes met hers, and she felt the heat of that gaze, the emotion behind it. As if he was saying he didn't approve of the way her father had treated *her*.

But that was ridiculous. Jameso might have heard some things from Reggie, but he didn't really know her. "But you kept coming around. Lucille told me you were the one who found him . . . when he died."

"Yeah." The creases around his eyes deepened. "I think he went quick. There weren't any signs of a struggle. It looked like he was working and it hit him. The coroner said it was a massive heart attack. He probably died instantly."

She sensed he was trying to comfort her, and the gesture touched her. "What happened to him?" she asked. "I mean, was there a funeral? Is he buried somewhere?" It embarrassed her that she didn't know these things, that she hadn't thought to ask them before.

"He wanted to be cremated. A bunch of us took his ashes up on top of the mountain here and scattered them. I guess we should have waited for you, but we didn't know."

"Of course you didn't know. It's all right, really."

"There were a lot of things in his past Murph never talked about," Jameso said. "I think he had a lot of regrets."

"Don't we all?" If she had a chance to live life over, would she have spent so many years devoted to making Carter's life easy? She'd thought keeping him happy was the key to her happiness as well, as if shaping her desires to match his was the sign of an ideal marriage. For years she hadn't even realized she *had* different opinions. She felt sick to her stomach remembering.

"Do you need help with those curtains?" Jameso asked, interrupting her self-flagellation.

"Help? Oh, no. I'm fine."

"How are you going to hang them?" he asked. "All that velvet's got to be heavy."

"Lucille suggested I use pipe and plumbing fittings."

"Good idea. You'll need tools to hang them."

"I'm sure my dad has some around here somewhere." She had no idea what fittings to buy or how she'd mount them on the wall, but wasn't part of being independent figuring that kind of stuff out?

"It would take me about half an hour to do the whole thing," he said. "You should let me help."

"Only if you let me pay you." Hiring someone was different from accepting favors from a man she hardly knew.

"Fine. I'll get the pipe and fittings and bring them back up here tomorrow." He started toward the stairs. "I'll go measure it now."

"Don't you have something else you need to do?" she asked, trailing after him. "A job?"

"The Jeep tours only run on weekends this time of year. Skiing season hasn't started yet. I only tend bar in the evenings. I have time."

Time and an interest in snooping as well? He stopped beside the bed and surveyed the empty metal box and the papers spread out around it. "Murph never did pay that traffic ticket," he said, plucking the citation from the pile of documents. He glanced over his shoulder at her. "If he didn't agree with a law or rule, he took the attitude that he didn't have to obey it."

"How did he stay out of jail?"

"I'm not sure he always did."

Maggie watched, afraid of disturbing his stillness. He was such a hard man to read; she couldn't tell if he was sad or angry.

He tossed the citation onto the bed. "I guess it doesn't matter now." He turned his attention to the window. "Where's your tape measure?"

"I don't have one," she said. She handed him the ball of twine. "Use this. You can cut it to size and measure it when you get back to town."

"Clever." He handed her one end of the string. "Hold this against the window frame over there."

He stretched the twine across the window and cut it, then began winding it into a ball. "I see you're making yourself at home here. Does that mean you're going to stay?"

"For a while. I don't know how long."

"When you make up your mind, let me know."

She stared at him. "Why? What difference does it make to you?"

He pocketed the ball of twine. "There's a pool in town on whether or not you're going to stick around."

"A *pool?*"

He shrugged. "It's a small town. We take our entertainment where we can find it." He started down the stairs.

"Wait," she called after him. "How did you bet?"

"Oh, I'll never tell." With a wave, he headed out the door. She stared after him, not sure whether to curse or laugh.

Chapter 7

"Wake up, Cassie. I brought you something."

Cassie started blinking, then hurriedly sat up. "I was reading," she said, frowning at the young woman on the other side of the checkout counter. She might, in fact, have fallen asleep for a moment. It was to be expected, given her insomnia last night. "What do you want?"

"Janelle made Linzer torte this morning and I brought you a piece. I know how much you like it." Danielle held out a square cardboard to-go container. The girl had a lush ripeness about her—all rosy cheeks and shining hair, perfect teeth, and impressive bosom. Cassie felt shriveled and aged in her presence.

"What do you want?" she asked again, standing and accepting the container.

At least Danielle didn't try to pretend the torte wasn't a bribe. "You have old issues of the *Eureka Miner* here, don't you?"

"If that's what you're after, why don't you go to the paper? I'm sure they keep back issues there."

"Rick went to Montrose for the afternoon and the office is locked up tight."

"What is in the paper that you couldn't wait for him to return?" As she spoke, Cassie came out from behind the counter and led the way to the shelves at the back of the room where the newspapers were stored. Nowadays, most modern libraries scanned the issues onto computer disks, but Eureka still kept the old issues in oversized portfolios stacked on flat shelves.

"I need a picture of Murphy. The one taken after he won the Hard Rock competition for the third time, year before last. I thought I could copy it on your copier; then I can scan it into my computer at home and Photoshop it into something that looks like a real photograph."

Jake again. The man had been dead a month and still he wouldn't leave Cassie alone. "Why do you need a picture of Jake?" she asked.

"For the memorial." At Cassie's blank look, Danielle nudged her. "You know, the service we're having for him at the Last Dollar. I know Lucille told you about it. It's at seven tomorrow night. You'll be there, won't you?"

"Why would I want to be there?"

Danielle's bright eyes clouded. "I thought Murphy was your friend. The two of you dated for a while, didn't you?"

"I don't know where you heard that, but it's a lie." They had gone out exactly twice. Well, three times if you counted the night she'd had him to her house for dinner—a night she still blushed to think about. She pushed the awful memory away. "Jacob Murphy meant nothing to me," she said.

"Okay. You can come to the memorial or not, makes no difference to me." Danielle turned her attention to the papers. "That would have been August. If you show me which folder, I'll look through them and you can go back to, um, reading."

"They're labeled." Cassie indicated the writing on the spine of each folder. "When you find the picture, let me copy it. I don't want you tearing the newsprint." She retreated to her desk and opened the takeout container. A six-inch square of Linzer torte rested on a paper doily, the cherry filling oozing between squares of crisp pastry, sugar sparkling on the top. There was even a little plastic fork alongside.

Stifling a moan, Cassie dug into the torte. Janelle made the best pastry in the county, perhaps in the state. But the Linzer torte was Cassie's favorite. It tasted just like the ones her grandmother had made when Cassie was a girl. She could remember sitting at the long, oilcloth-covered table in the kitchen of the Queen Anne house, eating slices of Linzer torte after school and listening to her grandmother complain about yet another business deal of her grandfather's gone wrong.

The table had disappeared somewhere over the years, and Cassie had taken for granted that the Linzer tortes had died with her grandmother. And then Janelle and Danielle had opened the Last Dollar and the tortes had reappeared. Cassie would give a tooth to know how Janelle had gotten hold of her grandmother's recipe.

"I found the picture." Danielle's voice rang out in the afternoon silence of the library.

Cassie pressed the back of the fork into the last crumbs of the torte and slid it into her mouth before she stood and made her way back to the paper. "It's a great picture, isn't it?" Danielle asked.

It was a great picture. Jake stood with the big sledgehammer over one shoulder, grinning at the camera. He looked strong and healthy and so handsome Cassie's heart ached.

"It's hard to believe he's gone," Danielle said softly. "I still expect him to walk into the café some morning and order breakfast."

When Cassie first heard Jake had died, she hadn't believed it. She'd invested so much in hating him, and in plotting revenge against him, that his death had left her feeling deflated. There was unfinished business between them, and now she could never know satisfaction.

"Why are you having a memorial service for him now?"

she asked. "He's been gone a month and his ashes are scattered."

"We thought it would be nice for his daughter," Danielle said. "Have you met her?"

Cassie shook her head and began twisting the brads to remove the paper from its folder.

"She came into the café this morning. She looks a lot like him, with his eyes and his hair. I meant to invite her to the service then, but I was so caught up staring at her, I forgot, so I had to send Jameso up to Murphy's place to tell her. Reggie says she never even knew her father. Can you imagine?"

"Can I imagine Jake abandoning a wife and baby without another thought? Yes, I can." The man she knew was just that coldhearted. Cassie carried the paper to the copy machine and positioned the picture facedown on its surface. "Do you want this original size or enlarged?"

"One of each, I think," Danielle said. "It is awful that Murph left his family, but he obviously had regrets. He left her everything and he didn't have to do that."

Cassie made a scoffing noise. "He left her a worthless mine and an old shack. I doubt she thinks he did her any favors."

"Murph had a beautiful place!" Danielle protested. "He could have pretended she didn't exist and no one would have been the wiser. Besides, she doesn't seem to harbor any hard feelings against him."

"She might feel differently if she really knew him." Cassie handed the copies to Danielle. "That will be fifty cents," she said.

Danielle hesitated. Cassie waited for her to point out that the Linzer torte sold for four dollars in the café, but instead, she dug in the pocket of her too-tight jeans and pulled out two quarters. "Thanks for your help," she said. "I hope you can make it to the memorial tomorrow."

"Maybe I'll be there." She wanted to see what Jake's daughter was like. And if the purpose of the service was to introduce the woman to her father, Cassie had a few stories she ought to hear.

Maggie spent the next morning in Eureka, washing clothes at the Laundromat and running errands. When she returned to the cabin shortly after noon, Winston was waiting on the front porch. She pushed past him and fetched the Lorna Doones. Her father must have bought the cookies by the case, but doling them out three and four a day, they wouldn't last forever. She'd have to see if the grocery store kept them in stock.

Then again, she probably wouldn't be here long enough to run out. After she was gone, Winston would have to go back to eating grass or brush or whatever it was bighorn sheep lived on.

Upstairs, the bedroom window was now framed by the red velvet drapes. Jameso had done a good job hanging them, even fastening a rod on each panel near the top to make it easier to pull the curtains open and closed. She'd thank him when she saw him tonight and make sure he sent her a bill for the supplies and labor.

She spent the rest of the day cleaning the cabin, scrubbing floors and dusting furniture and sorting through cabinets and closets. She boxed up most of her dad's old clothes to take to Lucille, who probably knew some local charity that could use the old shirts, coats, and blue jeans. She kept the jean jacket to ward off the chill. When she was done, the cabin felt emptier. Lighter. Maybe she'd ask Barb to ship a few of her own belongings from storage, just to make things more comfortable while she was here.

At five o'clock, she dressed in the gabardine suit she'd worn on the plane and drove into Eureka. She was less nervous negotiating the steep curves of the road, less worried about slipping over the edge as the route became more and more familiar. Driving back up tonight in the dark might be a different story, but she'd avoid thinking about that for now.

There was already a crowd at the café by the time she arrived. She was surprised by how many people she recognized: Danielle and Janelle, of course, and Bob and Jameso. Maggie joined Reggie and his wife, Katya, and Lucille at a table on one side of the room.

But her attention was drawn to the front of the room, to a slightly grainy portrait of a man with silvered hair and a thick moustache and brows. He stood with a large sledgehammer balanced on one shoulder as if it weighed no more than a golf club, and he looked right into the camera with a wide smile that was so warm and genuine anyone looking at it would have to smile back. Maggie stared at it, almost overwhelmed with longing and regret. This was the face of her childhood fantasies, grown older with years, but in so many ways unchanged.

"Murph was a handsome man," Lucille said.

"Did he have a girlfriend?" Maggie asked.

"No one serious," Lucille said. "He dated a few women, but nothing ever long term. He was friendly, but he was never the type to let anyone get too close."

"Yes, I guess not, living like he did, way up there alone." She fell silent, wondering again what sadness drove her father to separate himself from others that way.

"I take it you're not married," Lucille said. "Not that it's any of my business, but I noticed you don't wear a ring."

Maggie thought of the wedding band on the chain around her neck. "No, I'm divorced."

"Me, too. Though mine was a long time ago."

"Mine was just a few months ago." She knew she wasn't supposed to feel any shame for that. Divorce was as common as coffee shops these days, and this one hadn't been her idea anyway. But it still rankled to admit her marriage had failed—that she had failed.

"I didn't mean to pry," Lucille said.

"No, it's all right." The older woman inspired confession. "He left me for another woman."

"Ah." Lucille nodded. "Been there, done that, got the T-shirt. It does get better with time. The hurt, I mean. I moved to California after my husband left me. It helped, not living where I might run into him or his new wife in the grocery store or coffee shop."

Maggie could be sure she wouldn't run into Carter or Francine in Eureka, Colorado. The thought of either one of them cruising down the town's dirt streets in Carter's convertible BMW almost made her smile.

"Uh-oh." Lucille frowned.

"What's wrong?"

Lucille's gaze shifted across the room, then back to Maggie. "Don't look now, but here comes trouble," she muttered.

Maggie turned to follow Lucille's gaze and saw a small, thin woman with short, iron-gray hair coming toward her. The woman moved in a straight line, the crowd parting for her, and all Maggie could think of was a destroyer speeding toward a fight.

Cassie had fully intended to stay away from the memorial service. She had no desire to listen to people sing Jake Murphy's praises. She went straight home from work and decided to spend the evening cleaning house, to wash Jake out of her mind.

Once she'd mopped the floors and polished the glass, she decided to dust the bookcases. That was her downfall. The shelves were filled with her collection of family albums and volumes related to the history of Eureka County. While she'd donated some duplicates and other books to the library, this private collection contained her most valuable volumes. These were the documents that testified to her family's importance in the history of the area.

But looking at those books reminded her of the book Jake had stolen. It was one of the volumes she'd donated to the library, written by her great-uncle. Against library policy, she'd allowed him to take the rare book home with him, and she'd never seen it again. The theft of this part of her history hurt almost as much as his rejection of her as a woman.

Not bothering to change clothes, she'd dropped her dust rag and driven straight to the Last Dollar. That book had to be somewhere in Jake's belongings; she'd never forgive herself if she forfeited her best chance to get it back.

The street around the café was crowded with cars, so Cassie had to double-park in front of the saloon next door, beside a black SUV with Connecticut plates. She could hear the hum of conversation from the restaurant as she approached and had to squeeze past a trio of smokers on the front porch to get inside.

As Danielle had promised, Cassie had no trouble picking Jake's daughter from the crowd. She sat at a table near the front with Lucille and Reggie and Katya, her hair a shade darker than Jake's, without the smattering of gray. Even without the hair, there was something about the tilt of her head that was so familiar Cassie felt a pull at her heart.

Pushing sentimentality aside, she marched across the room. "Maggie Murphy," she called, her voice ringing above the hum of conversation.

The woman turned wide eyes to her. Jake's eyes, the same clear blue. "It's Maggie Stevens, actually," she said. "Murphy was my maiden name."

"Now, Cassie—" Reggie half rose from his chair, but Katya put a restraining hand on his arm.

"Hello, Cassie," Katya said pleasantly. "Maggie, this is Cassie Wynock, the town librarian."

"It's good to meet you," Maggie said carefully, her gaze shifting between Cassie and Reggie. Worry lines furrowed the lawyer's forehead as he stared at the older woman, as if he expected trouble.

"You're staying in Jacob Murphy's cabin," Cassie said. It was a statement, not a question.

"Yes."

Cassie took a deep breath, aware that conversation had

died around her, every eye fixed on her. Were they wondering why she was here? Did they think she was here because she mourned Jacob Murphy? Because she still carried a torch for him? "While going through your late father's belongings, have you come across a book that is marked as the property of the Eureka County Library?" she asked, her voice steady. She wanted everyone in the room to hear she'd come about the book, not about the man who stole it.

"I can't say that I've examined *every* book on my father's shelves," Maggie said. "Does this one have a name?"

"The name of the book is *History of the Mining Regions of Eureka, Colorado, and the Surrounding Territory* by the Reverend A. J. Kirkland. It's one of the oldest and rarest books in our collection."

"Is the book valuable?" Maggie asked.

What did that matter? Was she thinking she could take it back to wherever she was from and sell it? "A book's value is not necessarily measured in dollars," Cassie said, "but in the information that it conveys or the beauty of its prose."

Someone off to the side snickered. Cassie sent a withering look in that direction, but she couldn't be sure of the culprit.

"What makes you think my father had this book?" Maggie asked.

"Because he was the last person to check it out."

"When was that?"

Was the woman deliberately baiting her? She looked innocent enough, her face calm, a little weary even. "Jacob Murphy checked out that book on August 7, 2006," Cassie said, "and thereafter ignored repeated requests for its return. *When* you locate the book, I trust you will return it immediately. If you do so, we will consider waiving the accompanying fine."

Maggie arched one pale brow. "Any fine was my father's responsibility, not mine," she said.

"If you're his heir, you have a responsibility to settle the debts of his estate, and this is one of them." Honestly, did the woman have no sense of justice?

"Cassie, you can't hold Maggie responsible for a book she doesn't have," Reggie said. "Now, why don't you find a seat. I think the service is about to start."

As if on cue, Danielle struck up a melodic ringing with a spoon against the side of a water glass. "I want to thank you all for coming out tonight to honor the memory of Jacob Murphy," she said.

Cassie whirled and pushed her way toward the door. She had no interest in honoring Jacob Murphy. And no interest in being mocked by his daughter or his friends. They thought she was crazy for being so concerned about a book, but there was more to it than the mere volume. Jacob had stolen an important artifact from the county, and a Wynock family heirloom, but worse still, in walking off with that volume, he'd stolen Cassie's pride. She'd do whatever she could to reclaim it, and to destroy yet another bit of evidence of her folly with a man who didn't deserve to wipe her boots.

Chapter 8

Maggie watched the strange gray woman hurry out the door, then forced her attention to Danielle, who stood beside Jacob's portrait. "We have a very special guest with us tonight," Danielle was saying. "We want to welcome Murph's daughter, Maggie Stevens."

A smattering of applause greeted these words. Maggie flushed and offered a weak smile. Lucille took her hand and squeezed it, a gesture that made Maggie feel stronger.

"I thought we'd start by asking our mayor to say a few words," Danielle said.

Maggie started as the chair beside her scraped back and Lucille stood. "Jacob Murphy was a valuable member of our community," she said. "He had strong opinions that didn't make him popular with everyone. But he was definitely a man who stood up for what he believed in. He told me once if people were too afraid to speak up to right a wrong, terrible things could happen, so Murph always spoke up. And if you needed help, he was always there to help you."

Heads nodded around the room and Maggie heard murmurs of "That's right," and "That was Murph."

"I hope Murph is looking down on us all right now," Lucille continued. "I think he'd be especially happy to see Maggie here, in the place he loved so much."

Maggie blinked back tears and swallowed hard. Lucille sat and patted her hand again, and a lanky man with a patch over his right eye unfolded from his chair. "I was thinking today about what I wanted to say about Murph," he said. "I remember the first time I ever met him was when we competed against each other at Hard Rock Days. I'd won the competition the year before and I was the favorite to win again, when up steps this big redhead."

At Maggie's puzzled look, Lucille leaned over and whispered, "It's an annual celebration of the area's mining history. Men compete in things like drilling rock and swinging sledgehammers."

". . . said he was going to beat me and I swore to myself that wasn't going to happen. Sure enough, we set out neck and neck. He even fell behind a little, and I pushed harder, sure I'd bested him. I saw my mistake too late. I'd come on in such a rush, I'd burned up by the time we got to the end. Old Murph put on the steam and beat me, fair and square. He took home the trophy that year."

"And two years after that," someone added.

"Then he stopped entering," a woman offered. "I always wondered why he did that."

"I always figured it was because he knew he didn't have anything left to prove," Bob said. "Murphy liked to make a point, but once it was made, he moved on."

The stories continued: of Murph building Janelle and Danielle's chicken house, of skiing down Mount Garnet on a dare, of climbing Mount Winston to string a clothesline in front of an old miner's shack and hanging a pair of red long-handle underwear, a yellow flannel shirt, and blue jeans where they'd be visible to tourists on the highway below. "For the next year people would come into the café and ask who lived in that house way up near the top of Mount Winston," Danielle said. "We took turns making up outrageous stories about the Hermit of Mount Winston."

"The next summer Murph made the climb again and added a pair of ladies' bloomers and a calico dress to the clothesline," Janelle said. "He decided the hermit had gotten married."

Maggie listened to the stories, piecing together a picture of an outrageous, profane, generous, and courageous man—the kind of man she would have liked to have known. Bob told his story about Murph almost killing him, but it was presented as almost a badge of honor, as if he'd been singled out for special attention by the town's hero.

"He was mighty stubborn," someone said.

"If he didn't believe something was right, you can be sure you'd hear about it," said another.

When the talk died down, Janelle handed around plastic cups and Danielle poured everyone present a shot of Irish whiskey from a bottle she carried from person to person. "Let's drink a toast to the memory of Jacob Murphy," she said. "I hope he was in heaven a half an hour before the devil knew he was dead."

"Knowing old Murph, he's down there giving the devil a run for his money," Bob said.

Maggie cautiously sipped the whiskey. She wasn't ordinarily much of a drinker, and already she was thinking about the drive up the mountain in the dark. She pushed her cup toward Reggie. "You can have mine if you want it," she said.

"Why, thank you." He reached for the glass, but before he could take hold of it, the door to the café flew open.

"Big Mama's back!" shouted a boy of about sixteen who carried a skateboard tucked under one arm.

The buzz of conversation increased. As organized as any lifeboat drill, people began lining up by the kitchen. Janelle and Danielle handed pots, pans, and utensils over the counter of the pass-through. Someone shoved a saucepan and a wooden spoon into Maggie's hands. "What is this for?" she asked. "Who is Big Mama?"

"Big Mama's a big sow bear," Lucille said as she pulled Maggie toward the door. "She likes to raid the Dumpster behind the restaurant. Janelle and Danielle keep replacing the locks, but she manages to break them all."

"But what does that have to do with all these pots and pans?" Maggie asked.

"Bang on the pot with the spoon. The idea is to make so much noise she and her cubs won't want to come back."

They were outside now, and Lucille had to shout to be heard over the din of cookware and cutlery. Maggie stared at a fat black bear who stood beside a Dumpster, glaring at them like a nearsighted matron. Behind her, two rounded black shapes emerged from the shadows—cubs, peering from behind their mother at the crowd of noisy creatures who had descended upon them.

"Is she dangerous?" Maggie asked. "Will she attack?" The only thing she knew about bears were stories she'd read in *Reader's Digest* of campers who survived having their scalps ripped open by marauding grizzlies.

"Only to defend herself or her cubs," Lucille said.

"Then why are we trying to scare her away?"

"The Department of Wildlife has already tagged Big Mama once. If they catch her a second time, they'll shoot her."

"Shoot her? But—aren't bears protected or something?"

"A bear that thinks of people as a source of food will end up in trouble sooner or later. We're hoping we can reform Big Mama and her babies before it's too late."

Tonight, at least, the tactic was working. With a last, disgusted glance at the noisy onlookers, Big Mama ushered her brood off into the darkness, loping down the street at a surprisingly swift pace.

The crowd filed back into the café and their noisemakers

were returned to the kitchen. Maggie dropped into a chair and studied the glass of whiskey still before her. She wasn't drunk, so she hadn't imagined that a café full of people had banded together to drive away a bear—not because the bear was a danger to them, but to protect her, in a way, from themselves.

The same people who lauded her father, while readily admitting his faults. No wonder her father had chosen to settle here—where his dark side was welcomed along with the light. Where being different was something to be celebrated, not suppressed.

She felt embraced by them, too, at home in a way she had not felt since Carter announced he was leaving and turned her whole world topsy-turvy. "Welcome to a gang bang, Eureka style." Jameso spoke from behind her chair.

Maggie tilted her head to look up at him. "Thank you for hanging my curtain rod," she said. "It looks good."

"You're welcome. I'm thinking of adding to my business card: Jameso's Odd Jobs."

"What kind of a name is Jameso?" she asked.

"It's Jameson," he said. "My handwriting's not that great and when I hired on at the ski resort, someone in the office misread my application as Jameso, so that's what they ordered for my name tag. I decided I kind of liked it."

Danielle came to stand beside Maggie. "It was a good evening, wasn't it?" she said. "Everybody had good stories to tell about Murph."

"Thank you for doing this," Maggie said. "I learned a lot about my father I might not have otherwise known."

"Reg said you were pretty little when he and your mom split up," Danielle said.

"I was only a few days old, so I really have no memory of him at all."

"Still, you probably know things we don't," she said. "He never talked about his life before he came to Eureka."

"I know he was in Vietnam," Maggie said. "And something happened there that changed him. That's what my mother said, but how could war not change a person?"

"Vietnam was one thing he refused to talk about," Jameso said. "One year someone asked him if he'd march in a Veteran's Day parade and he went off on a rant about how we had no business celebrating something like that."

"When the U.S. declared war on Iraq, Murph was so upset," Danielle said. "He left town and was gone for over a week."

"Where did he go?" Maggie asked.

"He called them camping trips," Jameso said. "He'd buy a bunch of booze and go off in the mountains and stay drunk until he got it out of his system."

"Did he do that kind of thing often?" Maggie asked.

"Once or twice a year," Jameso said.

What kind of pain would drive a man to take such drastic measures to try to kill it?

"I don't want to give you the wrong impression," Jameso said. "He wasn't a drunk. He just had things that upset him and had his own way of handling them."

"Like beating up Bob to make a point." Maggie frowned.

Jameso shrugged. "Murphy wasn't into talking to people when he could use his fists. He didn't let his temper get out of hand very often, but when he lost control, it could be bad," Jameso said. "I think that's why he went off in the mountains to do his drinking, so no one else would be around to suffer the consequences."

"And after a few days or a week, he'd show up again all right?" Maggie asked.

"Sometimes I'd go looking for him," Jameso said. "To tell you the truth, I half expected to find him dead out there at one of his camps some day, not in his own front yard at a time when he'd been sober for months."

"But he was a good man." Danielle slid into a chair across

from Maggie and Jameso. "He had his troubles," she said. "But if his friends needed help, he would do anything for them."

His friends, but not his family, Maggie thought. She stood. "I'd better go. Thank you again for tonight."

"You okay making the drive up there in the dark?" Jameso asked.

"That's what headlights are for," she said, annoyed at his sudden solicitude. What did he care how she felt about the drive?

"I should come up someday soon and show you how to check the water lines," he said. "They can freeze up there all the way into July."

What was with this guy? He'd appointed himself her father's caretaker; now he seemed determined to take the same role with her. "If I need your help, I'll ask for it," she said. "You don't have to keep checking on me like I'm some idiot child who might fall down a well or forget to eat if you don't watch over me."

"Oh." Danielle's face clouded. "I'm sure Jameso didn't mean—"

"Maggie's right." Jameso's expression hardened. "I'm sure she can look after herself. After all, Houston isn't all that different from Eureka." He nodded. "Good night, ladies."

"Don't mind Jameso," Danielle said when he was gone. "He was probably closer to Murphy than anyone. His death hit him hard."

"They seem to have had an odd relationship," Maggie said, remembering Jameso's refusal to characterize their interactions as friendship.

"I think the two of them were a lot alike," Danielle said. "Jameso doesn't go on wild binges or beat people up, but there's a lot of emotion under the surface, like maybe he would do that stuff under different circumstances. I think he and Murphy understood each other, and that made things difficult between them sometimes." She made a face. "Then again, they were two guys; you know how weird they can be when it comes to emotional stuff."

Right. Though Maggie wasn't sure women handled the "emotional stuff" any better. If she'd punched Carter in the face when he told her he wanted a divorce, would it have made him think twice about leaving her? Would it at least have made her feel better?

When Lucille arrived home after Jake's memorial service, Olivia's SUV was no longer parked in the alley behind the house, and the house itself was dark and quiet. Lucille's heart sank as she stood in the shadow-filled kitchen and listened to the steady tick of the clock in the hall and the creak of the old house settling—sounds of emptiness. Her heart felt just as empty. Couldn't Olivia stand to be with her even twenty-four hours?

"Ma'am? Why are you standing here in the dark?"

Lucille started at the voice, and Lucas moved into the room, his round, worried face illuminated by the night light on the stove. Relief at the sight of him made Lucille feel almost giddy, and her hand shook as she leaned over and switched on the overhead light. "Lucas, I'm your grandmother," she said. "You can call me Grandma."

"All right." He took another step toward her. "Is something wrong?"

She shook her head, then nodded. "I saw your mother's car was gone and thought you'd left," she said.

"Mom went out."

"Where did she go?"

"I don't know." He adjusted his glasses on his nose. "Probably a bar. She likes to be with other people—other adults."

Lucille's heart pinched at the words. How often had Olivia left the boy alone like this, sending the clear message that she preferred the company of strangers to his? "I'm glad you're here," she said. "Will you sit a while and talk to me before it's time for bed?"

"Okay." He pulled out a chair and sat at the table.

Lucille sat across from him. "I was at a memorial service for a friend of mine," she said.

"I remember. You said at dinner that you were going."

So she had. "There were a lot of people there," she said. "Including the man's grown daughter. She hadn't seen him since she was a baby. None of us even knew she existed until a few weeks ago." She supposed Reggie had known, but as Murphy's lawyer he'd had a duty to keep the information secret.

"I haven't seen my father since I was two," Lucas said. "That's what Mom tells me. I don't remember."

"Does that make you sad?" Lucille asked.

"Not really. Mom says it's for the best." He sounded sincere, but his expression was so inscrutable, Lucille couldn't tell what he was really feeling. She had a vague memory of his father—Byron, she recalled his name now—as a big, brutish man who had once blackened Olivia's eye in a fight in which she'd stabbed him in the ribs with a steak knife. Olivia had had the sense to pack up and move back to her father's house the next day, and had started divorce proceedings that afternoon. Lucille had to hand it to the girl, she knew how to stand up for herself. "Tell me about D. J.," she said. "How long did you and your mom live with him?"

Lucas shifted in the chair. "About a year? He and Mom met at a bar where he worked as a bouncer."

"And you liked him?"

"Yeah, I did. He brought me books and stuff, and he'd talk to me about history and engineering and stuff I liked. He didn't treat me like a weird kid. He said I was smart and interesting."

Lucille didn't miss the note of longing in his voice. She remembered her own first impressions of him as awkward and unattractive and yes, strange. The men Olivia usually dated—the motorcycle riders and race car drivers, oilfield roughnecks and construction workers—would have had little time for a boy who favored books over baseball. "And D. J. is in Iraq now?" she asked.

"He's an engineer, building roads and bridges and stuff. It's what he did before he got laid off. That's why he was working as a bouncer, because he couldn't get a job in his field. He said the job in Iraq was a great opportunity, but Mom was mad at him for leaving."

That sounded like Olivia. She had always thought the world should revolve around her. She wasn't the nurturing type. No wonder Lucas was so independent; his mother hadn't given him much of a choice.

"I'm sorry D. J. went away," Lucille said. "But I'm very glad you and your mom came to live here. I hope you're going to like it. What did you do this afternoon?"

"I read some of the books we got at the library."

At lunch, he'd insisted she return with him to the library so he could get a card from "that witchy woman behind the counter"—a characterization Lucille had found apt, though she hadn't admitted as much to him.

"I tried to get on your computer, but I didn't know the password," he added.

She almost laughed out loud at this frank confession. "I'll give you the password, but if I find out you've been in any of my personal files or have been visiting Web sites you shouldn't be on, I'll take away the privilege," she said.

"I'm not interested in porn, if that's what you mean. I wanted to find out more about Eureka."

"I'll show you the password tomorrow." And she'd figure out how to establish some parental controls. Lucas might not be into porn at the moment, but she wasn't taking chances. "I suppose you'll need a computer for school," she added.

"I guess. I don't know what the schools are like here."

"Smaller than the one you went to in Connecticut, I'm

sure. But that can be a good thing. It will make it easier for you to get to know everyone."

"I doubt I'll have anything in common with them." He pushed his glasses up on his nose again. "It doesn't matter anyway. I like doing things by myself."

The words were spoken in a defiant tone, his chin jutted out, eyes hooded. Lucille had a sharp, painful memory of Olivia with the same expression. She'd been about the same age Lucas was now. Her glasses were square and black, not round and wire-rimmed, and her hair had been long and pushed back on her head with a plastic headband. But she'd had that same guarded yet fierce look in her eyes; the same I-don't-give-a-damn tone in her voice. She and Lucille had been sitting at a different kitchen table in the crappy apartment they'd moved to after the divorce. Lucille had been congratulating herself for finding ten minutes of "quality time" to spend with her kid after her shift as a cocktail waitress at a bar near the airport. She couldn't even remember what they'd talked about, some problem at school, she suspected. Olivia was always having problems at school. What came back to her now was her own feeling of relief that Olivia was doing such a good job of handling things on her own; that Lucille, already stretched to the end of her rope with two jobs and dealing with the emotional aftermath of her divorce, wouldn't have to wade in and try to fix things for her awkward daughter.

Now, twenty years later, she saw with startling clarity how utterly wrong she'd been. Behind Lucas's bravado—the same bravado she'd felt grateful for in his mother—she heard the hurt and fear. Yes, he was putting on a front of being brave and independent, but somewhere deep inside he was wanting help and maybe didn't know how to ask for it.

Sudden tears burned Lucille's eyes, kept back only by her determination not to lose it in front of this boy, who would no doubt think his grandmother as crazy and undependable as apparently every other adult in his life so far. All these years Lucille had spent wondering why Olivia was so messed up, and for the first time she saw clearly the role she had played in her daughter's undoing. Sure, it was a cliché of sorts for parents—mothers especially—to wallow in guilt over all the ways they'd failed their children, but Lucille really had failed Olivia. When the girl had needed her most—in a new school, coping with the loss of the life she'd known and her parents' divorce—Lucille had been off in a world of her own hurt. And when Olivia had rebelled a few years later, Lucille had gladly abdicated responsibility to her ex-husband, a man who had already proved he wasn't capable of anything like a permanent relationship.

Guilt choked her now and burned in her eyes. With aching clarity, she saw that Olivia was repeating a pattern she'd started, leaving Lucas to fend for himself. The boy looked okay so far on the outside, but who knew where things might lead?

She reached across the table and took Lucas's hand in hers. He tried to pull away, but she held it fast. "Lucas, I know I'm almost a stranger to you. I haven't been a storybook grandmother or even close. But I want you to know that I am here for you. If you need help with anything, I will do my best to give it to you."

He looked at her as if she was indeed crazy. Who could blame the boy? She let go of his hand and sat back. "I realize you're very mature for a boy your age," she continued, groping for the right words. "But you're not an adult and you shouldn't have to be. You need people you can depend on in your life, and I want to be one of those people."

He continued to stare at her, his expression guarded.

"I guess I can talk all I want, but the words don't mean anything unless I prove them," Lucille said. "I just . . . I hope you'll give me a chance to prove them."

"All right," he said. He stood, one hand gripping the back of the chair hard. "If it's okay with you I'll go to bed now."

She nodded. "Good night."

He started past her, then stopped and put a hand on her shoulder; she felt the briefest brush of his palm, like a breeze, across her shirt. "Good night, Grandma."

Then he was gone, leaving her sitting in her chair, tears sliding quietly down her face, smiling in spite of her sadness at the lovely sound of his last words.

Chapter 9

The mines in the Eureka Mining District yielded not only gold, but silver, lead, rhodochrosite, molybdenum, turquoise, and aquamarine in varying quantities. A few especially rich lodes, such as the— and—even produced significant quantities of gemstones such as sapphire and topaz, prized for use in both jewelry and industry.

Maggie held the *History of the Mining Regions of Eureka, Colorado, and the Surrounding Territory* by the Reverend A. J. Kirkland to the light, hoping she could see through the heavy black marker that had crossed out the names of the mines that had produced the gemstones, but the letters were thoroughly obliterated.

There were other such redactions throughout the book, either the names of mines or directions to them blotted out. Her father's work? Or some other book vandal?

No. If the book had come into the library in this condition, Cassie Wynock would have had the last borrower hauled to the prison in chains. Which also might explain why her father had refused to return the book. But why bother marking out the names of the mines? Was one of them the French Mistress?

Frustrated, Maggie set the book aside and went back to boxing up the paperback westerns and mysteries she knew she'd never read. Maybe she'd take them to the library and see what else she could learn about local history from Cassie.

Or she could try to find the key to the padlock on the mine entrance and explore the mine herself. But the thought of venturing into that dark cavern alone held no appeal. And she probably wouldn't know a vein of rhodochrosite or molybdenum from lead or fool's gold.

The library it was, then. She hauled the box of books to the car, along with the clothes and other items for Lucille.

The Eureka County Library was a neat white building with black shutters and a black iron railing along the handicap ramp leading to the double front doors. Cassie Wynock looked hopeful when she recognized Maggie. "Did you find my book?" she asked.

"I'm still looking," Maggie lied. She held up the box in her arms. "I'm cleaning out my dad's shelves and I found some books to donate."

Cassie accepted the box and glanced through it, the furrow between her eyes deepening. "We can't put the paperbacks in circulation," she said. "They fall apart after only a few months."

"Oh. Well, is there somewhere else I can donate them?"

Cassie dragged the box back across the counter, as if afraid Maggie might try to take them back. "We can put them in the annual book sale. I'll write you a receipt."

"Oh, I don't need a receipt," Maggie said.

"I have to give you a receipt." She filled out a form and tore it from the pad. "Are you sure you haven't seen my book?" she asked. "It has a brown cover. It doesn't look like much to most people, but it's an important part of the collection." She hesitated, then added, "And it's important to me, personally."

"Oh? Why is that?" She tucked the receipt in her purse, studying the librarian as she did so. Cassie wore a pinched look around her eyes, as if in pain.

"That book was written by my great-uncle," she said. "He was a Presbyterian minister and a noted historian of this area. He spent years compiling the information in that volume, which was hailed by reviewers as far away as Denver as the seminal work of its time." She lifted her chin. "Your father had no right to take that heritage away from me and from the people of this county."

"Why was my father even interested in that book?" Maggie asked. "Was he an amateur historian or something?"

Cassie sniffed. "He *pretended* that was his interest. He came in here, charming as could be, asking intelligent questions, flattering me with his attentions." Two spots of red bloomed on her cheeks. "I was foolish enough to fall for his act. But it was all a ploy to get around the rules. I should have known better. Jacob Murphy was famous for making his own rules."

"What did he do that was so wrong?" Maggie asked. "Besides not returning the book, of course."

"He persuaded me to lend it to him in the first place—against library policy. That volume was part of our permanent reference collection, to be used inside the library only. But I thought I could trust him and let him take it home. And then he refused to give it back." Her voice broke and she turned away.

Maggie felt queasy. She had an ugly picture in her mind of her father—what, *seducing* this woman? In order to rob her of a prized possession? And why? What difference did that book make to him?

"I'll keep looking for the book," she said. "But what if it's damaged? Would you still want it back?"

"It could be recovered. Pages can be repaired. It belongs in our collection. It's part of our history."

Maggie doubted anyone could repair the damage her father's marker had done to the book, but she'd find a way to return it to Cassie, though maybe not until right before Maggie left town. She didn't care to hear what the librarian would have to say when she saw what Murphy had done to her great-uncle's legacy.

"If you find the book, I want it back, whatever the condition," Cassie said. "Is there anything else I can do to help you?"

"Could I use the computers to check my e-mail?" Maggie asked.

"I'll need to see a driver's license, and you'll have to fill out a registration form."

"Of course."

After completing a form that asked for everything short of her blood type, Maggie sat down in front of a computer terminal and logged in to her e-mail. Three hundred messages greeted her, mostly spam or forwarded jokes and chain letters from well-meaning relatives and friends. She scrolled through the list, hitting Delete until she came to a familiar screen name.

FROM: TEXAS DOLL@LONESTARNET.COM

TO: MAGGIEMAE@DIGITEL.NET

SUBJECT: ACROSS THE GREAT DIVIDE

May I remind you, sweetheart, that you moved to Colorado, not the moon. You have got to get better about staying in touch with me or I will be forced to send out a search party to make sure you haven't been eaten by bears. Or are you merely having too much fun discovering your inner mountain woman?

Maggie smiled and typed a reply:

> Sorry I've been out of touch. I've been busy sorting through my dad's things and learning how to manage in a house without central heat, electric lines, or Internet. I'm answering this from the local library. The librarian deigned to let me sign on to their computer despite the fact that my dad stole a valuable library book. Yes, he was a thief, as well as a brawler and general scofflaw. Despite all that, people in town (with the exception of the librarian) seem to mostly like him. I think I would have, too. I want to stay a little longer and find out more about him.

In the back of her mind, she wondered if this was just a way of stalling, of putting off having to get back to her real life in Houston, of starting over without Carter or a job, or any of the things she thought she'd have right now. Focusing on her father was a welcome distraction, even if it wasn't a healthy one. For whatever reason, she felt driven to try to stitch together all the anecdotes and bits of stories to come up with some kind of whole picture of the man who had been a mystery to her her whole life.

She turned her thoughts back to the e-mail.

> Could you do me a favor and send me a few things from my storage unit? My stereo and CDs, the box of books marked Favorites, my laptop, and some of my clothes.
>
> Tell Jimmy I said hello.
>
> Lots of love,
>
> Mags

She hit Send, then skimmed the rest of her e-mail with the detachment of a stranger. She didn't really care anymore about discussions of local sports teams or politics. That was all part of another life that didn't feel like hers anymore.

She left the library and drove to Lacy's. Lucille was stringing chili pepper lights across the front of the store, perched on the top rung of a stepladder and wielding a staple gun to fasten the lights to the porch soffit.

"That doesn't look very safe," Maggie said, hurrying to steady the ladder as it wobbled.

"I'm counting on sheer stubbornness to keep me up here," Lucille said. "I can't afford health insurance, so I flat out refuse to fall."

"Maybe it would be smarter to invest in a taller ladder," Maggie offered.

"You're probably right, but then again, I think it does a body good to live dangerously every once in a while."

Maggie thought of her life in Houston, where she'd spent years playing it safe, never risking so much as an opinion if it might make anyone uncomfortable. Now she took her life in her hands every day simply driving to town, and started every morning with heart-stopping views that reminded her of how little excitement she'd known in her forty years.

"You didn't tell me you were the mayor," she said.

Lucille glanced down. "It's not the easiest thing to work into casual conversation."

"Still, I'm impressed," Maggie said. "Running a town is a big job."

"It can be," Lucille said. "Though Eureka doesn't have the problems larger cities do. Of course, we don't have the budget either. But I won't bore you with all that. What are you up to this morning?"

"I boxed up some of my dad's old clothes," Maggie said as Lucille climbed off the ladder. "I thought maybe you'd know someone who could use them."

"The Presbyterian Church runs a food and clothing bank. They'll make good use of them."

"Where can I find them?"

"There won't be anyone there today. You can leave the boxes with me and I'll see that they get them." She followed Maggie to the Jeep and helped her haul the boxes into the store. "Is there anything else you need up at the cabin?" she asked. "Are you staying warm enough?"

"I'm becoming a pro at starting a fire in the wood stove, and I've figured out the gravity-fed water system," Maggie said.

"That's the spirit," Lucille said. "You'll be a real mountain woman before you know it."

"Oh, I don't know about that." She couldn't see herself living in the cabin full time, though maybe she'd keep it and visit in the summer. It could be her special retreat—someplace Carter had never been. The idea pleased her.

"That was a nice get-together last night for your dad," Lucille said. "He would have gotten a kick out of it, especially when Big Mama stopped by."

"Oh? Did he like bears?"

"He liked all kinds of animals," Lucille said. "He had a cat for a while. He just called her Mama Cat. But I think some wild animal got her and after that he said the wilderness was no place for a pet."

"Instead, he made a pet out of a bighorn sheep."

"So you've met Winston." Lucille chuckled. "One of Murph's wilder eccentricities."

"Last night it sounded as if people really liked my dad," Maggie said. "But did they think of him as, well, *odd?*" Was that what her mother had meant when she said Jacob hadn't been well after the war?

"Not odd, exactly," Lucille said. "He was one to stick up for the underdog. You know how he came to build Danielle and Janelle's chicken coop, don't you?"

Maggie shook her head.

"There were people in town who didn't approve of the girls' 'lifestyle.' Most of the time it was low-level harassment—graffiti spray-painted on the back wall of the café; one time someone egged Janelle's car. But then someone set fire to their chicken coop. They lost most of their chickens and half a tool shed, too. Murph showed up two days later with a load of cinder blocks and tin. He built a fire-proof chicken coop and a new shed, and let it be known around town that if he ever found out who was giving the girls grief, that person would come to wish he'd never been born."

"And the trouble stopped?"

"Pretty much. Once Murph stepped up, others began to speak out in defense of the girls, too."

"People were that afraid of my father?"

"Mostly they respected him. He was a man who kept his word, whether he was promising to help you roof your barn or defending his friends."

Then why hadn't he kept his word to his wife and daughter, and honored his wedding vows and stayed to look after Maggie?

As far as Cassie was concerned, the sooner Maggie Stevens went back to wherever she was from, the better. She had as much business staying up there in Jake's cabin as a ptarmigan deciding to winter at the beach. If only she'd showed up in winter. Then the first blizzard to dump a couple of feet of snow up there would no doubt send her packing. Instead, she'd arrived on the cusp of summer, the prettiest time of year in the mountains.

Cassie could only hope the altitude would get to her. Or she'd miss her home in Houston and decide to head back. Then Cassie knew exactly what she'd do; what she should have done long before now. She'd drive up there and search the cabin. Jake had that book and Cassie would find it.

These thoughts filled her mind as she prepared to chair the

meeting of the Eureka County Historical Society the Friday evening after Maggie's visit to the library. She distributed copies of the night's agenda and the minutes from the last meeting around the long table in the conference room at the back of the library. Today's main topic was a proposal to revamp Hard Rock Days to more appropriately reflect the heritage of the county. Cassie had drafted the motion herself and was quite proud of the work.

Bob was the first to arrive. No surprise there. "No refreshments yet?" he asked, frowning at the side table, which was empty of everything but the water pitcher.

"Tamarin is in charge of refreshments this month and she hasn't arrived yet," Cassie said.

Bob pushed his lips out as if he'd just eaten something sour. "I hope she doesn't bring any more of that low-fat crap like last time," he said. "We ought to invite Danielle and Janelle to join. Then we'd have really good refreshments."

"I can't think those girls would be interested in the history of the county," Cassie said, disguising her horror at the idea. At least Bob, as disgusting as he was, had lived in the area fifty years. He knew more about mining in the area than almost anyone and was practically a historical artifact himself.

Tamarin Sherman and Shelly Frazier arrived together, with a pan of brownies Bob pronounced acceptable. The newspaper editor, Rick Otis, came with his camera slung around his neck, notebook in hand. As if anything ever happened at these meetings worth photographing.

Last to arrive was Lucille, that awkward grandson of hers shuffling after. "Lucas is very interested in history," she said, more by way of explanation than apology. "And his mother is working tonight."

"She got a job already?" Shelly smiled, showing a network of shiny braces. Honestly, Cassie thought. Why did a forty-something woman bother with braces? "Where is she working?"

"She's waiting tables at the Dirty Sally." Lucille wore a

pinched look, as if it hurt to say the words. And no wonder. Every low-life in town hung out at that bar. Jacob Murphy had been a regular.

Lucas helped himself to a brownie and slid into a chair next to his grandmother. The child was the oddest looking boy Cassie had ever seen. He caught her staring and glared at her. She quickly looked away. He had atrocious manners, too.

"I think everyone's here, so let's get started," she said. She pounded the little gavel on the table and checked her watch. "We'll note that the meeting officially began at 7:04 p.m."

Shelly scribbled away on her steno pad, and Rick snapped a picture that Cassie was sure showed her with her mouth wide open. Damn freedom of the press. Couldn't a person conduct business without having someone take her picture? She smoothed the front of her dress and continued, taking them quickly through approval of the minutes from the last meeting and discussion of the old business of a report from the State Historical Commission on new procedures for applying for historical designation for buildings.

"Rick, I want this information in the next issue of the paper," Cassie said. "Eureka has several buildings that would qualify for historical designation, if the owners would just put in the application. The Historical Society would be happy to help them through the process."

"Some people don't want that plaque on their homes," Rick said. "They don't want to have to answer to the government every time they want to paint the porch or change out a light fixture."

Cassie's own home had a prominent plaque by the front door, one that was a source of great pride to her. "Those regulations are in place to prevent people from changing the historic nature of the structure," she said. "People shouldn't think of them as intrusions, but rather as safeguards to the value of their home."

"I always said you'd make a good politician," Rick said,

grinning. At her look of fury, he chuckled. “Don’t get your panties in a wad. I’ll put the article in the paper and tell readers to contact you if they want to know more.”

“Fine.” She studied the agenda, regaining her composure. If it were anyone but Rick, she’d complain to his supervisor. But Rick had no supervisor. He owned the paper, edited it, and since Angela Zerbock had married and moved to Gunnison, he was the only reporter, except for the high-school boy who covered school sports. And people liked Rick. They didn’t feel that way about Cassie, she knew.

But as her grandmother had been fond of saying, life was not a popularity contest. People who were willing to be unpopular were the ones who got things done in this world. “Let’s move on to new business,” she said. “The proposal for a new addition to Hard Rock Days.”

“I still say we ought to have a beauty contest,” Bob said. “A Miss Hard Rock Days. A bunch of pretty young things strutting around in bikinis would bring in the crowds, I tell you.”

“That’s sexist and ageist,” Tamarin said.

“We could make the prize a scholarship,” Bob said. “That would make it all right.”

“No beauty pageants,” Cassie said. “My proposal is that we devote part of the day to honoring the pioneers who settled this area. We could produce an original play that tells the story of Eureka County. It’s the kind of thing people would return to see each year.”

“You don’t think it’s a little late in the year to be making changes to the festival?” Rick asked. “You’ve only got two months.”

“This won’t take any time at all to pull together,” Cassie said.

“A play might be fun,” Shelly said.

“Period costumes would be easy enough to find,” Tamarin said.

"Have you talked to the drama society about this?" Lucille asked. "They would want to be involved."

"I haven't talked to anyone yet," Cassie said. "But, yes, I would think the drama society would be involved."

"Have you written the play yet?" Rick asked, pen poised over his notebook. "And who do you want to play Festus Wynock?"

Cassie flushed. "Of course my great-grandfather would figure in the play, as would all the founders of the area. I've made some notes, but I'm certainly open to suggestions."

"When would we run the play?" Shelly asked. "We've already got the dance Friday night and the Hard Rock Games all day Saturday, and the awards banquet Saturday night, and the 1890s baseball game Sunday afternoon."

"There's no need to have the games go on all day Saturday," she said. "I thought we could eliminate the water fight."

Loud cries of protest rose up around the table. "Not the water fight!" "That's the most exciting part of the day!"

"What's the water fight?" Lucas asked.

"Teams of men or women go after each other with fire hoses," Rick explained to the boy. "The last team standing wins. It takes place right on Main Street. It's a blast—literally."

"What does that have to do with mining?" the boy asked.

"Exactly." Cassie seized on this objection. "It's an excuse for spraying a bunch of water around. It's a waste of resources and it's dangerous."

"You know as well as I do that one method of mining was to use high-pressure water to blast the ore out of the side of river banks," Bob said. "That's what the water fight recalls."

"Except that method wasn't used much around here," Cassie said. "So it has no place in a celebration of our mining heritage."

"You can't get rid of the water fight," Rick said. "It's the most popular event at the games. And the biggest fund-raiser, since some of the teams are pretty large and each individual has to pay to participate."

"You could present the play Sunday after the ball game," Lucille said. "It would be a nice way to end the festival. "

"It really should run all three nights," Cassie said. "To make it a centerpiece of the event."

"Try it on Sunday the first year and see how it goes," Lucille said.

"We don't even know if it will be any good," Tamarin said. At Cassie's scowl, she stammered, "I mean, I'm sure it will be good, but people want to be entertained, so you need to be sure and put humor and stuff in it, and . . . and stuff like that."

"I still say young women in bikinis beat out old codgers pontificating about the past," Bob said. "And I say that as a codger who can pontificate with the best of them."

"Rick, don't write that about Cassie suggesting doing away with the water fight," Lucille said. "It'll just get everyone up in arms for nothing."

"I'll admit I'm tempted," Rick said. "Except I don't have anyone to help me deal with the avalanche of angry letters to the editor I'd be sure to get. But I will mention the play. It'll be a good way to gauge what kind of interest you'll draw."

"Fine." Cassie slammed down her gavel, more out of frustration than out of any parliamentary need. "We'll table the idea of the play until next time, and I'll talk to the drama society and see if they want to take this on. Do we have any other new business?"

They all looked at each other, then at Cassie. "I move the meeting be adjourned," Lucille said.

"I second!" Shelly and Tamarin spoke together.

"Well, that was painless enough." Rick rose from his chair.

Cassie wanted to point out she hadn't officially adjourned the meeting yet, but everyone was already standing and milling about. She tapped the gavel on the table. "Meeting adjourned," she said, though by this time no one was listening.

Chapter 10

By the start of her third week in Eureka, Maggie felt less intimidated by the isolation of the mountaintop cabin. Every morning she built a fire in the woodstove to chase away the dawn chill that lingered even in June at this altitude.

She cooked breakfast, feeling very much like a pioneer woman as she made a cheese omelet from eggs Janelle had sold her—eleven perfect brown ones and one blue one from the estimable Arabella. She smiled as she cracked the shell on the side of the counter and watched the rich yellow yolk spill into the bowl, thinking of the hens snug in the fireproof chicken house her father had built in defiance of bigots. That was one good thing he'd done, though the threats that had accompanied the construction still made her uneasy.

She tidied the cabin, read, or explored the property. Sometimes she simply sat and contemplated the view out the cabin windows. She felt much like an invalid recovering from a long illness—a little fragile, craving stillness; weak, but feeling herself growing stronger every day.

Often various errands—and a craving for human contact—took her to Eureka. So it was that one Wednesday morning she headed down the mountain but had barely traveled two miles when she met a truck headed uphill. Before she could pass it, it swerved toward the middle of the road, forcing her to stop. She shoved open her door and climbed out, intending to give the driver a piece of her mind, but before she could approach, the driver's side window rolled down and Jameso stuck his head out. "I'm glad we caught you before you left," he said.

"Who's we?" she asked.

But just then the passenger door of his truck opened and Barb stepped out. "Darlin', when you said you were living on a mountain, you weren't kidding," she drawled. "This view is spectacular." She fanned her face. "But I have to say, the lack of oxygen makes me dizzy."

"It's just those high-heeled boots you're wearing," Maggie said, and rushed to embrace her friend.

Barb's arms wrapped tight around her, and to Maggie's surprise, her friend's voice was thick with tears when she spoke. "I've been so worried about you, woman," Barb whispered.

"Well, you wasted all the worrying for nothing," Maggie said. "I'm fine."

"You're more than fine." Barb stepped back to appraise her. "You look fantastic. This new style suits you."

"New style?" Maggie looked down at the worn denim jacket, faded jeans, and boots.

"Very Ralph Lauren," Barb said. "And the longer hair looks good on you, too."

Maggie put a hand to her hair, which she hadn't cut because she hadn't taken the time to find a hairdresser in Eureka.

"Now that we've all admired Maggie and praised her fashion sense, do you think we could drive on up to the cabin?" Jameso said. "We are blocking the road."

"You're the one parked in the middle," Maggie said, but returned to the Jeep.

Barb climbed into the passenger seat beside her. "Where

are you going to turn around?" Barb asked, eyeing the steep drop on one side of the gravel track and the cliff on the other.

"I'll have to back a ways," Maggie said, and proceeded to do so. Two weeks ago, such a feat would have terrified her, but now it seemed no big deal.

She backed about a quarter mile before she found a place to turn around, then led the way up the mountain to the cabin. When they arrived, Winston was on the front porch, his head stuck in the open window.

"What is that?" Barb shrieked.

"Winston, you get out of there this instant!" Maggie called.

The ram had to tilt his head almost sideways to withdraw it from the window. He did so with surprising delicacy and looked over his shoulder at her, his expression accusing. "What is that animal?" Barb asked again.

"It's a bighorn sheep." Maggie strode toward the front porch, waving her arms. "Get out of here, Winston," she called.

"I don't think he's going to leave until you give him his cookies," Jameso said. He stood by his truck, smirking.

"Fine." Maggie went inside and fetched the Lorna Doones. Winston took the cookies she offered and trotted away.

"You're giving cookies to a sheep?" Barb asked. Her expression said she feared for her friend's sanity.

"Not my doing," Maggie said. "My father trained the darn thing, and I don't have the energy to untrain it."

She didn't miss the look Barb exchanged with Jameso, but marched past them into the house. Barb followed, though Jameso remained outside. "This is amazing," Barb said, turning all the way around to take in the cabin. "It's like . . . like the world's best tree house."

"That's exactly what it's like." Maggie hugged Barb again. "I'm so glad to see you. I can't believe you're here. How did you get here? How did you find me? How did you meet Jameso?"

"One question at a time." Barb laughed. "I got your e-mail about mailing you your stuff, but I thought it would be so much better to surprise you and deliver it in person. So I rented a U-Haul truck and drove here."

"You *drove*? In a moving truck?"

"A small one. And I stopped on the way and spent the night in Wichita Falls."

"But how did you find me?"

"I figured in a town this small someone would know where to find a woman from Texas who was living in a cabin on the side of a mountain, so I stopped in the first café I saw and asked."

"That would be the Last Dollar."

"Yes, and the woman there told me where you lived but said I didn't want to drive up here in a moving truck, and then she sent the other young woman to fetch Jameso and he loaded everything into his truck and drove me up here." Barb leaned closer and lowered her voice. "Now, *he* is exactly what I imagine when I think of a sexy mountain man. And he seemed more than happy to drive up here and see you."

Maggie fought down a blush. "That's because he's nosy and wants to see what I'm up to."

"Where do you want this?" The man himself spoke from the doorway, from behind a stack of cardboard boxes.

The women rushed to relieve him of his burden. Maggie set the first box on the table and ripped off the tape, then pulled out a waffle iron? Maggie stared at her friend.

"I wouldn't want to live without mine," Barb said earnestly.

Maggie set the waffle iron aside and dug deeper into the box. Jeans, her favorite University of Houston sweatshirt, and a long, fluffy robe more than made up for the waffle maker. Other boxes contained her stereo, CDs, books, and her laptop computer. "Though I don't know what good that computer's going to do you if you don't have DSL or even a phone line up here," Barb said.

"Don't bother helping to unload the truck or anything, ladies," Jameso said as he delivered another stack of boxes.

"You don't look like you need our help," Barb said. "This way we get to stand back and admire your muscles."

"That's not all I saw you admiring," he said with a provocative twitch of his ass.

Barb and Maggie dissolved into laughter. "Where is the moving truck now?" Maggie asked when she'd caught her breath.

"Jameso's going to turn it into the dealer in Montrose for me," she said.

"He's going to turn—woman, what did you do to him?"

"I can be charming when I want." She fluttered her eyelashes. "Plus, I offered to pay him twenty bucks."

"With Jameso, I have a feeling the money was a better persuader than your charms."

"You're either underestimating me or Jameso," Barb said.

"Never mind that," Maggie said. "How long can you stay?"

"I figure I'll hang out with you as long as you'll have me; then I'll fly home."

"Or as long as you can stand to stay in a place without central heat and cable TV."

Barb's smile dimmed a few watts. "You *do* have indoor plumbing, don't you?"

"The finest composting toilet money can buy."

"A composting—" Barb waved away the words. "I don't think I even want to know. "

"It looks just like a regular toilet, but you don't flush," Maggie said.

"Oh God, this is sounding worse all the time."

"You just drove over a thousand miles in a moving van to see me," Maggie said. "You're tough enough to deal with a composting toilet. At least you don't have to hike to the outhouse out back."

"You have one of those, too?"

"I do. Apparently my dad kept it because it was convenient."

"Your dad sounds like quite the character. I can't wait to hear more about him."

"I've got plenty of stories to tell, though I'm not sure I believe half of them."

"This is the last of the load," Jameso said. He deposited two suitcases by the door. "If you're all set, I'll be going now."

"You don't have to run off," Barb said. "Stay and have a drink."

"I don't have anything here *to* drink," Maggie said. Except for the rest of the whiskey she and Jameso had shared her first night here.

"There are several bottles of wine in one of these boxes." Barb gestured to the packing cartons scattered around the room.

"That's okay, ladies, I'll leave you to it," he said.

"Be that way, then," Barb said. "Thanks for all your help."

"Yeah, thanks," Maggie said.

"Any time." His eyes met hers and she felt again the flash of heat.

"He's definitely hot," Barb said when he was gone.

"He's full of himself," Maggie said.

"There's a lot to be said for a man with self-confidence," Barb said. "There's a lot to be said for a *man*."

"I've spent half my life tied to a man," Maggie said. "Let me enjoy being single for a while."

"I never said you had to marry the guy," Barb said. "I'm talking about enjoying being single."

"I'm not interested in Jameso."

"You two are a real trip," Barb said. "I can't decide if you're dying to jump each other's bones or you can't stand each other."

"That's ridiculous!" Maggie felt her cheeks heat. "Why would you say something like that?"

"Don't tell me you haven't noticed the way he looks at you," Barb said.

"He doesn't look at me any particular way." Did he?

"I'll bet you look at him, too," Barb said.

Yes, Maggie had looked. But she wasn't about to admit this to Barb. Some things had to be kept secret even from best friends.

Barb insisted on opening the bottle of wine right away and helping Maggie unpack the various moving boxes. "You must have brought half my storage unit with you," Maggie said as she hung clothes in the closet. She had no idea when she'd ever have use for the dresses Barb had packed, but she wouldn't hurt her friend by saying so.

"You haven't even seen the best part yet." Barb gestured to the four largest cartons. "I brought the Steuben."

Maggie stared at the cartons, which she could now see were clearly marked: *Glass. Fragile.* "Why did you bring those?"

"Because I know how much you love them," Barb said. "I thought maybe you could put them around the cabin. To, you know, dress things up. Remind you of happier times."

The Steuben glassware would remind her, all right. Of all the times when she'd thought her life had been perfect, when she thought it would go on being that way. "Thanks." She gave Barb a faint smile. "We'll leave them packed for now, until I decide the proper way to display everything."

"I wanted you to have everything you needed," Barb said.

"I do have everything I need now that you're here," Maggie said, happy to change the subject. "Tell me how everything is going back home."

"Jimmy is busy as ever. We're thinking of taking a cruise after the first of the year. Michael is dating a nice young woman; I think it might be serious this time. My hairdresser is pregnant and wants to stay home with the baby, so I'll have to find someone new. And I have some other news you're probably not going to like."

Maggie froze in the act of unwrapping a ceramic teapot. "What kind of news?"

"I saw an announcement in the paper a few days ago. Carter and the Rich Bitch are getting married."

"Oh." Maggie couldn't say the news was unexpected, but before it had merely existed in the realm of possibility, not as fact. Knowing that Carter would have another wife hurt more than she'd expected. It wasn't that she wanted him back, not after all he'd done. But hearing this news made her feel the pain of his rejection all over again. She'd spent twenty years identifying herself as Mrs. Carter Stevens, and now she wasn't good enough for that anymore.

"At least now you don't have to worry about him asking you to take him back," Barb said. "You're well rid of him."

"Barb! I thought you liked Carter."

"I love you and you loved him, so I learned to put up with him, but I always thought he was much too concerned with his image and his own comforts. You know good and well the only reason he's with Francine is because she has all that money."

"We don't know that," Maggie said. "Maybe he really loves her." She coughed, trying to clear the knot in her throat.

"Carter only loves himself. Getting rid of him is the best thing that ever happened to you, you'll see." She patted Maggie's arm. "Let's have some more wine."

"The bottle is almost empty."

"Then we'll open another."

Lucille was minding the counter at Lacy's, but she had on her mayoral hat. She'd spent the morning trying to reach someone from the state to get an explanation for a letter she'd received that, as far as she could tell, reduced funding for highway maintenance in the area—again.

"That's Eureka," she said to the third person to whom her call had been transferred. "In Eureka County. This is not merely a local issue—we have thousands of tourists driving these roads every year, and the state's happy to take their cut of the sales tax money from them. I don't think it's asking too much to get part of that money back to maintain the roads."

To which the bureaucrat informed her the person to whom she needed to speak was out of the office for the week.

Lucille slammed down the phone and was massaging the bridge of her nose when the string of cowbells on the back of the shop door jangled and Olivia walked in. Lucille had scarcely seen her daughter since she'd arrived in town. She worked most nights at the Dirty Sally. When she wasn't working, she was there as a customer, or off somewhere else with the new friends she'd made. She was asleep when Lucille and Lucas left in the morning. Though she'd managed to get the boy enrolled in school, Lucille was the one who drove him there on her way to work. She'd told herself this was an opportunity for her to get to know her grandson better, but Lucas answered her questions with grunts and single syllables. He wasn't sullen or irritable, merely uncommunicative.

"I just got a call from the school," Olivia said by way of greeting. "Lucas is in trouble."

Lucas? In trouble? The boy was so quiet. Not the type to fight . . . but he did have a smart mouth on him. "I'm sorry to hear that," Lucille said. "Are you on your way to the school now?"

"Yes, and I want you to go with me."

Lucille wondered how much those words had cost Olivia. She had never been one to ask for help, especially not from her mother. "Of course I'll go. Though I'm not sure what I'll be able to do."

"You live here. You're the mayor, for God's sake. You ought to have some influence."

Lucille laughed. "You wouldn't think that if you could have heard me on the phone with the state just now. In Denver, they don't even know where Eureka is."

"The people at the school will know you. Maybe they'll listen to you."

Olivia drove, Lucille in the passenger seat of the big black SUV. The seats were leather and the vehicle still smelled new. "Have you heard from D. J. lately?" Lucille asked.

Olivia's hands tightened on the steering wheel. "No."

"So he has no idea you have his car."

"Let it go, Mother. I don't want to talk about it."

Lucille pinched out a brief flame of anger. No sense starting an argument she couldn't win. At school they found Lucas sitting in the front office, reading a book. He looked fine. No black eyes or signs of tears.

"What happened?" Olivia asked.

Before he could answer, the door behind him opened and the principal emerged. Dennis Kinkaid was a slim, balding man with a salt-and-pepper goatee and the perpetually exasperated look of a man who dealt with teenagers for a living. His gaze flickered over Olivia, then shifted to Lucille, eyes widening in surprise. "You know this boy?" he asked.

"Lucas is my grandson."

Kinkaid held the door wide. "Come into my office."

The three of them filed inside. "I want you to tell me what happened," Olivia said.

Kinkaid sat behind his desk, his expression grim. "I don't know about the situation where you lived before," he said. "But we don't tolerate troublemakers at our schools in Eureka."

"Lucas is not a troublemaker." Olivia's spiky hair practically vibrated with indignation.

"He disrupted his classroom this afternoon. We won't stand for that."

Olivia turned to her son. "What happened?" she asked.

"The teacher was wrong." He looked stubborn.

"Wrong about what?" Lucille could keep quiet no longer. She looked at Kinkaid. "What exactly happened?"

"Lucas's teacher, Mr. Brewster, was teaching a history lesson. Lucas apparently didn't agree with his explanation."

"He was wrong," Lucas said. "He said the Spanish were the first to mine gold in the area, but that's not right. The Ute Indians knew about the gold before the Spanish ever got here. I told him so."

Lucille could imagine how Lucas had told him. The boy was nothing if not blunt.

"You can say what you want about your school, Mr. Kinkaid," Olivia said. "But I'm not impressed when my son is smarter than his teacher."

"The smartest thing about your son is his mouth," Kinkaid said, his face reddening. "He was rude to Mr. Brewster in a classroom full of students and he owes him an apology."

"Why should I apologize when I'm right and he's wrong?" Lucas protested.

Olivia put her arm around Lucas's shoulder and Lucille knew she was gearing up for another defense of her son. Lucille put one hand on each of them. "Lucas, you owe Mr. Brewster an apology because he is your teacher. He may have been mistaken about this one matter, but he deserves your respect. If you believed something wasn't right, you should have addressed him in a respectful manner."

"I don't think—" Olivia began.

"We can discuss what you think later," Lucille said. She focused on Lucas. "Part of getting along in this world is recognizing when something is worth a fight and when it isn't."

"A teacher is supposed to know better."

She gave him a skeptical look. "Don't tell me you've never made a mistake."

"I think Lucas and I should talk to Mr. Brewster." Olivia glared at her mother. "Alone."

Between Olivia's short fuse and Lucas's reluctance to sensor his own emotions, their "talk" with the teacher was likely to be a disaster. "I don't think that would be a good idea," Lucille said.

"I didn't ask your opinion."

But she'd asked Lucille to come with her this morning. Why? Because she'd thought Lucille would back her up in her determination to thwart authority?

Mr. Kinkaid ushered Olivia and Lucas out of the office, presumably to meet with Mr. Brewster. When he returned, Lucille was pacing the small room—four steps across, four strides back, her head pounding.

"Your daughter has some very definite opinions about how things ought to be done," he said.

"Olivia has always been headstrong. Not that that's always a bad thing." Having done her own time as a single mother, Lucille knew the kind of strength and courage that took.

"No, I'd say she comes by her stubbornness honestly." He seemed to be trying not to smile.

Lucille stopped in front of him. "Lucas was wrong to call out that teacher," she said. "But what are you doing hiring teachers who don't know their subject matter better than a seventh grader?"

"I think it's safe to say Lucas is not your average seventh grader. Mr. Brewster is a good teacher. But even good teachers can't be experts in every area."

"I know Lucas needs help with his social skills," Lucille said. "He's had a . . . a difficult childhood." She had very little idea what kind of childhood he'd had, but it certainly couldn't have been easy. Olivia had moved a lot, and been involved with several different men. "He hasn't had a lot of stability."

"Maybe now that he's here with you he will have that stability."

"I hope so. I don't know how long Olivia plans to stay."

"It can be tough on everyone when grown children come home again," Kinkaid said. "I hear it's happening more and more in this economy."

"I'm glad to have her here, but I don't know how happy she is."

"Maybe the town will grow on her, if she can figure out how she fits in. The boy is smart; he just needs to learn how to get along with people. You can help him with that, I'm sure."

Lucille wasn't sure about that at all. She had done a poor enough job with Olivia; whatever the girl had made of herself had been as much in spite of Lucille as because of her. "I'll do what I can to help Lucas," she said.

Kinkaid was called to the phone, leaving Lucille the option of either resuming her pacing or sitting. She sat and looked out the window at a grove of aspen trees, like dancers in lacy green skirts. Summer came to the mountains in a rush of breathtaking brilliance, the hills awash in twenty shades of green, wildflowers like jewels scattered everywhere. It was Lucille's favorite time of year, all the more precious because its tenure was so short, the warm days giving way to cold once more after only two and a half months.

The door opened behind her and she turned to see Olivia and Lucas, followed by a tall young man with glasses and a goatee so black he looked like a boy playing dress up with shoe polish on his face. "Dan, this is my mother, Lucille Theriot." Olivia's cheeks bloomed with bright spots of pink and her eyes sparkled with an excitement that seemed out of place in this drab office.

"Hello, Mrs. Theriot. It's a pleasure to meet you," he said, offering his hand. "I'm Dan Brewster."

"Nice to meet you, Mr. Brewster." Lucille shook his hand, but watched her daughter. Olivia tucked a lock of hair behind one ear and straightened the collar of her shirt, glancing every few seconds at the man at her side. The teacher, likewise, could scarcely keep his eyes off her. Lucille had to fight to keep from laughing out loud. Olivia and Dan Brewster might have been two teenagers, for all the hormones on overdrive in the room. She turned her attention to Lucas, who was retrieving his backpack from the corner. The dark cloud had lifted from over him and he looked less sulky.

"Did you get everything worked out?" Lucille asked.

"I'm going to do a special project," he said. "On mining in the Eureka district. I'll present it to the class when school starts next fall."

At his age, Lucille would have seen classwork over the summer as punishment, but Lucas seemed pleased with the idea. "Whose idea was this?" she asked.

"Mr. Brewster suggested it. He thought since I was so interested in the subject, I should share my knowledge with the class."

"Did you apologize to him?" Lucille asked.

"I said I was sorry I called him out in front of the class. We agreed next time I thought he was wrong about something, I'd talk to him after class. Man-to-man."

She glanced at the teacher again, who was engrossed in conversation with Olivia, both of them smiling, eyes locked together. He might look like a boy to her, but he'd figured out a way to reason with her obstinate grandson.

Lucas shouldered the backpack. "I have to get to English," he said.

"I'll see you tonight, then." Lucille patted his shoulder awkwardly, then watched him shuffle out the door. He was still thin and long-limbed, but not really as odd looking as she'd thought when they'd first met.

"Are you ready to go?"

Lucille turned and found Olivia next to her, jiggling her keys. "Where's Mr. Brewster?" Lucille asked.

"He had to get back to class." Her lips curved in a sly smile, showing no teeth. "He's coming to take me to dinner later."

"To talk about Lucas?"

Olivia's smile broadened. "I'm hoping he'd rather talk about me."

Chapter 11

Maggie struggled into consciousness, wondering if she was back in college, awakening after a night of partying at the sorority house. Her head throbbed like a sore thumb, and her mouth tasted like a wet doormat. She rolled over and looked at Barb, who laid like a corpse on the other side of the king-size bed, on her back with her arms folded across her stomach, a pink satin sleep mask over her eyes. She looked entirely too serene for a woman who had drunk more than her share of two bottles of wine the night before.

Maggie crawled over and poked Barb in the ribs. "Wake up, sleepyhead," she said.

Barb groaned. "Go away," she mumbled.

Maggie prodded harder. "Wake up," she said louder.

"Not now, Jimmy. You know I'm not in the mood before I've had my coffee."

"I love you, Barb, but not in that way." Maggie shoved her again. "Wake up."

Barb lifted one corner of the sleep mask and glowered at Maggie with one bloodshot eye. "You look like hell," she said.

"You look like you're laid out for the undertaker."

"God, how much did we drink last night?" Barb draped one arm over her eyes.

"Too much." Maggie lay back on the pillow, but the room spun dangerously, so she opened her eyes and forced herself up onto her elbows, jaw clenched, fighting nausea.

"It must the altitude," Barb moaned. "I never get sick when I drink."

"So it had nothing to do with the *two* bottles of wine."

"We should call that handsome Jameso and ask him to bring us coffee."

"We don't have a phone, and the last thing I want is for Jameso to see me looking like this."

"See, you really do care about him."

"It's a small town, Barb. If Jameso came up here and found us in bed together looking like something the dog threw up, he could start all kinds of awful rumors."

"Which do you think would be worse: the rumor about us being lesbian lovers or about looking like something the dog threw up?"

"I'm getting up now. If you don't come down soon, I won't save you any coffee."

Holding on to the stair railing for support, Maggie dragged herself down the stairs to the restroom just in time to lose last night's dinner in the toilet. Stripping off the old T-shirt and jeans in which she'd slept, she turned on the shower full force and stepped under the scalding flow. Maybe Barb was right and the altitude did make a hangover worse. She hadn't felt this bad in at least two decades. Even her divorce hadn't seemed worth working herself into such misery.

Fifteen minutes later, she emerged from the shower feeling slightly more human. She dressed in jeans and a sweatshirt that had belonged to her father and thick cotton socks. By the time she had the coffee brewed, Barb had crept down the stairs.

"I can't believe this is how you repay me for going to all the trouble to come visit," Barb moaned. Holding her head with both hands as if she feared at any moment it might fall off, she carefully lowered herself into a chair at the table.

"What are you talking about?" Maggie asked. "Repay you how?"

"I drive all the way up here and you get me drunk." Barb's voice was wet, as if with tears.

"It was your wine." Maggie set a cup of coffee and two aspirin in front of her. "Drink that. You'll feel better."

Two cups of coffee later, Barb did seem to feel better. She stared out the window across the living room. "This must be what it's like to go hang gliding," she said. "Without all the wind and cold and the danger part of it."

"Other than that, it must be just like it," Maggie said.

"Oh, sure, be all blasé about it," Barb said. "For a flatlander like me, it's really something."

"It's really something for a flatlander like me, too," Maggie said.

Barb turned back to her. "I meant what I said yesterday. You look great. You look . . . happier."

"I'm not unhappy. I guess you were right. It was good to get away from Houston and Carter and all the memories. This has been a good distraction."

"Have your learned a lot of good stuff about your dad? Do you know what he was up to for the last forty years?"

"He came to Eureka seven years ago," Maggie said. "I've learned some things about his life since then, but nothing about the time before that. He apparently never talked about it, and there aren't many clues."

"What are the clues?" Barb asked. "I love a good mystery."

"I have a letter from my mom in which she hints that he came to the mountains because Houston reminded him too much of the jungle. The jungles of Vietnam, I guess."

"What else?"

"That's really about it. Something happened in the war to upset him or change him so that he felt he couldn't be a husband and a father anymore."

"And you have no idea what that was."

"No idea."

"What about his life in Eureka? What do you know about that?"

"He made a lot of friends and a few enemies. He could be a great guy and a real son of a bitch. He made his own rules and broke some others. He had money in the bank that no one knows the source of."

"Oh my gosh. This is so exciting."

"No, it's confusing. I don't know what to think about him."

"Do you have to think anything? Can't he just be an interesting character you know a lot of stories about?"

"It would be easier if he could, but he can't."

"Because he's your dad."

Maggie sighed. "Yeah, because he's my dad." She traced one finger around the rim of her coffee cup, around and around, wondering if her dad had drunk from this same cup. In the picture Danielle had had at the memorial, he had a moustache. Carter never had much of a beard and remained clean shaven throughout their marriage. She had no idea what it would feel like to have a man with a moustache kiss her cheek, as a father might have done to say hello or goodbye.

"When I was a little girl, I spent hours and hours imagining what my dad was like," she said. "What he looked like, what he sounded like, what he'd say to me if he were there. I'd have imaginary conversations with him and tell him about my day, and he'd push me on the swing or take me riding in his Cadillac and buy me hot fudge sundaes from Dairy Queen."

"A Cadillac?"

She nodded. "A Cadillac. My friend Celia's grandfather had one and I thought it was the most wonderful car I'd ever seen. So, of course, my father drove one. "

"And bought you hot fudge sundaes."

"Of course. And gave me silver dollars for my allowance and rode with me on the roller coaster at the fair and walked me down the aisle at my wedding."

"He did all the things a father is supposed to do for his daughter," Barb said.

"Yes, and he was perfect." She glanced at her friend. "I knew reality wouldn't be perfect, but I didn't realize the truth could be so unsettling. The more I know about my father, the more I see his flaws. And that makes me wonder which of those flaws he passed down to me."

"Sweetheart, I understand the arguments for nature versus nurture, but you can't honestly believe your father passed on a tendency to break rules or get into fights or any of the other unsavory things you've learned about him."

"No, but maybe I *do* have some of those traits, only they manifest in other ways. He ran away from a marriage and I ran away from my divorce."

"You didn't run away from a divorce. You made a fresh start."

"I spent my whole marriage letting Carter make all the decisions. I almost never spoke up."

"Which sounds like the opposite of your father, who apparently wasn't ever afraid to express an opinion."

"They're both ways of avoiding responsibility," Maggie said. "If Carter made all the decisions, it was never my fault when things went wrong. If my dad talked loud enough about how he didn't like the way things were being done, he divorced himself from the responsibility for the outcome, too. He could stand back later and say, 'I told you so.' "

Barb put a hand on Maggie's arm. "I think all that wine

you drank last night hasn't worn off yet. You are way overthinking this. So let's start over. What are we going to do this morning?"

Maggie took a deep breath. Barb was right. She was getting worked up over nothing. Her friend was here. It was a beautiful day. She should stop worrying about her father and focus on Barb. "What would you like to do?" she asked.

"I want to see the town," Barb said. "But first I want to see the French Mistress Mine."

Maggie blinked at Barb's pronouncement. "You do know mines are cold, dirty, and underground," she said. She studied the Michael Kors ensemble her friend had chosen for this morning, complete with matching kitten heels. She tried to picture Barb crawling through some filthy mine tunnel, but it was impossible.

"I'll change into old clothes," Barb said. "You must have something I can borrow."

"There's a locked gate over the mine entrance. I'm not even sure we can get in."

"Don't you have the key?"

"I have a whole bunch of keys. I just don't know which one opens the lock on the gate."

"We'll try them all. And if that doesn't work, bring a hacksaw."

Maggie couldn't hold back a laugh. "I never saw you so anxious to get dirty."

"I've never had a chance to see gold up close and in its natural state." Barb fingered the gold hoops in her ears. "Maybe you'll let me chip out a few nuggets, as a souvenir."

"We don't even know if there's gold left in the mine. There probably isn't."

"Don't you want to find out? I'd think you'd be dying to know. Instead, you're doing your best to talk me—and yourself—out of looking."

Maggie pressed her lips together. "I just get, I don't know, nervous whenever I think about it."

Barb put a comforting hand on her arm. "What are you afraid of? We're just going to take a look. We won't do anything dangerous."

That fear thing again. Maggie took a deep breath. "I guess I'm afraid of being disappointed." God knows she'd had enough of that emotion to last the rest of her life. "That there won't be anything of value in the mine and I'll be the proud owner of a big empty hole in the side of a mountain."

"Then maybe you can use it to grow mushrooms or raise bats or something."

"Raise bats?"

Barb shrugged. "I read an article about some guy in Texas who made a fortune selling bat guano out of caves for fertilizer."

"Bat guano?"

Barb grinned. "Just think. You could be the bat-shit queen."

Laughter bubbled up despite Maggie's best efforts to suppress it. "The bat-shit queen!" she repeated between guffaws. "Then Carter could tell everyone his ex-wife was truly bat shit." As crazy as her life had been lately, it was almost appropriate.

"Gold or guano, what difference does it make if you end up rich?" Barb said.

"Or it could just be an empty hole," Maggie said, sobering.

"Why would someone bother putting a locked gate over an empty hole?"

"Because it's dangerous. I'm sure there's all kinds of liability issues if a hiker or someone got trapped in there." Maggie shuddered. "Are you sure you want to do this?"

"Yes." Barb gave her a gentle shove. "Now find me some old clothes."

Half an hour later, the two women started out. Barb wore Maggie's oldest jeans while Maggie donned a pair of coveralls that had belonged to her father. She had to roll the sleeves and the pant legs up, and had cinched a belt around her waist to gather in all the extra fabric. "All that's missing is a pair of big shoes and a red nose," Barb said, surveying her. "You could be the clown at the circus."

"And you could be the ring leader. I can't believe I let you talk me into this. I just hope to God no one else I know sees me like this."

"No one will care how you dress when you're a millionaire." Barb picked up the foot-long flashlight Maggie had given her. "Let's go."

They started toward the door, but on the porch Maggie turned back.

"What now?" Barb called after her.

"I forgot Winston's cookies." She crammed half a dozen Lorna Doones in the pockets of the coveralls. "If he sees us and decides he wants cookies, we'll have to bribe him to let us pass."

"And you're worried being seen in baggie pants will harm your reputation?"

"Winston is my father's doing, not mine." Maggie marched past her down the steps.

"And those are your father's pants," Barb hurried to catch up with her. "If anyone accuses you of being eccentric, you can tell them it's in your jeans."

Maggie groaned. "If you're going to subject me to bad puns all morning, we can turn around now."

"It's almost afternoon," Barb pointed out. "So get a move on. I want to have a few gold nuggets in time for cocktails."

As they hiked along the path to the mine, Maggie began to feel a little better. The morning was crisp, but not too cold, and as always the view captivated her. "The tallest peak there is Mount Winston." She pointed the peak out to her friend. "My dad's ashes are scattered there."

"So he's still watching over you," Barb said.

A chill breeze blew Maggie's hair across her face. She turned away from it and raked hair out of her eyes. "He never watched over me in the first place, remember?" she said.

"Have you found any clues as to why he never got in touch?" Barb asked.

"Not really. Maybe he didn't think he was cut out to be a father."

They hiked in silence the rest of the way. Maggie began to feel better about the expedition. It would have been foolish to go into the mine by herself, but with Barb things would be all right. As soon as the situation got the least bit uncomfortable, she could count on Barb to want to leave. Maybe later Maggie would hire someone to investigate the mine for her. Someone who knew what they were doing. Someone with more guts than she had.

They stopped in front of the gate. "*No trespassing. Violators will be shot. Survivors will be shot again,*" Barb read the sign and laughed. "Who is Bob?"

"I told you about him. He's the old guy who thinks there's gold in the mine." She searched through the keys on the ring she'd found in a kitchen drawer. "Which one of these keys do you think is the right one?"

"Just start trying them." Barb practically vibrated with impatience, rocking back and forth on her heels.

Maggie inserted the first key into the lock. No luck. She repeated the process until the fifth key she tried slid smoothly in. "Houston, we have liftoff!" Barb cried, and grabbed hold of the gate as soon as Maggie slipped the lock from its hasp.

The gate was heavy. It took both women to pull it open, but it swung out quietly, with no ominous creaks and groans. Maggie stared into the opening. A tunnel a little taller than Barb with a smooth, narrow path extended into the darkness.

"This doesn't look bad at all," Barb said, playing the beam

of the flashlight along the gray rock walls. "No gold, though. It must be farther inside." She led the way into the tunnel.

Maggie reluctantly followed. She thought of the tourist cave she'd visited near San Antonio a few years ago. She'd been nervous at first about that, too, but had gotten so caught up in admiring the fanciful formations on the walls, ceiling, and floor that she'd forgotten her fright. Maybe this wouldn't be much different. She didn't think mining tunnels had formations to look at, but she could distract herself by thinking about her father. He must have spent a lot of time here. What did he see in this mine? What had he discovered here? Was this the source of those mysterious bank deposits?

The tunnel began to slope downward. It also grew narrower, the ceiling lower so that first Barb, then Maggie had to stoop. "My dad must have had to double over to get in here," Maggie said. She began to feel queasy, her breath coming in short, rapid gasps. Was this what claustrophobia felt like?

They turned a sharp corner. "Watch out," Barb called. "There's water on the floor. It's a little slippery."

Maggie flinched as an icy drop hit her face. She looked up and another splashed her in the eye. "Maybe we should turn back," she said.

"No, this is interesting. No bats, though. There goes the guano empire."

"Darn. I was already looking forward to designing batshit queen T-shirts."

"I don't see any gold yet either," Barb said.

"I don't think you're going to find nuggets lying around on the floor," Maggie said. "I think I remember they found veins of gold in rock. They had to cut the rock out, then crush it and process it with chemicals to get at the gold."

"What does the ore look like?"

"I have no idea."

"Fat lot of help you are. You own a mine and you don't bother to find out these things?"

"When we get out of here I promise I'll run right out and get that geology degree." She banged her shin on a rock. "This is ridiculous. We should go back."

"We haven't even gone that far yet. Come on."

"I'll leave without you."

"No, you won't. I've got the flashlight."

Maggie ground her teeth together but continued to follow her friend. Barb halted. "What is it?" Maggie asked, trying to see over Barb's shoulder.

"A fork in the road."

"Is this another pun?"

"No, there's a side tunnel."

"Don't take it. We'll get lost."

"We won't get lost. I have a very good sense of direction."

"Those are probably the last words of everyone who ever got lost in a cave."

"This tunnel definitely looks like it's been used more than the other." The flashlight beam wavered and dipped. "Look!"

"Look at what? I can't see anything but your back."

Barb turned sideways and shone the light on a niche in the wall. There, on a shelf of rock, sat a half-empty water bottle, a small colored piece of gravel, and a small silver disk.

Maggie reached past Barb and picked up the disk. "It looks like a religious medal," she said, recalling the St. Christopher medal a friend's mom kept hanging from the rearview mirror of the family car when Maggie was a girl.

"Which saint is it?" Barb asked.

Maggie studied the little figure. It was of a woman in a long gown, a halo on her head. She carried a glowing cup, and behind her was what looked like a tower. "I don't know." She replaced the disk on the shelf.

"Was your dad religious?" Barb asked.

"I don't know." Maggie shook her head. "I don't think so.

No one's said anything to make me think so, and there's nothing in the cabin to indicate that. Maybe he found it in here, from whoever owned the mine before."

"I think it's a sign we should explore this tunnel," Barb shone her flashlight down the passage.

All Maggie saw was more rock. "Since when do you believe in signs?" she asked.

"Since they point to what I want anyway." She started down the passage.

"What are we looking for?" Maggie asked as she followed her friend.

"Some sign someone's been working in here," Barb said. "Maybe some chunks of rock—ore. I'm thinking shiny streaks in the rock. I mean, we're talking gold here. It has to be shiny, right?"

"I haven't got a clue. Maybe we'll find another note for Bob: 'Leave this gold alone!' "

"Exactly. Uh-oh, it's getting pretty tight." The light dropped down and Barb with it. Something tugged on Maggie's coveralls. She gasped and jumped.

"Don't be such a ninny," Barb said. She was on her knees at Maggie's feet. "It's just me. There's a really narrow part here. We're going to have to crawl."

The only thing about Maggie that was crawling was her skin. "Honestly, Barb, I—"

Barb gave another firm tug and Maggie was on her knees. "This is what real cave explorers do," Barb said. "I saw it on public television."

Muttering under her breath, Maggie crawled after her friend. "Your butt looks a lot bigger from this angle," she offered.

"Go ahead and kiss it," Barb said cheerfully. "Oooh, look!"

She stopped abruptly and Maggie almost plowed into her. "What?" she asked.

"More of those colored rocks. Almost like some of that

colored aquarium gravel you can buy at the dollar store. But what would your dad be doing with that?"

Maggie looked at the half-dozen pieces of rock Barb held out to her. The largest was the size of a pea, the smallest a tiny chip, in various shades of blue and green. "You think that's aquarium gravel?"

"Yes, but I'm no expert. I haven't seen any since the boys were little. We had a couple of beta fish for a while. The cat got one and the other eventually succumbed to neglect."

"I can't imagine why my father would have aquarium gravel, and certainly not in this cave."

"Maybe they came from the mine." Barb's voice rose with excitement. "Maybe that's where aquarium gravel comes from—mines like this one."

"Or maybe it isn't aquarium gravel at all. Maybe it's some kind of gemstone."

"Gemstone?" The beam of the flashlight hit Maggie full in the face as Barb swiveled awkwardly in her crouching position to stare. "I thought this was a gold mine."

"It is. I mean, this is a gold mining district. But my dad had a book that talked about gemstones being found in some of the mines."

Barb squinted at the rock in her hand. It was tiny, tinier even than the diamond in Maggie's original engagement ring from Carter. "It's blue," Barb said. "Is it a sapphire?"

"I don't know. I guess I should find someone who can tell me."

Barb slipped the stone into the pocket of her shirt. "We should definitely do that. Maybe we can even find some more."

She started to turn around again, but Maggie caught her elbow. "I've had enough," she said. "We need to turn around. Give me the flashlight."

Barb sighed and handed over the light. "You're right. My knees are killing me."

They reversed course, Maggie leading the way this time. She decided she'd liked being behind Barb better. Up here the view of dark tunnel and encroaching rock unsettled her. She tried not to think about a whole mountain pressing down on her. Instead, she focused on how much her knees hurt and her back ached.

They'd been laboring a while when Barb spoke. "Shouldn't we be at that intersection by now?"

"I'm sure it's just ahead." Though she wasn't sure of any such thing.

"I don't remember all this rubble before."

"It was here, I'm sure. We were just too excited to notice."

"Oh. Good. Because I was beginning to think we were lost."

The word was like a jolt of electricity to Maggie. Her heart beat faster and she wouldn't have been surprised to know her hair was standing on end. "There's only the one passage," she said. "We can't be lost."

"There may have been some side passages between where we stopped and the intersection. In fact, I'm sure there were."

"But we haven't turned. We've been going straight down this one passage."

"We haven't turned, but we have sort of angled."

Maggie stopped and looked back at her friend. The flashlight illuminated Barb's smudged face, mussed hair, and muddy clothes. "You look like you've been mud wrestling."

"So do you," Barb said. "That doesn't make us any less lost."

"Stop saying that!" Maggie brandished the flashlight.

"I think we should turn back. Retrace our steps."

"We aren't walking."

"Retrace our crawl, then." She held out her hand. "Give me the flashlight."

"No, the last thing I want to do is crawl deeper into this god-awful cave."

"We should have brought that religious medal with us. We could say a prayer."

"We don't know who the medal is. Besides, I don't believe in that stuff."

"Not even a little?" Barb sounded wistful. "I do. At least I think I do. It's comforting."

Maggie turned so that her back rested against the rock wall, her knees drawn up to her chin. Barb assumed a similar pose. "When I was little I prayed every day for years that God would bring my father back to me. After a while, I decided no one was listening, because nothing ever happened."

"I'm sorry," Barb said. "I never realized you missed your dad so much. You never said."

"There didn't seem to be any point talking about it. And really, until all this happened, I'd pretty much stopped thinking about him."

"Yeah." They fell silent for a few seconds; then Barb nudged her. "Do you still have those cookies?"

"The Lorna Doones?" Maggie felt in her pocket. "Yeah."

"Let's eat them now. We should keep up our strength."

Maggie handed over three cookies and bit into a fourth. "They'd be better with milk," she said.

"Or coffee." Barb almost moaned. "My head is pounding again. I'd kill for a cup of coffee."

"We should set out again. I'm sure the intersection is ahead. We just haven't crawled far enough."

"Not yet. I want to finish my cookies and rest a little." Maggie heard the crunch of Barb's teeth on the shortbread, the sound magnified by all the rock around them. "I never told you," Barb said after a moment. "But Carter made a pass at me once."

Maggie almost choked on her cookie. "Carter made a pass at you? When?"

"Last year. At our annual Christmas party. He'd had a little too much to drink and caught me under the mistletoe. I think you were in the ladies' room. He kissed me; then he propositioned me. Said he was going out of town the next week, I ought to sneak off with him."

Maggie waited for the sick feeling of betrayal that should have come, but felt only a mild revulsion. A good sign, she thought. "What did you do?"

"I told him he was sick and if he didn't sober up and apologize, I'd tell you. He tried to act like it was all a joke and begged me not to tell you. He said it would only upset you and I realized it was true, so I kept my mouth shut. I felt guilty about that after he told you he wanted a divorce. If I'd confessed then, maybe it would have saved you some heartache later."

"I probably wouldn't have believed you," Maggie said. "It might have damaged our friendship, and then where would I have been when he did dump me?"

"I'm sorry." Barb gripped her hand. "I know you loved him, even though he didn't deserve your love."

"I despised him for what he did, and the way he did it—cheating on me for God knows how long, then announcing it so coolly." His callousness still hurt. "But we'd been together so long, more than half my life. I couldn't turn off my feelings for him like a switch." She studied her hand around the flashlight, the nails in sad need of a manicure. For twenty years she'd had an appointment every two weeks with a nail technician. Now her hands looked like those of a completely different woman. "Carter and I had sex the week before I left to come here," she said.

"Sex?" Barb's voice rose. "With that bastard?"

"Yeah, except when we were in bed together I wasn't thinking about him as a bastard. I was thinking about him as my husband—the only man I'd had sex with for twenty years." It had felt good, a physical release, if not an emotional one. Of course later, after he left her, she'd felt used and had cried even harder. "I think he was a habit I had a hard time breaking."

"I think I understand," Barb said. "I can't imagine suddenly losing Jimmy after all this time. It would be like losing an arm."

"Yeah," Maggie agreed. "But they tell me it gets better. And here in Eureka I don't think about him quite as much." She hefted the flashlight and pointed it down the tunnel. "Come on. I'm ready to get out of here."

She began crawling faster, ignoring the muddy gravel digging into her palms and the sharp pains in her knees. Barb was right; she didn't remember so much rubble before, but this had to be the right way.

Five minutes later, she felt a surge of triumph as the passage widened and they emerged into a corridor tall enough to stand. "This has to be it," she said, rising stiffly.

"Thank God." Barb stood beside her, massaging her back. "Much more of that and I'd have been crippled for life."

"I don't care what's in this mine, I'm not the one to get it out," Maggie said.

"You can hire others to work it for you," Barb said. "Maybe that Bob guy would help."

"Bob would pocket at least half the profits for himself," Maggie said.

They quickened their pace toward the entrance. Maggie's confidence rose as they approached the little niche with the water bottle and the saint's medal. They were definitely headed in the right direction.

A few steps more and she was blinded by a beam of light. "Hey!" she shouted, shielding her eyes.

"Maggie? Is that you?" called a masculine voice, distorted by the echo off rock.

"Who is it?" she called, squinting, spots of light dancing before her eyes.

Footsteps hurried toward her; then someone gripped her arm. "It's me, Jameso. Are you all right?" He sounded out of breath.

Maggie was having a little trouble breathing, too. She was torn between the urge to throw her arms around him and the fierce desire to hit him over the head with the flashlight. "What are you doing here?" she asked.

He put his face close to hers, the creases around his eyes sharp, his expression worried. "I was coming to rescue you," he said.

Chapter 12

Barb later said she thought it was romantic that Jameso, upon arriving at the house and finding her gone, though the Jeep was still in place, had followed their tracks to the mine and plunged in after them. Maggie, however, was annoyed.

"I don't need rescuing," she told him. "This is my mine and I have a right to be in here."

"It's dangerous," Jameso said, his mouth set in a stubborn line. They were back at the cabin by this time, Maggie drinking coffee and waiting for her turn in the shower while Barb cleaned up. "Murph told me he put that gate up because the mine tunnels were unstable."

"There's nothing unstable about solid rock," Maggie said, ignoring the flutter of fear in her stomach.

"What were you doing in there anyway?" He scowled at her as if she were a child who'd misbehaved. The expression infuriated her.

"It's my mine. I wanted to see what was in there."

"That's a stupid reason."

"Stupid? Are you calling me stupid?" Where was that flashlight when she needed it? She looked around for something else heavy to hit him with.

"It was stupid to go in that mine, where you could have been hurt." The lines along either side of his mouth had deepened, his nostrils flared. She'd rarely seen a man look so furious.

And so sexy. The thought ambushed her, weakening her legs so that she dropped into a chair to keep from falling. Was Jameso angry because he *cared?* She glanced at him, but he wasn't looking at her anymore. He'd moved over to the coffee maker and was refilling his cup.

"There's no gold in that old mine. Nothing of value. That's why Murph sealed it up."

"He didn't seal it," she said. "He put a gate over it with a lock. And I have the key. And how do you know there's nothing of value in there?"

"Because he told me there wasn't."

"And you think my father never lied?" All she'd learned of her father so far made her believe he wouldn't hesitate to make up whatever story he thought was necessary.

"He wouldn't lie to me."

Their eyes met and she saw the real hurt in his gaze. Because Murphy might have lied to him? Because Maggie was doubting him? The emotion in those brown depths made her uncomfortable. She looked away. "Why did you come all the way up here this afternoon?" she asked.

"I wanted to let Barbara know I returned the moving van. And to give her these." He reached into his pocket and took out a pair of black cat-eye sunglasses, rhinestones at the rim.

"You could have left them on the front porch."

"I started to when no one answered my knock. Then I noticed the Jeep was still here."

"You didn't think we might have gone for a hike?"

He made a face. "Barbara didn't strike me as the hiking type. But yeah, I might have thought that, if your tracks didn't lead down the path to the mine. On the way up here yesterday she peppered me with questions about the place. I figured she'd talked you into investigating."

"It's *my* mine," Maggie said again. "Why shouldn't I investigate it?"

"Suit yourself." He tossed the sunglasses onto the table. "I don't know why I bother trying to reason with you."

"Why *do* you bother?" Why did he give two cents what happened to her?

"Your dad meant a lot to me."

"The night we met, you made it sound like you didn't even like him much."

"I was angry at him for dying. He'd still be around if he took better care of himself."

"You can't know that. Maybe it was just his time." She winced inwardly at the words. She didn't believe that; it was just something people said as a kind of false comfort.

"Now you sound like Danielle," Jameso said. "She and Janelle think everything happens for a reason. That everything's connected."

If a person followed that way of thinking, Carter left Maggie so that she'd be on her own when her father died and left her this place. And she'd come here why? To get rich from what may or may not be gemstones in the mine? To meet Jameso?

The last thought sent a tremor through her that was definitely more fear than desire. The last thing she trusted right now was her ability to have anything like a healthy relationship with a man. Especially one she felt wasn't being entirely truthful to her, about his relationship with her father or his reasons for always showing up on her doorstep.

"My father wasn't overly concerned about my well-being, so I don't see why you should be either," she said.

She waited for him to offer up some defense of her father, readying her own reply, welcoming the opportunity to give full vent to her emotions.

Instead, he surprised her by stepping forward, his hand cradling her cheek, the tenderness of the gesture and the softness in his eyes like a blanket smothering the fire of her anger.

"You deserve someone who cares about you, Maggie," he said, his voice a rough caress. "You deserve the best."

Then he turned and left, leaving her wondering if she'd imagined the moment, though her cheek still felt warm where he'd held her.

"And in this blessed valley we shall found a town, Eureka! For here we have indeed found true treasure."

Cassie had no idea if her great-grandfather had ever said any such thing, and he hadn't exactly named the town. He'd sold a bunch of his land at bargain prices to a group of miners and their hangers-on, and a town had just sort of happened. But a play needed drama, so Cassie had no qualms about adding it when necessary. The basic facts were still there: without her great-grandfather, there wouldn't be a town, at least not right here.

"Excuse me."

Cassie stared at the computer screen, frowning. After the miners cheered, what should happen next? Should they carry Festus Wynock around on their shoulders? Or break into song?

"Excuse me. Lady?"

Cassie turned and confronted two watery blue eyes behind round spectacles. It was that strange kid again, Lucille's grandson. "What do you want?" she snapped. "Can't you see I'm busy?"

The boy didn't even blink, just continued to stare at her. "I have a paper to write," he said. "I need to see all your books on local mining."

First Indians, now mining. What was it with this kid? "I showed you before where the local history section is. Did you look there?"

"There's a sign that says some books are locked up behind the front desk and are available upon request." He nudged his glasses farther up his nose. "I'm requesting."

"You're not old enough." She turned back to her computer, but her train of thought was derailed. She'd moved the most valuable historical books—the ones that had belonged to her family—to a locked case after Jacob Murphy had walked off with one. If it wouldn't have been so much trouble explaining things to the library board, she'd have taken them all home.

"Are they porn or something?"

Of all the . . . Cassie whirled to face him. "We do not keep pornography in this library," she said.

"Then I'm old enough to read the books," he said.

Cassie was ready to refuse him, but she knew what that would lead to. He'd run tell his grandmother, the mayor. Then Lucille would show up to tell Cassie why she had to hand over the books. It wasn't worth the trouble.

She stood, deliberately taking her time, and pulled a clutch of keys from her pocket. "You may only examine the books in my presence, and you may under no circumstances remove them from the library."

"Whatever."

What was wrong with parents today, allowing such bad manners? Her father would have locked her in her room for a week if he'd heard her address one of her elders as this boy talked to her.

She opened the bookcase and indicated a trio of brown leather-bound volumes at the end of the top row. "Those books mention mining in this area."

"I'll need any books you have on Indians, too," he said, helping himself to the three books, plucking them off the shelf all three at once with hands that were surprisingly big for a boy his age.

Jake had had hands like that, with long fingers and bony joints, a smattering a red-gold hairs across the knuckles . . .

"Do you know if any of these say anything about the Ute Indians mining gold?" the boy asked, flipping through one of the books.

"The Indians didn't mine the gold," she said. "The miners did."

"The Indians did, too," he said, his expression hardening.

Whatever, Cassie thought, but she didn't say it. She didn't have time to spar with this boy. "You can sit at the table there and look through the books." She pointed to a wooden table closest to the checkout desk. "Let me know when you're finished."

She returned to her desk, and to the half-finished play on her computer, but her concentration had been destroyed. When she tried to write more dialogue for her great-grandfather, she heard Jacob Murphy instead, asking to see those same books about mining. He'd probably been the last person besides Cassie to crack them open. She'd been taken in by his big smile like everybody else. God, when she thought of the way everyone had carried on at his memorial service. You'd have thought the town's patron saint had expired. The man was nothing but a thief and a bully. Why was Cassie the only one who could see that?

"Is there anything in these books about mining other things besides gold?"

The boy was speaking too loudly for a library; he was too lazy to get up from the table and approach her like a considerate person. "Keep your voice down," Cassie hissed, in the loud whisper perfected by librarians everywhere.

"I said, is there anything in these books about mining stuff besides gold?" He copied her whisper, overenunciating in a way that might have been mocking. Was he mocking her?

"This is your paper. You do the research yourself." She turned her attention back to her computer, hands poised over the keyboard as if the words would pour forth at any moment.

She heard a chair scrape back against the floor and sneakers squeaking across the room. "What are you working on?" the boy asked, looming over her shoulder like a gangly bird—

an ostrich or an emu, something with a spindly neck and beady eyes.

It was too late to shield the screen from his view. "I'm writing a play about the founding of the town," she said. "For our Pioneer Heritage Festival." She's always thought heritage festival sounded better than Hard Rock Days, which had led more than one tourist to expect long-haired leather bands and giant amplifiers instead of pretend miners and water fights in the street.

"People sure talked funny in the old days." He squinted at the screen. "Who's Festus Wynock?"

"He was my great-grandfather. He founded this town. The land this building sits on used to belong to my family."

"If he had all that land, what are you doing working in a library?"

Cassie started to tell him it was none of his business, but when she opened her mouth, the truth came out instead. "Festus was a lousy businessman. He lost a lot of the family money through poor management, and my grandfather and father lost most of the rest." She still had the house and some old books and antiques, but the family history was her only real legacy.

"I don't even know my father," the boy said. "And my grandfather, at least the one I know, is a tool."

Cassie had no idea what he meant by tool, but apparently nothing good. "My grandmother was a wonderful person," she said. "She was smart and beautiful and kept my grandfather from making even bigger mistakes."

"I don't know my grandmother all that well, but she seems pretty cool."

Shrewd was the word Cassie might have used to describe Lucille—much like Cassie's own grandmother, God rest her soul. Cassie respected her, though the women would never be friends.

This boy intrigued her, though, even as he annoyed her. "Tell me your name again," she demanded.

"Lucas," he said, eyeing her warily.

"Lucas, I want you to be in my play," she said. "You can be the messenger boy who announces the discovery of gold in the mountains above town."

He shook his head, backing away. "I don't want to be in any play," he said.

"Nonsense. You'll be perfect for the role." She hadn't actually written that part yet, but she would. She turned back to the computer. "I'll notify you when rehearsals begin."

He might have mumbled another protest, but she was too engrossed in the words on the screen to hear. What this play needed was a villain. A good-looking, silver-tongued swindler who'd pull the wool over everyone's eyes. And a heroine, the courageous daughter of the town founder, who would see the handsome devil for the snake he truly was.

Barb emerged from the shower pink faced and dewy, her hair swathed in a bath towel turban, her body wrapped in a too-short terry robe. "Where's Jameso?" she asked, looking around.

"He had to leave," Maggie said. If he hadn't, they both might have said—or done—things they'd later regret. "He brought you these." She handed Barb the sunglasses.

"The darling man." Barb donned the glasses. "I couldn't imagine where I'd left them."

"He said to tell you he turned in the moving van."

"I knew I could depend on him."

"You knew no such thing," Maggie said. "You only met him yesterday."

"I have good instincts." She sat at the table, sunglasses still in place. "What else did Jameso have to say?"

"He said the mine is dangerous and we were idiots to go in there."

Barb pursed her lips. "He didn't really say we were idiots, did he?"

"No, but it was implied."

"He was just upset because you scared him."

"Why should anything I do affect him one way or another? I'm certainly not losing sleep over him."

"No? Too bad." She removed the sunglasses and gave Maggie a long look. "Did you show him the stones we found in the mine?"

"No."

"Why not? He might have known what they were."

Maggie busied herself lining up the salt and pepper shakers, avoiding Barb's gaze. "There wasn't a good opportunity. And I don't think we should tell anyone yet. I don't want a bunch of people like Bob up here trying to check things out for themselves."

"If you asked Jameso to keep a secret, I'm sure he would."

Maggie started to object that Barb didn't know any such thing, but why waste her breath? "After I get cleaned up, let's go into town. We can stop by the library and see if we can find any information about the stones."

Chapter 13

An hour later, Maggie parked the Jeep in front of the Eureka library. "The librarian, Cassie Wynock, can be a little touchy," she said as she switched off the ignition and pocketed the key. "My dad stole a library book and she's still upset about it."

Barb looked amused. "Oh my," she said. "I had no idea your old man was such a hardened criminal."

"If that's the worst thing I ever find out he did, I'll consider myself lucky," Maggie said.

Cassie was helping a mother and her young daughter when Maggie and Barb entered. They waited for their turn at the front counter. "Hi, Cassie," Maggie said when the librarian turned to them. "This is my friend, Barbara Stanowski. She's visiting from Texas and we'd like to use the Internet."

Cassie's expression was cold. "I'm afraid that isn't possible," she said.

"Oh." Maggie was taken aback. "Is the Internet down?" She glanced toward the row of computer terminals, where a teenager and an older man sat engrossed.

"You're not a resident of Eureka County," Cassie said.

"You don't have a library card. I can't allow you to continue to come in here and use the library's resources."

Maggie blinked, stunned. "You didn't have a problem before," she said.

"That was a one-time courtesy. I can't allow you to take advantage. The computer terminals are for our regular patrons."

"Excuse me." Barb stepped forward, a brilliant smile on her lips that made Maggie wince. She knew that smile. It was a smile that had annihilated snippy shop clerks and imperious committee members throughout Houston. "This lovely library is a publicly funded institution, is it not?" Barb inquired.

"Yes, but—"

"And those computers and the Internet service and even your salary are paid for by taxpayers."

"Yes, local taxpayers."

"Of course." Barb's smile never dimmed, though the look in her eyes sharpened. "But Ms. Stephens is living here now. So, you see, she is a taxpayer."

"She doesn't have a library card." Cassie's pout lent her face an unfortunate piggish look.

"Then perhaps you could issue her one," Barb said.

"Oh, yes," Maggie said. "I'd love a library card."

"I'll need proof of your legal residence," Cassie said. "A driver's license or a utility bill."

"I live off the grid," Maggie said. "You know that. I don't have a utility bill. And I haven't had a chance to get my driver's license changed over." Not that she had the slightest intention of doing so. She wasn't moving to Eureka; she was only here on an extended visit. Just until she got things settled.

"Then I can't give you a card." Cassie turned her back to them.

Maggie felt Barb stiffen. By all rights, the librarian should have been a steaming puddle on the floor from the heat of the gaze Barb shot her. "I'd like to speak to your supervisor," Barb said.

Cassie's smile was a low-wattage imitation of Barb's, but with just as much malice behind it. "I don't have a supervisor."

That couldn't be right, Maggie thought. She probably had to report to the county government. And there was probably a state library board. Fat lot of good that would do them today. "Come on, Barb." She tugged at her friend's sleeve. "We can use the computer at Reggie's office."

With a last, withering look at Cassie, Barb turned on her heel and marched out of the library, Maggie in her wake. By the time they reached the Jeep, Barb was muttering a steady stream of obscenity-laced invective against Cassie and her ancestors. "Who died and made her queen?" Barb asked as she buckled her seat belt.

"I don't know, but it doesn't really matter. Reggie said we were welcome to use the computer in his office." Though she hated to bug him.

"I can't believe she'd punish you for something your father did. You didn't even know the man. And over a stupid book. I should have just offered to pay for the thing and be done with it."

"It's not really about the book," Maggie said. "At least, I don't think it is. The book did belong to her family, and is probably irreplaceable, but I think she's more upset because my father pretended to be interested in her when he really only wanted the book."

"Did she tell you that?"

"Yes." Maggie remembered the hurt in Cassie's eyes when she'd told the story—the sting of false hopes and betrayal she knew all too well.

"Then you don't know that's what really happened," Barb said. "You only have her side of things."

"It's the only side I'll ever have, since my father isn't here." She pounded the steering wheel with her palm. "That's the frustrating thing about all of this. The deeper I dig into my father's life, the more of a tangle it becomes. Maybe I should just give up and go home."

"Then you'd always wonder and worry about those unanswered questions," Barb said. "Besides, where is home now? Some apartment in Houston? Not that I don't miss you, but you seem to be settling in well here. You're making friends, and you have a cute little cabin with a killer view."

"And five miles of road only navigable by snowmobile in the winter." Maggie found a parking space near the Last Dollar and guided the Jeep in.

"If that's a problem, I'm sure you could find a place in town this winter." Barb unfastened her seat belt. "I thought we were going to your lawyer's office."

"We are. He's upstairs from the café."

"Let's eat first. I'm starved."

Maggie started to protest, but her stomach growled. All she'd had since breakfast was coffee and a few Lorna Doones, and it was almost two. "All right," she said. Maybe food would improve her mood.

"Hey, Maggie!" Danielle greeted her with a wave, then came out from behind the counter to throw her arms around Maggie in a hug.

Maggie returned the gesture, touched and little taken aback. "This is my friend, Barbara Stanowski," she said. "Barb, this is Danielle, one of the owners of the café."

"Nice to meet you," Danielle said. "Jameso said Maggie had a friend visiting. Y'all come sit over here." She led them to the same booth Maggie had occupied before. "What would y'all like to drink?"

They ordered iced tea and she hurried back to the kitchen. "Friendly girl," Barb said, squinting at the chalkboard menu Maggie had directed her to.

"Wait until you see her partner, Janelle."

As if on cue, the blonde emerged from the kitchen. Today

a red beret topped her head, and she wore a matching cropped red sweater and black skinny jeans. "Dani said I had to come out and meet your friend," she said by way of greeting.

Maggie made the introductions. "It's nice to meet some friendly people after the reception we got at the library," Barb said.

"Was Cassie on one of her tears today?" Janelle asked sympathetically.

"She refused to let us use the library computers because Maggie doesn't have a library card," Barb said. "And she won't issue her a library card because her driver's license doesn't say she lives in Eureka County."

"If it's any comfort, she doesn't like me and Danielle either," Janelle said. "But if you get your driver's license changed, she'll have to give you a card. Meanwhile, Dani and I have books you can borrow, if you like paperback mysteries and romance novels."

"I should have given my dad's collection to you instead of the library," Maggie said. "He had a lot of mysteries."

"I know. We used to trade books a lot," Janelle said. "We'd be happy to trade with you, too."

"Thanks. I'll remember that. Today we just wanted to use the Internet."

"That's too bad. Now, what would you like to eat?"

They ordered burgers and Janelle returned to the kitchen. Barb watched her departure, then turned to Maggie. "See, you belong here. These people like you, the witch at the library excepted."

"Yes, it's a nice place. And I like it here. But what would I do for a living if I stayed? My dad didn't leave me enough to live on for the rest of my life."

"I'm still holding out hope for the mine," Barb said. "But there must be something you can do."

"I know how to manage an office, but there aren't that many businesses in Eureka."

"That's what you've always done, but is it really what you've always wanted to do?" Barb sipped her tea. "You've got a chance here to build a totally new life. What's your dream job?"

"You mean besides being George Clooney's kept mistress?"

"Besides that."

Maggie rested her chin in her hand and idly stirred her tea with the straw. "I used to want to be a writer. This sounds dumb, but reports and letters and stuff like that were my favorite part of running the office."

"Then you could write a novel."

"People don't just wake up one morning and decide to write a novel. It's a lot of work."

"That doesn't mean you couldn't try. In the meantime, we'll keep our eyes open for something else."

Maggie started to protest that it wasn't up to Barb to find her a job, but decided not to waste her breath. Barb liked to look after people and frankly, Maggie liked being looked after. Sometimes.

Danielle delivered their burgers, along with a bottle of ketchup and extra napkins. As she bent over their table, Maggie noticed the necklace of blue stones around her neck—stones like the ones they'd found in the mine. "Where did you get your necklace?" she asked.

Danielle put one hand to the circlet of stones. "Murph gave it to me."

Maggie exchanged a look with Barb. "Did he say where he got it?" Barb asked. "I've never seen one quite like it."

"He said he picked it up in his travels," Danielle said. "He was always doing things like that; going away for a while, then showing up with gifts and stuff."

"He didn't say where in his travels he got the necklace?" Maggie asked.

"No, but he gave one to Janelle, too."

The front door opened and a couple came in; Danielle

went to greet them. Maggie leaned across the table and spoke to Barb in a whisper. "So maybe the stones didn't come out of the mine at all," she said.

"Or maybe he wasn't telling the truth," Barb said. "We've already established your old man could lie when it suited him."

Had her father lied about the origin of the necklace, perhaps to keep the mine safe from poachers like Bob? She half hoped the old miner would show up so she could question him again, but no one she recognized came into the café while she and Barb finished their meal.

Stuffed and feeling in need of a nap, Maggie led the way up the stairs to Reggie's office, but before they were halfway up she spotted the Closed sign on the door. She finished the climb anyway, and tried the knob, but the office was shut tight and dark.

"We don't really need him now anyway," Barb said as they descended to the parking lot once more. "Tomorrow we can bring your laptop to the café."

"I know, but I wanted you to meet Reggie. He's a really nice guy. And I need to ask him if he has a date for probate yet."

"Maybe he'll be in tomorrow." Barb looked down the row of storefronts. "What else is there in Eureka that I shouldn't miss?" she asked.

"There's someone else I want you to meet. Come on. It's just a short walk."

At Lacy's, they found Lucille unpacking boxes of raku pottery. "Hey, Maggie," she greeted the newcomers. "Come see my latest acquisition." She held up a squat vase. "A collector near Cortez decided to sell some of his treasures and I'm handling the consignment."

"It's gorgeous." Maggie stroked the rough side of the pot. It shone with shades of copper and brown, and hints of purple. "Do you think you can sell it?"

"You'd be surprised what passes through here." Lucille

opened another box and began cutting Bubble Wrap away from another pot. "I have collectors who stop by here regularly, along with folks looking to furnish high-dollar homes in Telluride. And I have a Web site where a lot of the pricier stuff finds buyers. This may look like just a junk shop, but there's more to it than that."

"Oh, I didn't mean—" Maggie flushed. She had thought of Lucille as more of a junk dealer, but she could see now she'd underestimated the woman. After all, Maggie had seen all that Haviland china on her first visit. Apparently it hadn't been as out of place as she thought.

"Hi, I'm Barbara Stanowski." Barb stepped forward and held out her hand. "I'm visiting Maggie from Houston."

"Nice to meet you, Barbara. I'm Lucille."

"Lucille is the mayor of Eureka," Maggie said.

"Then do you have any authority over the town librarian?" Barb asked. "The woman isn't the best representative of Eureka hospitality."

Lucille set aside the pot and sent Maggie a questioning look. "What did Cassie do?" she asked.

"She refused to let us use the Internet in the library," Barb said. "She said it was because Maggie doesn't have a library card, but she won't issue her one without a utility bill, which you know she doesn't have, or a driver's license showing an address in Eureka County."

"I can talk to her, but the county commissioners are the only ones with authority, and they pretty much let her make her own rules."

"Why does everyone let her bully people?" Maggie asked, remembering Reggie's warnings about Cassie Maggie's first day in town.

"She's really not a bully," Lucille said. "She's great with kids. Her family has lived here for four generations, but she's the only one left. She has her problems, but she's really not that bad. Her biggest fault is that she holds a grudge."

"But Maggie hasn't done anything to her," Barb protested.

"The woman is mad at a dead man and taking it out on Maggie. That's sick."

"I'll see what I can do," Lucille said. "In the meantime, the easiest thing would be for Maggie to get her driver's license updated." She smiled at Maggie. "After all, you are living here now."

"I haven't decided yet to make it permanent." She shoved her hands in the pockets of her jacket and felt the two small stones from the mine.

She took them out and showed them to Lucille. "Have you seen any stones like this before?" she asked.

Lucille fingered the tiny stones and smiled. "I have a bracelet with similar stones that Murph gave me. Where did you find those?"

"Around my dad's place." Maggie put her hand, and the stones, back in her pocket. "Did he say where he got the bracelet he gave you?"

Lucille tilted her head, thinking. "I'm pretty sure he told me it was from a jeweler's in Montana." She nodded. "Yes, I'm positive that's what he said. Why?"

"Just wondering. I think these may have come from another bracelet or necklace that broke. If I find the rest of them, maybe I can get it fixed."

"That's a good idea." Lucille turned back to her boxes. "Is there anything else I can help you ladies with today?"

"No, thanks," Maggie said. "I'm just showing Barb all the sights of Eureka."

"You should take her out to Living Water," Lucille said. "There's nothing like that in Houston, I promise you."

Barb waited until they were back at Maggie's car before she asked the question Maggie knew had been burning on her tongue. "Living Water? Isn't that the naked hot springs you told me about?"

"Clothing optional," Maggie said as she slid into the driver's seat. "You can wear a swimsuit if you want."

"I didn't bring a swimsuit with me. Besides, you know

what they say about when in Rome. If people in Eureka go skinny-dipping at the hot springs, then I will, too."

"Barb!" The word came out as more of a yelp.

"Oh, come on, Maggie. What's the big deal? You don't have any parts no one else doesn't have. And after crawling around on my hands and knees half the morning in that mine, soaking in a hot springs sounds divine."

"I've never been there before." Maggie's stomach knotted and she gripped the steering wheel as if it were a life preserver.

"Then now's a great time to go, while I'm here to hold your hand." Barb laughed. "Come on. What are you afraid of?"

What was she afraid of? Of being embarrassed? It wouldn't be the first time in her life. Of being judged? There was that, but why should she care what people who were most likely strangers thought of her?

She glanced at Barb, whose smile was warm and encouraging. "The hot water would feel good," she said.

"That's my girl." Barb patted her shoulder. "Let's go try it out."

Maggie's stomach was doing backflips by the time she guided her car through the gate in Living Water's high wooden fence, but it calmed some as she drove through the beautifully landscaped grounds.

"This is gorgeous," Barb said as the car glided past flowerbeds filled with blooms and a stretch of manicured lawn. "It's like some European spa."

They parked by the office and went inside. A young woman with tattoos of flowers covering both arms greeted them. "Hi there. Is this your first visit to Living Water?"

Gee, how can you tell? Maggie thought.

"Yes," Barb announced. "We're virgins."

The girl giggled. "Don't worry. You're going to love it."

She explained the layout of the grounds and the various pools, issued towels, and pointed them to the changing room.

"You haven't been a virgin since tenth grade," Maggie said when they reached the changing room.

"Neither have you, but isn't it a lovely idea? To have an experience that's brand new?"

They stripped off their clothes and stuffed them in a locker, then, wrapped in towels, followed a hallway to the entrance to the soaking area.

Rock paths wound among more flower beds to the naturally heated pools. The stone was cold beneath Maggie's feet and she shivered a little, feeling vulnerable with only this thin towel between herself and the outside air.

"The main pond is this way," Barb said, starting down a path.

"I thought maybe we'd start somewhere smaller," Maggie protested. "Less public."

"Nonsense. We should dive right in."

Murmured conversation alerted them to their approach to the main soaking pond. They rounded a bend in the path and the large, kidney-shaped pool came into view. Steam rose from the surface, blurring the images of men and women seated around the edges or floating in the middle. A quick scan revealed not one person was wearing more than a hat.

"Oh, this looks divine," Barb said. Not waiting for a reply, she dropped her towel and headed for the water.

Chapter 14

Maggie froze, one hand clutching the front of the towel she'd wrapped around herself, the other clenched at her side. This was the story of her life—head full of ideas that sounded wild and daring, fear holding her back from carrying out any of them. When her friends in high school had skipped school to go to the beach, she'd stayed in class and suffered through Mrs. Prebble's feminine hygiene lesson. She'd bought a sensible sedan instead of the sports car she'd craved because her mother had told her sports cars were dangerous. When the urge to cut her hair in a stylish, slightly punk cut had hit, she'd let Carter convince her she wouldn't look like herself, though she could see now that had been the whole point. She was tired of being herself—dull, sensible, and safe.

"Come on in. The water feels wonderful," Barb called, smiling up at her like some middle-aged water nymph.

Heart pounding, Maggie let go of the towel and hurried into the water, submerging up to her neck in its warm embrace.

"Your face is all red," Barb said.

"It's the heat." Maggie put one hand to her burning cheek

and fought the urge to wrap both arms across her torso, as if that would somehow preserve her tattered modesty.

"This makes me feel like a teenager," Barb stretched her arms over her head and looked up at the sky. "Do you remember skinny-dipping out at the reservoir?"

"I never went skinny-dipping at the reservoir." Something else she'd been too chicken to try.

"You didn't?" Barb laughed. "Well, you can make up for it now. You can come here all the time."

"I'm only here now because of you."

"Come on now. Don't you think it feels great?"

The water flowed around her like warm silk. She could say the same thing about a hot bath, but the sensation of standing here in broad daylight, with the sun overhead and other people around, was oddly . . . invigorating. "It feels good," she admitted. "Just sort of . . . exposed."

Barb laughed. "You are too much, darling."

"I see you ladies are enjoying yourselves."

Maggie's head snapped around at the sound of the familiar voice. Bob was wading toward them through the water, his naked chest sprinkled with white hair like frost on a weathered log. She jerked her gaze away, determined not to look down. Even the thought of shriveled old man bits was enough to traumatize her.

"This place is divine," Barb cooed. "It must be the best-kept secret in Colorado."

"Oh, we've got plenty of secrets hereabouts." Bob turned to Maggie. "You take a look in the French Mistress yet?"

"We explored the mine this morning," Barb said before Maggie had a chance to open her mouth. "I was sadly disappointed. There was nothing there but a bunch of rock."

"Some of that rock can be worth a lot of money," Bob said. "If it's the right kind."

"I don't think there's anything valuable in that mine," Maggie said. "I think the only reason my dad bought it was because it was remote and nobody would bother him up there."

"Too lonely for you?" Bob asked.

"I'm not lonely." The admission surprised her. She'd been far lonelier in the house in Houston after Carter left than she'd been in her father's cabin on the mountain. "I haven't had time to be lonely," she said.

"You'll have plenty of time when you're snowed in this winter," Bob said. "If you decide to stay."

"Are you going to stay?" Barb asked.

The back of Maggie's neck prickled. Was it her imagination or had everyone leaned in to hear her answer? Had Jameso been serious about the locals placing bets on how long she'd stay in town? "I haven't decided," she hedged. "I still have to wait for my father's will to be probated."

"Probate's set for Friday." Reggie, wearing only a ball cap and sunshades—and a surprising amount of body hair—slipped into the water beside them. "I was going to drive up and tell you later today."

"Um, okay." Maggie covered her mouth to hold back a giggle. Yes, Eureka was a small town, but she felt as if she was in the middle of some wild farce. The only thing more ridiculous would be if the rest of the soakers in the pool broke into a Broadway-worthy song and dance.

"You must be Maggie's friend from Houston." Reggie offered his hand. "I'm Reggie Paxton."

"I see my reputation precedes me." Barb shook hands. "Nice to meet you."

"Jameso told us he took you up to Jake's place yesterday morning."

"Who is 'us'?" Maggie asked. Was Jameso sharing her schedule with everyone in town?

"Somebody commented on the moving truck parked behind Jameso's place," Reggie said. "It was either tell the truth or have a rumor spread about him leaving town."

"He should have gone for the rumor," Barb said. "That's much more interesting than I am."

"You seem pretty interesting to me." Bob waggled his eyebrows in the manner of some melodrama villain.

"What's Jameso's story?" Barb asked. "How did he end up in Eureka? Is he from here?"

"Almost nobody is from Eureka," Bob said. "Jameso showed up a few years ago and just sorta took. Like one of those windblown seeds that manages to take root in the rocks."

"Where's he from?" Maggie asked. "Why did he come here? Eureka's not exactly on the way to anyplace else."

"He might have come for the skiing or the fishing," Reggie said. "I drove through here on a motorcycle seventeen years ago and fell in love. Moved back permanent as soon as I could quit my job and sublet my apartment in Milwaukee."

"So your wife is from here?" Maggie asked. She'd heard of people doing stranger things for love.

Reggie laughed. "I moved here because I fell in love with the mountains. Katya came later."

"There's a saying around here that people who stay in Eureka are either running to or running from something," Bob said.

"Which are you?" Barb asked.

"I come here to prospect for gold," Bob said. "So I was running to."

"I guess my father was running from," Maggie said. She hadn't yet decided if he saw his cabin on the mountain as a refuge or an exile.

"What'll it be, Maggie?" Barb asked.

"What do you mean?" She blinked at her friend.

Barb winked. "Are you running from or running to?"

"I'm not running at all," she said lightly, but the words left her feeling heavy. She'd spent years moving her feet and going nowhere at all, treading water in a life that left her feeling empty. If nothing else, the divorce had forced her to think about moving, though where she'd end up she still hadn't a clue.

"Is Rick around here?" An older woman who walked with a decided limp hobbled to the edge of the pool. She wore khaki cargo shorts and a T-shirt with the Living Waters logo, and no bra, judging by the way her breasts hung somewhere near her navel. Maggie folded her arms under her own breasts, lifting them a little higher. They weren't sagging too much yet, but was it only a matter of time?

"Hey, Rick," the woman called.

"I'm here, Grace." A slight man with a tonsure of dark hair and a tattoo of an eagle on his shoulder waded toward the woman. "What is it?"

"I just heard on the scanner there's been a rock slide over near Hereford Pass. Couple of tourists got caught in it. Highway's closed."

"So much for my afternoon off." Rick started for the steps leading out of the pool.

"When are you gonna hire another reporter to help you out?" Reg asked.

"When I can find someone to work for the piss-poor salary I can afford." He hauled himself out of the pool and began toweling off.

"Cute ass," Barb whispered in Maggie's ear. "I wonder if he's single."

Maggie didn't care if the man was single. She didn't even care that he was naked. "Did you say you were looking for a reporter?" she asked.

He stopped with the towel around one thigh. "Who are you?"

"Jake's daughter," Bob and Reg chorused.

"Maggie Stevens," she said, a beat behind.

Rick narrowed his eyes at her. He had bushy eyebrows, like a melodrama villain. "Can you write?"

"She's a wonderful writer," Barb said. "And she's organized and reliable. She ran her ex-husband's business for years."

Rick glanced at Barb, then back at Maggie. "Can you talk for yourself?"

"Yes, I can talk." She frowned at Barb. "And I can write. I've never been professionally published, but I'd like the chance to try."

"And you're willing to work for twenty-three hundred dollars a month?"

"Yes." With the money her father had left her, she'd do all right. At least for a while.

"I'll give you a try." He draped the towel around his shoulders. "Get dressed and come with me."

"Now?"

"Yes, now. If you want the job."

"Go on." Barb patted her shoulder. "I'll be fine here."

Maggie hurried from the pool and into her clothes, marveling at the strange turn of events. She'd just interviewed for a job while stark naked. And been hired. Her heart raced and her hands shook as she zipped her jeans. But this time the sensations weren't caused by fear. Not entirely by fear, at least. After twenty years of putting her dreams on hold for other people, she'd impulsively done something solely for herself, just because it was what she wanted to do. The sensation was exhilarating.

"Come on," Rick said when they met outside the dressing rooms. "You can ride with me. Do you have a camera?"

"Just a small digital one. And not with me."

"You'll need a better one. And always carry it with you. Today you can borrow mine."

She'd buy a camera. And a printer for her laptop. And maybe one of those little handheld recorders for taping interviews.

"What are you grinning about?" Rick asked.

She forced her mouth into a somber expression. "I'm looking forward to the job," she said.

"It's a job." He jerked open the driver's door of a weather-beaten Land Rover. "Lots of grunt work for little reward."

As if working for Carter all those years had been particularly rewarding. At least now she was doing what she wanted, not what she was obligated to do for her marriage. She buckled her seat belt. "You won't be sorry you hired me."

"If you're anything like your old man, I won't be." Gears grinding, he threw the Rover into reverse and backed out of the parking lot.

"What do you mean?" she asked, raising her voice to be heard over the clatter of gravel against the bottom of the vehicle.

"Hardheadedness is a good trait for a reporter, and Jake was the stubbornest old mule I ever knew."

Maggie didn't think she was particularly stubborn but saw no need to point this out to her new boss. Everything she'd heard about her father led her to believe she'd inherited very little from him beyond his material possessions. But he had passed on one thing more valuable than an empty mine and mountaintop views: he'd given her the opportunity to start over, in a very different kind of life. She hoped she'd make the right choices this time and find some of the happiness she'd missed the first time around.

"I'm calling a family meeting tonight and I expect you to be there, with Lucas." Lucille was waiting for Olivia when the young woman emerged from her room shortly before noon on a Monday after school let out in mid-June.

Olivia blinked owlishly, and Lucille was struck by the resemblance to Lucas. Yet, what was awkward in the boy was beautiful in the woman. "What are you talking about?" Olivia said, and moved past her mother to the stairs.

Lucille followed her to the kitchen, where she'd put on coffee to brew. She let Olivia pour a cup before she spoke again. "I've hardly seen anything of you these past few weeks," she said. "I want us to all have dinner together and talk."

"I have a date." Olivia stirred two spoonfuls of sugar into her coffee, the spoon rattling against the side of the mug.

"Then cancel it. It's not as if you aren't out every night anyway."

"I'm not some kid you can order around."

"You will always be my daughter, and since you're living here now I think I deserve a little consideration."

"Don't talk to me about what you deserve." Olivia glared at her.

Lucille bit back her own angry retort. She took a deep breath, which she'd read somewhere was calming, but it only made her feel like the big bad wolf gearing up to blow a house down. "I want the three of us to have dinner as a family."

Olivia blew on the coffee, then took a sip. "We're not really the family dinner type."

"We all have to eat. I don't see why we can't do it together occasionally."

"Fine. I'll cancel my date. Though if you have something you want to talk about, why not tell me now?"

"There is something I want to ask you while Lucas isn't around. I want to know what really happened with you and D. J."

"That's none of your business."

"It is if his stolen car is parked in my driveway."

"The car isn't stolen."

"Does he know you have it?"

"I told you he does."

"Then what aren't you telling me?"

Olivia stared into the coffee mug, fingers white-knuckled on the handle. Lucille wondered if she'd hurl the coffee at her. She took a step back, recalling an incident when Olivia was sixteen and she'd launched a bowl of tomato soup across the room.

"He left us," Olivia said. "I asked him not to go, but he left anyway, so I took his car. He owed me that much."

She bit her lip, and Lucille could almost taste the metallic sting of blood in her own mouth. She stared at her daughter, but saw herself, not much older than Olivia was now. Mitch had just announced that he was leaving her for his secretary, a woman Lucille had considered her friend. The hurt and rage had washed over her in waves. She'd felt like a piece of trash tossed to the side of the road. She'd hated him for making her feel that way, and she'd hated herself for still loving him so much. After he left the house, to meet with his new lover, she'd gone into his room, to the top dresser drawer where he kept his cuff links and tie pins, and she'd taken out the box where he kept his father's watch. It was a gold pocket watch, engraved with the figure of an elk. He'd told her it was worth a lot of money. She took the watch to the pawn shop and pocketed the money and the ticket, planning to taunt him with it when he asked. Imagining the moment gave her a little relief from the pain that bore down so hard.

But he'd never asked about the watch. Whether he really hadn't noticed it was missing or he hadn't wanted to give her the satisfaction of acknowledging her revenge, she didn't know.

She'd spent the money long ago, and lost the pawn ticket, but that bitter ache of rejection was still buried somewhere inside her. "He was stupid to leave," she said. She meant D. J., but Mitch, too. She looked Olivia in the eye. "You deserve a man who will stay."

Olivia blinked again, the mask sliding away for half a second to reveal the vulnerable girl behind the tough façade. "Yeah, well, instead I got a new ride. That's something anyway." She turned and poured the rest of her coffee down the sink. "See you at dinner."

She took the stairs two at a time and in a minute Lucille heard the shower. She wondered if Olivia was crying in there, hiding her tears in the flow of hot water. Lucille had done that, standing naked under the spray until the water grew cold, trying to wash away the grief that bloomed anew every day like a cactus flower.

Other mothers gave their daughters family recipes and advice on raising children. The only thing she seemed to have passed on to Olivia was an inability to find the love she wanted, and the twisted belief that it was possible to steal happiness.

Chapter 15

Maggie survived the race to the rock slide in Rick's Land Rover. She took a few pictures of the scene and conducted her first interview, with an irate tourist whose car had been half buried by the avalanche of boulders and debris. He threatened to sue the county and the State of Colorado for not making the mountains safer.

Rick, listening in, had interrupted at this point. "Does your wife do what you tell her?" he asked.

"My wife? What the hell does my wife have to do with this?"

"I just want to know if she always does what you tell her."

"I'm not dumb enough to try to tell my wife what to do." The man glared at Rick.

"That's kind of how it is with Mother Nature," Rick said. "She's a real bitch, and we gave up trying to tell her what to do a long time ago."

Maggie had tried to use that line in her article, but Rick had edited it out. But he liked her writing enough to keep her on, and now she spent her days at a scarred wooden desk at the newspaper office or covering various meetings and the occasional auto accident. She loved the job, and as a bonus, it kept her too busy to think about Carter or her father.

"Hey, Maggie."

She hadn't thought much about Jameso in her first ten days on the job either, but now here he was, standing beside her desk, dressed in motorcycle leathers, his hair ruffled where he'd removed his helmet, tiny lines radiating from his chocolate brown eyes. How had she forgotten how impossibly sexy he was?

"Jameso!" The word came out in a squeak, so she modulated her voice. "What brings you here?"

"I hadn't seen you in a while. I wanted to know how you were doing." He sat on the edge of her desk, leather creaking with the movement.

"I'm doing great." She straightened a stack of press releases he'd shoved aside. "The job is great."

"Everything okay up at the cabin?"

"Everything's great."

"Probate go okay?"

"Great." What was wrong with her? Why couldn't she think of anything else to say? And why wouldn't he stop staring at her? Was her mascara smeared? Was her hair a mess? She put one hand up to check.

"You look good." He grinned. "Great."

"Now you're making fun of me." The old annoyance at his attitude crowded out some of her nervousness.

"No, I'm not." He shifted, leather creaking again. He wore jeans under the chaps, dark denim stretched across muscular thighs . . . *Don't go there, Maggie.*

"Barb make it back to Houston?"

"Yes." Maggie had driven her to the airport four days ago. She'd carried with her a chunk of rock from Maggie's front yard, a bag of Janelle's Linzer torte, and an all-over tan from her days spent at Living Water. "I'm sure she'll be back to visit. She loved it here." Though Maggie knew her friend was looking forward to getting back to her steam shower, satellite TV, paved roads, and, of course, her husband, Jimmy.

"What about you?" Jameso asked. "Do you love it here?"

"Love might be too strong a word, but you could say Eureka is growing on me." On chilly mornings she could start a fire in the wood stove in under a minute and she negotiated the winding road down from the mountain with hardly a qualm, and she was proud of that. There was something to be said for living in a place where the simple act of getting up and coming to work every day was worthy of self-congratulations.

"I won the bet," he said.

"The bet?"

"About how long you'd stay in town. I had my money on you deciding to stick around permanent."

How had he determined that when she hadn't even known it herself until she asked Rick to give her a job? "Permanent is a long time," she said.

"If you were only visiting, you wouldn't have taken the job."

"I guess not." She glanced at her laptop screen. She was writing a piece about a proposal to put solar panels on the city office building. Not exactly breaking news, but she did need to finish before she left the office today.

"Want to have dinner with me tomorrow night?" Jameso asked.

"Oh, well . . ." Was he asking her out? On a date? She put a hand to her chest, feeling the lump the rings made under her shirt, then jerked it away. "I don't think so. Thank you, but no."

The lines around his eyes deepened. "Why won't you go out with me?" he asked.

Because you're too sexy and too good looking and I can't think straight when I'm with you. "I'm not interested in dating anyone right now."

"What are you afraid of?"

"I'm not afraid!" But of course she was. She was afraid of losing herself in some man's orbit again, the way she had with Carter. She'd spent so many years doing what he wanted, she was just now figuring out what she really liked and disliked and thought and felt. She wasn't ready to give that up. "I don't want to date anyone right now," she said again.

She didn't want to look at him, but she couldn't help it. She'd expected annoyance or disappointment, or maybe even a little embarrassment, but the anger that flashed in his eyes when his gaze met hers made her catch her breath. Had her answer really mattered so much to him?

"Jameso, quit distracting the help."

Rick burst into the office with his usual bluster, papers flying in his wake. He shrugged out of his fleece jacket and tossed a stack of mail onto Maggie's desk. More press releases, probably, plus a few bills and some junk. Her job was to deal with the releases, toss the junk, and funnel the bills back to him.

Jameso slid off the desk. "I was just leaving," he said.

Rick turned to Maggie. "I need you to set up an interview with Cassie Wynock."

"The librarian?" Maggie had avoided the library since her last confrontation with Cassie.

"You know any other Cassie Wynocks? She's written a play about the town founders. The drama society's going to put it on as part of Hard Rock Days. Go ask her about it, then talk to a couple of drama club people. We'll run it as promo for the festival."

"All right."

"Cassie still got it in for you?" Jameso asked.

"She's upset about a book my father took."

"She's upset because she was crazy about Jake and he didn't return her feelings," Rick said. "The book's only part of it."

So Maggie's suspicions were true. "My dad and Cassie were . . . involved?"

"He took her out a couple of times," Rick said. "I don't think he was ever serious, but I guess Cassie fell pretty hard."

Maggie turned to Jameso. He'd known her father better than anyone. "Is that true?"

"Jake was never serious about women," he said. "But he let them believe what they wanted if it got him what he was after."

"What was he after from Cassie?" Maggie asked.

"I don't know," Jameso said. His face was grim, the way it often was when he spoke of her father. "It was one of the things we argued about."

Maggie felt sick to her stomach. It shouldn't matter to her what a man she'd never known had done, but Jake was her father. The man she'd spent too many years imagining as perfect.

"I'll talk to Cassie," she said. Maybe she'd find out what had happened with her father. Or maybe she'd decide to avoid the subject, to avoid being disappointed by him again.

Lucille's eyes kept straying to the envelope lying on the kitchen table. Made of the slender blue paper used for airmail letters, it was addressed to Lucas, from Daniel Gruber, with a return address in Iraq.

Was Daniel Gruber D. J.? And why was he writing to Lucas, and not Olivia? Lucille couldn't decide if this was a good thing or not. Was the man trying to get back at Olivia through her son? Was this unexpected communication going to upset Lucas, who had clearly thought a lot of the man? If Olivia and D. J. had truly severed their relationship, wasn't it a bad idea to put Lucas in the middle?

If Olivia had been there, Lucille might have asked her all these things. But having arrived safely at her mother's house, Olivia was acting more like a teenager than a responsible single parent, staying out all hours, showing up only long enough to bathe or sleep or eat. She seemed to have gladly relinquished all but a token responsibility for her son to Lucille.

I should talk to her about that, Lucille thought, still staring at the envelope, which she'd laid at Lucas's place at the table. *The boy needs his mother.*

But the truth was, Lucas didn't seem to need anyone much. Since school had let out last week, he'd spent his days roaming the town on his bicycle. When he was home, he read books he'd checked out of the library about Indians or mining, or researched these subjects online. He ate the meals Lucille cooked and, when prodded, talked to her about what he'd done that day. He wasn't unfriendly, just terribly self-contained.

More than once Lucille had formulated lectures about how she wasn't running a hotel here and she wouldn't let Olivia take advantage. But when the opportunity presented itself, the words eluded her. She was so grateful to have Olivia and her grandson back in her life, she was reluctant to say anything that might drive the young woman away.

Coward, she told herself.

The scuff of tennis shoes on the concrete back steps alerted her to Lucas's arrival. He pushed open the door into the kitchen, his cheeks sunburned, his hair wind-blown, one knee scraped bloody.

"Where have you been?" Lucille asked, trying not to sound accusing.

"I rode my bike up to look at some mines," he said.

The nearest mines were miles from town, up steep mountain roads. "You rode up there on your bicycle?" she asked.

"Yeah." He shrugged, as if this was no big deal.

"You need to be careful," she said. Some of the shafts were disguised by piles of rock. Others looked deceptively shallow, then plummeted straight down like deep wells. Fallen timbers, jagged rusted metal, and even unexploded charges of dynamite littered the old tunnels. "Those old mines are dangerous places. Promise me you won't go in any of them."

"I'll be careful," he said. "Ms. Wynock already warned me about them."

Cassie had warned Lucas about the dangers of mines? "Did you tell her you were going up there?"

"I was looking for books about mines. I had to listen to her safety lecture before she'd let me look at them." He took a bottle of juice from the refrigerator and poured a large glass. "Is supper soon? I'm starved."

"It'll be ready in about half an hour." She didn't say anything about the letter. She half hoped he'd go up to his room or to the living room to the computer without noticing it. But he'd already spied the envelope on the table.

"What's this?" he asked, picking it up and turning it over.

"It was in today's mail." She watched his face for some sign of recognition, or even alarm.

He studied the return address, and a smile transformed his face from overly serious and mature-for-his-age to all boy. "It's from D. J.!" He ripped open the envelope and pulled out the letter, eagerly unfolding the pages. "He sent a picture!" He waved a photograph. Lucille came to peer over his shoulder at the photo of a dark-haired man in desert camo standing beside a tanker truck. He wore aviator sunglasses and smiled at the camera, revealing white teeth in a broad mouth.

"He says . . ." Lucas scanned the letter. "He says it was a hundred and twelve there last week—and they have spiders as big as rats. But he says the people are nice and the money is good, so mostly he likes it." He fell silent, his smile fading.

"What is it?" Lucille asked. "Is something wrong?"

He shook his head, then made a furtive swipe at his eyes. "He says he misses me."

Lucille tried to swallow past the knot in her throat; at the same time, a protective instinct fierce as a mother bear's rose in her. Why was this man writing and upsetting the boy this way? Why try to maintain a relationship that was impossible, with the man thousands of miles away and things so unsettled between him and Olivia?

The back door opened and Olivia herself came inside. She wore skintight jeans and a Dirty Sally tank top, her hair in twin braids, pink feather earrings dangling almost to her shoulders. "Mom, I got a letter from D. J." Lucas waved the sheet of paper like a flag.

Olivia's face paled. "What?"

"D. J. wrote to me. And he sent a picture. See."

Olivia snatched the photograph and studied it, as if looking for some hidden message in the image. "What does the letter say?" she asked, eyes locked to the photo.

"He says it's really hot, but he likes the people and the work he's doing. They have really big spiders there. And he misses me."

Olivia's fingers on the photo tightened. "He misses you," she repeated.

"Yeah, that's why he wrote. I'm glad he didn't forget about us when he left."

Olivia took the letter and scanned it, then let the page flutter to the table. Lucille could read the hurt in her daughter's eyes and could feel it in her own chest. There was no "us" in D. J.'s letter. He may have missed Lucas, but he hadn't written a word about Olivia.

She turned and headed for the door. "Where are you going?" Lucille protested.

"Out." She was gone, the windows still rattling from the force of the door slamming, before Lucille could utter another word. She looked at Lucas, but he was rereading the letter, seemingly oblivious to his mother's departure so soon after she'd arrived.

"He says he's got e-mail there, so we can stay in touch that way." Lucas jumped up. "I'm going to write him now."

"Do you think that's a good idea?" Lucille asked.

Lucas looked at her as if she'd just suggested that chocolate tasted terrible. "Why wouldn't it be a good idea?"

"Well, your mother and D. J. aren't dating anymore. . . ."

"So? D. J.'s my friend. I can have friends of my own."

"Of course you can," Lucille said weakly. And God knows, the boy could use a man in his life. But did it have to be this one—the one who still had the power to wound Olivia with a word?

Or with his silence.

The long days of summer brought a stream of tourists to Eureka County. Like salmon spawning upstream, they came in caravans of motor homes or motorcycles, sports cars or sedans. They hiked and fished and rafted and Jeeped. They photographed mine ruins and wildflowers and every building in town, and piled into the Last Dollar and the Dirty Sally in loud, sunburned, and mostly smiling bunches.

On summer afternoons, the normally deserted roads around town became clogged arteries of traffic. Retirees towing camping trailers inched around the narrow curves, white knuckled, while impatient daredevils tried to pass on the smallest straightaway. Tempers flared, and the sheriff's office responded to both accidents and brawls with equal regularity. In their wake, Rick inevitably sent Maggie. "Get good photographs," he'd say.

"Why do you want to run photos of mangled vehicles on every front page?" she asked him as he hurried her out the door of the newspaper office for the sixth day in a row.

"The locals like to see the tourons get theirs," he said.

"If it weren't for those tourists, this town might curl up and die," she said, mindful that she herself was practically a tourist—though she hoped not a touron, that melding of "tourist" and "moron" that Rick used to refer to all but the most attractive female visitors.

"Then think of the photos as a public service, reminding our visitors what can happen if they don't take it easy on the road."

So once more she set out with her camera and notebook, but by the time she reached the site of this latest accident—a scenic overlook west of town—there was nothing left to photograph but a mangled bumper and a dented guardrail. Maggie dutifully photographed this evidence, then stood for a moment between a Winnebago from Arkansas and a minivan from Texas, and savored the view of a mountain peak whose name she couldn't remember. A golden spill of tailings stained its side, and the remnants of an old mine tram ringed its middle like a rusty belt.

"It's pretty amazing anybody ever got up there, much less built all that," a man in a battered fishing hat who stood beside the Winnebago said.

"I guess the thought of all that gold will lead a person to do almost anything," a woman in a matching hat replied.

Gold probably had something to do with it, Maggie agreed. But she had a feeling that, for some of the pioneers at least, gold wasn't the only thing that drove them to climb mountains and stake their claim. Maybe some of them were charmed by the idea of conquering something bigger than themselves. Of making their mark in a place few others dared to go.

Before coming to Eureka, she hadn't thought much about the legacy she'd leave behind, but whether it was her father's death or her approaching fortieth birthday or the precarious nature of life lived on a mountaintop, the question nagged at her more these days. Would she remain in Eureka? Write a novel? Have a baby? Some days she felt as if she was holding her breath, waiting to find out what would happen next. She had a home of sorts here in Eureka, but her life still felt impermanent and unsettled.

Reluctantly, she returned to the Jeep and headed back toward town. She still wasn't completely comfortable driving in the mountains, so all her concentration was on the road, and she registered only annoyance at first when she saw the motorcycle parked in the narrow pullout to her right. What was he doing parked there? It was the wrong side of the road for the view, snugged up against the rock, and pulling back into traffic he was liable to cause a wreck.

Then the rider turned his head and she recognized Jameso. He had his helmet off and a wrench in his hand, tinkering with something on the bike. She didn't want to think too much about the way her heart sped up before her brain could even register that it was him. He'd taken her refusal to go out with him so cavalierly, she couldn't believe he'd really been serious, but sometimes—especially alone in her bed at night—she wondered if she'd made the right choice, telling him no.

Chapter 16

Maggie switched on her blinker and eased the Jeep in behind Jameso, managing to squeeze in between the cliff and the road, her rear bumper a scant six inches from traffic. She rolled down her window and stuck her head out. "What happened?" she asked.

"Fuel pump."

Right. As if that made any sense to her. "Get in and I'll give you a ride to town," she said.

"Thanks, but I can't leave the bike up here."

"I don't think you have much choice." She watched in the side mirror as the traffic crawled past. "I don't think anybody will bother it."

"This is a 1948 Indian Chief," he said. "There are people who would sell their mother for a bike like this."

She would have accused him of making a bad joke, but it was clear he was serious, in that way men had of being serious about things like cars and guns and all kinds of machinery. "No one I want to know," she said.

"Yeah, but they're around. I won't take the chance."

"So you're just going to stay up here babysitting your motorcycle?"

He stowed the wrench in a compartment on the side of the bike and eyed her Jeep. "I'm wondering if we take your backseat out, we could—"

"No! You are not loading that motorcycle into my car."

He opened his mouth as if to protest, then shook his head. "You're right. It would never fit."

"Why don't you call a wrecker or something?" she asked.

"Phone doesn't work up here."

She flipped open her cell phone and frowned at the message: NO SIGNAL.

He walked around to the back of the Jeep and began rooting through the contents: her dad's jean jacket, a pair of his boots, a piece of tarp, a coil of rope, and more ore samples.

"I can't believe you still have all Jake's stuff in here," he said.

"I've been too busy to pay much attention to what's back there," she said. "You can have any of it you like, except the jacket." The jacket she'd keep, to wrap around herself on cool nights and remember what little she knew about her father.

He took out the tarp and rope. "I'm going to cover it up."

"All right." She waited while he swathed the bike in tarp and rope. Now if anyone tried to steal it, it would be giftwrapped for them.

Twenty minutes later, he stowed his helmet in the back of the Jeep and climbed into the front passenger seat. "Thanks for waiting," he muttered.

"No problem. I'll take you into town."

"Take me to my place. I'll get my truck and the bike trailer. That is, if you have time."

"I have time." Rick was probably expecting her back at work, but he'd understand she couldn't leave a friend stranded. Besides, she was curious to see where Jameso lived.

He was silent the first ten minutes of the drive, staring out the window. When he did speak, his voice was subdued. "Go ahead and say it."

"Say what?"

"That I'm too stubborn for my own good. That I was stupid to even think about trying to take the bike."

"You're talking to a woman who has four cartons of antique glass taking up space in my living room. I'm not one to criticize anyone for being attached to some personal possession."

"Antique glass? Really?"

She nodded, then tightened her grip on the steering wheel. She hadn't asked Barb to bring the glass to her, but now that it was here, she wasn't in any hurry to deal with it. Common sense told her to sell the stuff, or find a way to display it so at least she could enjoy it. But no, it sat in those boxes, every piece a memory she didn't want to look at every day, but something she couldn't bring herself to release. "It's Steuben glass. My ex gave it to me."

"I bought the bike off a dealer in Tucson," he said. "It was the first purchase I made after I got out of the army."

"You were in the army?"

"I was in the first wave of troops sent to Iraq after nine-eleven."

"So you and my dad had that in common—you'd both fought in wars."

"Yeah." He shifted in the seat, leather creaking. "Have you interviewed Cassie about her play yet?"

So the war, or maybe her dad, was off limits as a topic of conversation. She could take a hint. "No, I haven't interviewed Cassie." She'd been putting it off, hoping Rick would forget about it.

"You're not afraid of her, are you?"

"No!" What was the deal with him always accusing her of cowardice? "Every conversation I have with Cassie ends the same. She hates my father. She wants the book he took from the library and didn't return."

"Why don't you just give her the book?"

She opened her mouth to deny she had the precious volume, but the lie stuck in her throat. Something in Jameso's expression was too knowing. She cleared her throat. "The book's all marked up. Someone—I suspect my father—took a black marker and blotted out the names of a bunch of mines. I can't imagine why."

"Poor old Cassie might stroke out if she saw that."

"Exactly, which is why I can't give the book to her. I should just burn it and be done with it."

"You don't strike me as the book-burning type."

"What do you know?" Of course, he was right. She'd grown up in a home where books were at least as valued as currency and not to be folded, spindled (whatever that meant), or mutilated. "Why would Jake mark up that book that way?" she asked.

"Haven't a clue. He was a hard man to figure out sometimes."

"Yet you remained friends, despite all the things you didn't like about him."

The knowing look was gone, replaced by a darker emotion. She recognized the mixture of grief and anger as one she'd felt after the dissolution of her marriage—equal parts frustration that someone she cared about wouldn't behave the way she wanted, and dismay at herself for caring so much.

"Do you remember studying the Roman god Janus in school?" Jameso asked.

"The god with two faces." Was he saying her father was two-faced?

"In the story, the god has a young face and an old one. A beginning and an ending. Now we think of someone as 'two-faced' when they're hypocritical or double-dealing. Jake wasn't like that, but he had two faces he could show to the world. He could be as kind and generous as anyone you ever met. If you were poor or hurt or someone had done you wrong, there wasn't anything in the world he wouldn't do for you."

"But he had a violent side." She thought of Bob's shattered face—and her mother's broken heart.

"Yeah, that was his other face. He could turn as cold as ice. On days like that, I think he could have killed a man and not thought twice about it."

She shuddered. "Why was he like that?"

"I don't know. Maybe it was something that happened to him in Vietnam. Or maybe he'd been like that his whole life."

"How could you be friends with someone like that?"

He laid his head back against the seat and contemplated the ceiling a moment. "Sometimes I think you just connect with people," he said. "The day I met Jake I was angry at the world. Mad enough to do violence. I was shooting a pistol at tin cans up in the mountains, but I could just as easily have shot the next person I saw. Except that next person was Jake."

"I take it you didn't shoot him."

"No, he was up there on one of his camping trips. I didn't realize it at the time, but he'd been drinking. He wasn't drunk, but he was, um, 'lubricated,' he called it."

The word surprised a laugh from her.

Jameso's half smile was both sad and sexy. "It was a good way to describe it. The alcohol loosened everything up."

"What were you angry about?"

"I didn't always need a reason in those days. I think . . . mainly it was just that life hadn't worked out the way I'd planned."

"I know the feeling."

He glanced at her. "I guess I was up there in the mountains having my own pity party when Jake showed up."

"What did he do?"

"He pulled out a pistol and started shooting right along with me. Even with a few drinks in him, he was a good shot. When we'd used up all our ammunition, he turned to me and said, 'It feels good to plug a few sometimes, don't it? If only we could blow our troubles away so easily.' Then he offered me a drink of his whiskey."

Male bonding over guns and alcohol. She supposed friendships had been formed on a lesser basis. "What was the life you had planned that didn't work out?"

"I was going to go into the army to earn money for college. Instead, I ended up in a foreign country that might as well have been hell. I was there fifteen months, scared to death every second. I saw buddies blown up right in front of me. I couldn't eat. Couldn't sleep. I came home a wreck, and the girl I'd been seeing before I left had married someone else without bothering to tell me."

"Oh, Jameso . . ."

He glared at her. "Don't you dare feel sorry for me. I'm not telling you any of this because I want your pity."

She swallowed. "Fine. Then why are you telling me?"

"You asked me why I stayed friends with Jake. It's because he knew what that kind of hell was like."

"So I was right. Your bond was the war."

"It was more than that. The two of us were a lot alike. I had that violence in me, too."

"Do you go around beating people up?" Was there a side of Jameso she hadn't heard about?

"No, but maybe Jake is part of the reason why I don't. I saw how he'd let his emotions rule him—how the drinking and the rages and the depression ate at him. I didn't want to be that way."

"So you just what . . . stopped?"

"I got rid of that gun. I cut down on my drinking. I started skiing and running and found other ways to deal with the emotions. I tried to share some of that with Jake, but he didn't want to hear it. He said he was too old to change. And maybe he was."

"Did he ever talk about what happened to him in the war? Or what he'd done before coming to Eureka?"

"We talked a little about the war, but in general terms. I know he was in Vietnam during the Tet Offensive in 1968. He mentioned that once when I talked about being in Fallujah. He said he'd seen some bad things over there. I didn't have to know specifics to imagine what it was like."

"And he never mentioned me, or my mother?"

"No, I'm sorry."

"It doesn't matter now." Jake was gone, and no amount of questioning his life would ever bring him back or make him into the father she wanted.

"Turn up here." Jameso indicated a side road on the outskirts of Eureka. The Jeep bumped down the rutted dirt track, past a row of weathered miner's houses, the narrow wooden buildings stair-stepped up the steep slope. Each was painted a different pastel shade—pink, blue, green, orange. Jameso's truck was parked in front of a lavender house, a white lilac in full bloom beside the front door.

"Nice place," Maggie said as she stopped the Jeep beside his truck.

"The rest are summer rentals." He unfastened his seat belt and leaned behind the seat to collect his helmet. "Thanks for the ride."

"No problem. I hope you get your bike fixed."

He opened the door and she thought he would leave; instead, he leaned over and kissed her cheek, his lips warm against her skin, the scrape of his beard pleasantly abrasive. "Jake missed out, not knowing you," he said.

Then he was gone, out the door and up the walk past the lilac, leaving her to sit with one hand to her cheek, her heart pounding wildly in her chest.

Chapter 17

"Upon this spot I will found a great city, to be named Eureka." Doug Rayburn, who was playing the part of Festus Wynock in the Founders' Pageant, lowered the script and looked at Cassie. "That doesn't sound right," he said.

"What do you mean?" She tugged at the front of the boned bodice of the dress that had belonged to her grandmother, hoping to somehow make it easier to breathe in the confining thing. This wasn't a dress rehearsal, but she'd hoped wearing the outfit would help her to get into her part as Emmaline Wynock.

"Eureka's a nice little town, but no one would ever think of it as a great city," Doug said.

"Festus was thinking of the future."

"But a line like that just makes him seem foolish."

In so many ways, her great-grandfather was a fool, but that certainly wasn't the point of the play. "Then what do you think the line should be?"

"I don't know. Maybe just 'I'll found a town named Eureka after my great discovery.' "

"All right." She winced as the boning in the dress dug into her sides. "Let's take the scene from the top."

Lucas Theriot ran to the center of the meeting room they were using as rehearsal space. "Gold! Gold!" he shouted.

"You there. Boy." Doug/Festus pointed at Lucas. "What's this nonsense you're shouting?"

"It's not nonsense, Mr. Wynock. Old man Haney's found gold."

Everyone waited, looking expectantly across the room. "Bob?" Cassie called. "Bob, that's your cue."

The old man shambled into the room. "Sorry, Cassie. I was busy." He tugged at the waistband of his pants.

"What's everybody so excited about a little bit of gold?" Toby Mercer stumbled into the scene, shirttails half untucked, hat askew. "There's a lot more valuable things in these hills than gold." He leered at Cassie and the others laughed.

She frowned at her script. "You came in too soon, Toby," she said. "And cut the leer at the end."

"Aww, come on, Cass," Toby said. "The leer is funny. And you told me this character, Jake, the town drunk, is supposed to be funny."

"Yes, but he's not supposed to steal every scene he's in."

"Never work with drunks, animals, or children," Toby said. "They'll always steal the show."

"Too bad the real Jake isn't here," Bob said. "He'd have gotten a kick out of seeing himself in a play."

"The character isn't Jake Murphy," Cassie protested, her face heating. "It's just a drunk who happens to be named Jake. Now everyone go back out and we'll start over." She looked around the room to make sure everyone was ready. "Where's Shelly?" Shelly Frazier played the part of Lucas's mother.

"Shelly can't make it." Tamarin spoke up from behind the backdrop of early-day Eureka she was helping to paint. "Sorry. I was supposed to tell you and forgot. Her dad in Miami is having hip surgery, and she had to fly down and take care of him."

"Then who's going to play the part of Annie?" Cassie tried to hide her annoyance. "Tamarin?"

Tamarin shook her head. "If I have to speak in public I get so nervous I throw up."

"Why don't you ask Janelle?" Bob said. "She's the right age, and I heard her say once she'd done some acting."

"Janelle wouldn't be right for the part," Cassie said.

"Why not?" Bob asked. "The boy and she are both blondes, though if you want a brunette she could wear a wig."

Honestly, Bob was so dense sometimes. "There were no lesbians in Eureka at the time this play is set," she explained.

"How do you know?" Bob asked.

Cassie scowled at him. "Never mind. Let's get on with the rehearsal. We'll leave out Annie's part for now. Lucas?"

Dutifully, the boy stepped forward. "Gold! Gold!" he shouted so loud Cassie fought the urge to cover her ears.

"You there. Boy." Doug/Festus pointed at Lucas. "What's this nonsense you're shouting?"

"It's not nonsense, Mr. Wynock. Old man Haney's found gold."

Bob started forward, but Lucas turned to Cassie. "Is that really how it happened?" he asked. "If I'd been the first to find gold, I'd have kept my mouth shut so no one would try to jump my claim."

"Bob couldn't keep his mouth shut to save his life," Toby said.

"It'd be hard to keep a secret like that in a small town anyway," Doug said. "Somebody would notice you were acting different, throwing more money around. They'd figure it out before too long."

"Where was that first mine?" Lucas asked. "And why did Festus say it was his discovery if old man Haney's the one who found it?"

"The mine was on land that Festus sold to Mr. Haney," Cassie said. "So he felt he'd played a part in the discovery."

"He should have gone out and found gold on his own, instead of trying to take credit for someone else's discovery," Lucas said.

"He's right," Doug said. "Festus owned the land the town was on, but not the mines. Maybe we should change the dialogue."

"We are not changing the dialogue," Cassie said, raising her voice to be heard over the clamor of discussion. "Say your lines as written. And no more questions. Bob, let's take it from where you come in."

She turned toward the door, but instead of Bob, Maggie Stevens stood in the doorway, a little notebook in her hand.

"Hello, Cassie," Maggie said, tilting her head in a way that was so reminiscent of Jake, Cassie's heart skipped a beat. "Is this a bad time? I wanted to talk to you about the play."

"We're in the middle of rehearsal," Cassie said.

"No problem. We can talk afterward." She moved to a chair along the wall and sat.

Finally, Bob came in and said his line, followed by more declaiming from Festus and a repeat of Toby's drunken protests, complete with leer, which again drew a big laugh.

Maggie rose from her chair. "You named the town drunk after my father?" she asked, two spots of red high on her pale cheeks.

"The character is *not* Jake Murphy," Cassie said, aware that no one believed the lie. "Jake is a very common name."

"The real Jake would have gotten a kick out of it," Bob said.

"He's the best part of the show," Toby smirked.

Maggie sat again, though she continued to glare at Cassie. Flustered, Cassie missed the cue for her line. "Somebody's got to feed and house all the miners who'll be pouring into town," she finally managed, after an uncomfortable pause.

"They're goin' to be thirsty, too!" Toby declared. "What we really need is another saloon."

"I'll drink to that," Bob said.

"Why don't we all head to the saloon and celebrate," Doug added.

"None of that is in the script!" Cassie protested.

"Too bad," Bob said. "It's pretty funny. I'll bet the audience would like it."

"This is not a comedy," Cassie said. "This is a serious presentation about the history of this town."

"Oh, lighten up," Toby said. "You don't want to bore people to death."

"I still say we need a few dancing girls or something," Bob said. "Eureka had its share of bawdy houses back in the day."

"What's a bawdy house?" Lucas asked. "Do you mean prostitutes?"

"Everyone shut up!" Years of quelling noisy patrons at the library stood Cassie in good stead, as everyone froze at her words, some with mouths half open. "We are going to present this play as written," she said, her tone cutting. "Now, one more time from the top—and no improvisation, unless you all want to stay here until midnight."

Meekly, everyone obeyed. The read-through went off without a hitch, though some of the actors delivered their lines with all the enthusiasm of prisoners. Cassie trusted that when the time came to perform for the public, the egotism that had drawn them to acting in the first place would assert itself and they'd present a competent enough performance.

"That was fine," Cassie said. "We'll work more next week. I want everyone to have their parts memorized by then."

As everyone filed out, Bob sidled over to her. "Don't you worry about a thing," he said. "I've got a surprise planned for the end that'll knock everyone's socks off."

"No surprises, Bob," she said, alarmed. "That's an order."

"Don't worry." He patted her arm. "You'll like this one, I promise."

She stared after him, too stunned to speak. No telling what

the old coot was planning. But she had three weeks to talk him out of it. Or she'd get someone to watch him and keep him out of trouble. Yes, that was probably the best approach. . . .

"Cassie? Can we talk now?"

She'd forgotten about Maggie, who stood beside her, wearing the expression of someone being forced to complete an unpleasant task. The woman should never play poker, that was for sure.

"What do you need?" Cassie asked.

"The paper is running a story on the Founders' Pageant. Want to tell me a little about it? How did you come up with the idea?"

Cassie launched into her prepared spiel—the one she'd written for the program to be handed out at the pageant—about how she wanted to honor the town's founders, and recognize its heritage and preserve its history for younger generations.

"And you thought portraying my father as town drunk was an important part of that history?"

She had thought it would be a satisfying way to take revenge on Jake, by reducing his memory to a caricature, but it wasn't turning out that way. Toby was turning the role into the favorite one in the play. "It's just a part," she said. "A bit of comic relief. It's not your father."

"Then why not change the name? Why not call him Casey?"

"Casey? No, I don't think . . ."

"Oh, forget it." Maggie shoved her notebook into her purse. "I'm tired of your little games. I don't know what went on between you and my father, and I don't particularly care, but get over it already. He's dead and you should let him rest in peace." She jammed a pair of sunglasses over her eyes, then turned and left.

Cassie let out a breath and sank into the nearest chair, the boning in the dress stabbing her ribs. Maybe she should change the name of the drunk from Jake—just in case his crazy daughter decided to sue.

As for the rest, yes, Jake was dead. But there were some things a woman could never forget.

The first Monday in July was a day off for Maggie, who'd worked the previous Saturday covering a massive bicycle race through the mountains. She planned to spend the day cleaning house, maybe even unpacking the Steuben, and deciding once and for all what to do with it.

Instead, Jameso stood on her doorstep, a modern-day mountain man clad in hiking pants and T-shirt, radiating testosterone and sex appeal in the brilliant sunshine. "Good morning, Maggie," he said when she opened the door. "I need your help."

Twice in one week this anything-but-helpless man was asking for her help, as if he'd honed in on her greatest vulnerability. "Did your bike break down again?" she asked. "Or do you have an elephant or a small tank you'd like to haul around in the back of my Jeep instead?"

"I'll be chauffeuring you today." His gaze swept over her, and she was painfully conscious of the faded black leggings and oversized sweatshirt she'd donned for today's role as charwoman. "Change into something suitable for a hike."

Just when she was beginning to feel fondly about the man, he did something jerky like ordering her around. "I'm really busy today," she said. "You'll have to find someone else to help you."

She started to close the door, but he shoved out one hand and stopped her. "Nope, you're the only one who can help. We need to get started, though. We don't want to be on the side of a mountain when the afternoon thunderstorms roll in."

"I live on the side of a mountain. If I was afraid of a thunderstorm, I'd have left a long time ago." The first time she'd experienced the violent onslaught of lightning, thunder, and hail that was a summer mountain storm, she'd been caught between abject terror and fascination. Once she'd persuaded herself she was safe inside the cabin, she'd perched on the edge of the love seat and stared out the window at the light show that rivaled any professional fireworks display. Electricity crackled in the air and lightning arced from the clouds like the flash of cameras that hailed the arrival of an A-list celebrity. Thunder like crashing surf shook the cabin, and hail beat on the roof as if some angry god were pelting it with rocks. Afterward, the world outside had glowed, washed clean and smelling of ozone.

"You don't want to be outside on the mountain during a lightning storm." He pushed the door the rest of the way open and moved past her. "You still have Jake's flag, right?"

"His flag?" She followed him into the living room. "What are you talking about? And I did not invite you into my house."

"He used to keep it under the stairs." He poked his head into the shadowed alcove beneath the risers. "Yep, there it is." He pulled out a long cardboard tube.

"Are you listening to me at all? You can't just come in here and make yourself at home, uninvited."

"I've got extra rope and carabineers in the truck, in case the ones from last year have gone missing," he said. "Hurry up and change. Jake always insisted we start at dawn, but I thought I'd better let you sleep in."

Maggie was not a violent woman, but he gave her no choice. She pounded on his back with both fists. "Listen to me. I am not going anywhere with you. Get out of my house."

"Don't you even want to hear what I'm proposing?"

"So far you haven't *proposed* anything. You've been ordering me around as if I was some dim-witted child."

"I never think of you as dim-witted." His gaze lowered to the vicinity of her chest and the corners of his mouth quirked up. "Or as a child."

She had to fight back a smile, which only irritated her more. She focused on the cardboard tube he held. "What is that?"

He popped the plastic cap off the end of the tube and shook out a red-and-white striped roll of fabric, which turned out to be a large American flag. "Jake flew it at the hermit's cabin, up on Mount Winston, every Fourth of July," he said. "I thought you and I ought to continue the tradition."

"Why did my father fly a flag at the hermit's cabin?" she asked.

"He said he wanted people to know the hermit was a very patriotic guy."

"You talk about it as if there really was a hermit," she said. "Was there?"

He shrugged. "Someone lived in that cabin a long time ago, but not for years. It was just a joke Jake played on the tourists."

"That doesn't mean I have to be part of the joke."

Jameso re-rolled the flag and slid it back into the tube. "Come with me. Please?"

She hesitated. What would be the worst thing that could happen if she spent the day with Jameso? That she'd stop resisting the physical pull between them? Barb would vote for that option. *You deserve to have fun after the hell Carter put you through.* Maggie could practically hear her friend whispering in her ear. But there would be nothing fun about getting hurt again. Jameso definitely had pain potential.

But if she turned him away, then every time she saw the flag flying on Mount Winston she'd play an awful game of what-if? "I'll go," she said. "But only because you asked nicely. And because I want to see this hermit's cabin up close."

She retreated upstairs to change. When she came down, dressed in jeans, hiking boots, and a flannel shirt over a T-shirt, she found Jameso leaning against the tower of packing boxes. "Is this your famous glass collection?" he asked.

"That's it."

"Nice." He looked at the boxes. "I can see why you love it so much."

"How's the motorcycle?" she asked.

"Repaired and safely in my garage. If we didn't have so much to carry with us this morning, I'd have brought it and given you a ride."

The idea of thundering down the road clinging to Jameso's muscular back sent a tremor through her stomach. "I'll pass," she said.

"Oh, you haven't lived until you've been on a ride with me."

The sexual inference was so overt Maggie had to believe it was deliberate. She turned away. "Let's get going. I have other things to do today."

Though Mount Winston was just across the valley from the cabin, the route there was a circuitous one, over bumpy back roads that navigated shallow stream crossings and wound along narrow ledges. "Why does everything around here take three times longer to get to than it should?" Maggie groused as the truck growled its way up yet another steep gravel slope.

"Maybe it takes just the right amount of time to get there," Jameso said. "And everyone else is in too much of a hurry."

"I used to feel as if my life was crawling by," Maggie said. "Lately it's rushing. I've heard that's a sign of getting old."

"You're not old," Jameso said.

"I'll be forty in September."

"Age is a state of mind."

"Do you have any other clichés you'd like to share?"

"I'm serious. I felt a lot older at twenty-six wearing full battle gear and staring down a kid with an IED in Fallujah than I do now at thirty-two."

Thirty-two. So she'd been right to think he was younger than her. Eight years wasn't that much, but still . . .

"We'll do something special for your birthday," he said. "Your first birthday as a free woman."

She didn't feel that free, not really. She was living in a different place, working a different job, but it didn't feel as if much inside her had changed. She was the same woman, with the same uncertainties and fears she'd always had. The impact of Jameso's words registered. "What is this 'we'?" she asked. "I told you I wasn't interested in going out with you."

"I've got a few months to change your mind."

She started to tell him he couldn't persuade her, but she wasn't exactly avoiding the man, was she? For all her resolve not to get involved, she kept tangling with him. He was like one of those sticker-filled vines she used to pull out of her garden in Houston: persistent and impossible to shake off. "I might not even be here in a few months," she said.

"Where would you go?"

"I was thinking of traveling. I've always wanted to do that."

"Could you really leave here, now that the mountains are in your blood?"

He made Eureka sound like some sort of communicable disease. "I'm sure people leave here all the time. Otherwise, we'd be overrun with tourists who showed up in June and never went away."

"People seldom leave once they belong here."

"I'm not so sure I belong here."

"You've settled in nicely. You have a home, a job."

"If that was all it took to belong somewhere, I could go to any state in the Union and have those things. That wouldn't make any of them home. And don't say my father's cabin is home. I'm not crazy about the idea of spending the winter up there."

"So get a place in town. I wasn't talking about the cabin, just that you fit in well with Eureka. Not everyone appreciates our quirks, you know."

"Imagine that." Just last week she'd written a story for the paper about a clash between summer residents who'd started a petition drive to install iron gates over every mine entrance in the district, and locals who'd pointed out attempting such a task would bankrupt the county in no time. But it wasn't only spending the money that people objected to, Maggie had learned. "The mountains aren't supposed to be as safe as a kindergarten," one man had explained. "It's dangerous up here, and people need to respect that." People in Eureka *liked* the danger; they were proud they'd survived it.

"We're almost there," Jameso said. "Or at least as close as we can drive. We'll have to hike the last three miles."

She started to protest that her idea of a fun day was not hiking three miles straight up the side of a mountain and then back down, but then she'd have to endure a pep talk from Jameso about how she could do it. Or worse, he'd accuse her of being afraid. So she kept quiet. The hike wouldn't kill her, and once she'd done it, her curiosity would be satisfied and she wouldn't have to do it again.

He parked his truck at a narrow pullout past the faint tracks of an old mine road and then pulled a backpack from behind the seat. "What's in there?" Maggie asked.

"Emergency supplies. Lunch. A few other things we'll need."

"Emergency supplies? I thought you said this was only a three-mile hike."

"If the weather changes suddenly, or one of us gets hurt, we could end up having to spend the night out. It's always a good idea to be prepared."

That whole danger thing again. Or maybe he was trying to impress her. She followed him up the trail, which quickly grew steep. "If . . . anybody . . . can hike . . . up here," she panted. "What's . . . to keep . . . anyone . . . from coming . . . up here?"

"It's not a trail on any map," Jameso said. "It's not even a real trail—more of a goat track. You have to really know where you're going to get there."

"And you're sure . . . you know . . . how to get there?"

He stopped and looked back over his shoulder. "Are you saying you don't trust me?"

Did she trust him? She'd tossed the remark off as another sally in the war of words they always seemed to end up in, but his questions forced her to think. "I believe you care enough about your own skin you wouldn't risk it on a climb you weren't sure about," she said.

"I'm much more likely to risk my own skin than yours," he said.

She flushed, searching and failing to come up with some flippant reply to diffuse this weighted remark.

"If I let anything happen to you, Jake would come back to haunt me," he said, and started up the trail again.

Chapter 18

When Lucas grew bored with riding around town on his bicycle or staying home with his books and computer, he liked to stop by Lacy's and look through all the old things. His grandmother would give him little jobs to do, and while he worked the two of them would talk. The conversations were rarely serious, but she enjoyed the insight into the way his mind worked. He was both sweetly innocent and scarily smart, both tough and vulnerable in a way that moved Lucille almost to tears at times.

Today he was sorting through a carton of yellowing newspapers that had been part of an estate Lucille had purchased in Montrose. She'd been ready to throw the box out when Lucas had asked to look through it. He pulled out a copy of the *Eureka Miner* dated August 1916. The headline was about a battle in France, but Lucas's focus was on a photo at the bottom of the page. The picture showed a train of burros weighted down with timbers and stovepipe and baskets of supplies for the booming gold and silver mines.

"Do you think there's still gold and stuff in the mines?" Lucas asked.

"I know there is," Lucille said. "The problem is, what's there costs too much to get out of the ground."

"Gold's worth a lot of money," Lucas said. "How could it cost too much to get out?"

"It takes expensive machinery. And there aren't roads up to some of the places, so they'd either have to build them or use helicopters. That costs tremendous amounts of money."

"What if there's something really valuable up there they don't know about yet—like some really rare mineral they can use to make nuclear weapons or something? That would make it worth spending the money to get it out, wouldn't it?"

Lucille smiled. The boy definitely had an imagination. "I suppose so."

"Then somebody should be up there looking in some of the mines, to see if they can find things like that."

"Maybe someone will someday." She set aside the set of silver candlesticks she'd been polishing, part of the same estate that had yielded the newspapers. "Are you about done sorting those papers?"

"Almost." He pulled out another sheaf of yellowing newsprint. "Can I take some of these home with me to read through?"

"If you want."

"There's a lot of funny old ads and pictures," he said. "I could scan some of them into the computer and send them to D. J.," he said. "He'd get a kick out of them. He likes machinery and stuff."

"So you've heard from D. J.?" Lucille had hoped, since the boy hadn't mentioned him, that the two hadn't kept in touch.

"We e-mail all the time." He refolded the paper, set it aside, and pulled out the next issue from the box—from the 1940s, Lucille saw. "I don't talk about it much 'cause it upsets Mom."

So he'd picked up on that. "You know, Lucas, your mother isn't upset with you," she said.

"She's mad that D. J. wrote to me, but he wasn't just her friend—he was my friend, too. Just because she got mad at him for not staying with us doesn't mean I was mad." He spread a section of paper out on the table and studied the photograph on the front page, of a narrow-gauge locomotive half buried in an avalanche. "Maybe when he's done working in Iraq he'll come to see me, and Mom won't be so mad at him anymore."

Lucille didn't think she imagined the wistfulness in his voice. Time to change the subject. "I'm looking forward to seeing you in the Founders' Pageant," she said. "Are you excited about it?"

He lifted his thin shoulders in a shrug. "I'm mainly just doing it because Ms. Wynock couldn't find anybody else."

"So she nagged you until you said yes." That was Cassie's usual approach to anything, from getting more shelving for the library to a historical survey of the town buildings. People gave in because they grew weary of listening to her.

"Not really. She asked me and I thought I should do it because she helps me find books at the library, and I don't think she has very many friends to help her."

Did Cassie have friends? Everyone in town knew her and most of them tolerated her, or accepted her as part of the fabric of the community. But Lucille could not think of a single person she would say was Cassie's friend. Had there ever been anyone? Were some people simply destined to always be apart?

She studied Lucas, his fair head bent over the old papers. He hadn't had a haircut since arriving in Eureka, and the blond locks curled around his ears and the nape of his neck. Lucille thought the longer style suited him, disguising the roundness of his head and the height of his forehead and size of his ears. "Have you made any friends here in town?" she asked. "Are there any boys or girls your age you, well, hang out with?"

"I know some kids." He pushed his glasses up the bridge of his nose. "I'm not really much for hanging out."

She resisted the urge to reach out and smooth the back of his head, as one would soothe a small child. "It's good to have friends," she said. "The longer you're here, the more people you'll know and the easier it will be for you to make friends."

"How long are we going to stay here?" he asked. "Mom hasn't said."

Olivia hadn't said anything to Lucille about her plans either. She was still dating Dan Brewster, though Lucille doubted the seriousness of that relationship; she'd also been seen in the company of at least two other men who frequented the Dirty Sally. Maybe that was for the best. If Olivia wasn't serious about any one man, she wouldn't feel the need to leave town if things didn't work out with one or the other. Lucille knew from experience a broken heart was a powerful motivation for travel.

"I hope you'll stay a long time," she said.

"Yeah, me too." His gaze remained fixed on the photo of the buried train engine. "Can you imagine what it would be like to wake up one morning and everything you knew had been swept away in an avalanche? Just wiped out by all that snow."

"No, I can't." Though her divorce had been like that: One day her world had been familiar and warm, the next it was empty and cold, home and family and her picture of the future wiped out with a single sentence: *I don't love you anymore*. The words were as cold and obliterating as a cataract of snow. She did reach out to stroke Lucas's head now. "No more avalanches for us," she said. "We'll stay here where it's safe and warm."

"It isn't always warm here," he said, turning over another page in the paper. "With all that snow, I'll bet it gets really cold in the winter."

Her winter would be a lot warmer if he and Olivia stayed, but the boy wouldn't understand such sentimentality. "You'll like it here in winter," she said. "You can learn to ski. Or snowboard."

"That would be cool." He straightened a stack of papers. "I'll take these home."

Home. She hadn't given the boy much in his life, but she wanted to give him that. She hadn't realized before he and Olivia moved in how empty the old house had been. How empty *she'd* been. She hadn't minded being single all these years, but the maternal side of her that had screwed up so badly years ago longed for a second chance. A chance to be a grandmother to Lucas—and the mother Olivia had never really had.

After the first mile of climbing the steep, barely discernible track, Maggie silently cursed Jameso for ever talking her into coming with him on this fool's errand. After another half mile, during which she turned her ankle twice on loose stones, she switched to cursing out loud.

"Who cares if the damn imaginary hermit flies the flag on the Fourth or not?" she asked.

"It's a tradition," Jameso said. "People would miss it if it wasn't there."

"Then those people should climb up here and hang the flag."

"Jake would have gotten a kick out of knowing you were carrying on something he started."

If Jameso had caught her in a more sentimental moment—say, after a few glasses of wine, or some time when every bone in her body didn't ache from the climb—she might have been swayed. In her current state, she could think of few things less absurd. "Do you really think I'm concerned with impressing a dead man?" she asked. "One who couldn't be bothered to have anything to do with me while he was alive?"

Jameso stopped and waited for her to catch up with him. "Good for you," he said.

"Good for me what?" She stopped beside him, bent forward, hands on her knees, trying to get more oxygen into her lungs.

"I was wondering if you'd been honest with yourself about what a bastard Jake was to you."

"I might have once had illusions about my father, but living here in Eureka has opened my eyes." She straightened. "Nice to know you've been so concerned about my mental health, but I'm fine. My father may have been the first man to disappoint me, but he certainly wasn't the last."

If they'd been on level ground, she might have swept past him in some grand gesture, but that was impossible on this slope—not to mention she wouldn't know which way to head if she did take the lead.

He took her arm and helped her up the trail beside him. She didn't resist, instead enjoying the strength and warmth of his grasp. It felt . . . supportive, not coercive. The difference was subtle, but important. "Tell me about these other worthless men," he said. "I assume your ex-husband is a chief offender. What was his name?"

"Carter. Carter Stevens. We met my freshman year in college. A friend introduced us. She told me he would be perfect for me and I was dumb enough to believe her."

He frowned at her, dark brows drawn together in reproach.

"Okay, not dumb," she amended. "But naïve. I was nineteen years old and had my life all planned out: I was going to get married, have children, and live happily ever after, and anything that didn't fit with that picture I ignored. The truth was always there right in front of me, but I refused to acknowledge it. It was as if I wore blinders for twenty years."

"What was the truth?" Jameso asked.

"That the thing Carter cared about most was Carter. He didn't want anything to inconvenience him, ever, and I played right along. I ran his business for discount wages, cooked his meals and kept his home, and let him convince me that children would be just too much trouble." Her breath caught on the last words, the injustice of it too much to bear.

Jameso's hand tightened on her arm and she swallowed hard, determined not to break down in front of him. "You'll make a great mom," he said.

"It's a little late for that now."

"My mother was forty-one when I was born and I turned out all right, though I suppose some would say that's debatable."

"Is your mother still alive?"

"Seventy-three and she swims two miles every morning and teaches a seniors' exercise class at the Y in Clearwater, Florida. She'd read the riot act to anyone who tried to tell her she was too old to do anything."

"She sounds like a remarkable woman."

"I have an affinity for remarkable women."

She chose not to acknowledge what might or might not be blatant flattery, but his words had cheered her. "Are we almost to the top?" she asked.

"Almost. The hermit's cabin is over this rise and to the left."

Sure enough, two minutes later, they topped the rise and Maggie saw a flash of red, which turned out to be a pair of bloomers flapping on a clothesline strung between two trees. She laughed. "I don't think I realized before that red was a pair of bloomers."

"Lucille's idea. She contributes the hermit and his wife's wardrobe every year."

The cabin itself was little more than a façade tucked up against the cliff, an old washtub anchored by a large rock beside the door. "Where does the flag go?" Maggie asked.

"Over here." Jameso led the way to a flagpole anchored in cement just beyond the clothesline.

"Who hauled a bag of cement up here?" Maggie asked.

"Who do you think?"

"Jake?" She glanced back at the path they'd just climbed. "But how?"

"When he put his mind to do something, he did it." Jameso took out the flag and let it unfurl in the breeze. "Come here and hold this while I fix it to the rope."

He fit carabineers into grommets along the edge of the flag, then fastened these to a rope on the flag pole. As the breeze caught the Stars and Stripes, snapping the banner in the wind, Maggie fought the urge to put her hand over her heart in salute.

"It looks nice up there, doesn't it?" Jameso came to stand beside her.

"How long do you leave it up?" Maggie asked.

"For a week after the Fourth; then I'll come up and get it. Jake originally thought he'd leave it up here year-round, but the sun and wind tears it up pretty quick, and it bothered him to see it falling apart like that. So he decided to just put it out for the holiday."

"Sounds like the hermit wasn't the only one who was patriotic."

"The two of them had a lot in common. Come on, we need to do the rest of it."

"The rest of it?"

He slipped the pack from his back. "Time to put fresh laundry on the line. Can't have the hermit and his wife going another year in those rags."

On close inspection, the garments on the line were in sad shape. The overalls were bleached almost white, and the bloomers had a long tear in the backside.

Maggie helped Jameso take the old clothing from the line. Instead of clothespins, the garments were held in place with spring-loaded clips that Maggie had to use both hands to open. Regular clothespins probably wouldn't have stood up to the gales that must assault this lonely spot, she thought.

They hung up a new pair of overalls, a white man's shirt,

and a green gingham dress. Lastly, Jameso extracted a pair of bloomers from his pack—white with large pink polka dots.

"Polka dots?" Maggie laughed.

Jameso grinned. "Lucille made them up special. I thought you'd get a kick out of them."

"Mrs. Hermit is certainly a colorful dresser."

When they were done, they stood back once more to admire their handiwork. If Maggie hadn't known better, she might have thought she had stumbled upon a remote homestead. All the scene needed was smoke curling from the stovepipe to be complete.

Why had her father gone to all the trouble to establish this elaborate tableau, with the cabin and the clothesline and the flag? He'd said he did it to fool tourists, but maybe he was really entertaining himself with this picture of a happy little life on the mountaintop, where a man had everything he needed to be content—the things that had eluded Jake himself.

"I'm glad you asked me to come with you," she said. "I never would have had a chance to see this otherwise."

"I'm glad you came, too. I was really dreading coming up here by myself this year. I thought it would be too hard, thinking of Jake."

"You really did love him."

"I did. The bad in him made the good that much easier to embrace. He was struggling with something, some secret, right up to the end. I always thought I'd get the chance to find out what that was. It doesn't seem fair that he didn't have more time."

"A secret? Do you mean me?"

"That was one secret, but I don't think it was the thing that troubled him so much—something in his past."

"Something that happened in the war?"

"That seems most likely, doesn't it? But I guess now we'll never know."

"I'm sorry I said what I did earlier, about it not mattering if the hermit flew the flag or not. It does matter."

"I was wrong, too," he said. "The past matters, but not as much as the present. Not as much as the future." His eyes met hers, intense and searching, as if looking for answers to a question she couldn't discern.

He took a step closer. "What do you want from me?" she asked.

"Too much, probably."

The admission startled her, and she might have stepped back, but he put his hand on her arm, steadying her. "I always want too much," he said. "But I'm learning to accept whatever you can give."

He leaned in and kissed her before she had time to think or move. When his lips met hers, she reacted instinctively, sliding one hand up to caress the nape of his neck, the other pressed against his chest, curled into the soft fabric of his shirt. His lips were firm, yet soft, teasing awake every nerve of her mouth, surprising a soft moan from her. In that moment, she was sixteen again—and twenty-six and almost forty, innocent and knowing, thrilled at the possibilities and terrified at what this might mean.

Jameso broke the kiss, resting his cheek against hers. She could feel the pounding of his heart beneath her fingers and was grateful for the strength of his arms around her, afraid she was too weak to stand on her own. After a long moment, he spoke. "I've been wanting to do that since the first night I saw you, standing on Jake's porch, defending yourself with a stick of stove wood."

"Was it the stove wood that did it for you?" Her voice didn't sound nearly as shaky as she felt.

"No, it was you. So beautiful and brave and . . . unexpected." He slid both hands around to the back of her neck and lifted her hair off her shoulders. Then he bent and kissed the soft skin at the side of her throat, and she felt her knees begin to buckle.

But he held her upright, and traced kisses down her throat

and along her collarbone, pulling the flannel shirt and the T-shirt out of the way to bare her skin. She arched her neck and moaned softly with pleasure. "What are you doing to me?" she managed to gasp.

He stilled. "You don't like it?" The words vibrated against her skin.

"I like it." Her hands slid up to clutch at his head, keeping him against her. "Very much."

He pulled his head up, grinning at her. Then he kissed her again. She melted against him, letting her regrets about the past and worries about the future recede. She wanted to act not because it was what someone else expected of her or what someone else said was right, but because it made her feel good right now, in this moment. Just being able to admit that felt like a powerful victory.

Jameso's hand slid beneath her shirt to rest on her stomach, the skin heated. Rough. "I'm wishing like hell there really was a bed inside that cabin," he growled. "Or that there was even a cabin."

"There's a bed at my place," she said.

His eyes met hers, but she held his gaze, a calm she hadn't imagined she could feel washing over her. All her anxiety and dithering was over. She wanted Jameso. And she wanted him as soon as possible. "Is that an invitation?" he asked.

"It is."

"Then I accept." He smiled, a look as sweet as any he'd ever given her, and she felt her heart pound, her emotions soar dangerously. She struggled to rein in her feelings. This wasn't about fantasy or commitment or any of those feelings. It was about lust and need and pleasure.

He took her hand and pulled her toward the trail back down the mountain, but she hung back, needing to know he understood. "I want to be with you," she said. "But don't expect too much. I still have a lot of baggage I need to deal with."

"Four boxes of Steuben glass."

"That, and other stuff." Internal stuff she wasn't ready to look at any more than she wanted to unpack that glass.

He turned to her again and traced one finger along her jaw, down the soft curve of her throat, where the edge of the chain stopped him. "What's this?" he asked, fishing the rest of the necklace from her shirt.

"Rings." She fought the urge to snatch them from him and tuck them away again, out of sight.

"Wedding rings." He rubbed his thumb along the curve of the thicker gold band and squinted at the engraving inside it. "Carter and Margaret, December 12, 1992," he read. Then he carefully tucked the necklace back into her collar. "More baggage?" he asked.

"Maybe." It wasn't as if she needed to wear the rings anymore; she just felt naked without them after so long. "Does it make a difference?"

His eyebrows drew closer together, a small V forming above the bridge of his nose. "It probably ought to, but where you're concerned, none of the rules seem to apply." Then he pulled her to him and kissed her again, more roughly this time, a kiss full of need and longing and all the emotions that she knew too well.

When he broke the kiss, they were both out of breath. Maggie looked away. She had to, or she might have pulled him down onto the rough ground to make love with him there on the cold mountainside. That wasn't what she wanted their first time to be. "We'd better go," she said.

"Right." He shouldered his pack and led the way down the trail. Maggie stopped at the edge of the trees and looked back at the little tableau of cabin, laundry, and flag. The pink polka-dot bloomers flapped smartly in the breeze, a comic salute to her father, who maybe enjoyed a last laugh from the grave.

They didn't speak on the way down the mountain, as if trying to give words to their feelings would break this spell.

He raced the truck at dangerous speeds over the rough roads, but she didn't protest. Already she felt cold away from his heat; she didn't want to delay being back in his arms.

When at last he pulled in front of the cabin and shut off the engine, she let out a sign of relief. Keys still in hand, he turned to her, his expression grave. "You haven't changed your mind, have you?"

"No, have you?"

"No, I just thought I ought to pretend to be a gentleman and give you a chance to back out of this—even though I'm not. A gentleman, that is."

"I probably wouldn't like you half as much if you were." She'd spent twenty years with a gentleman. Carter wouldn't have dreamed of making a crude statement or openly stepping across society's lines. His affair had been conducted with the utmost discretion, after all. But good manners hadn't made his betrayal any less painful, and there was something to be said for a man who'd go after what he wanted, damn the consequences.

"Good." They climbed out of the truck and she led the way up the steps to the porch, but before she opened the door, she turned to him, a question entering her mind that had to be asked. "This . . . this attraction between us—it doesn't have anything to do with my father, does it? Because you thought so much of him and I know you miss him and—"

His expression twisted somewhere between laughter and disgust. "My feelings for Jake didn't run in that direction—at all. Besides, I was drawn to you the first time I saw you, and I didn't even know Jake had a daughter."

"Good. I mean, I just wanted to be sure."

"Don't overanalyze this," he said. "Sometimes the feelings between a man and a woman—they're below the level of thought. More primal."

The words sent a shiver of arousal through her as powerful as his kiss.

And then they were inside, in each other's arms again, the

door still standing open behind them. She was dimly aware of him kicking it shut, even as he pushed the flannel shirt off her shoulders and tugged at the hem of the T-shirt.

Laughing, giddy with the joy of his exuberance, she tore herself away from him and grabbed his hand, then tugged him toward the stairs. She stumbled on the narrow risers and he caught her, his hands firm at her waist. She flashed him a look of thanks and felt her heart climb into her throat at the heat and anticipation in his eyes.

They undressed quickly and fell onto the bed, scrambling beneath the covers, the sheets cool against fevered flesh. She molded her body to his, reveling in the feel of the hard muscles of his arms and chest and thighs. "God, you feel good," she said.

"We're just getting started," he said, sounding amused.

"I was merely making an obser—" The word was strangled in her throat by a gasp as he fastened his mouth around one of her nipples and she thought she might very well shatter then and there.

The man knew what he was doing, that was clear. She didn't want to think too much about where he'd garnered such experience, except to be grateful that she was the lucky beneficiary of his talents now. Not that she didn't have a few talents of her own—enough to make him gasp and his eyes glaze over with a pleased, distracted look.

By the time he knelt over her and slid inside her, they were both half-crazed with wanting, the kind of wanting that left no room for embarrassment or self-consciousness—only room for pleasure, laced with a touch of tenderness that took her over the edge as much as the physical sensations he gave her. As she drifted down from that incredible high, the words of old wedding vows drifted to her—not the vows said at her own wedding, but ones she'd read in a book somewhere, or heard recited in a movie: "With my body, I thee worship." That's what she felt at this moment—worshipped. Like a goddess.

* * *

Even goddesses have to come down from the throne and deal with the mundane world. In this case, a bladder that was screaming for relief when Maggie awoke two hours later. Jameso snored softly beside her, stretched out on his stomach. She took a moment to admire his naked body before reluctantly pulling on a robe and heading downstairs to the bathroom.

As she washed her hands, she studied herself in the mirror. Hair mussed. Beard rash on one cheek. Lips slightly swollen. She grinned dopily at her reflection. One look and anyone would know what she'd been up to. And would be up to again, as soon as she woke up the sleeping stud in her bed.

But when she reached the bedroom again, Jameso was already awake and getting dressed. "Hey, where are you going?" she asked, wincing at the accusing note in her voice.

"Sorry." His look was full of apology, but his gaze shifted away before meeting hers. "I have to get to work."

When will I see you again? She thought the words, but she didn't dare say them. Hadn't she been the one to emphasize that she wasn't ready for any kind of serious relationship? Of course, that was before he'd rocked her world two hours ago. She hugged her arms across her chest, suddenly cold. "I had a great time," she said. "Not just the sex, but the hike, too."

"I had a great time, too." He stood, buttoning his shirt, then came forward and kissed her. Not the passionate kiss of a lover, but the tender kiss on the cheek of a friend. The way he might have kissed her if they'd never slept together at all.

She studied his face, trying to read the emotion there. The lines around his eyes seemed more deeply etched, but that might have been a trick of the fading light. "Is everything okay?" she asked.

"Everything's great." He patted her arm. "I'll call you later," he said. Then he shrugged into his jacket and headed past her, down the stairs and out the door.

She listened to his truck start up and drive away, and tried to figure out why she suddenly felt so rotten. Of course he couldn't stay here twenty-four hours a day. He had a job. He had a house. She'd told him not to expect too much from her, so she shouldn't expect too much from him. But this afternoon had been so . . . so *incredible.* Didn't that count for something? Didn't that change things—the way they had changed her?

She'd expected more than him just . . . walking away. Was it just that men always ended up walking away? Or that she was a woman who was easy to leave?

Chapter 19

Olivia liked her job at the Dirty Sally, especially on nights like this, when the customers didn't keep her too busy. The crowd was light, a mix of locals and tourists. A friendly bunch, nobody too drunk or too loud. She was making good tips. It wasn't what you'd call a career. She knew her mother didn't approve, but Lucille looked down her nose at pretty much everything Olivia did.

Her mother didn't understand that Olivia needed time to get her head together. She had a lot to deal with, with a kid like Lucas who, let's face it, wasn't a typical little boy. For one thing, he was scary smart, brilliant in a way Olivia knew she'd never been. But all those brains were too much for his own good sometimes. You couldn't fool a kid like that, couldn't convince him you always knew best just because you were the parent. Lucas saw through that bullshit like it was nothing more than tissue paper, which left Olivia scrambling sometimes to make the right decisions.

It wasn't as if anybody gave you a handbook on how to be a parent. God knows Lucille hadn't been much of an example. In those first days after she split with Mitch, she was either off working or locking herself in the bathroom to cry, leaving Olivia to pretty much fend for herself. The lesson Olivia got from that little episode was that she couldn't count on anyone else to pick her up when she fell down, which was fine until you fell so far down you really needed a hand, and then what?

She'd give Lucille credit for one thing anyway. She hadn't blinked about letting Olivia and Lucas move in with her now, and she looked after the boy. Lucas had really taken to his grandmother. He was one of those kids who got along better with adults than he did with other kids.

There was one adult she'd just as soon he not be so friendly with. D. J., damn him. Where did the man come off writing to her kid? Short of cutting off Lucas's Internet connection, there wasn't anything she could do about it, though. And if she tried that, Lucas would make her life holy hell, she knew. Better to just forget about it. Pretend it didn't matter. Because hell, why should it? All men were bastards. D. J. was just the latest in a long line, starting with her father.

"Take it easy on the glassware," Jameso said from the other end of the bar. "You keep slamming those mugs around, one's going to break."

"Yeah, yeah." She waved him away. Jameso was all right. The hottest guy in town probably, but he'd made it clear he wasn't interested in her. She'd been a little miffed at first, but he'd managed to be charming, not insulting, so she'd come to think of him sort of like a big brother.

A balding man in a new-looking Windbreaker that practically screamed tourist leaned against the bar. "Hello," he said in Olivia's direction, though his gaze shifted constantly, taking in the room, almost as if he was searching for something. Or someone.

"What can I get you?" Olivia asked.

"Bud Light." He pulled out his wallet.

Olivia drew the beer and set it before him. "You want to run a tab?"

"No, that's okay."

"Three bucks, then."

He laid a five on the bar. "Keep the change."

"Thanks." She rang up the sale and slipped the change into her pocket. "First time in Eureka?" she asked. Not that she was really interested, but it paid to be nice to good tippers.

"Yeah." His gaze roamed the bar again. "It's not what I expected." He turned back to her. "I mean, it's nice and all, just not the kind of place someone from the city would choose to live."

"You here on vacation?"

"Not exactly." He sipped the beer, then set it down again. "Maybe you can help me. I'm looking for someone."

Olivia stiffened. "Are you a cop?"

"A cop?" His laugh was loud. Abrasive. "No, I'm not a cop. I'm looking for an old friend. I heard she was living here now and wanted to say hello."

"What's your friend's name?" Olivia hadn't been in town long enough to know everyone, but the stranger was right about one thing—Eureka wasn't that big.

"Maggie Stevens. Do you know her?"

"What do you want with Maggie?" Olivia would have sworn Jameso wasn't paying any attention to the stranger, but the mention of Maggie's name brought him down the bar to stand in front of the stranger, his expression forbidding.

The stranger had balls, because he didn't back down in the face of Jameso's glare. Then again, he didn't know about the baseball bat under the bar. Olivia had never actually seen Jameso use the weapon, but she'd never doubted he would if circumstances warranted.

"Who are you?" the stranger asked.

"Jameso Clark. Who are you?"

"I'm Carter Stevens."

The name meant nothing to Olivia, but the effect on Jameso was remarkable: He paled, then flushed, and the muscles of his jaw tightened. Olivia got ready to duck, in case the bat came out. "Maggie doesn't want to see you," he said.

"If that's the way she feels, she can tell me to her face. Do you know where I can find her?"

"No." Jameso sent Olivia a look that made it clear he didn't want her opening her mouth about Maggie's whereabouts either.

When Carter turned to her, Olivia shook her head and stepped back. "Can't help you," she muttered.

She could see in his eyes that Carter wanted to say something, maybe something not nice, but he thought better of it. He slid the half-empty beer mug across the bar. "If you see Maggie, tell her I'm looking for her," he said.

He turned to leave, but in a moment of sheer bad timing, the door opened and Olivia's mother walked in, followed by Maggie.

"Hey, Olivia. Jameso," Maggie called, smiling. She had her red hair piled up on top of her head and wore a blue gauzy top that brought out the color in her eyes. The stony look on Jameso's face made her falter, and only then did she see the man at the bar.

"Maggie! It's so good to see you again." The stranger strode forward and enveloped her in a hug. Olivia thought Maggie looked like she wanted to throw up.

"Carter," she said when he released her. She stepped back, putting distance between them. "What are you doing here?"

"I've missed you, Maggie," he said. "I've been doing some thinking, and we need to talk."

If she'd set out to script a bad dream, Maggie would have been hard-pressed to come up with a more nightmarish scenario than standing in the Dirty Sally with her ex-husband while what seemed like half the town—including her new lover—looked on. She'd had no plans to come here tonight anyway, but Lucille had called and suggested a drink, and knowing Jameso would be working behind the bar had been an extra inducement to accept. She wanted to remind him of what he'd so recently left behind.

But any prospect for a fun, flirtatious evening vanished as soon as she stepped in the door. When Carter threw his arms around her, she'd felt paralyzed, able only to make a strangled noise in the back of her throat.

He released her, his expression filled with concern. "Are you all right? You're not going to be sick, are you?" He took a step back.

"Maggie, is this man bothering you?" Jameso had moved out from behind the bar and stood behind Carter, glowering with menace.

The very last thing she wanted was for Jameso to make a scene. "Everything's fine. Thanks." She managed a weak smile. Jameso's stony expression didn't waver.

"Maybe we could go somewhere more private." Carter looked around with the expression of someone who's afraid to sit, for fear of getting something nasty on his trousers.

"Maybe a table . . ." Maggie looked around the bar, but the only empty spot was a table by the front window. She and Carter might as well have their reunion in the middle of Main Street.

Behind her, the door opened, admitting Bob and Rick. Was it coincidence, or had word already gone out on the small-town grapevine that Maggie's ex was in town asking for her? "Hey, Maggie." Bob waved. "Who's your friend?"

"Maggie." Carter's voice held a note of warning—the same tone he'd used when they were married and she wasn't behaving the way he wanted. The tone a disapproving parent might use with a child. It should have made Maggie angry; instead, long-ingrained habit made her cringe. She took his arm.

"Excuse us," she muttered, as she dragged him toward the door.

Jameso didn't say a word, but she felt his eyes on her all

the way out the door. The street was full of people this time of evening. Danielle waved from the porch of the Last Dollar, and Reg lifted a hand from across the street. They had to get out of here, to someplace they could talk without an audience. "Where are you staying?" she asked Carter.

"I haven't decided yet." He glanced around. "This place doesn't appear to have much in the way of accommodations. Nothing suitable anyway." This from a man who insisted on staying with relatives on vacation because he was too cheap to spring for a hotel.

"You can follow me to my place," she said. The cabin was one spot she could be fairly certain she wouldn't be followed or spied on. Not waiting for an answer, she hurried to the Jeep and started the engine.

Carter was driving a nondescript rental, small and white and probably the cheapest thing he could find. Maggie tore out of town with him close behind, allowing herself a grim smile of satisfaction as her tires kicked up gravel and slung it back toward him. He'd be lucky to get down off the mountain without at least a cracked windshield. That is, if he could keep up with her.

She didn't make it easy, driving the road at a reckless speed that would have been unthinkable a few months before, when she first arrived in town. The Jeep's engine whined as she took the grades, tires skidding around curves. Carter faded farther and farther into the distance, the lights of his rental barely visible in the dust and growing darkness.

She parked the Jeep in front of the cabin and waited, absently fingering the rings on the chain around her neck. He rolled into the yard a full three minutes behind her. "Were you trying to get me killed?" he demanded, jumping out of the car as soon as he cut the engine.

"Don't tempt me," she said. Up here at the cabin she felt a little sturdier on her feet. "What are you doing in Eureka, Carter?"

"I told you. I missed you." One hand on the car, as if he feared he might fall, he took in the surroundings. "Where the hell are we?" he asked.

"This is the cabin my father left me. How did you find out I was here?"

"I saw the address on a letter Barb sent you."

"You were snooping through Barb's mail?"

"It was lying on the counter when I stopped by to see Jimmy."

"If Barb knew you were going through her mail, she'd scratch your eyes out."

"She doesn't hate me nearly as much as you think." He looked smug. "She even made a pass at me at their last Christmas party."

"She told me *you* made a pass at her."

"So who are you going to believe—a friend, or the man you were married to for twenty years?"

"The man who cheated on me for the last five years we were married? How is Francine, by the way?"

He cleared his throat. "Francine is well, thank you."

He let go of the car and took a few steps toward the cabin. "So this is the mountain retreat your father left you?" He looked smug. "I heard there was a gold mine also."

"Yes." Let him think what he wanted about that. "You said you wanted to talk to me, so talk."

"Maybe we should go inside." He started up the steps to the cabin.

"No." She raced over to block his way. The last thing she wanted was to have him inside her home—the only place she'd ever had that was truly hers alone. "We can talk out here. Say what you have to say and get out."

"Maggie." His tone was placating, his smile one she once had thought charming. "I realize we've had our differences, but I really want us to be friends." He glanced over his shoulder at the cabin once more, then to the battered Jeep in the drive. "I think I'm in a position where I can really help you."

Maggie could practically see the dollar signs turning over in his head as he calculated the worth of all her possessions. He'd scarcely noticed the spectacular view, as if something she could get for free wasn't worth acknowledging. "You don't have anything I want," she said. Not his money or his name or his company—all those things she'd once valued were worthless to her now.

"Oh, but maybe I do." He stepped forward and tried to take her hand, but she jerked away. He frowned, but went on. "I can see you've really settled in here. Made a new life for yourself. I'm glad."

She folded her arms across her chest, silent.

"Colorado really suits you." He nodded. "You look great, Maggie. Really."

He sounded sincere. Maybe even a little . . . wistful? No, Carter wasn't the wistful sort. "Get to the point. You didn't come all the way to Colorado to flatter me."

"No, I came because I've been feeling guilty."

The starkness of the confession caught her off guard. Guilty? Carter? "You should feel guilty," she said.

He ignored this. "I feel I wasn't generous enough in our divorce settlement. I was shocked to hear you weren't able to sell the house for a profit."

She fought the childish urge to make gagging noises. "And how do you know how much I got for the sale of the house?" she asked.

"Sales records are public," he said. "I asked my new secretary to look it up."

The fact that he saw nothing wrong with this snooping showed his true character hadn't changed a bit. "You had no business doing that," she said. "You're not a part of my life anymore."

"I wanted to do something to make your situation more equitable," he said. "I was thinking I could make an additional cash settlement."

Right. Mr. Cheapskate was going to waltz in here and

offer her more money. "Fine. Write me a check and I'll run and cash it before you can stop payment."

"I'll be happy to write a check. In return, you could do me a little favor."

"I knew there was a catch."

He looked wounded. "No catch, Maggie. I just thought that in exchange for the money, I could take the Steuben collection off your hands."

"You want the glass?" The idea made her a little dizzy. Of all the things Carter could have demanded from her, she never would have suspected the Steuben. "You gave me that glass."

"And since we don't have a relationship anymore, I thought you'd be happy to give it back. It doesn't really fit the lifestyle you're living now and instead of all those reminders of the past, you could have a nice sum of cash in the bank."

"That glass was a gift. You don't just take back a gift."

"I'm not proposing to take back the gift. I'm prepared to pay you for it. Ten thousand dollars."

She narrowed her eyes. "The last insurance appraisal was for twenty thousand dollars."

"Yes, but that's replacement value. Wholesale is only half that, so I thought . . ."

"Get out." She pointed a finger toward his rental.

"All right, all right. I won't argue with you. Twenty thousand." He pulled his checkbook from his back pocket. "Is the glass still in storage in Texas or do you have it here?"

"You are not getting that glass. Now get out before I push you off the side of this mountain."

Her rage finally got through to him. "What's happened to you?" he asked. "You've changed, and it's not for the better."

"I don't give a fuck what you think of me anymore."

"Maggie! Language!" His eyebrows rose.

She laughed. "Have I offended your sensitive ears?" she

asked. “The man who was fucking another woman while he was married to me?”

“There’s no need to take that tone with me.” He’d reached the car now and opened the door. “I’ll come back when you’ve had more time to consider my offer. I’m sure you’ll make the right decision.”

“I don’t ever want to see you again!” she shouted. She clenched her hands at her sides, shaking with fury. For the first time she understood the kind of rage that could have moved her father to violence against another person. “I won’t be responsible for what happens if you come near me again.”

But she doubted he heard the last; he’d slammed the door and the rental was lurching down the road, dust billowing in the red glow of the taillights.

Maggie stood in front of her steps, swaying a little with the same sense of vertigo and incipient panic she’d felt at ten years old when her pet goldfish had died and her mother had flushed its golden body down the toilet. She’d wanted to reach into the bowl and fetch it back, even though she’d known it would be a bad idea. Having anything more to do with Carter was also a bad idea, but the reflex of years made her want to keep even an antagonistic hold on that remnant of the woman she used to be.

Chapter 20

"So what's the story on you and this ex-husband who's hanging around?" With the directness of an investigative reporter grilling a corrupt politician, Rick confronted Maggie two days later at her desk in the *Eureka Miner* office.

"There is no story. My mother always told me if you couldn't say something good about someone, you shouldn't say anything at all, so I'll keep my mouth shut." She stared at her computer screen, trying hard to give the impression that she was focused on her work and had no time for interruptions.

"So why is he still in town?" Rick perched on the side of the desk. "Olivia Theriot tells me he's been in the Dirty Sally every night."

"I don't know why he's in town. I'm not speaking to him."

"Bob thinks he's still carrying the torch for you, but my theory is he heard about the French Mistress and thinks you've come into money."

"Right, Rick. If I'd really come into money, would I be driving a ten-year-old Jeep and working for you?"

"Maybe you're one of those eccentric millionaires who doesn't like to flaunt her wealth. Danielle thinks he's consumed by guilt over how he treated you and wants to make amends."

Maggie gave up her pretense of work and glared at him. "Why is everyone discussing my business behind my back?"

"Well, we all had to decide where we wanted to be in the pool."

"The pool!?" She rose. "My personal life is not to be a source of public entertainment."

Rick slid off the desk and retreated to the door. "We wouldn't open it up to anyone who didn't know you," he said. "If it makes you feel any better, Jameso refused to place a bet."

Jameso. There was another man who was on her trouble list. He'd been conspicuously absent since that evening in the Dirty Sally. His avoidance of her was a wound that cut deeper than she wanted to acknowledge. She'd been a fool, thinking sleeping with her had meant anything to him. He'd got what he wanted and now he was backing off. So typical.

But that didn't mean she hadn't cried herself to sleep two nights running over his betrayal.

"Look at it this way," Rick said. "The gossip mill turns both ways. We'll be sure to let you know if we hear any dirt on your ex."

"The subject is closed," Maggie said.

Rick shrugged, then sauntered into his office and closed the door. Maggie waited until she was sure he was settled, then pulled out her cell phone and did what she should have done two days ago.

"Hello?" Barb answered on the second ring, though Maggie could hardly hear her.

"You sound like you're in a wind tunnel," she said.

"Sorry." The sound of fumbling, then Barb returned, her voice clearer. "I'm at the salon and I was seated next to the dryers. It's better now."

"Should I call back?"

"No, I moved into a massage room. No one will bother us

here. I'm just waiting for my pedicure to set before I put on my shoes."

Once upon a time Maggie had spent long afternoons at the salon with Barb, reading celebrity gossip magazines and pondering the fashion implications of Cherry Bomb versus Pink Party toenail polish. She felt only a twinge of nostalgia, remembering. Opportunities to show her toes here in the mountains were so few as to make toenail polish inconsequential.

"What have you been up to?" Barb asked. "How's the job going? How are Jameso and Reg and Danielle and Janelle? Does everyone miss me?"

"Everyone misses you, including me."

"My tan is fading, so I'll definitely have to get back up there soon. Not to mention it would be divine to escape this killer heat. It's been over a hundred degrees for fifteen days in a row."

"The high in Eureka yesterday was seventy-eight."

"Stop being so cruel while I sit here melting."

"Did you know Carter is in Eureka right now?"

"Carter? No! What's he doing there?"

"I was hoping you knew. I know why he *says* he's here."

"Because he realized what an asshole he was, and he's come to beg your forgiveness and shower you with riches in an attempt to mitigate his sins."

"That's not too far off from the line of bull he tried to feed me."

Barb laughed. "You're kidding. He actually said that?"

"Not in so many words, though he did say he thought the divorce settlement might have been a trifle unfair and he wanted to make it up to me with a check."

"Maybe he got religion. Or joined a twelve-step program. Aren't they supposed to try to make amends to all the people they harmed in the past?"

"I don't think Carter is particularly religious or sober." Definitely not the latter if he'd become a regular at the Dirty

Sally. "He offered to pay me if I'd do him a little favor in return."

"What was the favor?"

"He wants the Steuben."

"The Steuben?" Barb's voice rose in a squeal.

"Yes, all of it. For a mere ten thousand dollars, he was willing to take all those painful reminders of the past off my hands."

"The crook. Didn't it appraise at twice that?"

"He did up the offer to the full twenty grand when I turned him down the first time."

"Are you going to take it?"

"Barb! Why would I sell the Steuben to him?"

"You're right. It is beautiful glass. I bet it looks fabulous with all those windows in the cabin."

Maggie groped for some believable lie. "It will look fabulous, I'm sure," she said.

"You haven't even unpacked it, have you?"

"No."

"Then why not sell it to Carter?"

"If I was going to sell the glass—and I'm not saying I would—but if I did, it wouldn't be to Carter. Why should I give the man anything he wants?"

"Good point. Why *does* he want the glass, anyway?"

"I was hoping you could tell me. He let drop that he and Jimmy still see each other. What does Jimmy say?"

"That Carter cheats at golf as badly as he ever did. I promise you that's the only time they see each other. You know they've been in the same foursome for years. But I haven't had him and the rich bitch to the house or anything."

"He must have stopped by before or after a golf game when you weren't there. He said he saw my address on a letter you'd addressed to me."

"Probably the thank-you card I sent after my visit."

The card had featured a full frontal nude of an extremely, um, *virile* young man. Barb's idea of a thank-you. "You don't have any idea why he wants the Steuben bad enough to come all the way to Eureka to try to get it?"

"No, but I'll ask around. You say he's still there?"

"Yes, but I have no idea why. He hasn't been stupid enough to approach me again."

"I'll get right on it and get back to you. And, honey?"

"Yes?"

"If you do decide to sell the Steuben, I can help you find a good buyer. One you don't have any emotional ties to."

All well and good, Maggie thought. But what about her emotional ties to the damned glass? She didn't want to have to look at it every day, but there was something to be said for having it.

Cassie parked her car behind the giant lilac bush down the street from the offices of the *Eureka Miner* and pulled her grandfather's fishing hat down lower on her head. Her grandmother's best friend, Sue Ellen Partridge, had planted the lilac slip in 1943, emptying her dishwater on it twice a day and wrapping it in old quilts all winter to keep it alive. The bush had thrived under her care, and when the city had threatened to chop it down in 1966, the Garden Club ladies had marched in protest in front of the mayor's house. The mayor had argued the bush was a traffic hazard, but the Garden Club ladies had argued that people ought not to be driving so fast in a residential neighborhood anyway. They'd offered a compromise in the form of a hand-painted warning sign. *Hazard Ahead,* it read, with a picture of a bush looming over the sidewalk and a driver craning his head to see around it. The sign had vanished long ago, stolen by vandals, but when she was a little girl, Cassie had thought it meant the bush was liable to leap out and grab unsuspecting passersby. For years she'd insisted on crossing the street on this side of town.

A familiar red Jeep pulled to the curb in front of the office and Maggie climbed out. There wasn't a trace of the city girl in her hiking boots and jeans and summer-weight sweater, though the silk scarf she'd wound through her coppery hair had a stylish flair to it. She didn't even glance toward the lilac bush before she went into the newspaper office and shut the door behind her.

Cassie started her car and cruised past the office. If anyone saw her, they'd merely think she was out for a drive. She'd left her assistant, Gloria Sofelli, in charge of the library for the afternoon, telling her only that she had "personal business" to attend to. Not a lie. She couldn't imagine anything much more personal than her errand this afternoon.

Out of town, she picked up speed and headed up the road toward Mount Garnet. Today was Tuesday, the day the weekly issue of the *Eureka Miner* went to press. Barring breaking news—a rare event in Eureka—Rick and Maggie would work until at least six compiling the paper.

Traffic lessened the higher Cassie climbed on the mountain. She saw no one she recognized, only tourists gaping at the view, hands white-knuckled on the curves. The last half mile to Jake's place she passed no one at all. Perfect.

She pulled into the rutted drive leading up to the cabin and nosed the car alongside the house, where it was mostly hidden from the road. She wasn't worried about Maggie interrupting her, but she didn't want anyone else to take note of her car there and report back to the newspaper office.

Before she went inside, she took a moment to look around. She'd never been to Jake's place, though she'd imagined it often enough. Some people might think of it as little more than a shack, but she recognized the little touches of a true mountain man—the sturdy rock pillars, the carved railings on the porch, the elk antlers mounted over the door. The cabin was like Jake himself—rugged and handsome and strong.

She tried the door, annoyed to find it locked. Who locked their door way up here? Certainly Jake never had. Reaching up, she felt along the door lintel until she found the spare key. Did Maggie even know about this one? It was tradition in these parts to keep a spare key over the door. Such a key could save the life of a lost hiker or a traveler stranded in a blizzard. She fit the key in the lock and shoved the door open. The cabin was small but neat, and smelled of vanilla. Definitely a woman's home. The quilts on the back of the sofa and love seat probably came from Lucille's shop, as did the wavy mirror on the wall. A couple of books shared space on the table by the sofa with a teapot, one of those little computer drive thingies, and a little vase of mountain pinks.

The only things out of place in the room were four large cardboard boxes that occupied most of the space between the love seat and the kitchen counter. *Fragile* was scrawled on the side of each in bold black marker.

Cassie checked the two books on the table. Cheap paperback romances, the kind favored by Janelle and Danielle. Nothing of concern to her. She moved on to the alcove under the stairs. This was crammed with a jumble of everything from an old oil lamp to a cookbook that dated from the 1950s, plus half a dozen cardboard boxes that would be worth looking into.

She set aside her purse and opened the first box. It was full of paperwork—letters addressed to Maggie, bank statements, a copy of Jake's will. Cassie examined the sheaf of legal papers. Jake's middle name had been Charles. "Jacob Charles Murphy." Cassie said the name out loud. A nice, dignified name.

Of course, Jacob had been anything but dignified. She set the will aside and pulled the next envelope from the carton. Really, Maggie ought to keep these things in a safe. Or a deposit box at the bank. Anything could happen to them in this cabin.

The envelope contained three photographs. Snapshots, really, the kind with white margins all the way around the picture, and the date in block letters in one margin. *Septem-*

ber 6, 1972, read the date on a photo of a very young Jake holding a swaddled baby. Jake held the baby slightly away from his body, the fingers of one big hand splayed to support the head. He grinned at the infant, such joy in his expression it made Cassie's throat ache. This was what Jake looked like when he was in love.

She'd wanted him to look at her that way, but of course, he never had.

The sound of a car engine whining up the grade made her freeze. The sound grew louder; then the vehicle turned into the drive of the cabin and stopped.

A door slammed, followed by the crunch of shoes on gravel. Not a woman's footsteps, though. These were too heavy. They clumped up the steps, across the porch to the door, and stopped. Cassie held her breath, waiting for a knock. It must be a friend of Maggie's who didn't realize she wasn't home. That, or an annoyingly enterprising salesman.

But no knock came. Instead, the knob rattled and the door creaked open. Too late, Cassie realized she'd forgotten to lock the door behind her. She peered around the opening of the alcove and stifled a gasp.

A man she'd never seen before stood beside the love seat. He was short and balding, with a small paunch showing beneath his golf shirt. He wore bright white tennis shoes, the kind that always make men's feet look like small boats. He glanced around the room and zeroed in on the boxes marked *Fragile.* He headed straight for them and pulled the top box from the pile and ripped it open.

Cassie watched, fascinated, as he lifted out what looked at first like a basketball-size wad of Bubble Wrap. He pulled at the tape that held the wrap in place, but it refused to give.

He turned away from the boxes and Cassie ducked back into the alcove just in time to avoid being seen. But the man moved into the kitchen and returned a few seconds later with a large knife. He sawed at the tape and began unwinding the

Bubble Wrap. Finally, like the heart emerging from an artichoke, he held up a fluted glass vase, the pale green of seawater.

Smiling to himself, the man clumsily wrapped the vase once more in about half the Bubble Wrap he'd removed and stuffed it back in the box. Then he picked up the box and headed toward the door.

He was going to steal the vase and whatever else was in the box. Of all the nerve! He couldn't just waltz in here and help himself to someone else's belongings. Cassie had come to take back what belonged to her, but she couldn't stand by and let him *rob* Maggie. She stepped out from the alcove. "Stop right this minute!" she called.

The man yelped—actually yelped—and juggled the box frantically before clutching it to his chest. He turned and stared at Cassie, wide-eyed. "Who the fuck are you?" he asked.

"That is no way to address a lady," she said primly. Her grandmother had taught her that etiquette, if wielded with the proper attitude, could be as effective a weapon as a sword. She moved farther into the room. "Where do you think you're going with Ms. Stevens's belongings?"

He drew himself up to his full height—all of five-eight, from what Cassie could tell. "These don't belong to Maggie. She was merely storing them for me."

Was he seriously suggesting someone who lived in a 600-square-foot cabin would offer to store something for someone else? Cassie couldn't see it. If someone as tidy as Maggie was going to have boxes taking up precious space in her home, they were going to belong to her, not some dumpy guy. "I don't believe you," she said.

The man scowled, wrinkles cascading all the way up his forehead. He resembled one of those wrinkly dogs—a bloodhound or a Shar-Pei. The image made Cassie less afraid. "What business is it of yours?" the man asked. "Who are you?"

"A friend." Not exactly the truth, but if he was going to lie, she could do so, too. She took a step sideways, toward the kitchen knife he'd discarded on the floor. "If Maggie was storing something for someone, she would have told me," she said.

"What are you? Her roommate? Fine. Then I'm the ex-husband. The bastard she's probably told you about. I gave her this glass and now I'm taking it back. And you can't stop me."

Without looking back, he balanced the box on one hip and turned and opened the door.

Cassie stooped to pick up the knife. She didn't know what she'd do with it, exactly, but maybe he'd respond to a threat. At least she'd be able to protect herself if he tried anything.

"Aarrgh! What the fu—?"

Cassie looked up from reaching for the knife in time to see the box slide down the man's leg and bounce on the floor. She caught a glimpse of brown and white—was that fur?—and heard the scrabble of footsteps on the front porch. The man's arms windmilled and he flailed wildly at the door, throwing himself against it until it closed.

Ashen faced, he gaped at Cassie. "What the fuck was that?" he gasped.

Cassie clucked her tongue. "Profanity is the sign of a poor vocabulary."

"I don't need a grammar lesson here, Grandma. Just tell me what the hell that is on Maggie's front porch."

At that moment, a large pale snout pressed against the window beside the door. The man shrieked and backed up toward the love seat, tripping over the box of glass as he did so, which sent him sprawling. No better than he deserved for calling her Grandma. But the fall put him a little too close to the knife. She kicked it across the room, where it slid under the stairs. Then she turned and stared, fascinated, at the bighorn ram that looked back at her with soulful eyes. "It's a bighorn sheep," she said.

"It attacked me," the man said, still prone on the floor.

"Bighorns aren't generally known to attack humans."

"I don't give a fuck what they generally do. This one attacked me as soon as I tried to go out the door."

The ram did seem to be guarding Maggie's door. When Cassie moved toward it, he left the window and she could hear his hooves scrabbling on the floorboards on the other side of the door. "Apparently he doesn't want us to leave," she said.

The man sat up. "Well, make him leave. I've got to get out of here."

Cassie sat on the edge of the love seat, as far from the man as the small room allowed. "I don't think there's anything I can do about the ram," she said. "Until it decides to go away on its own, we're stuck here."

"Well, shoot it. I thought all you mountain people had guns."

"No, that's all you Texans." She immediately wished she could take the words back. He didn't have a gun, did he? Surely not. He was the type of little man who would have felt the need to wave it around before now. "It's illegal to shoot a sheep without a tag," she said. "And right now is not hunting season."

"We're talking self-defense. That animal attacked me."

"If I did have a gun, I'd just as soon shoot you," she said coolly. "After all, you did break in and were stealing Maggie's glass."

"It's my glass. I told you. I paid for every damn piece of it."

Cassie could have made a similar argument about the book she'd come to retrieve—well, except for the payment part. But in her case, it was the truth. "You said earlier you gave the glass to her." She had certainly never *given* Jake the book, only loaned it, with the understanding that he'd return it. Which he hadn't. So in this case, he was the thief.

She forced her attention back to the man. "If you gave it to her, the glass belongs to her."

"Goddammit!" The man rose and took a step toward her. Cassie's heart hammered so hard she thought it must be visible through her clothing, but she kept her gaze steady on the man and fixed him with her best librarian's glare. "If you lay one finger on me, sir, I will kick you in the balls so hard you will be tasting them for the rest of your unnatural life."

The man froze, then swallowed hard. Cassie continued to glare. She didn't know if she could really kick him that hard, but what man wanted to risk finding out?

Chapter 21

"I know why Carter was so anxious to get the Steuben." Barb's voice rang with triumph across the crackly cell phone connection.

"Why is that?" Maggie steered with one hand around the first curve up the road toward the cabin. She didn't believe in driving while talking on the phone, but there was no place to pull over on this narrow stretch, and she was in a hurry to get to the cabin and back to town to finish putting together the paper. She couldn't believe she'd left her flash drive with the story on last night's town council meeting on the table by the sofa. Rick had pitched a fit when she told him. Then again, Rick was always pitching a fit about something, and since no one else would work for the wages he paid—and certainly no one would do as good a job as Maggie did—she didn't think her position at the paper was in jeopardy.

Still, she needed to grab the flash drive and hurry back to the office, or they'd be there until midnight putting the paper together. "I'm sorry, Barb, we had a bad connection there for a minute. Could you repeat that last part?" And this time, Maggie would pay attention.

"Francine wants the glass."

"Francine?" The woman already had more money than God, and she had Maggie's husband—now she wanted the Steuben, too?

"Yes, I heard from Jillian Patel, who heard it from Francine's cousin Michaela Jarvis, that Francine's best friend and chief rival, Anita Dickson, has this fabulous collection of Lalique glassware. So Francine decided that she needs to one-up Anita with a collection of vintage Steuben. Carter's job is to get the Steuben. She doesn't care how, but you can bet she's reminded him that he bought his first wife a collection of Steuben, so doesn't she deserve the same consideration?"

"And Carter, being the lazy cheap bastard he is, decided the easiest solution is to give her *my* collection."

"Exactly. He'll buy it off you and present it to Francine, fait accompli."

"Thanks, Barb. I'll let you know how it goes." She hung up the phone and tossed it onto the seat beside her. She'd throw every piece of glass down a mine shaft before she'd sell it to Carter to give to Francine.

She rounded a curve faster than she should have, gravel flying. "Calm down, Maggie," she told herself. "Deep breaths. You can handle Carter."

A single taillight glowed ahead. As the dust settled, she recognized a familiar figure on a motorcycle. Jameso hunched over the bike, the set of his shoulders kindling a mix of longing and fury in her. Maybe she'd chase him down and confront him about the way he'd slept with her, then proceeded to ignore her. Or maybe she'd skip the conversation altogether and pound him with a tire iron.

She followed Jameso for more than five miles, fingers white-knuckled on the steering wheel. Maybe he was headed to her cabin right now, to apologize for ignoring her and to beg her forgiveness. She enjoyed a pleasant few moments fantasizing about making him grovel before she granted his wish. But then he turned off on a side road, giving no sign he'd ever seen her behind him.

Fine. Let him be that way. The last thing she needed in her life right now was another damn man.

The anger that had been simmering since Barb's phone call exploded when she turned into her drive and saw a familiar white rental parked crookedly in front of the cabin. Carter! Damn the man, what was he doing here? She'd tell him exactly what she thought of him and his selfish ass, and then she'd chase him off the property with an ax if she had to.

She skidded to a halt beside the rental and was out of the vehicle while the engine was still backfiring. Winston greeted her at the bottom of the steps, butting her playfully. "Not now, Winston," she said. "I'm busy." The ram followed her onto the porch. She shoved him aside to get into the house.

"It's about damn time you got here!" A familiar, irritated voice greeted her. Carter stalked toward her. One of the boxes of glass sat in the middle of the floor and he shoved it aside with one foot to get closer to her. "Between that damn animal on your front steps and your roommate here, I can't get out of this town soon enough."

"Roommate?"

He looked over his shoulder and Maggie stared at Cassie Wynock, perched on the edge of the love seat like an old-fashioned schoolmarm come to tea. "Hello, Maggie," she said coolly. "I didn't expect you home until this evening."

"I forgot something." Maggie marched to the table and snatched up the flash drive. She addressed Carter first. "What are you doing in my house, uninvited?"

"I came to talk to you about the Steuben. The door was unlocked, so I let myself in."

"He was going to steal those boxes," Cassie said. "He would have, too, if I hadn't stopped him."

"You had nothing to do with it, bitch. It was that damned wild animal out there on the front porch."

"Don't you dare call me bitch!" Cassie rose, but Maggie's glare silenced her. She'd deal with the librarian later. For now, she wanted to focus her wrath on Carter.

She moved closer to him and stared directly into his beady little eyes. "You are not getting the Steuben," she said, her voice soft, so that he had to strain to hear. "You are going to leave this house and this county and this state, and never come back."

"It's a free country. I can go anywhere I want."

She leaned closer. "If you *ever* come near me again, I won't bother calling the police. Do you know how many mine shafts there are in these mountains? You would disappear and no one would ever see you again."

His eyes looked less beady, widened in alarm. "You'd be the first person the police would suspect of murder," he said.

"I don't think so. After all, I'm just meek little Maggie Stevens. I never so much as hurt a fly. But you could be the first. Now get out before I throw you out."

He scrambled toward the door but stopped with his hand on the knob. "What about that beast out there?"

She laughed. "What about him?"

"He attacked me before."

She went to the kitchen cabinet and took out three Lorna Doones. Then she took out three more. Winston deserved a reward for keeping her two intruders at bay. "While he's eating the cookies, you can leave," she said to Carter as she passed.

She felt him scoot past her while Winston nibbled the cookies from her hand. The engine on the rental squealed; then the car fishtailed out of the drive, sending up a rooster tail of dust.

Maggie returned to the house and Cassie, who was seated on the love seat once more, as still and upright as an artist's model. "What are you doing here?" Maggie asked.

"I came to look for my book," she said. "That man interrupted me before I found it."

"How did you get in? I always lock the door."

"There was a key over the lintel."

Maggie didn't want to know how Cassie knew about the

key. "And you thought you'd use it to come in and help yourself to my belongings."

"The book belongs to me," Cassie said. "I wouldn't have laid a finger on anything else."

"Wait here a minute." Maggie went upstairs and retrieved the book from the shelf by the bed. She took it to Cassie. "It's all marked up inside," she said. "That's why I didn't want to give it to you. I knew it would upset you."

Cassie paged through the book, the lines around her eyes deepening as she took in the obliterated text. "Why would Jake do something like that?" she asked.

"I don't know," Maggie said. "I didn't know him and I don't understand him—any more than I understand any man."

Cassie closed the book and nodded. "That man who was here—you were married to him?"

"Yes." Sometimes it was difficult to believe now.

"He's not very nice."

"No."

"I heard what you said to him. That wasn't very nice either."

"No, it wasn't."

"But it was very good." A small smile played around Cassie's mouth. "It doesn't pay to let a man get away with too much."

"No, it doesn't." She ran her thumb under the chain around her neck. She'd let Carter get away with too much for too many years. She smiled, remembering the shocked, scared look in his eyes when she'd threatened him. He hadn't been expecting that from meek little Maggie.

She really hadn't expected it from herself. But the rage and frustration had taken over. Or maybe she'd been channeling the ghost of her dead father, who no doubt would have tossed Carter out on his ass, and maybe Cassie, too.

She glanced at the woman beside her, who was running her hands over and over the cover of the book, stroking it. She didn't know what her father had said or done to hurt Cassie; she didn't want to know. But the cruelty of men could drive a woman to do strange things, so Maggie would overlook this particular lapse in judgment. "Are we even now?" she asked.

Cassie looked up. "What?"

"You have your book back. Are we even now? No more enemies."

"Of course." She stood, not meeting Maggie's gaze. "Come into the library tomorrow morning and I'll issue you a library card." She walked to the door and let herself out without a glance back.

Maggie picked up the box of glass and stacked it back with the others. So far the stuff had brought her nothing but trouble. She thought about opening the box and checking to make sure the pieces were intact. Maybe she'd take out a few and find a place to display them. But the idea roused no emotion—not sadness or curiosity or anything at all.

Carter had tried to steal the glass from her, but in the end he'd taken something else. Any sentiment she'd associated with the collection had left with him. She might even say he'd done her a favor. That and a library card weren't bad for an afternoon's work.

"How does this stuff get into such bad shape sitting in a box for a year?" Danielle attempted to unfold a clump of red, white, and blue bunting that looked as if it had been run over by a car before being stuffed into the cardboard carton.

"It's like this every year." Lucille pulled out a banner advertising Hard Rock Days. "But once everything goes up, it doesn't look so bad."

"How old is all this stuff anyway?" Olivia wrinkled her nose at a string of red and blue pennants, their pointed tips bent back on themselves.

"Probably older than you are," Lucille said. "Is the iron hot? We're going to have to iron all of this."

"How did I get appointed to the decorating committee?"

Olivia asked. She wet a finger and touched it to the iron, which sizzled satisfactorily.

"You were in the store when I decided it was time to get out the decorations," Lucille said.

"Lucky us." Danielle smiled and laid the bunting over the ironing board. "We don't have to actually hang this stuff, do we?"

"No, the power company sends someone over to handle that." Lucille smoothed the banner over her front counter. "I think I've got some black paint somewhere, to touch up the lettering on this banner."

"Why doesn't this cheapskate town spring for some new decorations?" Olivia asked.

"Because we're broke. And cheap. And these will look fine once we work on them a little."

The bells on the door of the shop jangled and Maggie backed in, her arms wrapped around a large carton. "Another volunteer," Danielle said.

"Lucille, you take consignments, don't you?" Maggie asked.

"I do. What do you have there?"

Maggie deposited the box on the front counter, on top of the banner. "Steuben glassware. I've got four boxes I want to sell."

"Steuben?" Lucille frowned. "You'd get more money for something like that selling it on eBay, or at a shop in Denver."

"I don't want to fool with that. Can you sell it for me? I don't mind paying your commission."

"I can sell anything eventually. And I know a few collectors who might be interested. Let's see."

Maggie ripped the tape off the top of the box and took out several wrapped bundles. Olivia and Danielle put aside their work to watch as Lucille peeled away layers of Bubble Wrap from around delicate vases, goblets, figurines, and bowls in orange, green, blue and pink.

"This is gorgeous," Olivia breathed, stroking the rim of a

pink and white bowl with the tip of one finger. "Why would you ever want to sell it?"

"My ex-husband gave me that bowl for my birthday two years ago," Maggie said. "The next day he left town on a 'business trip.' Turns out he went to Cancun with his mistress. I got the bowl; she got a vacation at the beach."

"Bastard," Olivia said. "If I'd known that, I could have slipped something into his drink while he was here."

"I heard he left town in a hurry," Danielle said.

"Good riddance." Maggie replaced the glass in the box. "Can you sell this for me?" she asked Lucille.

"Sure. You say you have more?"

"Three more boxes out in the Jeep."

"We'll help you unload it."

"Only if you stay and help us with the decorations for Hard Rock Days," Danielle said.

Maggie took in the wads of bunting and pennants. "What do you need me to do?"

"Iron, sew, paint, or join in the general griping about the sad state these things are in," Lucille said. "You don't have to stay if you don't want to, but we could certainly use the help."

"Sure, I can help. Just show me what to do."

The women carried in the rest of the boxes of glass, then turned their attention once more to the decorations. Olivia ironed while Danielle and Maggie tugged the bunting into shape and Lucille repainted the lettering on the banner.

"How long have Hard Rock Days been going on?" Maggie asked.

"This is the sixty-third or sixty-fourth year," Lucille said. "They may be older than that, but they started out as just informal competitions among the crews from various mines. Over the years it's grown into an all-weekend affair. But the highlight is still the mining games."

"I hope Jameso will be back in town by then," Danielle said. "I've been trying to talk him into competing this year."

"Jameso's out of town?" Maggie dropped the section of bunting she'd been holding.

"He left a few days ago," Olivia said. "Came into the Dirty Sally one day and asked for the time off."

"He didn't bother saying good-bye to Janelle and me," Danielle said. "That really isn't like him. Last time he left town, he asked us to watch his house for him."

"I got the impression something came up suddenly," Olivia said. "He was in a big hurry to leave."

Maggie had gone pale, though Lucille thought she was the only one who'd noticed. She'd suspected there was something going on between those two for some time. Had they had a fight? Something to do with Maggie's ex-husband?

Maggie noticed Lucille watching her and flushed. She focused on the bunting once more. "So what do y'all think of the Founders' Pageant?" she asked. "That's new this year, right?"

"I'm worried the tourists will think it's a big joke," Danielle said.

"No, they won't," Maggie said. "Tourists love that small-town stuff. They expect it to be amateurish and comical."

"Cassie will be crushed if people laugh," Lucille said. "She takes this sort of thing very seriously."

"Poor Cassie takes everything seriously," Danielle said.

"Lucas is excited about it," Olivia said. "He's been practicing his lines all over the house. 'Gold! Gold!' " She chuckled. "When he's not doing that, he's talking about mines and Indians and all that. My little historian."

Lucille didn't miss the note of pride in her voice. "Lucas is a remarkable boy," she said. "And I don't say that just because he's my grandson."

"I got a good photograph of him at the rehearsal," Maggie said. "I'll have to get you a copy."

"I guess you'll be covering Hard Rock Days for the paper this year," Danielle said.

"Yes, I'll have the best of both worlds—the inside track of a local and the experience of a Hard Rock virgin."

"You're definitely one of us now," Lucille said. "I hear you even have a library card."

"Yes, Cassie has apparently decided I can be trusted with that privilege."

"Are you going to stay in the cabin this winter?" Danielle asked.

"I don't know."

"A lot of the summer places become available after Labor Day if you want to rent one of them," Lucille said. "I could make some calls."

"Thanks. I'll think about it." She set aside the section of bunting she'd been working on and fished another from the box. "Or I could go back to Houston for the winter."

"You wouldn't stay? But you fit in so well here." Danielle leaned over and touched Maggie's shoulder. "You're one of us now."

Maggie shook her head but didn't elaborate.

"I've been thinking about moving on this winter, too." Olivia said.

Lucille stared at her daughter. "I thought you liked it here," she said. "And Lucas already knows the school and your job . . ."

"The Dirty Sally probably won't be as busy after the tourists leave, so they might not even need me this winter. And it's not like Lucas wouldn't do well in any school he's in."

"Where would you go?" Lucille asked.

Olivia shrugged. "I don't know. I could go anywhere."

Lucille wet her lips, aware of the others watching her. Had Olivia chosen this setting to drop her little bomb because she knew her mother wouldn't be able to start an argument? But she didn't want to fight with her daughter. "I'd hate to see you go," she said quietly.

Olivia ran the iron over the point of a pennant. "I figured you were tired of us by now."

"No, I've enjoyed having you here."

"We'd all love it if you stayed," Danielle said. "The town's different in winter."

"Because the tourists are gone?" Maggie asked.

"That. And when the snows start, sometimes the passes get blocked and we get cut off from the rest of the world for days at a time. You learn who you can rely on for help in those times. We all look after each other. It's sort of like a big family. There aren't many places left where you can say that."

"Just what I always wanted," Olivia said. "A bunch more relatives."

Danielle laughed. "Well, there are always those people who annoy you, but you learn to get along. And you're wrong about the Dirty Sally not being busy in winter—everyone holes up at the saloon during a snowstorm. There are times when I don't think Bob comes out of there for days."

Olivia looked doubtful but said nothing. The door to the shop opened and all the women turned to look at Rick. He had a sheaf of papers in one hand, and a pen tucked behind one ear. "Are the decorations ready yet?" he asked.

"Just about," Lucille said. "The power company doesn't need them until in the morning."

Rick turned to Maggie. "Do you have Jake's trophies?"

"His what?"

"His Hard Rock trophies. We're putting together a display of all the trophies we can find. They're all different, you know, and we thought it would be interesting for everyone to see them."

"Who's 'we'?" Maggie asked.

"The Hard Rock Days committee. Jake won three of the things. Can you bring them to the office tomorrow?"

"I don't remember seeing anything like that at the cabin," she said. "What do they look like?"

"They look like trophies. One of them has a guy with a

hammer, I think. Another may have a miner's helmet. I don't know. But they've got to be somewhere in Jake's things."

"I'll look," she said. "But I can't promise they're there."

"They're somewhere. Jake wouldn't have just thrown them away." He paused, then added, "Maybe you should go now. We don't have time to waste."

"Stuff it, Rick. I'll look for them tonight."

He opened his mouth as if to argue, then shook his head, turned, and left, slamming the door behind him. The other women waited until he was gone, then burst out laughing. "Maggie, I didn't know you were so feisty," Lucille said.

"I didn't use to be, but I've decided I'm through with men ordering me around."

Lucille smiled. Jake's daughter was definitely coming into her own. She glanced across the room at Olivia, who was bent over the iron, lost in thought. If only Lucille could find a way to get through to her. She didn't want to lose Olivia again, but she hadn't a clue how to keep her.

Chapter 22

The cabin definitely seemed bigger without those boxes of glass taking up room. Maggie wondered if she should have kept one or two of the nicer pieces. The teardrop candlesticks, or the lotus vase, maybe . . . She shook her head. Better to make a clean break. She had a new life now; she'd collect new memories.

Her father certainly hadn't been one to accumulate a lot of souvenirs and knickknacks, unless you counted the rocks, fossils, and ore samples scattered about. Just the other morning she'd found more of the little blue stones, tucked into a coffee mug at the back of a kitchen cabinet.

Now she was searching for the mysterious Hard Rock trophies. It wasn't as if she hadn't looked through Jake's things already; she'd have noticed three trophies if they were here. But Rick could nag worse than any woman when he had an idea in his head, so she'd look again and hope the trophies would magically turn up.

The only place she hadn't explored was the trap door under the stairs. She assumed it led to the crawl space—an unlikely storage space. Weren't crawl spaces damp and cold—

and full of spiders and other creepy crawlies? If Jameso was here, she'd ask him to go down there.

But of course he wasn't here, the bastard. Running out of town without a word to her, and why? What had she done wrong? Nothing. But that was just like a man. You couldn't depend on them. She didn't need him, not even to go down in the damn crawl space.

She shoved a toolbox out of the way to reveal the trap door. Standing behind the door, she grasped the ring and tugged. It came open much easier than she'd expected, flying back and landing against the floor with a bang. She jumped back and waited, staring at the opening. But no monsters, or spiders, crawled out. She tiptoed to the edge and aimed the beam of a flashlight into the opening.

A metal footlocker sat to one side of the opening, army drab beneath a layer of dust. Maggie's heart pounded as she studied it. Why was this hidden down here? Simply because it was convenient—or because Jake hadn't wanted to be reminded of his army days?

If she lay on her stomach, she could just reach one handle on the side of the footlocker, but one tug told her it was too heavy to haul through the opening. She'd have to go down to it. She played the light all around the area, but saw no signs of bugs, rats, snakes, or other undesirables. The space was cold, but dry, lined with rock. She studied the footlocker again. It looked as if it hadn't been disturbed for a long time.

Curiosity won over squeamishness. Flashlight firmly in hand, she lowered herself into the opening and knelt in front of the trunk. It wasn't locked; the lid lifted easily.

In the very top of the box lay a rifle—black and sinister, with an army green sling. Maggie balanced the light on one side of the box and carefully lifted out the weapon. It was heavy and cold in her hand. She shuddered and set it to one side, the barrel pointing away from her. Next came an army jacket, with a sergeant's stripes on the shoulder and a patch that read MURPHY over the breast pocket. She stroked the jacket, then put it to her nose. It smelled of musty canvas, no trace of the man remaining.

She laid the jacket across her knees, then reached into the locker and took out at leather case. It turned out to contain a row of medals: a Purple Heart, a small silver medal with a target on it, and a bronze medal with the image of a dragon and the words *Republic of Vietnam Service.* Why did he hide these away down here?

A brittle brown envelope proved to be Jake's discharge papers. He received an honorable discharge on July 11, 1973. She'd have been ten months old; why hadn't he come home after he got out of the army? What had happened to drive him away? The mystery tainted everything, unanswerable but demanding an answer all the same.

Next came a yellow envelope full of photographs. Jake as a skinny young man, posing in uniform with a rifle. The rifle she'd just taken from the locker? He grinned at the camera, all youth and bravado. Longing clutched at her—longing to have known her father when he was so young and happy. How would her life have been different with him in it?

Some of the pictures were labeled with unfamiliar names and places. Son My, Quảng Ngãi, and My Lai.

My Lai. The name rang a bell; some fragment from high-school history classes and those papers she'd written about the Vietnam War. My Lai was the site of a horrible massacre, American troops killing Vietnamese civilians. Had her dad been there?

She set the pictures aside. Near the bottom of the locker she found two photographs of herself, tucked into an envelope with a folded sheet of paper. The photos had been taken several years before. One was before a formal banquet—her and Carter. They were standing arm in arm near an arrangement of flowers. She was looking up at her husband; he was looking off to the side, out of the picture. How telling that pose seemed now; she'd spent so many years focused on that man, while he looked everywhere but at her.

The second photograph was of her alone. It was her favorite picture of herself, taken in her mother's backyard on a summer day. She was seated on the steps, legs stretched out in front of her, looking over her shoulder at the camera and smiling. She looked young and happy and almost beautiful. She stared at the image, feeling a great tenderness for the woman in the photo. She'd been through a lot since that image was captured; her mother's death, divorce, the revelations about her father. She was a different person now, and yet the same. She still wanted that happiness.

She tucked the pictures back in the envelope. These must be the photographs her mother had mentioned in her letter. Why had her father put them here, at the bottom of this box—because they were memories that were too painful to contemplate?

She removed the paper from the envelope and smoothed it out. The sheet had obviously been torn from a spiral notebook, with a ragged fringe down one side. Crooked writing covered half the page—looping, leaning letters a barely decipherable scrawl. She squinted and shone the flashlight on the page.

Dear Maggie, the letter began. She sat back on her heels, heart pounding.

> *I've written a lot of times over the years, but never had the guts to send the letters. I don't know if I'll send this one. You probably think I'm an asshole, and I guess I am. You probably think I never cared about you and if you think that, you're wrong.*
>
> *The first time I held you in my arms was the biggest miracle of my life. I couldn't get over how*

beautiful and perfect and pure you were. And all I could think of as I looked at you, lying there in my hands, was all the awful things those hands had done. I didn't deserve something as innocent and wonderful as you in my life.

I told myself if I went away for a while, I could get my mind together and make things right. Then I'd come home and be a good dad to you and a good husband to your mother. But things didn't happen that way. I wanted to come home, but I never could. The longer I stayed away, the easier it was to never go back.

I don't expect you to understand it. I don't understand it either. It was another terrible thing I did, another thing I have to live with.

The letter ended there, the words trailing away. Maggie stared at it, tears making hot paths down her face. She wasn't crying for herself this time, but for the man who'd spent his life so tortured. "You should have sent the letter, Dad," she whispered. "Maybe I could have found a way to make things better."

After a while the tears stopped flowing. She tucked the letter back into the envelope with the pictures and set it aside with the jacket. Then she leaned over and took the last items from the trunk: the three Hard Rock trophies, each wrapped in an old T-shirt. One depicted a miner with a pick, one was a miner's helmet mounted on a stand, and the third was a miniature hammer. *Hard Rock Champion, 2010,* this last one proclaimed.

She replaced the rifle and the medals and all the photographs except those of herself in the trunk, and carried the trophies, jacket, and the letter and pictures up into the cabin. The trophies made a whimsical display, set in a row on the table. Maybe after Rick was through with them she'd keep them up here. They fit the cabin—and her life now—better than the Steuben.

"People! People! Our first performance is less than a week away and I can't believe you all still don't have your lines memorized." Cassie climbed onto the set that served as the front porch of the general store, on the stage of the Eureka Opera House, and scowled at her cast. Doug Rayburn slumped in a chair in the middle of the stage, looking half asleep. Bob preened in the reflective glass of the storefront, Toby Mercer had a cell phone to his ear, and Lucas stood with his back to her, reading old advertisements taped to the wall. "Don't any of you care about this play?" She raised her voice, her throat tight, eyes stinging.

"Aww, Cass, it'll be all right." Toby hung up the phone. "It'll all come together opening night. You'll see."

"I ought to cut your part from the play altogether," she said. "I warned you about stealing scenes."

"I can't help it if I've got all the best lines," Toby said.

"You can't cut his part," Tamarin said from her seat on the front row. "The programs have already been printed."

"Not to mention he has half my cues," Doug said.

"Why don't we take a little break." Bob moved over from the window to stand beside Cassie. "You go freshen up a bit and when we come back it'll be better. You'll see."

She turned away, mortified that he'd recognized she was on the edge of losing it. "Ten minutes," she called over her shoulder. "You might use the time to study your lines."

She stalked off stage and out a side door that opened into a hallway leading to the lobby. Her great-grandmother had been the president of the committee that raised the money to build the Opera House back in 1898. The granite had been mined near Gunnison and hauled over the mountains by mule. The original stage lights had been oil-filled smudge pots, and the red velvet stage curtains had been special ordered from Denver. The building had been closed for thirty years when the historical society, led by Cassie, badgered the town council into setting aside funds for its restoration. Cassie knew her great-grandmother would have been proud.

But there was nothing to make Emmaline Wynock proud in the train wreck of a production due to debut on the Opera House stage in four nights. Half the actors hadn't learned their lines, and the other half looked ridiculous. Cassie was so nervous half the time she forgot her own part, which only flustered her more. And despite her best efforts to lose a few pounds, her grandmother's suit was still so tight she could scarcely breathe.

She'd intended to head straight for the ladies' room to bathe her face with cool water, but the scene in the lobby diverted her. Rick Otis had emptied out the front display case—which had held a tasteful collection of antique opera glasses, ladies' fans, a silk top hat that had purportedly belonged to Horace Tabor himself, and an original brass spittoon from the Opera House—and was arranging a motley assortment of figures on the shelves. "What are you doing?" she demanded, marching toward him.

"Hey, Cassie." Rick grinned at her—her first clue that he was up to no good. Rick never grinned at anyone.

"What are you doing?" she asked again, eyeing the items on the shelves. On closer inspection, they appeared to be trophies, though no two looked alike. They were gold and silver, tall and short, featuring human figures and inanimate objects. Rick had arranged some framed pictures among the trophies: front and center was a large photograph of Jake, looking much as he had the first time she saw him, strong and virile, an ax slung over one shoulder.

"The committee thought it would be a great idea to showcase the history of the event," Rick said. "So we got together as many trophies as we could from past winners, along with some photographs. It'll fit in well with your play about the history of the town, don't you think?"

She couldn't keep her gaze from the photograph of Jake. Looking at him still made her heart beat faster. "I didn't give you permission to use that display case," she said.

"The building—and the display case—belong to the town, not you."

"Almost everything in that case belonged to my family," she said. "And I am president of the historical society, which oversees the operation of the Opera House."

"You don't have to worry about the stuff in the case." Rick nodded to a cardboard box and a pile of tissue paper on the floor beside him. "I'm going to box it up and store it until after Hard Rock Days. Then I'll put everything back. I promise."

The plan seemed sensible enough, and it wasn't as if anyone would miss the antiques, except her. But that wasn't the point. The point was that Jake Murphy was horning in on her big moment. The man was dead, and he was still stealing attention for himself.

"Who's the guy in the picture?" Lucas Theriot wandered out of the men's room and over to them. He leaned toward the case, squinting in that nearsighted way of his. Cassie noted he came just past the top of her head, and his jeans were an inch too short at the ankles, as if he'd just had a growth spurt. "Did he win all these trophies?"

"Just three of them," Rick said. "That's Jake Murphy. He died earlier this year, but he was quite a character."

"What did he do?" Lucas asked.

Rick arranged the last trophy in the case and shut the door. "Jake did a lot of things, though I guess, officially, he was retired. He had a cabin way up on Mount Garnet, and he owned the French Mistress Mine."

"He owned a mine?" Lucas's eyes lit up. "A gold mine?"

"Well, I don't know if there was any gold in the mine or not, but Jake owned it."

"There wasn't any gold in the mine," Cassie said. "And Jake was just a man who drank too much and liked to make trouble."

"Now, Cassie—"

She turned away. Rick could say what he wanted in defense of Jake, but having a charismatic personality and an imposing body did not make a man a good person, and certainly not one to hold up as an example to an impressionable boy like Lucas.

Before Cassie could reach the hallway leading back to the stage, the front door of the Opera House opened and Maggie came in, camera around her neck. "What took you so long?" Rick called. "I want you to get a picture of this display."

"Hello, Cassie," Maggie called. "What do you think of the Hard Rock trophies? Aren't they a hoot?"

"I think they're ridiculous." Even though she was Jake's daughter, Maggie seemed to have a little sense. Maybe she could persuade Rick to move his display out of the Opera House. "They certainly don't belong here," she said. "Why don't you display them at the newspaper office?"

"Nobody comes to the newspaper office if they don't have to," Rick said. "I don't even like to go there." He moved the carton of antiques out of the way. "Back up for a wide shot, Maggie. And angle the flash. You don't want it bouncing off the glass."

"Rick, why don't you take the picture?" Maggie handed over the camera and stepped back next to Cassie. "That's what he wanted anyway," she whispered.

"I guess Jake's trophies were at the cabin," Cassie said. Despite her best intentions, her gaze kept straying back to the photograph of Jake, in the center of the case. Even in a picture he looked more alive than everyone else.

"I found them in the oddest place," Maggie said. "Wrapped up in some old shirts in the bottom of his army footlocker, along with some old pictures and medals."

"Jake was in the army?"

Cassie thought Lucas had wandered away, but there he was again, the little eavesdropper.

"You know Jake?" Maggie asked.

"Mr. Otis was just telling me about him. He said he owned a gold mine. What did he get medals for?"

"I'm not sure. He had a Purple Heart and a Vietnam campaign medal. I think the other might have been some kind of marksmanship medal."

"He fought in Vietnam? I've been reading about Vietnam in some old newspapers my grandmother gave me."

"I thought you were interested in local history," Cassie said.

"I like all kinds of history." He turned to Maggie. "Can I see the medals some day?"

"Maybe one day," she said.

The door into the auditorium opened and Doug leaned out. "Are we gonna finish rehearsing today or not?" he asked.

"Of course we're going to finish," Cassie bristled.

"You said ten minutes and that was twenty minutes ago."

"Come along, Lucas." Cassie took the boy's arm and towed him into the auditorium.

An hour later, Cassie had the beginnings of a migraine. Doug kept messing up his lines, which he complained were too pompous even for a man like Festus Wynock. Toby kept making horrible jokes and puns that weren't in the script at all, though he insisted they were all right because they always drew a laugh. Cassie finally threw down her script in disgust. "That's enough for today," she said. "Between now and Thursday's dress rehearsal I want everyone to memorize the script. You are to deliver your lines *as written.*" She scowled at Toby. "If you don't, I promise you will be sorry."

"Ooh, I'm scared." Toby drew back in mock terror. "Please, Cassie. Don't take away my library card."

The others laughed. Cassie turned away and almost collided with Bob. He put out a hand to steady her. "Don't worry, Cass," he said. "The play's going to be great. And that little surprise I told you about is going to work out fine. People will be talking about this show for months."

"No surprises, Bob." But she couldn't muster much heat for the warning. The play was going to be a disaster. And it was all Jake's fault.

Back at the paper, Maggie uploaded the photos Rick had taken. Her father grinned back at her from the framed portrait in the display case, a man in his prime without a care in the world. He certainly didn't look like someone with dark secrets.

But most people were adept at hiding the things inside of them. She'd spent years concealing her own dissatisfaction with her life from everyone around her—even from herself.

She zoomed in on the next photograph, of Lucas solemnly staring at the row of trophies. A cowlick waved from the back of his head, and the tag from his shirt stuck out. Such an odd little boy. How many children his age knew anything about the war in Vietnam?

Her stomach knotted as she thought of those other photographs of her father, of a tall, thin young man in fatigues, beard stubble darkening his face like soot, the handwritten legend *My Lai*.

She exited Photoshop and pulled up the Internet. A search engine request produced thousands of hits for My Lai. *"U.S. soldiers murder between 347 and 504 unarmed Vietnamese citizens,"* she read. She shuddered as she read further. Most of the dead had been women and children, many of them sexually abused or mutilated. Twenty-five officers and enlisted men were eventually charged in the massacre, though many other soldiers in Charlie Company were thought to have been involved. Only Lieutenant William Calley was convicted.

Charlie Company, First Battalion. Her father's unit. He had been there, in that horror. Was that the reason he couldn't come home, the reason he'd exiled himself to a mountaintop?

The massacre had occurred on March 16, 1968. She'd been born September 6. Jake had come home for the last time then and left soon after.

What had he thought when he looked at his newborn daughter? Had he remembered the babies killed in that little South Vietnamese village? Had he been responsible for any of those deaths?

She disconnected from the Internet and turned away, feeling sick to her stomach. Whatever had happened there in Vietnam, it had made her father unable to live in Houston, the steamy heat of the Gulf Coast reminding him too much of the jungles of South Asia. Whatever horrors he had lived through there kept him from being comfortable with those who loved him.

Had her mother known about My Lai? Had Jameso?

She stared out the window at the street in front of the newspaper office, willing a black-clad figure on a motorcycle to ride by. Dammit, where was the man? Why did men—her father, Carter, Jameso—always leave? She used to worry some flaw in herself drove them off, but now she saw it was a defect in them. They were cowards, every one of them.

Yes, cowards. What else to call a man who ran away from his responsibilities, who refused to face the consequences of his actions? Her father had hidden himself away in the mountains rather than allow himself to be vulnerable enough to face the truth and begin to heal.

Love was like that. Maybe that was why some people were

so afraid of it. Love zeroed in on the hurting places and ripped them open, exposing them so they could heal. It took courage to open yourself up to that pain—strength to be honest enough to expose your flaws and past mistakes. Maybe that was why love was easier for the young. They didn't have as many wounds to bear. They didn't need to protect themselves as much.

She shut down her computer and collected her purse. As she left the office, Rick was coming in. "Where are you going?" he asked.

"Home."

She drove the route up the mountain like a sleepwalker, negotiating the twists and turns from memory more than sight, her mind too full of everything she'd learned about her father and everything she'd realized about herself.

At the cabin she climbed to the loft and sat on the side of the bed, staring out at nothing and everything.

How much different would her life have been if her father had stayed in Houston? How would he have been different if he'd been able to talk about what had happened over there, to get the help he needed? He wouldn't have owned a gold mine or been a Hard Rock champion, but what other trophies would he have had instead?

And Maggie wouldn't be here now, waking up to this forever view and feeling stronger than she had in years. Was there really such a thing as fate? Did a divine Providence move people around like pieces in a cosmic chess match? She'd never believed it. She didn't like the idea of being anyone's pawn.

Yet she sat in her mountaintop aerie, grateful she'd found her way to this place, where she could heal and start over. Her father must have felt that way, too. Looking out at the world falling away from the top of a mountain gave a person a new perspective. Everything—even big problems—seemed smaller against that vastness. Possibilities seemed as endless as the horizon.

Her father's ashes were out there somewhere in these mountains, scattered across the land he'd loved. "Rest in peace, Daddy," she whispered. She stood, then wiped at the tears that brimmed in her eyes. Time to stop judging the man. He'd done the best he could. The best any of them could do.

Chapter 23

A man from Lake City won the Hard Rock competition, a hulking twenty-something who flexed his muscles for Maggie's camera, then filled his trophy with beer and spent the rest of the afternoon drinking from it.

Maggie went to the street dance, intending only to photograph it and go home, but Bob grabbed her hand and tugged her into the crowd. "A young woman like you shouldn't work so much," he said. "Life's hard enough as it is. You've got to dance whenever you get the chance." Then he led her in an energetic polka that left them both too winded to speak.

"You . . . all right?" she asked, when the song had ended and they stood puffing on the sidelines. The old man was red-faced and wheezing alarmingly.

He nodded. "Fit . . . as a . . . fiddle." He wiped his forehead with a red bandana. "Can't keel over now. Got the play tomorrow. Cassie'd never let me rest in peace if I died before I'd said all my lines."

"Is Cassie here?" Maggie searched the faces lining the dance floor for the little librarian.

"Her people never held with dancing. At least not public

dances like this, where everyone mingled together. The Wynock's always held themselves above all that. The most damning thing they could say about something was to call it common. They were always after Cassie to not be common."

"If they thought they were too good to associate with everyone else, who were Cassie's friends when she was growing up?" Maggie asked.

"Oh, she had friends. Her parents didn't always approve, but she was a typical teenager and didn't care. She dated a real nice boy in high school, I recall. Son of the family who owned a plumbing business. But that ended when he went off to college. Cassie's mother was ill by then, and Cassie stayed to take care of her."

"How sad." Maggie pictured a younger Cassie, caught between her parents' aristocratic fantasy and the rest of life in a small mountain town.

"Yeah, she had it pretty rough. But then, so have a lot of folks." Bob stuffed the bandana back in his pocket. "Blaming everything that happened in the past for how you are now only gets you so far. When it comes down to it, some people are mean just 'cause they want to be."

"Then what's your excuse, Bob?" Lucille slipped between Maggie and the old man. She handed Maggie a plastic cup of yellow liquid. "Lemonade," she said. "Though if you want something stronger, Rick has a flask he's passing around."

"I think I'll find Rick," Bob said. "Ladies." He nodded good-bye and pushed his way through the crowd.

"Bob's an enthusiastic dancer, even if he isn't a very good one," Lucille said. "I thought I'd come save your toes before he suggested another round."

"Thanks." Maggie curled her toes in her shoes. Bob had only tromped on them once, but that was enough.

"I haven't seen Jameso," Lucille said.

"Who said anything about Jameso?" Maggie felt her face flame.

"I thought that's who you were looking for."

She hadn't realized it, but she had been scanning the crowd, searching for that familiar black-bearded face. She sighed. "I'm furious he left without bothering to say good-bye."

"Maybe an emergency came up," Lucille said.

"Or maybe he was just being a bastard."

"Grandma, can I have money to buy a hot dog?" Lucas poked his head up between the women like a mountain pika emerging from the rocks.

Lucille smoothed the cowlick at the back of his head, though it refused to lie flat. "I thought your mother gave you money for dinner."

"She forgot. I was looking for her, but I saw you first. Hello, Maggie."

"Hello, Lucas. I think I saw your mother dancing with a tall blond man."

He frowned. "She's dancing with a lot of men. That's why I thought it would be easier to get the money from grandma."

Lucille opened her shoulder bag and took out her wallet. "How much do you need?"

"Ten ought to be enough. I might need two hot dogs. And something to drink."

While Lucille fished out the money, he turned to Maggie. "What was the name of your mine again?"

"The French Mistress." It still seemed odd to say she owned a mine, even an empty one.

"Did they mine things besides gold there?" he asked.

"What kind of things?" she asked.

"I don't know. Some places around here got silver, and even uranium."

The idea of radioactive material steps from her back door was unsettling. "I hope there's no uranium, or anything else dangerous."

"It's not that dangerous, trapped in the rock," he said. "You have to refine it before you can use it to make fuel or bombs or anything."

"Maggie isn't interested in bombs or nuclear power," Lucille said. She handed the boy two fives. "Meet me in front of the store at ten," she said.

"He seems to be a very intelligent boy," Maggie said when the women were alone again.

"Too smart for me or his mother," Lucille said. "I worry about him."

"Has Olivia said anything more about leaving town?"

The lines between Lucille's eyes deepened. "No, and I haven't asked her. Speaking of which . . . I sold a bunch of your Steuben this morning."

"You did? To whom?" Dread washed over her. What if Carter had returned to town and bought the glass for Francine. . . .

"A collector from Scottsdale in town for Hard Rock Days. He saw the glass in the window of the store and ended up buying most of it. Stop by the store Monday and I'll write you a check."

"That's great." Maggie felt a little weak at the knees. "Thanks."

"It ought to be enough to rent a really nice place for the winter," Lucille said. "I can put you in touch with a friend who's a realtor."

"I don't know . . ." She wasn't sure she was ready for a mountain winter—the cold and snow and isolation. "I haven't decided what I want to do yet." She could go back to Houston, to mild weather and movie theaters and Barb. She felt strong enough for that now.

"Whatever you decide, remember you've always got friends here." Lucille squeezed her arm. "This little town may not have much to offer, but there's that."

Maggie nodded. Eureka had given her a lot of gifts beyond the friends she'd made. For the first time in her life she had real choices, and the freedom to decide for herself. Where once the prospect of relying on her own judgment had frightened her, now she found it thrilling.

* * *

The baseball game the next afternoon was postponed due to elk on the field. Maggie stood on the sidelines with the other spectators and stared at the two dozen or so shaggy beasts grazing around the pitcher's mound or lounging in the base paths. Bulls with massive shoulders and towering spreads of antlers ambled among the brown and buff cows and long-legged calves.

"Can't they just shoo them away?" Maggie asked.

"Do you want to tell one of those bulls shoo?" Rick asked.

She studied the gleaming tips of the antlers again. Even without those intimidating weapons, each bull stood six feet tall at the shoulders, towering over even the tallest man here. "I guess not," she said.

"The elk are more interesting than the game anyway," Rick said. "It's supposed to be a replica of circa 1900s baseball between teams from the various mining camps. They played without gloves, with home-whittled hickory bats, and no protective gear. Everybody's so afraid of getting hit they play like a bunch of fifth-grade girls."

"I heard that!" Doug Rayburn protested. He moved over to stand beside them. "Two years ago, I broke my hand playing third base."

"If it's that dangerous, why don't you make it a regular baseball game and wear gloves and helmets?" Maggie asked.

"Then it wouldn't be authentic," Doug said.

"And you wouldn't have an excuse for playing so poorly," Rick said.

"It's just as well the elk showed up," Doug said, turning his attention back to the grazing animals. "Jameso's our best hitter. With him and Jake both gone, odds didn't look good for the Tommyknockers to win this year."

The mention of Jameso in the same breath as a dead man made Maggie's heart stop for a minute. "Where is Jameso?" she asked.

"Don't know," Doug said. "I figured he'd be back by now, but maybe he's not coming back."

The thought made Maggie feel as if she'd swallowed ice. Of course she was furious with Jameso for running out on her, but she'd never imagined she wouldn't get the opportunity to tell him so. Would he really leave so abruptly, so she'd never see him again?

"You ready to wow the crowd as Festus Wynock tonight?" Rick asked.

"I think everyone's going to be pleasantly surprised by this play," Doug said. "Festus wasn't the smartest mule in the stable, but he did a lot of good for the town."

"According to Cassie," Rick said.

"She might be a little biased, but she knows her history. Come to the play and you might learn a thing or two."

"Oh, I wouldn't miss it," Rick said. He turned to Maggie. "If you've gotten enough shots of the elk, let's head over to the food booths. We'll get some crowd shots and I'll buy you dinner."

"Make him pay for the buffalo burger," Doug called. "Not the cheap-ass dollar hot dogs."

Rick winced. "Maybe Maggie prefers hot dogs," he said.

"Oh, a buffalo burger sounds perfect to me," she said, grinning.

They started to make their way away from the ball diamond when Olivia stopped them. "Have you seen Lucas?" she asked.

"No," Maggie said. "Is something wrong?"

"No, but he's supposed to be at the opera house in half an hour and I haven't seen him all afternoon."

"He'll probably ride his bike over there," Rick said. "I see him all over town on that thing."

"You're probably right," she said. "I just thought he might like a ride in the SUV so he doesn't get all dusty and sweaty."

"He's playing a nineteenth-century ragamuffin," Rick said. "The dirt and sweat will look authentic."

Olivia nodded, distracted. "If you run into him, tell him I'm looking for him."

"We will," Maggie promised.

Rick watched Olivia walk away. "Best legs in town," he said.

Maggie rolled her eyes. "If you're interested, why don't you ask her out?"

"Who said I was interested? Besides, she's too young."

Maggie hadn't expected Rick to be so discerning. "Are you seeing someone?" she asked.

He arched his eyebrows. "Why? Are you making a play for me? I don't date women who work for me."

She flushed. "No, I'm not interested."

"You don't have to sound so disgusted. Besides, I thought you and Jameso had a thing going."

"You thought wrong." She took his arm. "Come on. You owe me a buffalo burger." From now on, her policy was to take what she wanted from men, but to never assume anything.

Perched on a wobbly stool in the Opera House ticket office, Lucille had a view of the display case filled with Hard Rock trophies. Jake grinned at her from the photograph in the middle—even dead he was at the center of things. She wished he were here right now. If nothing else, he'd have kept her entertained as she sold tickets to the tourists and locals who dribbled in in twos and threes.

A late-afternoon thunderstorm had blown in, typical for August in the mountains. Every time new theatergoers arrived, they brought with them the scent of wet pines and the astringent tang of the mag chloride the county put on the dirt streets to keep the dust down. "The show starts in half an hour," she told a trio of middle-aged women in matching sweatshirts that advertised a town in Texas. "Enjoy."

"Lucille! Where is Lucas?"

Cassie, face peony pink from too much blusher, leaned

into the ticket window. "Where is Lucas?" she demanded again, and scanned the tiny office, as if she suspected Lucille of hiding the boy.

"Isn't he backstage with the rest of the cast?"

"No, he is not."

"Then I'm sure he'll be here shortly. I know he's been looking forward to the play." He couldn't enter a room this past week without declaiming his opening lines, accompanied by various dramatic gestures.

"He's late. I told everyone to be here an hour before the curtain."

Lucille leaned closer, studying the black fringe around the older woman's eyes. "Cassie, are you wearing false eyelashes?" she asked.

"What if I am?"

"Nothing. I'm sure they'll look great from the audience." Though some people might wonder at the town's founding matriarch's resemblance to an aging cheerleader.

"When you see Lucas, you send him right backstage. We don't have a minute to waste."

"I will." Lucille tried to push aside her uneasiness. Lucas was usually a very responsible boy. What if something had happened to delay him? What if he'd fallen on his bicycle in the rain or a driver hadn't seen him . . . ?

"What time does the show start?"

A man's deep voice pulled Lucille from her reverie. She forced a welcoming smile for the imposing figure in front of her. He was tall and broad-shouldered, with closely cropped dark hair and an erect, military bearing. "The play starts at seven. Give or take a few minutes. We're pretty informal around here."

"I just didn't want to be late." He pushed a five-dollar bill toward her. "One ticket, please, ma'am."

Odd that, a young man by himself choosing to attend a small-town play. "Are you in town just for the festival?" she asked.

"Not really." He returned his wallet to his back pocket and accepted the ticket. "I came here to look up a friend."

"Oh. Who—" But the young man had already moved away, his dark head barely visible in the crowd flowing into the auditorium. Lucille stared after him, the hairs on the back of her neck standing at attention. Something about him had been so familiar . . .

"I hate to see a pretty woman frowning. Is there anything I can do to help?"

The bass voice had a radio announcer's smoothness, with just enough gravel to add sincerity. The voice's owner smiled at Lucille—a gentle smile framed by a neatly trimmed goatee frosted with silver, beneath sparkling blue eyes. "Thank you. I . . . I'm fine." She fumbled with the roll of tickets, flustered.

The man kept his eyes fixed on her. "One ticket, please," he said. "I'm a visitor here and thought it would be interesting to learn more of the town's history."

"Are you by yourself?" she asked, then wanted to take the words back. It really wasn't any of her business.

"For the moment, yes." He looked down at her hands. Was he checking for a wedding ring? The idea made her warm all over. "Gerald Pershing." He reached through the window, she thought to take his ticket, but instead he grasped her hand. "May I ask your name?"

"Lucille Theriot." She disengaged her hand from his, reluctantly.

"Perhaps I'll see you again, Lucille."

Then he was gone, replaced by two teenagers from town, and an Asian family who wanted seats in the balcony. Lucille sold them their tickets, in a fog as she counted their change. Had the handsome stranger—Gerald—been flirting with her? She couldn't remember the last time that had happened. Amazing!

"What are you smiling about? You look like you just got away with something." Olivia stepped up to the window, Dan Brewster in tow.

"Nothing in particular." She tore off two tickets for her daughter and Dan. "Have you seen Lucas? Cassie's been looking for him."

"I'm sure he's backstage somewhere. When I saw him this afternoon he said he didn't need a ride, that he'd peddle over on his bike."

"Maybe something happened in the rain. An accident or—"

"You worry too much. He'll be fine." She took the tickets and moved away, arm looped in Dan's as if she was afraid he might decide to run away.

"You don't worry enough," Lucille murmured. But if anything had happened to Lucas, someone would find her and tell her. It wasn't as if people didn't know where to find her. That was one of the beauties of being mayor of a small town—people kept track of you.

At seven on the dot, an usher pulled shut the doors to the auditorium and Tamarin Sherman came to relieve Lucille at the ticket window. "I know you want to see your grandson's big debut," she said.

"Then he did show up?" Relief washed over her.

"Did who show up?"

"Lucas. He's here?"

"Well, where else would he be?"

"Earlier, Cassie said he hadn't shown up yet."

"Oh, you know Cassie. She's always in a tizzy about something."

Lucille slipped through a side door into the auditorium. She thought about searching the crowd for Gerald, but the house lights were already down, so she slipped into the first vacant seat she spotted near the back. The auditorium was small enough that even from here she had a good view of the stage, and the set painted to look like Eureka circa 1890, a collection of wooden false-fronted buildings lined up along a single dirt street.

The actors were in their places: Doug Rayburn in the center, resplendent in a black frock coat and striped morning trousers; Cassie beside him, furiously twirling a parasol and blinking rapidly, false lashes fluttering like insects trying to find a place to light; Toby Mercer and Bob lounged to one side, wearing the flannel shirts and suspendered canvas pants of miners.

Lucas had the first lines of the play. Lucille leaned forward in her seat. She hoped Olivia had remembered to bring a camera. Or maybe Rick or Maggie would get a shot for the paper and she could get a copy.

"Gold! Gold! Old man Haney's struck gold!"

But instead of Lucas, Doug's daughter, Sylvia, blurted these words from the side of the stage, then ducked back into the wings. Doug struck a pose and began declaiming as Festus Wynock and the play was off.

Lucille sat back, deflated, and more worried than ever. Where was Lucas? Should she rush out of the theater and look for him? But where? Again, she tried to comfort herself with the knowledge that if something had happened, the sheriff or someone would come to the theater and tell her, but what if no one knew yet? What if . . . ?

Laughter from the audience signaled the arrival onstage of Toby Mercer, in the rôle of "Jake." "There's a lot more valuable things in these hills than gold." He leered at Cassie and the crowd roared.

As Toby continued his comic monologue, Cassie sent him looks that would have felled a weaker man. Her face was redder than ever and she clutched the parasol like a club. Lucille wouldn't have been surprised if she clobbered Toby with it. Meanwhile, he was clearly ad-libbing and stealing the show.

Bob took over now, showing off a nugget as big as a doorknob. Lucille knew it was, in fact, a large wad of aluminum foil, spray-painted with gold radiator paint. Lucas had several like it in his bedroom—rejects Cassie had deemed unacceptable for one reason or another. Where was that boy?

Thank God Doug was making his final speech—the one

about founding a town and naming it Eureka. Of course, Cassie wouldn't let him get away with the last word. She twirled the parasol and stepped up beside him on the make-shift dais in the center of the street and declared Eureka would be a place of learning and education and blah, blah, blah.

Just as most of the audience had begun to murmur and shift in their seats with restlessness, Bob strode to the center of the stage. "Enough of that pontificatin'," he declared. "If you're gonna found a town, then you ought to start with a celebration. And I say we ought to do it in style."

A cheer rose up from the audience, and from Doug and Toby onstage. Cassie glared at all of them and opened her mouth as if to protest, but about that time a deafening *Boom!* shook the building, and a cloud of black smoke poured in from offstage.

Stunned, the audience stared as the smoke billowed their way. Then someone up front stood and shouted "Fire!" and the stampede was on.

Chapter 24

From her seat in the front row, Maggie could see figures backstage wrestling with what looked like a large wooden crate—the source of the acrid smoke. She tried to get closer to investigate, but the smoke drove her back.

Behind her, the theater was in chaos, though Rick and some of the other men were doing a good job keeping everyone calm, directing them to exits. She listened and didn't hear the crackling of flames or the crash of falling timbers, or feel any heat, so maybe there wasn't a fire after all. Maybe this was just someone's idea of a prank.

She started toward the stage again, intending to mount the stairs on the sides and duck into the wings for a closer look, but just as she set her foot on the bottom step, a pair of strong arms pulled her back. "Where do you think you're going?" Jameso's face was very close to hers, the creases around his eyes deeper than she remembered, his voice a menacing growl.

"What are you doing here?" she asked, struggling against his iron grip. "I thought you left town."

"I'm back." He loosened his hold but didn't release her

completely. "Just in time, it looks like. Come on, let's get out of here."

"I want to see what's going on." She started up the stairs again and once more he pulled her back.

"No, you don't. One spark and this whole place could go up."

She started to argue there was no fire, but at that moment Bob raced by, carrying a fire extinguisher. "Don't worry, folks," he shouted to no one in particular. "We'll have her out in a jiffy."

Reluctantly, Maggie let Jameso lead her out a side door into the street, where most of the audience still milled about, studying the building for signs of flames. By this time, most of the smoke had dissipated.

Jameso stopped Toby as the actor ran past. "What happened?" he asked.

"Bob thought it would be a kick to set off fireworks at the end of the show. He said he had it all under control—a lot of noise and some confetti and glitter and a big finish. Go out with a bang, you know? But I guess he overloaded the charge. That black powder can be kind of touchy."

"He's lucky he didn't blow up the whole place," Jameso said.

"Aww, it's all right." Toby shrugged. "Cassie's a little upset, I guess. She ran home, but Bob said he'd fix things with her. Other than that, though, the play went real well, I thought. See ya." With a wave over his shoulder, he plunged back into the milling crowd.

Maggie finally shook free of Jameso's hold. She faced him, arms crossed, fury overwhelming her earlier relief at seeing him. "Where the hell have you been?" she demanded. "And why did you leave without saying a word to me—or to anybody else?"

His expression grew sullen. "It wasn't anybody's business where I was going and what I was doing."

"Oh, it wasn't? Did it ever occur to you there were people who might be worried about you? Did you ever think of them, or are you so self-centered you couldn't be bothered to concern yourself with anyone else's feelings?"

"Who were all these people who were so concerned about me?" His gaze bore into her.

"Danielle was asking about you. And Rick and Lucille . . . and lots of people."

His lips compressed into a tight line. "So nice to know they care."

"Jameso! You're just the person I need. And, Maggie, you can help, too." Lucille was out of breath. She clutched Jameso's shoulder, leaning on him a little.

"What's wrong? What do you need?" Jameso put his arm around her, holding her upright.

"It's Lucas. No one's seen him since this afternoon. He didn't show up for the play and he'd been looking forward to it for weeks. I'm afraid something has happened to him."

"Where could he have gone?" Maggie asked, alarmed. Children went missing in big cities, not in little mountain towns.

"I don't know." Lucille twisted her hands. "When I saw him at the ball game, he was eating hot dogs and talking about the Hard Rock competition."

"Do you think he ran away?" Jameso asked. "Back to where he lived before?"

"Why would he do that? He was happy here. And there was no one at his old home he ever talked about. He's still in touch with Olivia's former boyfriend, but D. J. is in Iraq. Lucas would know he couldn't go there."

"Did he say anything when you saw him last?" Jameso asked. "Did you see him with anyone you didn't know?"

"He wasn't with anyone. And he didn't say anything special."

"He was talking about mining." Olivia joined her mother.

Dressed in a pale blue tank top, her hair pulled back in a ponytail, she looked very small and very young beside her tall, broad mother.

"I remember he asked about the French Mistress," Maggie said. "He was fascinated with mining."

"Maybe he went up to the mine," Jameso said.

"The French Mistress? But it's so far."

"He might have hitched a ride part of the way with someone," Jameso said.

"But there's a gate over the entrance," Lucille said. "Jake told me he had one installed to keep out trespassers."

"A boy Lucas's size might squeeze through the bars," Jameso said.

"We've got to find him." Olivia's face was pale, her voice tight.

Jameso pulled keys from his pocket. "Maggie and I will go in my truck. The rest of you stay here in case he shows up. He might have gone somewhere with a friend, or decided to take a nap, or stuck his head in a book and forgot to keep track of the time."

"Yes, I'm sure he's all right," Lucille said, no conviction in her voice.

Maggie squeezed her friend's shoulder. "We'll call as soon as we know something," she said. "I'm sure he's fine." Then she hurried to catch up with Jameso's long strides. He was the last man she wanted to spend time with at the moment, but Lucille was right. For all his faults, Jameso was a man you could count on in a crisis.

Cassie sat bolt upright in her grandmother's rocking chair in the corner of the parlor, lights out, tears streaming down her face. She made no move to wipe them away. She was too paralyzed with fear and shame. All these weeks she'd worked so hard to present her family's story to the town in a dignified manner, and she'd been made a laughingstock. A fool! Festus was probably rolling over in his grave, and her grandmother—if her grandmother were alive, she'd probably never speak to Cassie again.

"Cassie, open up!" The sudden pounding on the door made her jump, as much from the recognition of Bob's voice as anything else. She glared at the door, which shook with the force of his blows. "I've come to apologize, but I can't do it proper if you won't open the door."

More pounding. He was going to break the door down if she didn't stop him. "Go away!" she called. "I don't want to talk to you."

"You're going to have to talk to me. Open up or I'll find my own way in."

"You wouldn't dare. I'll call the sheriff."

"He won't come. He and everybody else are off looking for Lucille Theriot's grandson, who's gotten himself lost or kidnapped or something."

"Lucas was kidnapped?" She'd been furious when he hadn't shown up in time for the play, but it had been unlike him.

"Well, probably not kidnapped, but he's off somewhere and everybody's trying to find him. Now, let me in."

Reluctantly, Cassie stood and went to open the door. Bob was still in his miner's costume of bright flannel shirt and canvas trousers held up by leather suspenders. He held a broad-brimmed hat in one hand, his white hair ruffled. "I can't apologize proper if you don't let me in," he said.

She stepped aside and he strode into the living room past her. "Looks like a museum in here," he said. He looked back at her. "Maybe you ought to give tours. You could charge admission."

The thought of strangers filing through the rooms where her family had lived made her shudder. "This is my home," she said. "Now say what you have to say and get out."

"I'm sorry about the explosion," he said. "It wasn't supposed to come off like that at all. It was just supposed to be a little boom, then a shower of confetti and glitter. It was gonna be real pretty." He looked glum.

"What happened?" she asked.

"I think I measured the black powder wrong. Or else the proportions were off. I'll have to experiment a little to get it right next time."

"There won't be a next time," she said.

"Why not? Except for the little fuss at the end, I thought it went really well. People liked it."

"They laughed." She would never forget the sound of that laughter washing over her.

"Only at the funny parts. They liked it. And they learned a lot about Eureka's history, thanks to you."

"Toby Mercer put in all those extra jokes—they weren't in the script."

"He was just trying to help out—improvising, they call it in the theater world. And it fit well with the character. It's the kind of thing Jake would have done."

"Damn Jake!" she said, and burst into tears.

Bob stared at her, blinking, and she thought he might bolt back out the door. She wouldn't care if he did. She didn't want to cry like this, but she couldn't help herself. It was all too much.

But instead of running, Bob pulled an oversize red bandana out of his back pocket and shoved it at her. "I thought you were a mountain woman," he said.

She stiffened, then snatched the bandana and loudly blew her nose. "You know good and well I've lived in these mountains all my life," she said.

"Then why are you carrying on so over a worthless cuss like Jake Murphy?"

She could have denied she was crying about Jake at all, but what was the use? "You wouldn't understand," she said.

"I sure as hell don't. What was Murph to you that you'd be carryin' on so when he's been in the ground four months?"

She sniffed and dabbed at her eyes. One of the false lashes came off and lay against the bandana like a dead centipede. "I thought Jake was cremated."

"So he was. And what does that have to do with anything?"

"You said—"

"Never mind what I said. It's time you toughened up. If Jake treated you bad, well, he treated a lot of people bad, not the least of which is that daughter of his you've given such a hard time."

"Maggie and I have made our peace." Sure, Jake had been a lousy father to her, but what he'd done to Cassie was worse. "You don't understand," she said again.

"You already said that. Are you going to explain things or keep blubbering about it?"

"I'm not blubbering!" she protested, even as more fat tears slid down her cheeks. She blew her nose again. "Jake took advantage of me," she said at last.

"What does that mean, exactly?" Bob squinted at her.

"He . . . he had sex with me and he . . . he was my first." Her face grew hot, but she managed to hold back a fresh flood of tears.

Bob frowned at her. "Did you tell him you were a virgin beforehand, or just let it be a surprise?"

"What difference does that make?"

"It makes a hell of a lot of difference. A man likes to know these things."

She'd been too embarrassed to admit to Jake that he was her first, afraid he might reject her if he knew how inexperienced she was. "He figured it out after—well, during." She stared down at the floor.

"And he couldn't handle it."

"I thought he'd be pleased. Instead, he left and never spoke to me again."

"What did you expect?" Bob looked at her with disdain.

"He took what you offered, thinking you'd have a little fun—and right in the middle he finds out you've been saving yourself for nigh on fifty years and he realizes this means a lot more to you than it does to him. He can't handle the responsibility."

"What kind of man runs away from a woman like that?" The words emerged as a wail.

"The kind of man Jake was. He'd already left one woman and a baby, so why should he treat you any better?"

She knotted the bandana in her hand. "It was a horrible thing to do."

"You springing that surprise on him wasn't such a great thing either, Cass."

She lifted her chin. "I didn't set out to trick him, if that's what you're implying."

"All I'm saying is there was sin on both sides. It's time you grit your teeth and get over it."

Those were the same words her father had told her when the boy she'd dated in high school had gotten engaged to another girl. He'd also told her there'd be other men, but he'd been wrong, as he'd been wrong about so many other things.

"Jake hurt me and I'll never forgive him," she said.

"I doubt a dead man is much worried whether he gets your forgiveness or not."

"People think he was such a hero," she said. "But that's wrong. He did some horrible things."

"Wouldn't surprise me a bit," Bob said. "But in case you haven't figured out by now, most people aren't much interested in the past. If you'd let things die down, people will mostly forget about Jake in a few months or a year."

But Cassie would never forget. "It doesn't seem right he was never punished for the awful things he did."

"My God, woman!" Bob's voice was sharp. "The man took himself off to a mountaintop to wrestle with his demons. You don't think alone up there in the cold and dark with only a bottle for company he wasn't in a special kind of hell?"

"I thought Jake liked it up there. He wanted to be alone."

"I imagine he liked it well enough sometimes. Maybe even most of the time. But it ain't natural for a man to separate himself from people like that. If you ask me, Jake was punishing himself. He spent a lot of time alone with the memory of things he'd done."

She had an image of Jake up there in that cabin, staring out into the darkness, alone. Just as she'd spent so much of her life alone. "Maybe he was ashamed and too embarrassed to face me," she said.

"Or maybe he was afraid you'd try to rope him into marrying you," Bob said. "The thing is, you'll never know. And it don't matter. He's gone. Let it go."

She hated to admit a man who annoyed her as much as Bob was right. She sniffed and dabbed her eyes again. "I'm fine now. You can go."

He didn't hesitate, but grabbed hold of the doorknob.

"Bob?"

"What is it now?"

"If you breathe one word of what I told you to anyone, I won't wait until you're dead to take my revenge."

She expected him to leer at her, or to make some kind of a joke. Instead, he nodded solemnly. "I'd never tell a lady's secrets," he said.

She was still gaping after him when the door swung shut. She sank into the rocking chair once more, all the strength drained from her. She looked around the parlor, at the books and mining tools and china crowded together on the shelves. All that fuss over Jake Murphy, and where had it gotten her? She was still the same person, in the same house.

She felt a little foolish. Maybe she had made too much of the whole affair. Yes, Jake had been a jerk, but that didn't make him special. Lots of men were weaker than the women around them. She nodded to the portrait of her father that hung over the fireplace mantel. He'd been a kind man, but so foolish. The women in Cassie's family were always the strong ones. The ones who kept everything together.

She stood and smoothed her hair, then reached up and carefully peeled off the other set of false lashes. Time to stop mooning about and get to work setting things to rights. After all, she was a mountain woman.

Chapter 25

Jameso didn't say a word on the way up Garnet Mountain. Only his rigid posture and the speed with which he drove, the truck fishtailing around every curve, gave a clue to his emotions. Maggie gripped the edge of the seat with one hand and the armrest with the other, staring out into the darkness and trying not to think of what might happen if they missed a curve. Or of all the horrors that might befall a boy out there alone in the darkness. Finally, she could bear the tension no longer. "If he's at the French Mistress, he'll be okay," she said. "When Barb and I were in there, we didn't see anything that would hurt anyone."

"You didn't explore the whole mine," Jameso said. "You don't know what's down there."

"No, I'm just an ignorant city woman who doesn't know anything, is that it?"

"I didn't say that."

"You didn't have to. You've made it clear from the first night we met that you think I'm incompetent."

A muscle in his jaw twitched, though he continued to stare straight forward, focused on the road. "You might have been ignorant of a few things, but I never thought you were incompetent."

"Then what do you think? I'm sick of the whole inscrutable male shtick. Tell me what you really think of me." Her voice rose, on the edge of hysteria. She purposely goaded him, craving a fight. She was tired of always being calm and reasonable and adult—of letting men walk away unscathed while she suffered.

He glanced at her for half a second, but it was too dark for her to read anything in his eyes. "How did it go with your husband?" he asked.

Her *husband?* Did he know how lucky he was she didn't have a weapon handy right now? "My ex-husband. You know that."

"He came all the way to Eureka to find you. Sounds to me like he didn't want to be your ex anymore."

Maggie couldn't believe what she was hearing. "Is that why you left town? Because you were jealous?"

He didn't answer, but he gunned the truck up a particularly steep slope, throwing her back against the seat. Maggie's stomach hurt, and so did her heart. Maybe Jameso did care for her, but he was about as trustworthy as a bear. And he clearly didn't trust her.

But she wasn't going to let him off the hook so easily. "You didn't answer my question," she said. "Did you leave because you were jealous—of Carter?"

Frustration choked her as he remained silent. She leaned forward, ready to strike words out of him, but the seat belt held her back as the truck jounced over ruts in the dirt road. "I left because I realized we don't belong together," he said, his voice hard and flat.

"And you decided this while we were making love? Or after?"

He glanced at her, but she couldn't discern his expression

in the dark. "That afternoon with you was the best afternoon of my life," he said. "But you're better off without me."

"So you get to decide that, and you get to leave. And I get to pick up the pieces." She wanted to shake him out of all his macho certainty. "What if I'm pregnant?"

The truck swerved and she had to clutch at the dash to steady herself. He slowed and then steered straight again, but she heard the shock in his voice. "Are you? Isn't it too soon to tell?"

"Yes. I mean no. I mean I don't know. But I could be." She knotted her hands in her lap, her heart fluttering wildly. *Was* she expecting a baby? Stupidly, they hadn't used any protection, too caught up in the moment to think straight. She'd always wanted a baby more than she'd been able to admit, even to herself. But she hadn't wanted to conceive one this way.

"If you are, I'll do right by you." His voice was stronger, but not reassuring.

"Meaning what?" she asked.

"Meaning . . . I'll . . . I'll . . . pay for the baby and . . ."

"I don't want your money. I just want to know why you ran."

Silence again, only the whine of the truck tires on gravel filling her ears. She swallowed hard, refusing to give in to tears. He wasn't worth crying over anymore.

"I ran because I'm a coward."

"A coward?" She'd accused all men of being cowards, but in her heart she couldn't believe the adjective applied to Jameso. He was so masculine, so stoic and strong. Not the type to back down from a challenge or a fight.

"I looked at that ex-husband of yours and I realized what you were from—the kind of life you were used to. I'm a part-time ski bum whose most valuable possession is a motorcycle. I can't give you anything like the life you're used to."

"I'm here because I don't want that life anymore."

He shook his head. "I'm bad news, Maggie. I'm thirty-two years old and I still don't know what I want to be when I grow up. I'm still fighting my demons. Jake and I had that in common."

Jameso may have been her father's best friend, but she refused to believe they were alike. "You're stronger than my father was. He drank and resorted to violence. You turned away from that."

"That doesn't mean I don't fight it inside. You deserve better."

Maybe he was right. But this wasn't about what she deserved. If people always got what they deserved, there would be a lot more miserable people in this world. All she could think of to say was, "You shouldn't have run out like that."

"Yeah."

So much for getting any real answers out of him. She stared out the window at the darkened landscape as the truck rattled past the entrance to her driveway. "Where are you going?"

"There's another road, takes us closer to the mine."

If this "road" really existed, she couldn't see it in the dark, and she didn't know how Jameso did either. The headlights of the truck barely made a dent in the blackness, lighting up a spot barely five feet in front of them, revealing uneven ground scattered with rocks. Maggie had to clench her jaw to keep her teeth from rattling as Jameso guided the vehicle over this moonscape. She held her breath as they descended a steep slope, the nose of the truck pointed straight down. "You can get out and walk if you like," Jameso said.

She glared at him in answer.

At last they came to a wall of old tree stumps and boulders, and what looked like a rusted set of box springs, all held together with barbed wire. "Jake put that up to keep folks from driving back to the mine," Jameso said. He shut off the engine. "We'll have to walk from here."

Maggie climbed from the truck on shaking legs and prepared to follow Jameso to the mine. But instead of striking out ahead, he waited and took her arm. "The trail's pretty rough," he said. He flicked on the flashlight he held in his other hand, revealing more of the same uneven terrain.

She jerked away. "I'll be fine." Then, recognizing something like hurt in his expression, she softened her tone. "It'll be faster if you go ahead. Lucas might need help."

They hiked for perhaps a quarter mile, picking their way around rocks and the remains of old mining equipment. The rain had stopped, but clouds still obscured the moon and stars. The air was icy, the ground rimmed with frost. Maggie's ears and fingers soon grew numb. She shoved her hands in her pockets and prayed that Lucas had some way to keep warm. That he was safe and they would find him.

They descended a small hill and the beam of Jameso's light caught something shiny. "We're here," he said, and shone the light on the mine entrance. Her heart leaped when she spotted the blue bicycle on its side in front of the gate.

"Lucas!" Jameso shouted.

"Lucas!" Maggie cried. She turned to Jameso. "We forgot the key. It's at the house." She could have wept in frustration at this new delay.

"There's a spare." Jameso reached behind the NO TRESPASSING sign and brought out a metal box, the kind with a magnet on the back, designed to attach a spare key to the bumper of a car. He fit the key in the lock and the gate swung open with a groan.

He focused the light on the floor of the mine entrance. The dirt was scuffed, but Maggie couldn't make out any distinct footprints. "Lucas!" she called out.

The word was swallowed up in the empty reaches of the mine.

While Emergency Services quickly organized groups to search for Lucas, Lucille and Olivia returned to the house.

Lucille hoped they'd find the boy asleep or engrossed in a book or a computer game. But the rooms were dark and silent when they entered, and cold in spite of the gas furnace that hummed in the background.

Olivia led the way up the stairs to her son's room under the eaves. She switched on the light and wrinkled her nose at the sight of the unmade bed, quilt half-trailing on the floor, a pair of jeans hanging from the closet doorknob, another draped over the back of the desk chair. She walked to the desk and began rifling through the papers stacked there.

"What are you looking for?" Lucille asked.

"I don't know. A note. Something to tell us where he's gone." She picked up a book and read the title on the spine, then set it aside.

"You don't think he's run away, do you?" Lucille asked.

"I don't know what to think." Olivia looked back over her shoulder at her mother. "I can never figure out what goes on in his head."

"I remember feeling the same way about you when you were only a little older than him."

Olivia's eyebrows rose. "I was never as smart as Lucas is."

Lucille plucked a shirt from the end of the bed and folded it, as if busying her hands would help quell the fear growing inside her. "You didn't like school or books, but you were very intelligent. Smart enough to see through me."

Olivia frowned. "I don't know what you're talking about."

"You saw through my feeble attempts to be the mother all your friends had—June Cleaver in high heels and pearls. I was never like that."

"And I never wanted that." She gave a harsh laugh. "Please!"

"I know I made some mistakes." Lucille forged on. "I just want you to know I'm proud of how you've turned out. And I'm proud of the job you've done with Lucas."

"Give yourself some credit, too." She turned back to the desk, opening drawers and rifling through the contents. Her shoulders stiffened and she drew out a bundle of letters. Lucille recognized the handwriting on the envelopes.

"Are those all from D. J.?" she asked.

Olivia nodded and thumbed through the pile. "Why did he write to Lucas and not to me?"

"Maybe he thought you didn't want his letters."

"I told him I didn't, but that didn't mean I was telling the truth."

"What will you do when he comes back to the States?"

"There's nothing to do."

"He might decide he wants his truck back."

"Then he can have it. I don't care."

But she did care. Lucille could read that so clearly, in the tight set of her daughter's shoulders and the slightest trembling in her lower lip.

Olivia returned to her search of the desk drawers. "What's this?" She held up a strand of blue beads.

Lucille accepted the trinket and turned it over in her hand. "It looks like the bracelet Jake gave me for Christmas last year. Why would Lucas have it in his room?"

"I don't know. Where did Jake get it?"

"I always assumed he'd picked it up in his travels. But Maggie said she found stones similar to this around the house."

"Could they have come from the mine?"

"The mine?" She shook her head. "I doubt it. It's a gold mine."

"But Lucas said people mined other things around here. Silver and lead. That's what all these books he's been reading are about." She gestured toward the desk. "Maybe they mined stones, too. I'll bet he did go up to that mine, to try to find out."

"But why would he go today, with the festival going on, and the play—?"

"He probably thought it was the best time to get away

with no one noticing. And I'm sure he planned to get back home in time for the play." She swallowed, fear dimming her eyes. Lucille felt the same fear. If Lucas hadn't gotten home in time for the play, it meant something must have prevented him from doing so.

"We should call the sheriff and let him know," Lucille said.

"Maggie and Jameso headed up to Jake's mine, didn't they?"

"Yes, we'd better go, too. In case they find . . ." She swallowed hard, choking off thoughts of a boy's broken body lying at the bottom of a mine shaft. "In case they find him. We can both read him the riot act for running off this way." She started down the stairs, leaving Olivia to turn out the lights in Lucas's room and follow.

Olivia caught up with her mother near the front door and slipped her hand in the crook of Lucille's arm. "What you said up there, about being proud of me," she said. "I'm proud of you, too."

"Whatever for?"

"I know it wasn't easy looking after me by yourself. I didn't appreciate that when I was a kid, but now . . ." She shrugged. "Sometimes when I think that I'm the only one in the world Lucas has to depend on, it scares me sick."

"I know. But you don't have to be scared that way anymore. You and Lucas both have me. And right now he has a whole town looking for him."

"I hope they find him . . . and that he's okay."

"He will be," Lucille said. He had to be. She refused to think anything else.

Jameso moved down the mine tunnel, Maggie close behind. Before too long, he had to hunch over to keep from hitting his head on the low ceiling. Neither of them said anything until they came to the niche in the wall, with its collection of rocks and the shiny medal. Jameso examined the medal in the light. "Saint Barbara," he said. "Patron saint of miners."

"Why is it here?" Maggie asked. "Jake didn't strike me as particularly religious."

"He wasn't . . . and he was." Jameso put the medal back on the shelf. "More spiritual than religious, maybe. He'd talk about God sometimes, when he'd had a few drinks. But it was the way some men talk about women they want but can never have." He turned and started walking farther into the mine. "He told me once that he'd done too many bad things to ever make it right with God."

"Did you know he was at My Lai? The massacre in Vietnam?"

"My Lai?"

"It's a village in Vietnam, where a bunch of American soldiers killed Vietnamese women and children. More than three hundred died there—maybe as many as five hundred. Jake was there. Or, his unit was. He had to have been there, too."

"He never mentioned it."

"I think it's the kind of experience no one talks about." She put her hand out to touch the wall as the passage narrowed. Jameso's back loomed ahead of her, solid as stone. "I read about it on the Internet. There'd been a lot of casualties in the weeks leading up to that day, and the soldiers just . . . snapped. They killed everything that moved. Pictures showed bodies and blood everywhere." She shuddered. "How could anyone do such a thing?"

"When you're in a war zone, constantly under attack, it does things to your mind. I'm not saying it excuses anything he may or may not have done, only that none of us can know how we'd act in similar circumstances. It's not like the real world over there. All the rules go out the window."

She remembered that Jameso had fought in Iraq, that he'd said it was hell. That he'd been afraid all the time he was there. "You're right," she said. "I shouldn't judge. He was nineteen, thousands of miles away from home . . ."

Jameso stopped, then angled his body to reach back and take her hand. He squeezed it, hard. "Don't think about it," he said. "There's nothing you can do for him now."

She took a deep breath, sucking in the cold, dusty air of the mine shaft. "I can't not think about it. It explains so much. How could anyone go through something like that and not be different? Damaged."

"We're all damaged in one way or another," Jameso said. "Some more than others. Jake had his faults, but he did his best. Try to remember that."

How are you damaged? she wondered. What had happened to him in Iraq—or before that—that made him think he wasn't the man for her? But she couldn't think of a way to ask such a question. And now didn't seem the time to be baring their souls. So she merely squeezed his hand, then released it. "Come on. We've got to find Lucas."

They reached the passage where Maggie and Barb had turned off. "Lucas!" she leaned into the passage and shouted.

"Let's try straight and if we don't find him, we'll come back," Jameso said.

Not anxious to navigate that narrow tunnel in the dark, Maggie agreed. This main shaft was still tall enough here for her to walk upright, though Jameso had to hunch over. Little avalanches of dirt and debris spilled into the passage at intervals, forcing them to scramble over them. Maggie's hands and arms were scraped and bruised. "At least it's not too cold down here," she said, thinking again of the boy.

"Not exactly warm either. Do you know if Lucas had a jacket with him?"

"I don't know."

He stopped. "Lucas!"

They waited, holding their breath. Maggie heard only the pounding of her pulse in her ears. Jameso cursed under his breath and they moved on.

"How far back into the mountain does this go?" she asked as they scrambled over yet another mound of debris.

"I don't know. Could be miles."

"Miles?" The idea exhausted her. They'd already passed two other side passages; Lucas could be in any one of them. "Maybe we should go back to town and get some help."

"We'll search a little longer. Lucas!"

A sound—little more than a squeak—drifted down the corridor. "What was that?" Maggie gripped Jameso's back.

"Lucas!" he shouted again.

The squeak came again, stronger this time. Jameso ran toward it, hunched over, his feet pounding hard on the packed dirt of the passage. Maggie stumbled after him, slamming into him when he stopped suddenly.

He put out an arm to steady her. "There's a drop-off here," he said. "I think it's a vertical shaft."

She peered over his shoulder as he shone the light down into the hole. A pair of wide, scared eyes stared up at them from about ten feet below. "Lucas!" she cried.

When Lucille and Olivia arrived at Jake's—now Maggie's—cabin, they found a crowd of people, but no Maggie or Jameso. And no Lucas. Olivia had called the sheriff, and he said he was sending a search and rescue team up to go into the mine. Meanwhile, those gathered outside the mine were arguing over whether they should wait for the sheriff or go in on their own.

"The last thing we need is a bunch of amateurs going in there and getting hurt and adding to the rescue squad's work," Rick said.

"Who are you callin' an amateur?" Bob countered.

Lucille wondered if she was going to have to tear the two apart, when a third man stepped between them. She was startled to recognize the dark-haired young man who'd bought the single ticket at the Founders' Pageant. "Does anybody have a map of the mine tunnels?" he asked.

"Who are you?" Bob demanded.

"I'm—"

"D. J.!" Olivia's voice rang clear above the murmur of the crowd. Everyone turned to look at her. She stood five feet away, mouth open, face pale as she stared at D. J.

"Hello, Olivia," he said, his voice low, his expression solemn. But his gaze searched her, wanting yet wary.

"What are you doing here?" Olivia asked.

"I heard Lucas was missing. I came to see if I could help."

"No. What are you doing in Eureka?"

"I came to talk to you."

She looked away. "If this is about your SUV, I didn't steal it. I was only borrowing it."

"I never said you stole it. I don't give a damn about the car." He took a step toward her, but she held up her hand to stop him.

"We don't have anything to talk about," she said.

"I think we do."

"I don't have time for this now. My son is missing."

"I want to do what I can to help find him."

"The best thing you can do is to leave us alone."

D. J.'s expression clouded. "Are you saying you don't think Lucas wants to see me?"

Lucille was certain Olivia wanted to lie, but she couldn't. Not about Lucas. Or maybe not to this man. "Lucas would love to see you."

"Then I'll stay."

"Suit yourself." She turned away, though she must have felt the heat of his gaze on her back. The look was searing.

Lucille stepped forward. "I'm Lucille Theriot," she said. "Olivia's mother."

He glanced at her. "I wondered when I saw you at the theater. There's a resemblance."

Lucille flushed. "Do you really think so?" Olivia was so slender and delicate and beautiful. All things Lucille had never been.

He nodded. "Something about the eyes is the same."

He was talking to her, but his eyes followed Olivia as she paced back and forth in front of the mine entrance, arms folded over her stomach. "She was pretty upset with me last time we spoke," he said.

Lucille said nothing.

He sighed. "I guess now's not the best time for a reunion."

"Probably not. Are you back in the U.S. for good or merely on leave?"

"I'm back for a while." His gaze remained fixed on Olivia. "It depends."

Depends on what? she could have asked. But she had an idea she knew.

"When's that damn sheriff going to get here?" he asked in a sudden burst of emotion.

"He should be here soon," Lucille said.

"Not soon enough. What was the boy thinking, going off by himself to explore a mine?"

"We don't even know for sure he's in there."

"I bet he is," D. J. said. "His last letter to me was full of stuff about mines and minerals and Indians. . . ." He shook his head. "He wrote the most incredible letters, long and full of details, almost stream of consciousness, just pouring out of him. He's an incredible kid."

"Yes, he is." Emotion tightened the bands around Lucille's heart as she thought of Lucas, lost and alone in a cold, dark mine tunnel, maybe injured . . .

"I fell for Olivia practically the first moment I met her."

Lucille was grateful for D. J.'s voice, giving her something to focus on besides what-ifs, and he seemed to need to talk. "Olivia has that effect on men," she said.

"It wasn't just physical attraction," he said. "She was so smart and funny and fierce—how could I not love her? But Lucas . . . I never expected to fall for him, too."

"Then why did you leave?" Wasn't that the question women always asked?

His eyes met hers briefly, dark and glittering with anguish. "I wanted to be able to give them something. A future. That wasn't going to happen if I stayed a bouncer at a bar. I left for them. I tried to explain that to her, but she wouldn't listen."

Olivia had never been very good at listening, but what woman wanted to hear that her man would rather be away from her—working? Lucille wasn't naive enough to think money didn't matter, but sometimes it didn't matter enough to make up for being left behind.

"That sheriff better get here soon," D. J. said. "I lost them once, but I'll be damned if I lose them again."

"I'm stuck!" Lucas wailed. "My ankle . . ."

Jameso directed the beam of light down, and they saw the boy's foot was wedged between two rocks. "I've tried and tried to pull it out," Lucas said. "It won't budge."

The light showed a long scratch on the boy's face and the tracks of tears. "Other than the ankle, are you all right?" Maggie asked.

"I'm thirsty," he said. "And cold."

Jameso stripped off his jacket and dropped it down to the boy. "Put that on," he ordered.

Lucas did so. "What are we going to do now?" he asked.

"I'm going to find something to move those rocks." He pushed past Maggie and retreated down the corridor.

"Wait," she called, but he was soon out of sight. She swallowed, the darkness closing in around her. "I'm still here," she said to the boy. How many hours had he been waiting in this darkness alone? She'd have been terrified.

"I missed the play," he said.

"Sylvia Rayburn said your lines, but she didn't do nearly as good a job," Maggie said. "Everything else went pretty well, until the end. Bob wanted to set off fireworks, but instead he almost set the theater on fire."

"I'll bet Ms. Wynock was pissed."

"I imagine she was. The rest of us were worried about you."

"Is my mom really mad at me?"

"More worried than mad right now. And your grandmother. Why did you come all the way up here by yourself?"

"I wanted to see a mine, and I figured with everybody involved in the festival, now would be a good time to see it without anyone trying to stop me. I guess it wasn't such a smart thing to do."

"No, but it will be all right now." Though she still had no idea how they would free him.

The beam of Jameso's light glowed bright down the corridor and she turned to greet him. He carried what looked like a rusted iron fence post. "Hold the light." He handed Maggie the flashlight. "Shine it down into the hole once I'm down there."

Before she could protest, he lowered himself into the hole, landing heavily at the bottom. Maggie crouched beside the opening and focused the beam of light on him. Jameso was trying to move the rocks by hand, grunting and straining. "Owww!" Lucas wailed. "You're just making it worse."

"Sorry." Jameso glanced up at Maggie, his face anxious. "I'm going to try to pry the rocks off. It might hurt."

"Lucas, look at me," Maggie said. "Try not to think about the pain. Tell me what you want to eat when you get out of here."

"Eat?" Lucas winced as Jameso moved toward the rocks that trapped his foot.

"Look at me," Maggie commanded. "Do you like burgers? I had the best buffalo burger this afternoon."

"Cheeseburger," Lucas said. "With fries and a chocolate shake. My grandmother never lets me eat stuff like that.

'Course, I'm so hungry right now I'd even eat vegetables. Broccoli with cheese sauce is goo—ahh!"

"It's moving!" Jameso shouted.

Lucas screamed. Maggie wanted to cover her ears, but she had to keep hold of the light. "Got it!" Jameso cried. He tossed aside the fence post and gathered the boy in his arms.

Maggie looked away, then peeked into the hole again. Lucas's face was pale, and she caught the glint of fresh tears, but he was conscious and breathing. "Everything okay?" she asked.

"His ankle's pretty scraped up and swollen, but he'll be okay." Jameso addressed the boy. "I'm going to boost you up. Think you can crawl out on your own?"

Lucas nodded. Jameso grasped him around the waist and lifted. Maggie dropped the flashlight, grabbed the boy's shoulders, and helped him scramble out of the hole. Then she turned to help Jameso, who was already heaving himself over the side. He brushed himself off, then turned his back to the boy.

"Climb on," Jameso said. "You can't walk on that ankle, so I'll give you a ride out."

Maggie led the way back down the tunnel, the flashlight weakly illuminating the passage ahead. They walked quickly, up the slight grade, past the side tunnels and the niche with the saint's medal. Soon she saw the glow of light from the entrance. She frowned. Where was the light coming from?

She discovered that the combined headlamps and flashlights of half a dozen people made for quite a bright glow. As they emerged from the tunnel, a cheer went up, and Olivia and Lucille rushed forward to embrace both Lucas and Jameso.

"I'm fine, really. I just . . . I think I sprained my ankle." Lucas leaned on his mother, balanced on one foot, and rubbed at his dirty cheek, perhaps to brush away fresh tears.

Rick hovered around, snapping pictures for the paper. "Put that damn camera away before you blind someone!" Lucille ordered.

"What were you thinking, going down in that mine by yourself?" Olivia scolded.

"I know I shouldn't have done it. I promise it won't happen again."

"Hey, big guy, you okay?"

A young man Maggie didn't recognize stepped forward.

"D. J.!" Face alight, Lucas threw up his arms and hobbled toward the man. D. J. swung him into his arms and held him tightly.

"You okay?" he asked again.

"I think my ankle's busted, but I'll be okay. When did you get here?"

"This afternoon. I wanted to surprise you, see you in your play."

"I'm bummed about missing it."

"This is better," Rick said. He snapped another photo. "You'll be on the front page."

"We need to get your ankle looked at," Olivia said. She'd been standing to one side, arms crossed, frowning at the man Lucas had called D. J.

"Will you come with me?" Lucas asked D. J.

"If your mom says it's okay." He glanced at Olivia.

She hesitated, then nodded. But as he and Lucas moved past her, she touched his arm. "We're not going to pick up where we left off," she said.

"I didn't think we would," he said.

"I almost forgot!" Lucas whirled around. "Mama, look what I found." He reached into his pocket and pulled out a handful of blue stones. Maggie moved closer.

"What are those?" Olivia asked.

"They're from the mine," Maggie said. "Barb and I found some like them when we went down in there."

"I'm pretty sure they're turquoise," Lucas said. "There's a

lot more down there, where I was stuck. I bet they're worth a lot of money."

"Money that doesn't belong to you," Lucille said. "You were trespassing, remember? And the mine doesn't belong to you."

"I don't care about the money," Lucas said. "I just think it's neat that I discovered something." He glanced at Maggie. "Can I at least keep the stones I found?"

"Yes, you can keep those," she said. "But you have to promise me you won't go into the mine again unless I or someone I've given permission to goes with you."

"I promise." He replaced the stones in his pocket and started to move forward again, but cried out as his ankle gave way beneath him.

"Not so fast," D. J. said. He swept the boy into his arms. "I'll carry you."

Without waiting for a reply from anyone, he started down the trail toward the cabin. The rest of the crowd set off behind them, except Maggie, who stayed behind with Jameso.

"So who was that?" Jameso asked, when they were alone.

"I'm not sure," Maggie said. "But I'd say he and Olivia once had feelings for each other."

"I'd say they still do." He closed and locked the gate and returned the key to its holder behind the sign. "You'd better go on in," he said. "It's getting colder." Lucas still had his jacket, so Maggie knew he must be chilled, though he showed no signs of it.

"I thought I'd walk back with you," she said. "Come up to the house and I'll give you a ride to town. You can get your truck in the morning."

He fell into step beside her on the trail. The clouds still obscured the moon, forcing them to walk slowly, picking their way by the beam of the flashlight. "What will you do now?" he asked.

"Do about what?"

"The mine. Lucas is right—that turquoise could be worth a lot of money."

"That explains where Jake got his money. He was mining the turquoise a little at a time and selling it in Montana or Denver or wherever."

"It's your money now. You could travel, buy a new place. What do you want?"

She looked at him, wondering if she was being a fool. "I don't want Carter. And all he wanted was the Steuben glass collection he'd given me over the years. When I wouldn't give it to him, he tried to steal it." She laughed, remembering. "Winston kept him here until I came home and threw him out." She didn't mention Cassie, something in her wanting to protect the poor woman. "You've got nothing to be jealous about."

He stopped, pulling her up short. "You asked me what I thought of you. That first night, when I saw you standing on the porch of Jake's cabin, that stick of kindling in your hand, all that red hair tumbling around your shoulders and fury in your eyes, I thought you were the most beautiful woman I'd ever seen. And you were way out of my league."

The sincerity of his words shook her. "We're not playing sports," she said. "Leagues don't matter."

"You can say that because you're the woman with a turquoise mine. I'm a man with nothing."

"If money was that important to me, I'd have stayed in Houston and let Barb introduce me to her rich friends."

His grip on her tightened. "What is important to you, Maggie?"

"You are." She kissed him, all the anxiety and confusion that had tormented her washed away by those two words of truth and the feel of her lips against his.

His arms came around her, crushing her to his chest. They kissed for a long time, there in the chilled darkness, warm in each other's arms.

"I'm sorry I ran out on you," he said, his voice rough against her hair when they finally came up for air. "It was a shitty thing to do. I wish I could promise I won't do anything like that again, but with my record, it probably won't be the last time I screw things up." He shifted and moved back enough that his eyes met hers in the dim light. "But know I will never deliberately hurt you," he said. "I love you, Maggie. I love you so much it scares me."

"It scares me a little, too," she said. "But we can be brave together."

They started back toward the cabin, holding hands. She was glad of the weight of him holding her to the earth—her heart felt light enough to send her soaring off the mountain. "Do you think Jake would approve of us together?" she asked when they reached the cabin.

"If he didn't, he'd kick my ass. But I wouldn't care." He pulled her close again and cradled her head on his chest. "I promise I'll treat you better than he ever did."

"I know you will. And if you don't, I'll be the one doing the ass kicking."

He slid his hand up to her neck and stroked softly. "You aren't wearing the rings anymore," he said.

"No, I took them off after I kicked Carter out of town. I realized I didn't need them anymore." Like the glass, the rings were ties to another life. One where she'd depended on other people for her happiness. She'd tucked them in the back of her jewelry box, like souvenirs she could look at from time to time to remind her how far she'd come.

Jameso kissed her again, his lips hot, tongue twining. Desire flared. "Come inside," she murmured, and tugged him toward the door.

As they crossed the porch, she felt something wet and cold on her cheek. She blinked into the darkness. "Is that snow?"

"I think it is." He aimed the flashlight up, at the shower of flakes drifting down on them, like glitter in a snow globe.

"Welcome to fall in the mountains," he said. "Snow now, warm again next week. The aspen will turn before you know it. The elk will start bugling. It's my favorite time of year."

"I can't wait to see it." She smiled at the swirling flakes and thought of all the wonders she had yet to discover. "I want to see it all."

Chapter 26

"This is the last of the clothes, but there's still a lot of books and stuff." Barb shoved the cardboard carton into the back of the truck they'd borrowed for the move.

"The books can stay." Maggie deposited another carton next to Barb's. "Most of them were here when I got here, so they'll be all right."

Barb leaned against the back bumper of the truck. "We should have asked Jameso for help," she said. "This is a job that could use some muscle."

"I don't want his help." Maggie knew she was being stubborn, but that's who she was. Considering all she'd learned about her father, her obstinacy was probably at least partly genetic. "Besides, I've got you." She hugged her friend. "Thanks for helping."

"I wouldn't have missed it. I've been dying to get back up here. Besides, I never knew a mining heiress before. I want to be sure you remember me in your will."

"It's not a diamond mine," Maggie protested. "Just a pocket of turquoise. A semi-precious stone." Though the first estimates of the money the mine might yield had been precious enough for her to live comfortably for years to come.

"Have they started mining the stones yet?" Barb asked. "When do I get that turquoise necklace you promised?"

"I hired Bob to oversee the job." The old man had very solemnly sworn he would never cheat a lady. "He's working with a couple of engineering students from Montrose. We want to keep the operation small and minimize the disruption to the area."

"Just don't forget my necklace." Barb straightened. "I guess we'd better get back to work."

"We're almost done." Maggie followed Barb back up to the cabin. It was a lot emptier now than when she'd first arrived. She was leaving the furniture, but she'd decided to take some of her dad's quilts and the pie crust table that had sat by the sofa. Little things to remember him by; not that she was likely to ever forget.

While Barb carried out the last packing box, Maggie went into the kitchen and pulled a box of Lorna Doones from the cabinet. She carried them out onto the porch and shook the package. In a few moments, Winston came trotting down the path from the mine and clattered up onto the porch.

"What is that old goat going to do when you're not around to feed him cookies?" Barb asked, watching from beside the moving van.

"Sheep. Rocky Mountain bighorn sheep. And he'll be fine. He doesn't need the cookies, he just liked them."

"I don't need chocolate, but I wouldn't want to live without it."

Maggie fed the last cookie to Winston, then showed him the empty box. He licked at the crumbs, then gave her a reproachful look and trotted off. She turned to Barb. "I guess that's everything."

"We'd better get going, then. Not to rush you, but I don't want to be driving this truck after dark."

"I just need to lock up." Inside the cabin, Maggie grabbed her purse and turned off the lights. She'd promised herself she wouldn't linger. She'd had plenty of time before Barb arrived to say good-bye.

She shut the front door behind her and turned the key in the lock. Then, after only a moment's hesitation, she reached up and put the key above the door.

Barb drove the moving van, while Maggie followed in the Jeep, down the winding road toward town. The top of Mount Winston was shrouded in snow, though the lower elevations were clear once more. Golden groves of aspen dotted the landscape; while clumps of purple aspen lined the road. Fall in the mountains was more beautiful than anything Maggie had ever seen; she had to swallow down a knot of emotion as she studied the view out the windshield.

They rumbled into town, past a row of deserted tourist cabins and down the quiet main street. Rick's truck was parked in front of the newspaper, but he didn't come out to salute the moving van. Lucille waved from the porch of Lacy's, where Lucas was helping her to string a row of skull-shaped lights. She'd heard Olivia had decided to stay in town. D. J. was apparently still here, too.

They passed the library. Cassie wasn't exactly friendly these days, but she was distantly polite. Since that or open hostility seemed her two attitudes for dealing with everyone, Maggie counted herself among the lucky.

Barb turned down a side street three blocks from the library and headed up a small hill. She parked the van in front of a towering blue spruce and shut off the engine. "Not half the view of your dad's place, but not bad," she observed.

Maggie smiled at the little blue house with the wide front deck. "It has electricity, a gas heating system, and indoor plumbing," she said. "Everything a girl could want."

"I'll say." Barb nudged Maggie in the side as the front door of the house opened and Jameso emerged. Clad in flannel shirt and canvas trousers, he might have been a lumberjack, or a miner. "I got the bed set up and the new microwave installed," he said.

"My hero." Maggie hugged his neck and kissed his cheek. "Thank you."

"Everything go okay up at the cabin?"

"It's fine. Winston's stuffed full of Lorna Doone's and I shut the water off like you showed me."

"You know I'll go up there later and check."

"I know." There was a time when she'd have been highly annoyed at him checking up on her that way, but she was learning to accept his need to look after her, and even to enjoy being looked after. "Thanks for letting me say good-bye today on my own."

"Only because I love you."

"I know. And I love you."

"Could you two lovebirds tear yourselves apart long enough to help me unload this truck?" Barb asked.

Maggie reluctantly moved out of Jameso's arms and headed down the walk toward the moving van. Too many times in the past year she'd packed her things and moved away from something—her marriage, her sadness, her life back in Houston. It felt good to be moving toward something now—love and possibility and a life she couldn't have imagined before.

A READING GROUP GUIDE

The View from Here

Cindy Myers

About this Guide

The suggested questions are included to enhance your group's reading of *The View from Here.*

DISCUSSION QUESTIONS

1. One of the themes of the book is finding a home. What does "home" mean to each of the main characters in this story? What does home mean to you?

2. Both Maggie and Olivia arrive in Eureka to start life over, essentially from scratch. If you were in a situation like that, would you find the prospect thrilling or frightening? Have you ever fantasized about starting over in a new place?

3. Several characters in the story have to deal with how the choices they, or others close to them, made in the past have affected their lives. Do you think the past shapes us, or do we shape our memories of the past to fit how we see ourselves?

4. Jameso tells Maggie that people in Eureka are proud of being independent and surviving sometimes harsh conditions. Do you think you'd enjoy living that way?

5. One of the reasons Maggie hesitates to get involved with Jameso is that he's younger than she is. Do you think society still frowns on women who are in relationships with younger men, or is it more accepted?

6. Maggie and Cassie have a prickly relationship. They share a link through Maggie's father, Jake. What qualities do Maggie and Cassie have in common?

7. The character of Jake influences much of the action in the story, even though he isn't alive when the story takes place. What do you think of Jake and the choices

he made in his life? Have you ever known anyone like him?

8. Lucille has mixed feelings about her daughter and grandson moving in with her. Have you been in a similar situation—either as the child who moved home or the parent who had to adjust to the return of a grown child? Was your experience positive or negative?

9. Maggie holds on to her wedding ring and the Steuben glass long after she needs or really wants them. Letting go of these items from her past is a turning point for her. What items in your life do you hold on to or have you held on to? Why do we keep things associated with painful times?

10. If you visited Eureka, which character or characters would you most want to meet and why?